Dark Dragon

Volume One of the Cosmic Warrior Series.

Paul M Chafer©

Author's Notes

This book is a work of fiction and,
except in the case of historical fact,
any resemblance to actual persons, living or dead,
is purely coincidental.

Many thanks to my family, without their support,
this book would not have been possible.
Thanks also to those who have read this book,
in one of its many forms.
Their constructive comments proved to be most helpful.

Special thanks also go to Amanda J Fuller.
Not only for editing this book,
but for all helpful suggestions.

All rights reserved.
No part of this publication may be reproduced,
stored in a retrieval system, or transmitted,
in any form or by any means,
electronic, mechanical, photocopying,
recording or otherwise,
without prior permission of the author.

This work conceived and written and produced,
by Paul M Chafer.
Copyright remains with the author © 2015
Subculture Publications © 2015

First Edition

For my daughters
Kerry and Rachel

By same author in this series,
and available as E-books on Amazon.

Dark Dragon: volume one
Wizard's Wrath: volume two
Stone Sorcerers: volume three - released 2015
Echoes Of Heroes: volume four - released 2016

Available in paperback from CreateSpace

Dark Dragon: volume one
Wizard's Wrath: volume two - summer 2015
Stone Sorcerers: volume three - winter 2015
Echoes Of Heroes: volume four - summer 2016

mrwizard@hotmail.co.uk

On Merm, one of four known worlds, momentous changes are afoot. Intrinsically linked to these changes and unaware how much her life of fifteen summers is to be shattered and reshaped beyond all imagining, is a girl, Ionuin. Incredible powers, so devastatingly strong that if they should be unleashed in their entirety, whole civilisations will be blitzed from existence. Personifications of Dark and Light are indulging themselves, attempting to force the outcome they desire.

Half a world apart, a seeker, Taj, responsible for finding gifted inhabitants in this arid land, strives to connect with Ionuin, but he has monsters of his own to conquer. The Dark Dragon has broached Merm's ancient defences and plans total destruction. Taj and Ionuin, aided by the remnants of a once great dragon race, are the last hope of the Light, and all worlds await the outcome of the looming titanic battle, knowing that if they fail, all life is lost.

The Clysm begins, the Reckoning and the eternal struggle between Dark and Light forces erupts in a frenetic war. Can Ionuin and Taj possibly survive and withstand the unbearable pressures placed upon their young shoulders? Can they unravel the conundrums facing them and escape enemies seeking to sway them or slay them? They must, or the four known worlds, including our Earth, are doomed.

"A reader lives a thousand lives before he dies," said Jojen.
"The man who never reads lives only one."
George R.R. Martin, A Dance with Dragons.

Creation Tale

When mighty symbols clashed,
The Universe was born,
The Minstrel Strummed,
The Piper Hummed,
And the Wizard blew his horn.

The Great Game had begun,
Chaos burst onto the stage,
To the tune of war,
Peace reigned no more,
Space and Time, came of age.

Kings, Queens and Bishops
Seek a sacrificial Pawn,
A Rook, a Cosmic Knight,
Darkness against the Light,
When the Wizard, blew, his horn.

Lyondell: The Scribe, Poet and Teller

Prologue

The sun dipped below the mountainous horizon, giving over the rule of the heavens to a full moon and an array of stars studding a pale, red sky. The moon was bright, with an orange hue insinuating itself over the pock-marked, cratered surface, whilst the stars resembled a scattering of glimmering diamonds spilled upon a damask cloth. These natural celestial wonders sailed and wheeled across the steadily darkening blanket of the night, illuminating a rare meeting of cosmic powers, far below.

Sireena strolled around the inside of the large stone circle, playing her pipes. Moonlight caught her shimmering blue hair that brushed against pale, but shapely, shoulders. It was a cold evening, but this personified female force of nature appeared not to notice as she concentrated on her music, her slim hips swaying gently to a melodic tune of her own creation. Her strapless, translucent gossamer gown shimmered as various pastel colours floated through the wispy fabric, giving the garment the impression of constant motion.

'You should try to wear more clothes,' said a calm voice directly behind her. 'Then you would not resemble the Numina that we really are, and perhaps you would even blend more easily with the humans, who we are supposed to be imitating, as previously agreed.'

Sireena turned, smiled, and inclined her head. 'Cai, dear brother, you should not be so concerned about my welfare.' She blew haughtily on her jewel-encrusted pipes. The notes eclipsed each other, building to a crescendo of achingly haunting sound that trip-hammered along the soul with exquisite delicacy. 'Tell me, dear brother; are those tight-fitting leathers comfortable? Or, like your brash personality, do they chafe in all the wrong places?'

'Ooh, sister, I can see that you are taking this persona of a human female to the limits, and are prone to emotional tantrums, but do you have to be such an unpleasant bitch?' Cai did not wait for a reply, but slid an arcing golden bow along the spider-silk strings of his own instrument. A sonorous wail vibrated around the ancient stone circle, bouncing back, echoing, sounding as if a string quartet were actually playing.

Sireena laughed at the acoustic effect. 'Brother, let us not fight. It has been too long since we last met. I must also offer you a compliment, your playing has improved so much!'

Cai leapt onto the altar in the centre of the stone circle and dashed off a few flashy riffs with a dramatic flourish, before offering his sister a deep bow. 'Compliment accepted, dear sister. Although; I did not consider myself all that bad prior to this evening.'

Sireena jumped up onto the altar stone beside her brother, hooking her forefinger beneath his chin. 'Oh, I did not say you were bad, brother, only that you have progressed. Why, soon you shall be on my level. Then of course, being a female, I may feel vulnerable and be forced to kill you!'

Cai gasped. 'Sireena, of all the terrible things to say! If I did not know you better I would accuse you of taunting me! No, I take that back.' He slapped her hand away, her nail drawing blood where it had raked his skin. 'You are taunting me, you sassy minx!'

Sireena sprang high into the air, flipped over and landed on the lintels of the inner horseshoe ring, sucking a drop of blood from her nail, closing her cerulean eyes in ecstasy. 'Hmm, yes, tastes so good. Do you imagine any of the human species are perhaps drinkers of blood, dear brother?'

'No, at least, not yet,' Cai replied tersely, dabbing his palm on the small wound. 'And let us ensure that it remains that way. We have enough to contend with, do you not think?'

Sireena blew on her pipes, a jaunty mocking tune. 'For a splitter of worlds, you are no fun, brother, no fun at all. I expected more from you and I insist that we indulge much more in the lives of others. I refuse to play fair if we are limited to humanity and those lumbering fire-breathing lizards of which you are so absurdly fond.'

'Dragons!' Cai snapped. 'Please, try and respect the life-forms that have sprung forth to fight for the survival of the universe. As a representative of the Light, I demand that you honour our agreement, and, for the record, I never expected you to play fair.'

Sireena pulled a sulky face. 'Aw, really? Am I so obvious? Now, you have hurt my precious feelings and for such a terrible act, you must be severely punished.'

Cai leapt up beside his sister. 'As my opposite, and the representative of the Dark, I know you so well, but punished?' Cai tutted and wagged his finger in Sireena's face, grinning as her luminous eyes, as if lit from within, flared with anger. 'Sireena, you amuse me. How could you even think about taking one such as I, an accomplished breaker of whole planets, to task?'

Sireena blew on her pipes and leapt to the grassy floor with casual grace. 'You have so much to learn, Cai. Do you really believe your male persona to be the stronger of the two of us? You poor deluded fool! You know nothing of the wiles and ways of womanhood, do you?'

Cai looked down on his sister, his previous confidence in disarray. He tried to marshal his thoughts. Somehow, beyond his reckoning, the discussion had escaped his control. 'I do know it is not in your interests to consider yourself above me. Nor is it your place to threaten!'

'Whatever!' Sireena hissed, contemptuously, offering Cai her best smile and a little wave with her delicate hand. 'See you on Merm, brother. Oh, and do not be late, or I might just slay one of your precious champions without warning. Would that be punishment enough, do you suppose?'

'You would not dare!' Cai shouted, but he was addressing empty air.

His sister had vanished without even offering a proper goodbye, leaving behind only the scent of her lilac perfume. He pondered upon her parting words and knew, or thought he knew, what must be done, but there was time yet. Many years would pass before the forecast champions arose, and in that time, he decided, he would plan, plot and scheme. He slid his bow across the spider-silk strings; of course, he would also indulge in the greatest of all endeavours, he would play!

Chapter One

Ionuin swerved as she ran, cursing her decision to take only a few arrows with her that morning, as she sensed another spear whipping through the air, aimed at her legs. She skipped high, her feet scissoring, kicking up dust and loose stones that skittered along the hard, arid ground as she landed. With a solid thump, the steel-tipped shaft plunged into the thin soil where her feet had been only moments before. She considered stopping, snatching up the weapon, but did not want to break her momentum, so continued onward. The stinging sand grains that peppered the tanned skin at the back of her knees, leaving small red marks above the tops of her deerskin boots, were an annoyance, but of little concern. What did concern her was being captured, having to suffer chains and shackles, the loss of her freedom.

She risked a quick glance over her shoulder and saw only two slavers from the caravan still in pursuit. The other half-dozen or so seemed to have given up, probably through sheer exhaustion. Despite an arduous chase in the pressing afternoon heat, it would appear, at least for these remaining two, that the prize of a teenage girl was not one to be yielded so easily.

She was beginning to feel tiredness creeping through her limbs, and her mind dallied with indecision; should she turn and fight, or continue to flee? With only open barren country before her, and at least one more night sleeping rough in her makeshift camp, the choice soon became a forced decision. The low grassy hills surrounding her secluded valley home were beyond immediate reach, so she decided to fight while she retained enough energy to do so. One more glance over her shoulder told her that until they reclaimed the weapon that had just been thrown, her would-be captors were out of spears. They had no bows, but she could see wickedly long blades in their hands and she supposed they would know how to use them.

Unfortunately, while hunting earlier that day, venturing into flat desert scrubland, she had come upon the snaking caravan quite by chance. Usually, such bands of nomadic traders were harmless, and Ionuin had ignored them, until she saw a small group of men suddenly detach themselves and move towards her, fanning out across the dusty plain. She had instantly seen the potential danger and fled, aware that this was a slaver's caravan, and not the carnival variety she was so used to seeing.

It was only by chance that she had travelled so far west in the pursuit of a large hare. Normally, she kept to the thinly grassed plateau bordering her home valley. With her breathing becoming increasingly laboured, she now regretted her foolishness. The chase, that had begun in the late morning and continued through into early afternoon, had taken a lot from her reserves of strength, but one by one, she had outdistanced all but these last two pursuers. Now, she intended to employ alternative tactics and put the combat teaching of her father to a stern test.

She knew she needed the element of surprise to increase her chances of surviving relatively unscathed, so taking care, she stumbled over her own feet and

11

allowed herself to go sprawling onto the floor. She rolled once, twice, her bow seemingly flying from her hand, landing on her left side, legs akimbo, her right hand flopping behind her within easy reach of her sword-hilt. Now it was just a matter of waiting. Peering through slitted eyes, hidden by loose strands of lank brown hair that had fallen over her face, she could see she would not have to wait long.

Taj awoke with a start, his mind trying to snatch at the remnants of his dream that were quickly dissipating beyond recall. A girl was being chased; hunted by a group of savage looking men. The whole scene was overlooked by a strange black splotch of cloud that appeared to be floating in an otherwise cloudless sky. The girl, dressed in clothes which looked as though they were made from wolf skin, her hair wild and windblown, seemed very tired. 'And they are catching her!' he blurted out, sitting upright.

'Ah, awake are you, sleepy head?' said a voice to his left.

Taj glanced round to see Beulah, one of the clan matriarchs, sitting before a large bronze mirror, admiring her own reflection. Taj, a boy of just fifteen summers, knew he was not really allowed to spend the night in the chamber of a matriarch. He did, after all, have his own chambers, but Beulah's rooms were comfortable and well lit with bright glowing crystals, so where was the harm? She was also the kindest female in the clan and she understood him better than anyone else. Even better than his master and protector, Lord Nexus, who had become the head of all the clans since the death of his father, High Lord Shogun.

Taj rubbed sleep from his eyes and stifled a yawn. 'Beulah, I was having a dream, of sorts.'

'Of sorts?' Beulah replied. 'Whatever does that mean, dear boy?'

'One of those lucid dreams. You know, as if it is happening, as if it is real,' said Taj, throwing back the fur covering swamping the whole bed, swinging his legs to the stone floor. 'There was a girl and-'

'Oh, a girl!' Beulah interrupted. 'One of those dreams! You should have said. A young boy like you having lucid dreams about girls, why, it's quite natural.'

Taj frowned. 'What?' he said, puzzlement evident in his voice, his mind still a little drowsy from oversleeping. 'What do you mean, lucid dreams about girls are natural?'

Beulah smiled and reached over to pat his hand. 'Exactly what I said. Although, I'm not sure you should be sharing such dreams with me, Taj. I know we are friends and everything, but I am much older than-'

'No, no!' said Taj, snatching his hand away, getting to his feet, his face aghast as he understood Beulah's allusion. 'You misunderstand! The dream was quite innocent, in that respect. The girl, well, she was being chased by men, desperate looking men.'

Beulah laughed. 'Ooh, desperate you say? Well, a girl who runs away will always have males chasing her; mark my words. And of course, many of them will be desperate, stands to reason, don't you think?'

Taj sighed, his shoulders sagging. 'Forget it, Beulah.'

12

'No, please, Taj, do tell me about her! You have raised my interest now.'

'Too late,' said Taj, leaning over and looking in the mirror. 'What was left of the dream has gone! I'm sorry, there's nothing really to tell about the girl: it has all gone!' Then another image reared in his mind. He paced across the chamber before turning to Beulah, unable to hide his surprise. 'Although, there is one aspect I would like to share. In the sky, above the girl, there loomed a dark shadow, a kind of figure, an unnatural entity watching the chase. What do you think it could have been, Beulah, hmm?'

Chapter Two

Ionuin observed the men closely as they slowed, drawing ever nearer to their fallen victim, their breathing ragged, swords at the ready, a retrieved spear in each hand. She knew they only had one spear apiece, and she had gambled that they would not stab her, not immediately anyway. On this sparsely populated desert world of Ancient Merm, a young, fit girl would fetch a high price at the flesh fairs, and undamaged goods were highly sought after. She allowed a moan to escape, rolled her head slightly as the pair split, pulling her legs to a more natural position from which she could lash out if needed.

'Maybe unconscious?' gasped one, a youngish fellow by the look of him, sporting a lean, naked torso that was deeply tanned.

'Nay, she be awake,' said his companion, an older, more solidly built man. 'Come on lassie, on yer feet. Yer nabbed, and you know it! There be no fooling us, we come too far for such malarkey.'

'Aye,' said the first man, still breathing hard. 'Yer gave us a good run, so you did, but you be ours now. On yer feet, keep them hands off that queer sword you got there and we won't hurt you none; will we, Edan?'

'Nay, we won't hurt her,' Edan laughed. 'Why, we shall be most gentle, young Jord.'

They are very wary, thought Ionuin. They took care not to come within striking distance, but she made no attempt to acknowledge them, drawing steady breaths into her burning lungs, preparing for action. Her father, Tharl, had taught her how to defend herself, but she thought that two fit opponents, both armed with swords and spears, would prove far too much for her in a straight fight. The only advantage she had over them was that they probably thought she was only a slip of a girl. A vulnerable, exhausted victim; disorientated and injured. At least, she hoped they thought this, or she could be in deep trouble.

'I reckon she be hurting, a mite,' said the one called Jord, crouching down by her legs, his head canted at an unnatural angle.

Falling stars! Thought Ionuin, observing him from beneath fluttering lashes. Was the disgusting pig trying to look up her wolf hide dress? Stinking stools! The words of Edan, claiming they would be gentle, now carried a more sinister threat, and fear exploded in her mind. With a guttural scream, she rolled her hips from the floor and flipped her legs over her head, pulling her curved sword from its scabbard in one easy movement. As she came upright with a savage snarl, she grabbed her boot knife with her free hand, steadying her balance, settling into a slight crouch. She was greeted by looks of utter surprise from both men and she wasted no time springing into action by attacking Edan.

She went for the older man first as she considered him to be the most dangerous, and battle commenced with an outpouring of fury as her blade cut and slashed at the man. He retreated under the sudden onslaught, parrying her blows with sword and spear, his eyes betraying fear and uncertainty. Ionuin got the better of the first exchanges but failed to thrust home her advantage. Killing a

14

man, even one who might dishonour a girl before selling her into slavery, was very different to bringing down game animals.

'Don't just stand there gawping!' Edan yelled to Jord, as he retreated beyond her reach. 'Bring her down, for pities sake!'

Ionuin scrambled to one side, trying to keep both men in sight. Jord had rushed towards her with speed, probably intending to backstab her, but she skipped away, wrong-footing him, then slashed at his face, a blow he easily dodged. He made a clumsy jab with his spear as he ducked low, which she parried with her knife before again slashing at his face, but she knew her blade would not bite home.

It seemed that for all her training, the very first time she needed to defend herself in a real life or death situation, she could not even maim, never mind kill! This was something that her father, with all his worldly wisdom, had apparently overlooked in his training schedule. In frustration at her predicament, she kicked out wildly. The sole of her boot, by accident rather than design, thumped into Jord's exposed ribs, knocking him to the floor with a gasping whoosh of escaping breath.

'Ooh, she kicks like a moon mad mule,' Jord hissed through clenched teeth, rolling away from her before scrabbling along on hands and knees.

Instead of following up and finishing him, as she should have done, Ionuin hesitated. The words of her father, *those who hesitate are lost,* echoed in her mind as she stepped back, wondering what to do next. Then Edan came at her with sudden urgency, screaming a fearsome battle cry, jabbing his spear at her legs while thrashing around wildly with his blade at head height. Ionuin easily sidestepped him, parrying the spear with her knife while her sword, Fyrdraca, which according to her father, meant 'Fire Dragon' in some ancient forgotten language, easily blocked all his strikes.

Edan was a powerful man, but Ionuin knew she had been wrong with her first assumption; these men did not know how to use their weapons. They were slow, blundering, and only of average skill, while she was very fast, accurate, and had been taught by an old swords-master. Still, she had the problem of winning the fight, as, apart from cutting her father by complete accident, she had never wounded a man before, let alone indulged her natural curiosity about death by actually slaying one.

She found herself falling into routine swordplay, performing as she had been taught. Even when Jord got to his feet, nursing his ribs, and joined Edan in the attack, she had no difficulty holding them both at bay, but she wondered how much longer she could fight before fatigue took its toll on her strength and energy.

'I imagine that the dark shape in the sky . . . was probably you, Taj,' said Beulah.

'Me?' Taj snapped, jabbing his forefinger into his chest.

'Yes you, dear boy. Would that be so strange?'

'I, I don't know,' answered Taj, pacing in a circle. 'I never even considered such a thing, for I sensed darkness within the shape, a horrible detestable darkness.'

Beulah grinned. 'It makes perfect sense to me, Taj. The dark shape could have been you and you felt guilty about enjoying your observation of the chase. Maybe wishing that the girl would fall, and maybe, just maybe, be caught by those chasing her!'

'No, no, I would not have wanted that,' Taj protested, flapping his hands around in rejection of Beulah's words.

Beulah inclined her head and appeared to consider Taj's response. 'No, no, maybe not, but perhaps, you would have then swooped down and rescued her?'

'You really think so?' Taj asked.

'Of course, and I imagine she would be very grateful and would undoubtedly, show you some small appreciation, um?'

'Appreciation?' Taj quizzed, then he realised what Beulah was actually saying. 'Oh, now look, I told you Beulah, it was not that sort of dream. Do you ever really listen to me?'

'Ooh, touchy, touchy,' said Beulah, pinching his cheek. 'Maybe the patch of darkness was nothing at all. Some dreams, you know, are just dreams; nothing more.'

Taj shook his head. 'No, no, I don't think so, Beulah. I feared for the girl, it was real!'

'Well, it could be your inner desires awakening, coming to the fore,' said Beulah.

Taj scowled. 'I already told you, for the last time, it was not that kind of dream!'

'Oh, yes, so you did. Oh, well.' Beulah shrugged her shoulders and got to her feet. 'I suppose you'll work it out, sorry I cannot be more helpful.'

'You've nothing to be sorry for, Beulah. I just wish I knew what it all means.'

'If it means anything at all,' replied Beulah, walking to the chamber door, patting Taj on his shoulder. 'Never mind, you poor boy. I'm sure there will be other girls being chased in other dreams. Now, you have overslept again and Lord Nexus is expecting you to make an appearance before visiting dignitaries at some point today. So, look sharp, tidy yourself up, and do not forget to make my bed. I know I rarely have use for it, but when I do fancy a nap, I want to be able to just flop down and not have to mess around with the covers. Is this understood, Taj?'

'Fully understood,' said Taj, sitting down on the seat Beulah had just vacated, staring at his wild mop of unruly dark hair in the large mirror.

'And do not be late. Nexus hates to be kept waiting, as you well know,' said Beulah, finally leaving the chamber.

'Whatever,' said Taj, under his breath, teaselling out the tugs and knots of his wild mop of hair with his fingers while running Beulah's words through his head. She was known as something of a seer, and in some respect, she had been right about his dream. He had not wanted the girl to fall, but he was fairly certain she had fallen! He asked himself again; what did the dream mean? Who was the girl and why was she being chased? Beulah had to be wrong about the dream not meaning anything. He was positive there was portent in there somewhere, but what, if anything, was he supposed to do about helping the girl?

Tharl heard the water bubbling, so he swung the metal hook from over the fire, and using wooden handled tongs, lifted the boiling pot clear, setting it on the hearth. From a tin caddy, which he always kept in a pouch by the side of his rocking chair, he scooped two spoons of loose tea-leaves and dropped them into the water. Even with his fading eyesight, he could see it was past noon from the way shadows were falling through the cottage windows, and his stomach growled, seconding his opinion.

As he stirred the pot and grabbed his dark stained mug, he wondered if Ionuin would return today. Fresh meat would be nice, he thought, and he knew his beloved daughter would not fail to bring home a good few kills after being away for several days. Even though game was scarce, she was a fine huntress and a true shot with her bow. He had taught her everything she needed to know about survival in the wilderness, and she was more than capable of looking after herself.

He stirred the pot, sniffing the aroma given off by the tea, his hairy nostrils twitching at the scent.

'Can't beat a good mug of char,' he murmured, half rising from his chair and reaching for the bread and cheese he had prepared earlier, his mouth watering at the thought of the simple, but wholesome food.

He blew across the top of the tea, cooling the surface before sipping gingerly; making a slurping sound, happy at that moment that Ionuin was not present. She always scolded him for not using his manners and eating and drinking noisily.

He bit down into the bread, knowing it would have tasted better with some butter, but the goat had gone wandering since Ionuin's departure and had not yet returned, so he had settled for eating his food dry. He sipped his tea again, thinking it tasted good without milk, and how he should have it black more often; then it happened.

An extremely loud buzz thrummed across his mind, zipping through his head from ear to ear, building to a high, humming crescendo, pulsing at a resonant pitch, before suddenly fading. Somewhere, somehow, an enemy had breached the defences of their valley and were approaching the path to Ducat, the secretive home he and Ionuin had shared since she was a babe in arms.

'Impossible!' he shouted, getting to his feet. He had been assured by the best mage to ever visit Merm that Ducat was impenetrable. The only explanation was betrayal of the worst kind, which meant either that the mage was dead, or had somehow been tricked into revealing the whereabouts of the valley.

His meal and tea forgotten, he snatched his weapons from the wall, strapped on Ironwolf, his ancient sword, gripped his axe tightly and stepped through the cottage door into the dusty yard. He sniffed, scenting the air, and did not like what he could smell. Intruders were definitely coming and they stank to the skies of their own filth.

17

Chapter Three

Ionuin was thankful that she had the advantage of youth and fitness, an advantage that was beginning to pay dividends. Edan was puffing and blowing and could hardly bring any speed or power to bear with his sword strikes. Jord was not quite so tired, but his skills did not match his admirable stamina. Ionuin danced around, making them crash into each other, until Edan, in sheer frustration, shoved Jord out of his way, giving Ionuin a perfect opportunity. She darted forward and flicked the tip of her blade at Jord's wrist, making him yelp and drop his weapon.

'Pig muck and rope burns!' Jord wailed, wringing his hand, watching amazed as blood spurted from the gash. 'The lucky little demon! She got me!'

Ionuin wasted no time in bringing Fyrdraca round in an arcing backswing; smashing the spear from his other hand, breaking the shaft into two pieces.

Edan's mouth formed a perfect 'O' as he observed his injured partner. Ionuin dipped low and rolled, slashing Edan across his thigh with her knife before rolling clear and jumping back to her feet.

'Stinking, rotten offal!' Edan cursed, falling to the floor, casting away both his weapons. 'You wet-neck wench!' he shouted, rocking back and forth, clasping his hands to his leg, blood seeping through his fingers. 'I'll kill you for this! Just see-'

Ionuin jabbed her sword beneath Edan's ear, the point hitting a sensitive spot, making him hiss with pain, drawing a bead of blood. 'I'd be quiet if I were you, Edan,' she said, her voice low, threatening, calibrated for command. 'I might slice off your particulars, cut out your eyes, you know, the sort of thing that happens in your worst nightmares.'

'I've had enough,' Jord declared, picking up his sword, abandoning his broken spear and walking away. 'Come on, Edan. Little rat-tail isn't worth it, let's get back to the caravan, sun's way past midday already.'

'You don't frighten me with your empty threats,' said Edan, gently pushing her sword away. 'Oh, you are good, very good, but you don't have what it takes to cause serious damage, do you?'

Ionuin knew he was right, but she forced herself to smile. 'If I see you on my trail again, Edan,' she said, edging her voice with venom, 'You'll have more than a sliced leg to worry about; it will be your throat next time. On your feet, and move your arse. Your friend Jord has given you good advice. I'd follow it if I were you.'

Edan stared back up at her, squinting in the harsh sunlight. 'I'm injured; you can't expect me to walk away! You bested us, so you are the victor. Now, in the rules of war, you have to take care of-'

'Don't push it!' Ionuin snarled, jabbing Fyrdraca into his fleshy nose, nicking the skin slightly, grinning as his protuberant eyes widened considerably.

Edan yelped and scuttled backwards on his behind. 'Screaming scorpions!'

Ionuin sheathed her sword. 'Scorpions indeed. I dare say there are some around, so stay here and roast in the setting sun for all I care. Take your 'rules of war' and shove them in a dark place. Know what I mean; fool!' She turned and walked away, her senses on full alert for any danger, but she knew neither of the men would bother to follow. Edan was right about one thing, she had bested them; they would not want to retry capturing her, just yet.

A few moments later she heard Edan shouting to Jord, but she was already too far away to discern the words. She had quite a trek if she was going to arrive back at her camp before nightfall, but knew she must reach her hideout and get some much needed rest. She delved into a pouch on her belt and pulled out a small, rounded stone; this she popped into her mouth as a means of generating saliva, extending the time she could go without water. Then she broke into a light jog with no fear that she would be pursued anytime soon. Even if they did give chase, Edan was in no fit state to fight and she thought she could defeat Jord with just her boot knife.

It did bother her that she had failed to strike home fatal wounds, or even telling wounds, for that matter. Was it a weakness she needed to worry about? Was it something which she should talk through with her father on returning home? She glanced over her shoulder to see two distant figures leaning on each other for support, and wondered if she would regret allowing them to live.

Taj straightened the large fur cover on Beulah's bed and prepared to leave her chamber. Lord Nexus was not someone to be messed with, and Taj knew he was due in the throne room that very morning to report any news his wandering thought quests could deliver. It was Taj's task to scour the minds of people and locate any who had a talent for extrasensory perception. So far, he had found no others with talent akin to his own, and he did not expect that to change anytime soon. His gifts were rudimentary at best, but the dark shape in the dream did give him cause for concern, so before he left to meet his Lord and master, he closed his eyes and pushed out his thoughts.

Taking shallow breaths, he relaxed as his senses whirled, spiralling away from him in an out-of-body experience, pouring through various dizzying vortexes that appeared and vanished with unerring frequency. He sought out the blue skies of his dream vision and pictured the dark shape, trying to recall how it had looked hovering in the sky above the chase taking place below. At first, he found nothing resembling that amorphous, troubling presence, and he was just about to withdraw when a nebulous figure whipped across his vision.

'There you are,' he murmured, gripping Beulah's dressing table for support as his mind gave chase. 'Only, now I have found you, what are you?' he wondered.

Taj focused all his power on the figure, trying to draw closer; his thoughts forging ahead through the nether world where dreams and lost souls wander side by side. Shapes shifted within darker shapes, shadowy forms rose and fell, grey mists swirled and eddied, sheets of pale colour blossomed, expanded and dissipated, and then he found the target he was seeking. A large, billowing,

19

writing, pillar of churning darkness, that spread before him, curling around itself.

Taj reached out and it shimmied away. He wondered if it was fearful of him? Maybe he had been wrong all along, perhaps it only looked sinister, but was actually friendly; he knew looks could often be deceiving. He flexed his mind and sent a message into the roiling snake-like, foggy plume. *Do not be afraid, I mean you no harm.* Then he wished with all his heart that he had simply brushed his hair and followed Beulah to the throne room where Lord Nexus awaited him. The darkness was indeed, as he had first suspected; an unnatural, detestable entity. It was savagely malicious, and it had snared his mind in a cunning trap.

Taj heard a sinister chuckling as he strained to break away from the unfurling mass.

Words tumbled through his mind in an ominous avalanche of rumbling hollow sound that boomed inside his head. *Taj! That be your name! 'You mean me no harm?' Hmm, tis very seldom that I ever chance to hear words such as those. A shame really, as I mean you harm. Lots and lots of harm. I am Dark Dragon! I am also lethal and you, little boy, are all mine!*

Taj shuddered at the sound of the voice and tried again to wrench his thoughts free. Mentally, he kicked, punched, bit, scratched and wrestled to break away, all to no avail. A coldness filtered into his mind, a numbing spike of freezing ice stabbed into his consciousness and he screamed, and screamed, and screamed, writhing with excruciating agony as he tumbled into an abyss of empty blackness.

Tharl rubbed crumbs of bread from his lips. Having realised the trespassers would be quite some time stalking their way up towards Ducat, he had remembered his sandwich and drink and returned for them. He took a large gulp of his tea, belched loudly and rubbed his belly, wondering if he would lose his winter-fat this summer. He supposed Ionuin would make sure he at least tried, giving him plenty of chores to keep him exercised. He then wondered why the approaching men smelled so odd. Their sweat stank strangely; it was downright weird, like nothing he had ever smelled before. He smiled, realising it hardly mattered; they would soon be dead.

He felt the warm sun on his face as he tossed the dregs of his tea on the floor and heard a bird singing high above, probably a skylark in its first season, he mused. The valley where he and Ionuin lived had always thrived with such life, it was the only place in the southern hemisphere that still had an abundance of small birds and he always found their songs satisfying and soothing. Another sound acquired his attention now though, a loose pebble rolling along the ground, probably scuffed accidentally by a careless boot, the owner of which was perhaps too intent on where he was going and not watching his footsteps as he should have been.

Tharl absently tossed his metal mug into the goat's water trough and yawned, stretching his arms to the sky. Without warning, using a quick overhand throw, he launched his axe towards where he thought the intruder stood and was rewarded with a hissing yelp, then a thunk, as the axe blade bit into the trunk of one of the skinny pines shading the yard.

'Stone the damn crows!' a voice screamed. 'He gone and cut off me bleeding finger!'

'Shut your silly hole, Grog!' shouted another voice, situated somewhere to Tharl's right.

'It'll be your head that comes off next,' Tharl warned as he drew his sword, listening intently for the slightest sound. There were at least two of them, probably more, he thought as his nostrils flared, picking up myriad scents. Not more than four, he considered, because if there were more than four, they would not have been so cautious. 'I know what you're all thinking,' - he took a calculated gamble - 'all three of you. You're thinking, you are facing a blind old man, a doddering warrior long beyond his best days, but I advise you now; leave this place and I'll not kill you for trespassing.'

'Sterner, he can see!' yelled the one who had lost a finger, who sounded fairly young to Tharl. Young or old, he would have to die.

'I told you, Grog, keep your slobbering gob shut, will yah!' snapped the second voice, who Tharl knew was creeping closer with every passing moment. An older, wiser man, with caution edging his voice making him more dangerous than the other two put together.

'Now!' shouted a third voice, and the fight began.

Tharl parried the first strike from the one he thought was called Sterner, ducked low to avoid an expected attack from the one who had shouted 'now', and set about the intruders with gusto. He jabbed his blade where he thought his enemies might be, was rewarded with the sound of steel clashing against steel and got into his stride with determined enthusiasm as he took the measure of the three men surrounding him.

Relying on what little sight he had remaining, using shadows and sunlight, his ever alert ears and his nose, that possessed the scenting capabilities of a wild animal, he set about defending himself and trying to kill his opponents. He had always enjoyed a good fight, battling with weapons, or even just fists and feet, was something at which he had excelled since he had first learned to walk.

Until now, he had never met anyone who could best him. He had known a few who were his equal with certain weapons, but the sword was his speciality. There was not a man alive who could have defeated him when he was in his prime and even now, almost blind, able to see only vague shadows, there were still few who could match him blow for blow.

The fight was going well, he had felt the tip of his sword slice into flesh several times. He had picked up a few minor cuts himself, but none of the wounds were serious. He was even goading them, asking them if this was the best they could do, taunting their manhood by calling them weak old women, but in the end, it was one of their voices that became his undoing.

'Crudder, get the girl!' the one called Sterner had whispered, just loud enough for Tharl to hear and he had a momentary vision of Ionuin walking upon the scene unexpectedly and being taken unaware.

21

The next thing he knew there was a terrible pain rioting in his chest, a sudden burning, quickly followed by numbing coldness. He gasped and fell to his knees, dropping Ironwolf, his ancient battle-worn sword, his hands now clutching the blade that had cut so deep, piercing the hardened pectoral muscle above his heart, sliding between his ribs. He hissed in agony as another blade stabbed through his back, going directly into his lungs, and he knew it was all over for him. After a life of battling for survival, continually triumphing over his enemies, he had finally met with defeat and he could hardly credit that such a thing was happening.

As he keeled over, his face twisted with pain, his head slamming hard into the dust of the yard, he realised that they had beaten him by using the one thing he had never expected. They had taken the fatherly love that he held for his daughter and turned that love against him.

There were further blows, blades hacking into his body, boots and fists smashing into his face and head, but he was beyond feeling as his mind slipped free of its moorings and drifted into a calm, bewildering nothingness.

Chapter Four

Ionuin set off in the middle of the night, not waiting for dawn; taking a small amount of the meat she had hunted, burying the remainder in a deep pit before covering it with cool sand where it would remain fresh, even through the heat of many months.

She slept fitfully, dreams rearing up and assaulting her mind, bringing her wailing into wakefulness until she could stand it no more.

By keeping a steady pace she made good time and on reaching the edge of the valley she called home, she knew immediately that something was terribly wrong. The warm, welcoming sensation that usually greeted her as she passed from scrubland to verdant greenery was curiously missing. There was the usual birdsong, but it was not light and trilling, harmonious and melodic, but harsh and strangely chaotic. Butterflies danced on the wing, scraps of blue, red and white flitting hither and thither, but not fluttering playfully; they were darting around, crashing into things. Some were even floundering on the grassy slopes as if disorientated and breathing their last.

'My world has changed,' she whispered, casting out her mind, trying to sense other noticeable differences. Her stomach rumbled, tightened, and she knew it was not the lack of breakfast that troubled her, but something else entirely. Fear, cold and unwelcome, tingled within her very core, lurched in her gut, making her feel nauseous, and for the first time in her life, Ionuin was scared to go home.

Taj wiggled his toes as water lapped around them, the small wavelets foaming with bubbles as he pushed his feet into the soft, black sand. He looked out across the dark water, wondered at the starless sky, and sighed. It felt so peaceful here, but, he had no idea where *here* actually was, or how he had arrived. He also knew that it hardly mattered. Nothing mattered, not anymore, not now, not ever again, for he had achieved ultimate tranquillity. A sensation of blissful restfulness had settled deep within his very being.

He wondered if the aggressive looking, muscular man, standing nonchalantly by his side, felt the same. He was very quiet, unmoving, so he supposed that it was likely. He had the urge to ask the man, but resisted saying anything when he noticed that there was an unsettled, troubled expression, creasing his craggy old face.

'He is a wandering soul in torment,' said a voice behind Taj that brimmed with soothing calmness. 'He cannot hear you, or see you, and he is unaware that he is even here.'

Taj turned and looked at the speaker, knowing instantly that the words spoken were the truth. He found himself observing a slightly built woman with skin the colour of midnight roses and a white smile, so stunningly bright, it appeared to be quite dazzling.

'Do you understand what I am saying, Taj?' she asked.

23

'Yes, yes, I do,' Taj replied. 'You speak the truth, for now I see that this man is indeed a wandering soul. You say he is in torment, and sadly, I have to agree. He is certainly distraught, as if he has lost all he knows.'

The woman nodded. 'Yes, you see, he is compelled to be here, he suffers with crippling anguish. I do speak the truth, Taj. This place is called Aztalan, and nothing but the truth can ever be spoken here.'

'Yes, yes, of course, Aztalan,' said Taj, slapping his forehead with both hands, actually staggering a few steps from the sudden impact.

The woman reached out and took his hands within her own. 'You are familiar with this place?' she asked.

'Oh, no, not really, but I have heard of Aztalan. Writers have mentioned it in some of the books I have been fortunate enough to read. A fabled place, steeped in legend, supposedly sacred and populated by dreamers, lost souls, astral-travellers, and such.' The woman smiled and Taj found himself squinting. 'Woman, you are very beautiful. Are you available?' he asked, then gasped at the boldness of his words.

She laughed. 'Taj, I am old enough to be your mother, but I sincerely thank you for what you consider a compliment. I am called Freon, and whether or not I am available is my own business.'

'Yes, yes, of course it is. I am sincerely sorry, please forgive me,' said Taj. 'Freon,' he repeated, listening to the sound of the name, as if trying to discern some hidden meaning.

'I'm nothing so mysterious that you need wonder so. I am what you might call a dreamer of experience, or, an astral-traveller, as you termed it, and I heard and responded to your call.'

'You heard me calling? How odd, I don't remember doing any such thing.'

'That does not surprise me, Taj. Aztalan is a strange place, a law unto itself. There will be many things you do not remember; even when you leave this place, much will remain beyond recall.'

'Oh, I won't be leaving,' said Taj, pulling his hands free of her grasp. 'I like it here so very much! It's better than . . . better than . . . do you know, I don't know where I was before I came here. How peculiar! Let me think. I was . . . hmm?'

Freon took his hands again and clasped them tightly. 'Do not think, Taj. Do not try to remember. Trust me, you were in a bad place, a very bad place. Your mind has become traumatised, blocking out that which it cannot, or will not, accept.'

'How very curious,' said Taj, agreeably. 'I have no idea to what you are referring, although it sounds most ominous; you say I was calling?'

'When I said calling, I really meant screaming,' admitted Freon.

'Screaming!' Taj exclaimed. 'Really?'

'Yes, really. You were screaming, and you were in terrible pain. Your thoughts were being shredded and your soul was crying out in such torment that I was pulled from my dreams. I saw you struggling with another, so I slipped into the fray unnoticed and quickly whisked you away.'

'You did?' Taj said, puzzlement furrowing his brow.

Freon nodded. 'I move swiftly through the dream realms. I was much too fast for the one who had captured you, we were gone before it even noticed. In Aztalan, you can heal quickly from the damage that was done to you, and hopefully, you will soon be as good as new.'

Taj found himself nodding knowingly, though he barely understood what had happened, still, it seemed he owed Freon a great debt. 'I am very grateful, Freon. If nothing but the truth may be spoken here, perhaps a reward is in order,' he said, wondering exactly what form this reward might take.

'There is no need for any reward, Taj, and you will be leaving this place in a few moments. You do not belong here, you must go back to your life. I sense a remarkable future awaiting you, one that is fraught with danger, but also full of choices. How things transpire will depend upon the decisions you take, the choices you make.'

Taj laughed. 'I don't know what you're talking about, Freon, but look, I can see right through my arms! How weird is that?' He glanced around. 'Talking of weird, how come I can see at all? Where is the light source for Aztalan?' He gazed at the blank sky. 'Does the sun ever rise here?'

Freon released his hands. 'We are the light source, Taj. Our very thoughts, do you have a light source in your dreams?'

'Ah, I understand,' said Taj, holding up his hands. 'Look, Freon. No fingers!'

'Yes, you're fading quickly, but I feel we may meet again.'

'Oh, I do hope so,' said Taj. 'Perhaps next time we meet we can kiss each other?'

Freon laughed as Taj gasped at his own words; then he was gone. She walked over and stood by the man who was still staring intently at the lake, and took one of his hands. She forced her thoughts to touch his and recoiled at the savagery she found there. Unassailable anger raged in his mind, akin to a wild beast running rampant, barely held in check by a poorly built cage constructed of civility. This was not something with which she would willingly engage: not yet.

'Not good to lose, is it, Tharl,' she whispered, patting his arm with gentleness. 'But everyone must lose, from time to time. This is what makes the winning so worthwhile.'

Freon thought she heard Tharl grunt, but she was unsure. She caressed his fingers. 'You'll adjust, Tharl, move on, and you will realise your defeat paved the way for the future of others. Unexpected good things often arise from tragedy, so try not to despair, you have all the time you have ever needed, for Aztalan is practically eternal.' She glanced down and saw that her own hands were fading to transparency.

'Goodbye,' she whispered, her words a faint echo drifting across the darkling waters.

'Ionuin,' murmured Tharl, his voice a barely audible whisper that was swallowed by the lapping of the susurrus waves, as he continued to stare across the emptiness of the vast lake.

Ionuin rolled away from the cliff edge, her eyes burning. She felt completely cried out, totally lost and extremely vulnerable. She was uncertain what had happened in their home valley, but she was positive that her father was dead. She took some deep breaths, wishing that the strangling ache in her throat would go away, and scrambled back to her previous position where she could again observe the yard around the cottage.

Keeping low, so that her dark outline could not be seen against the morning sky, she stared intently at her father's unmoving body, willing it to lurch into life, but she knew that it would not, not ever again. She cast her mind around the yard, questing for life, and found nothing bigger than a mole-rat scurrying along its underground burrow. She continued searching around the cottage for any other signs of life, desperately wishing that whoever had killed her father, would step out into the sunlight. In her distress, she had forgotten that wishes were only for little girls who knew no better, and cursed herself for her own stupidity.

That her father had been killed, murdered, was not in doubt. Items from the cottage were strewn over the dusty ground along with various sets of boot prints, and even from this distance, the wounds on his body indicated that her father had fought hard for his life. The one saving grace was that now, she knew the questions she had wanted to ask him had already been answered. She was certain, beyond all reasonable doubt, that she could now dig deep within herself and find the elusive ingredient required to actually maim and kill another human being.

At first, she had thought that she would wait until darkness fell before going down to the cottage, but she changed her mind in an instant. She had scouted the immediate area and found no large life forms, apart from the goat, that always seemed to be here when not wanted and never around when needed, but she still sensed some sort of danger lurking close by, a danger beyond anything she had ever known before. Despite this, she decided to face whatever fate had in store, and leapt to her feet.

Determined not to shed one more tear, she ran down the narrow animal trail. The truth of the matter was that she could not bear one more moment of seeing her father's body lying out in the yard. The goat ran bleating as she rounded the gable-end of the cottage and skidded to a halt, falling onto her knees, throwing herself across her father, hugging him, cradling his head in her hands. Her determination instantly crumbled. She released a yell so loud, so shrill and piercing, that birds flapped squawking from trees, bushes, bracken and briar, their beating wings filling the sky.

As Ionuin wept, she swore retribution for the life that had been taken and the great wheel of karma turned, setting itself upon a new course.

Taj stretched, yawned, and opened one bleary eye to see Beulah staring at him with an odd expression on her face. 'Beulah? Is everything all right?

Beulah shrugged. 'I don't know, Taj. Is everything all right? You failed to show at the throne room yesterday and Nexus is furious! I came home early this morning to find you here, lying on my chamber floor with your eyes wide open, staring off into space. You were cold; shivering, so I put you in bed and covered you up.'

'You did?' Taj said, sitting up, massaging his temples. 'I, I don't understand. I was sitting before the mirror, thinking about what you had said concerning the dream and then . . . I just don't know!'

'Think, Taj. Something has happened to you, but what?'

Taj slid out of the bed and began pacing. 'I tried to find the girl from the dream and something did happen. Something bad.' The memories of the dream stirred, feeling awkward, heavy in his mind, clogging cognitive reasoning, denying him access. 'I just don't know, Beulah,' he said at last. 'Whatever happened is beyond my recall.' He turned to Beulah. 'Is Nexus really angry?'

Beulah nodded her head. 'Not raving, but um, quite cross.'

'Well, cross is not too bad, I don't suppose,' Taj said.

'Yes, um, when I say *cross*, I mean that you can feel his annoyance simmering beneath his thoughts.'

'Oh,' said Taj. 'That bad, eh?'

Beulah sighed. 'Well, maybe I'm exaggerating a tad. I don't think it's that bad actually. Thing is, there are still many visitors here so, if I were you, I'd go bouncing into the Great Cavern as if everything is normal. Nexus can hardly show anger in front of other clan leaders, as it might undermine his authority, and that would be most unbecoming.'

'Then what?' Taj asked.

'Well, try and ingratiate yourself with him, wait on him, be at his every beck and call and if he asks anything of you, do it instantly.'

Taj walked over and hugged Beulah. 'You're the best, but do you think it will work?'

Beulah shrugged 'Maybe, maybe not, but such behaviour will certainly lessen his anger,' she advised. 'When the time comes to face the music, tell him what happened, or tell him you don't know what happened, but don't lie to him. Never lie to Nexus.'

'Beulah, give me some credit!' Taj laughed. 'I would never do such a foolish thing,' He wondered why the fabled realm of Aztalan had suddenly popped into his mind. He gave Beulah another big hug, thanked her and ran from her chamber as fast as he could. He would do exactly as Beulah suggested and get himself in the good graces of Nexus, then, when he had a spare moment, he would visit the library and check out . . . check out what, he wondered?

Chapter Five

The pale sun cleared the distant mountains as Ionuin, one rogue tear trickling slowly down her cheek, placed the final stone on her father's grave. Slanting rays of weak sunshine streamed through the lower boughs of the few surrounding scattered pine, the mild heat dispersing the thin silver mist, gently warming the tanned skin of her exposed arms and legs. After spending a few moments in reflective silence, she cinched her father's ancient leather belt around her middle, securing her wolf-hide dress, and tied back her light brown hair with twine. She slid Fyrdraca into its scabbard, and glanced back at the old stone cottage for one last time before setting out in search of the killers.

During the two days she had been absent on a hunting trip, her life had changed irrevocably. Her father had once been a great warrior, battling freely with all challengers, fighting dragons, rescuing maidens and generally, having an exceptionally good time.

Towards the end of his life, having lost one eye and with blindness claiming most of the vision in his remaining eye, he had become something of a recluse, withdrawing from the wild life of daring escapades. This dying world was not a place where the strong protected the weak, and throughout his life, Tharl had made many enemies while indulging in what he liked to think of as *his heroic adventures*. Ruthless, vicious enemies who would not allow a disability such as the onset of premature blindness prevent them from exercising their revenge. To kill a warrior of Tharl's status would be a great coup. Even though the man was past his prime, he was still a living legend, and to defeat him would bring exceptional kudos to any warrior. Regrettably, that time had now arrived. Tharl's blood had been spilled, the fire of his life-force quenched. The man who had become a myth in his own lifetime, was no more.

When Ionuin was born, her father had given up his wayward lifestyle and settled in the mountains on the edge of what remained of civilization. They had made their home in a secluded little valley where opportunist cutthroats, travelling bandits, and mercenary soldiers of fortune were rarely encountered. Ducat, Tharl had called their isolated cottage and meagre gardens, which in the old language meant *Lion's den*. When Ionuin had asked why they never had any visitors, or ever saw travellers passing through their valley, Tharl had claimed they were granted a protection spell by a great wandering wizard. This wizard had cast a ward over the whole valley to keep trespassers at bay, making the cottage virtually invisible, so that they would always be safe. Ionuin had never believed the story, but she had never openly questioned it either.

The years had passed peacefully and Tharl had taught his young, determined daughter all she needed to know about the art of combat, survival, the ways of the wild and the world. He had instilled the wisdom of countless generations into her eager mind, taught her how to depend upon her own intuition, take major decisions for herself, and to trust gut instinct when dealing with others. In a harsh drought-like environment, where life was tough, trust was a precious commodity that could not be given lightly, as it could mean the difference between extinction and survival.

Ionuin's mother had died while giving birth, so Tharl, representing both parents, had raised Ionuin to the best of his abilities. The task, she knew, had not been easy for him, as she had developed into a wayward child with an inherent mischievous streak. She was wilful with an independent nature, confident in her own skills, harbouring a toughness that was tempered by a veiled kindness of spirit. She expected things to be done the right way, but could be forgiving if they went amiss, so long as attempts were made at correction.

Ionuin remembered schooling being the worst part of her upbringing, as Tharl would be the first to admit, he was never the best of scholars. He had known his letters and basic mathematics, and Ionuin had proved to be a quick learner, but still, teaching often proved difficult. By the age of twelve, Ionuin was even teaching him a thing or two, so Tharl accepted, that as far as education was concerned, no more could be done. Ionuin had rebelled against the idea of teaching herself, claiming that, as he was her father and guardian, it was his duty. Tharl had countered that once the pupil exceeds the master, no more can be taught.

In a stubborn protest, Ionuin refused to further her education by herself, hoping her father would relent, but Tharl was an old master at the fine art of stubbornness and reused to be swayed. Eventually, to quench her aching thirst for knowledge, Ionuin had returned to studying the score of books they possessed, and her education continued, perhaps not in ideal circumstances, but in the situation at hand, the best that could be hoped for. As a peace offering, whenever Tharl did venture into any of the scattered settlements that remained, he endeavoured to find books for his daughter. Invariably, he was successful, until by the time Ionuin was in her fourteenth summer, they had four shelves full of volumes on various topics that they jokingly referred to as, 'The Little Library'. What Ionuin adored even more, was when her father returned from his travels with quills and coloured, inks. Sheaf's of blank paper; paper from which Ionuin would make her own books, filling them with thoughts, ideas and wayward musings. Personal books that she now must leave behind, with the intention of returning for them once she had performed what she saw as her family duty.

Sighing loudly, she reminisced further, urging the fond memories of their daily life to surface, to give her the courage of conviction to do what must be done. Recalling how at the beginning of each day, they had indulged in ritual combat instruction. If Tharl had been honest with himself, it was only the size advantage he held over his daughter that stopped her getting the topside of him during their routine swordplay. Admittedly, he was almost blind and Ionuin took it relatively easy, but she knew that in his own mind, he still represented a formidable opponent. Ionuin also knew that her father's fighting days were over, leaving the exploits of his youth to become the comfort of old age and the folly of many a stretched yarn. Old age is a familiar friend to those managing to avoid premature death, becoming the ultimate price man pays for his reprieve from an early grave.

Ionuin had spent many a chilly evening seated by the fire, listening to her father's tales of his misspent youth, his daring and bravery pitted against seemingly insurmountable odds. Now, these recounted adventures were nothing more than memories that belonged in a bygone era. Tears threatened to overwhelm her in a gushing flood, but Ionuin drew in a deep breath, forcing her emotions under control. Reminiscing was a fine thing, but she had unfinished business that needed tending in the present before she could finally close the door upon the past.

Her father had been brutally slain, and from scuffed markings along the ground, Ionuin estimated that there were at least three in the murderous party. Along with the trail of tracks, there were other markings too. Animal prints, but they were very faint and Ionuin could make nothing of them. There was something else too; the heavy scent of blood that was not her father's, it smelled different, spicy.

Just like her father, Ionuin had always possessed an incredible sense of smell, something her father often enjoyed remarking upon. She sniffed around the markings on the ground, her nose hovering over blood spatters. It seemed her father had delivered at least one telling strike before he fell, as the blood had dripped in more than one place. Not a fatal wound, but she knew his killers had not gone away unmarked.

In her hand, she squeezed the dismembered finger she had found by the pines earlier, examining it closely before placing it in the pouch slung across her shoulders. At least one of the killers would be easily recognizable, a youngish fellow by the look of the finger, and if he had his companions with him, the more the merrier as far as Ionuin was concerned. Boiling anger reared its ugly head as she thought of the murderers. She felt like lashing out wildly, but there was nothing upon which she could vent her displeasure. Instead, she breathed deeply, letting each breath ease away the pain until slowly, her self-control was reasserted.

'You shall be avenged father, or I shall die trying,' she promised, touching the top stone of her father's cairn. 'On this, you have my word of honour.'

The king remained, silent, motionless, his chiselled features giving no indication of the turbulence raging within. His worried eyes locked firmly on the impassive, yet beautiful face, of his slender queen, and she returned his measured gaze, her calculating eyes conveying to him some much needed assurance. The king relied heavily on his queen's judgement. She kept control of his court and oversaw the running of his small empire. Their world was constantly under threat from the forces of darkness residing on the far side of this unassuming world, and their very existence was seemingly in the hands of the Gods; supreme beings that had allegedly shaped them all and created the divine rules by which they lived, and more often than not, died.

The king had become distressed because men had been sacrificed, for the greater good, his queen would say, but still sacrificed. Often, usually at night, when the dark blanket of silence had descended, he thought of peace and what the world would be like if peace reigned supreme. However, when he saw his magnificent troops preparing for war, his knights mounted and ready to lead the charge, all thoughts of peace disappeared in an all-consuming blitz of battle fever. He wanted victory, demanded victory, and with his powerful queen by his side, marshalling his forces, it was win or die.

Across the cacophonous fervour of the tumultuous mayhem being waged, he surveyed the situation, and saw, above the sharpened points of clashing weapons, a possible weakness along his enemy's flank. He hoped that there was not a cunning ploy afoot to lure him into a trap, and prayed that with the help of the omnipresent Gods, that he would win this battle.

However, before he could capitalize on the situation, catastrophe struck a decisive blow in the enemy's favour. Charging out of nowhere, a knight, clad in full battle armour, his sword raised, leapt through the defensive line and slaughtered his queen without mercy. The king reeled back in shock as the knight wheeled around and threatened him. He was trapped with no possible escape. With his queen dead, all was lost and he retained no desire to fight on, or even live. Somewhat lacklustre, he capitulated and slumped to the floor. *So this is death*, he thought as his senses seeped away, leaving only a terrible numbing coldness that welcomed the dark, as once again, he had lost the game.

'Another checkmate, I believe,' said Lord Nexus as Taj pushed over his white king.

'No, I-I conceded,' Taj argued, his lavender eyes darting around the board. 'I could have moved, my lord, only . . . well, I thought I saw-'

'He's a poor loser, aren't you, Taj?' interrupted Bollfur, relaxing on a nearby stone couch. 'I suppose it's only to be expected, considering your heritage.'

Taj sprang to his feet, anger flashing in his lavender eyes. 'What do you mean, Bollfur?'

'Now, now, sit down, Taj,' said Nexus. 'You did not mean anything, did you, Lord Bollfur? Do try and remember that young Taj is my ward and under my protection. An insult to him is an insult to me. We don't want any upset, now do we?'

The whole cavern had suddenly gone very quiet. Three dozen pairs of eyes were fixed on the unfolding tableau before them.

31

Chapter Six

Ionuin gathered the few precious belongings she possessed, securing them along with her bedroll - a massive bear hide sewn together by her father - and set off on the trail left by the murderers. Mountains, their peaks lightly capped with snow, loomed in the distance. She considered that perhaps, somewhere amongst these natural rocky giants, the killers were hiding. Or maybe not, she thought, assessing the easy clues left along the path, reasoning that they were just careless amateurs. Probably bandits from the Valley of Caves seemed to be the most likely answer, rather than men from the mountains. According to her deceased father, the men who inhabited the Valley, and the vast rock-strewn wastelands beyond, were mostly lowly brigands and unscrupulous outcasts. Robbers and killers, taking what they wanted whenever they liked and answering to nobody.

The cottage had been rifled and two gold bracelets had been stolen. Along with her long-handled, curved-blade sword, Fyrdraca, the bracelets had been birth gifts to Ionuin from a great benefactor, her father had told her. Now that she had attained her fifteenth year, she had intended to wear them permanently and not just use them as playthings as she had done during childhood. She now wished that she had done just that, then they would not have been stolen, although, it was not so much the bracelets that she wanted returned, this was a murder hunt.

She scrambled up a set of worn steps her father had cut into the mountain side when she was still a little girl, then halted. She drew her sword, whiplash-quick, glancing all around. She had the unnerving sensation that she was being watched. No-one could be seen in the immediate vicinity and all she could hear was the buzz of insects. Ionuin was not usually so jumpy, but during her hunting trip, while being chased by the slavers, she had sensed the presence of another; but again, had seen nothing.

In her heart, she hoped that it was the killers, that they had laid a false trail, planning on trapping her, but she knew this was just wishful thinking. Over several days and nights, this unknown watcher had avoided being seen, and in Ionuin's estimation, was far more dangerous than a bunch of cowardly opportunist cutthroats.

Unable to see the watcher, and relatively certain that she was in no immediate danger; she sheathed Fyrdraca and continued up the steps to the mountain path. She felt uneasy; stirrings from deep within informed her that she was about to be confronted by matters of some concern.

'How I need my father's advice now,' she mumbled, because any sense of what those matters might be, completely eluded her. She brushed loose strands of dirty brown hair from her eyes, catching a whiff of her body odour. 'I need to bathe too,' she told herself, teasing bits of gorse and bracken from her fringe. 'It'll have to wait.' She continued to climb and tried to control the turbulent feelings of danger and impending adventure. There was something else too, she thought, as she left the steps and ran at a crouch along the trail. An acute awareness resting in the back of her mind, just beyond reach. A hushed call, trying to attract her attention, attempting to make contact. A voice, vague and distant, but insistent, trying to connect, but not quite able to break through.

'Who are you?' she asked herself, stopping and glancing around, resting on her haunches, pressing her palms to her temples.

Exasperated by the experience, she scratched at the prickling sensation irritating her scalp, turned off the trail and began the ascent of a winding path that climbed the rocky shoulder of the mountain known as *Flathead*, the name earned when its summit had been removed by a huge explosion long, long, ago. From this vantage point, she could scan the surrounding land. There was nearly a full day's light left for her journey, that would almost certainly be doomed to end in death, either for her, or those she pursued. Brimming with confidence, one way or the other, she hoped the end came soon.

Behind her lay the scattered remnants of a once great civilization that had torn itself apart far back in history. The reasons why had been lost in time, only jumbled stories remained of what had really happened. Exaggerated stories steeped in myth and legend that contradicted each other, becoming nothing more than fairytales told and retold to entertain small children. Before her were the Badlands, where only brave men and fools ever ventured, and only the extremely lucky returned to tell the tale. Journeying through the Valley of Caves, it was into the Badlands that Ionuin suspected she must go if she were to keep her belated promise to her father.

As she crested the summit of Flathead, with her hands resting on her knees, she caught her breath. The rocky hills around her were ideal for hiding, but Ionuin looked further ahead towards the vast ancient floodplain that lay before the entrance to a snaking valley that had been carved out of the rock by water that was long gone. She sniffed the air and caught a whiff of something stale on the light breeze. Sweat, rank with the filth caused by living an unclean life - and there it was again, that strong spicy odour she had found in the blood back at the cottage. She checked under her arms, her nostrils flaring. 'No, I do smell, a bit, but that stink on the wind is not coming from me.'

She observed the inhospitable landscape until the sun reached its zenith, but could see no movement, so guessed that the killers were sleeping away the hot daylight hours somewhere on the floodplain. Either that, or they had fled at speed and were already in the valley, and she was almost certain this was their destination. She was travelling light and estimated that she could reach the valley entrance in a couple of days. She sniffed the air again, the unmistakable scent of unwashed bodies was so light that it was barely detectable, and she reasoned that they were at least a day, maybe two, in front of her.

She quenched her thirst from her water-skin, placed a small pebble in her mouth to keep her body fluids circulating, a trick her father had learned from the desert men of the high plains far to the south, and set off at a light trot. The hunt was truly underway.

High above Ionuin, unseen, circled a black speck. The speck observed her and knew the dice of destiny had taken a big tumble. How they rolled out was still undecided, but the speck hoped to influence the outcome. Perfect timing was crucial for a successful conclusion in this matter, and in its favour, it had essential knowledge, while the pathetic girl creature scrabbling about below remained ignorant of the truth. If it could have grinned maliciously, it would have done, instead, the black speck peeled back its scabrous lips to reveal many sharp teeth before it banked and wheeled away. There was much to do and vital preparations to make before the coming conflict exploded into life.

Lord Bollfur scratched at the bony ridge above his piercing blue eyes. 'No, we don't want any upset,' he said, getting to his feet, stretching to his full height so he towered over Taj. 'I was only joshing with the lad. I meant no offence to Little Squeaker.'

Taj hated the nickname, *Little Squeaker*. It had plagued him ever since he first learned to talk. His voice had been so quiet that it came out in barely intelligible squeaks that brought mockery from those around him. He sprang forward, leapt over the chessboard and jabbed his fist into Lord Bollfur's rotund stomach. 'I challenge you, Lord Bollfur,' he shouted, trying to make his voice strong and manly.

Bollfur threw back his head and peals of laughter echoed around the cavern. His amusement was infectious and others joined in the merriment. 'You challenge me? Why, my dear boy, don't talk such foolishness! I'll crush you in an instant!'

'Taj,' Lord Nexus said cautiously. 'Once again, you have allowed your impetuous nature to get the better of you. Withdraw the challenge, stop acting like a deranged mutant, and sit down this instant!'

'No, I won't!' Taj snapped with vehemence. 'I'm tired of this fat sack of rancid offal mocking me at every turn, just because I'm different. The challenge stands, Bollfur. Do you accept?'

The edges of Lord Bollfur's light blue scales flushed a darker blue, indicating anger at Taj's insult, but he only sighed. 'All right, Little Squeaker, if you insist, I accept.'

'And if I win,' Taj shouted, so all could hear, 'if you ever call me, Little Squeaker again, you will perform penance at my bidding! Understood?'

'Indeed!' said Lord Bollfur. He pushed his nose squarely into Taj's face; his breath hot and reeking of rotten flesh. 'Rancid offal, you called me, Little Squeaker. You like hurling insults, don't you? So, if I win,' he growled, 'you shall inherit the name, Little Squeaker, officially, for all time; understood?'

Taj clenched his fists into tight balls. He had not considered how Bollfur would react to his ill-thought out demand of penance for the loser, but the challenge had been laid and accepted, so he had to win. The mockery of being called, 'Little Squeaker', for all time, would make his life unbearable. He snatched up two pawns of opposite colour, switching them behind his back, exchanging the pieces before thrusting them before Bollfur.

Bollfur tapped Taj's right hand and the colour was revealed. 'Black! Hmm, ah well, the advantage is yours, but not for long, Little Squeaker.'

Lord Nexus vacated his seat for Lord Bollfur and the rest of the clan gathered around to watch. There was nothing like good entertainment before the approach of the crack of doom. Nexus watched the game begin and agreed to adjudicate. Both Lord Bollfur and young Taj were skilful players and predicting the winner was not easy. Bollfur was old and wise and had proven to be a great tactician in his time on the battlefield, whilst Taj was young and full of vigour and so much like his dearly beloved mother that it actually pained Nexus to have to stand by and watch the boy grow up ignorant of his parentage. Taj displayed so many of his mother's traits, that the current situation seemed grossly unfair; but that was how it had to be, for now.

These were the rules he had agreed to abide by when he took custody of the child. No one in the whole clan even suspected who Taj really was or where he had come from. Only a select few knew the truth, and most thought the boy was just a talented orphaned waif Nexus had found wandering the empty desert settlements. They knew he could prove useful to the clan as they were aware of his natural gifts. He possessed the ability to mentally project, link minds, seek out trouble makers who might threaten the clan, and he also provided amusing entertainment on dull evenings when they gathered for various feasts. Even so, most knew nothing of his true importance, for if they did, they might treat him with more respect. Although, Nexus knew, as with all clans, real respect could not simply be given, it had to be rightfully earned.

'Check!' Taj shouted, as he slid his king's bishop across the board.

'Interesting,' muttered Lord Bollfur as he blocked the move and appeared to be lining up his pieces for a cunning counter attack.

Taj allowed a cautious smile to escape, and Nexus knew the boy had already seen what was afoot. Yes, such a keen wilful mind, thought Nexus, just like his dearly departed mother.

Chapter Seven

Since discovering the brutally battered body of her father, Ionuin had travelled the whole day, through the night, rested in the morning and travelled again during the afternoon, finally stopping beside a stream near an up-thrust of rock. Meltwater trickled over the slippery stepping stones, thoroughly wetting her deerskin boots while fording the brook. Apart from the springs in her home valley, this rivulet was the only known fresh source of the precious liquid this side of the Valley of Caves. Once inside the valley, which led directly into the outskirts of the Badlands, she knew fresh water would be scarce. Not non-existent, just hard to find. She quickly filled her skin bottle, tying it off with a twine thong, and stood staring into the distance. Night was fast approaching and she needed to acquire a gut feeling for her immediate surroundings.

She had passed one camp in the night where three forms had clearly flattened the ground, and found places where the killers had urinated and defecated. She now knew that the spicy stink she had smelled on the bloody-finger and the stale sweat carried by the wind came from their diet of strange meat and the scented giant cacti that grew in scattered clumps in this part of the world. Her determination to catch the killers had only increased, and as she walked along the stream's edge in a crouch, scenting the ground, looking for signs of their passage, she caught the strange scent again. Very faint this time, but it was definitely the same smell. It did not take her long to find their crossing-point, and she guessed that they had left that very morning, so she was perhaps a little more than half-a-day, two thirds at most, behind them. By now though, they would be approaching home territory.

Considerable caution would be required as she crossed the remainder of the broad plain leading into the valley. Her father had warned her never to use the valley, because packs of lychyaena hunted there, and certainly never to enter the Badlands, but his well-intentioned advice would now go unheeded; this task was necessary. Her hunting skills were very useful when it came to remaining concealed, and her prey remained unaware they were being tracked. Or, she wondered, were they unaware? If they were in the habit of checking their back trail they may have seen her following; they may even be waiting up ahead!

What bothered her more, was why they had come to their cottage in the first place. What were they doing in the secluded valley that she and her father had called home? If the valley was protected by the wizard's ward - as her father had alleged - why had it failed? Or was this wizard just part of her father's fanciful imagination? She pondered these questions as she knelt by the water and doused her upper body liberally, slaking away days of travel dirt, then snatched up a handful of stones and casually threw them at her own reflection, watching as her image wavered in the ripples. She realised they could have found the cottage by accident; or were they actually looking for something else?

'Or someone else,' she murmured, as the last stone plopped beneath the water, 'maybe someone in particular?'

Females were scarce on this world, especially young ones; what if they had perhaps seen her out hunting and followed or tracked her? Once they had the location of the cottage, it would be easy to just turn up one morning and take her and her father by surprise. 'I bet they were very angry when they discovered I was not home,' she mused. She began speculating how the scene had played out, but could draw no firm conclusions. If she got the chance, she would question the men before she killed them, just to satisfy herself that her father's death was pure chance and that her carelessness when returning home was not to blame.

She gave a little shiver. The onset of early evening had quickly darkened the pale sky, and the sun had disappeared behind the high range of mountains in the far west. Ionuin returned to the up-thrust of rock, made camp and began scanning the horizon for signs of life. At first there was nothing, but as her eyes became accustomed to the eerie gloom, she saw exactly what she was looking for. In the far distance, glimmering through the rapidly increasing darkness, a pinpoint of light appeared. Ionuin knew it had to be the killers and if so, they were within striking distance and from the careless advertising of their whereabouts, they were not expecting trouble.

'Soon, father,' she whispered into the cooling night. 'Soon you shall rest in peace.'

Sitting down, legs thrust out straight before her, Ionuin placed palm against palm and began to meditate. Taking shallow breaths, she felt her heart rate slowing, and cleared her mind so that she had an unobstructed view of the way ahead. On the edge of her thoughts, she heard the call of a beast that had loomed large in her mind, savage and scary, but Ionuin remained unafraid of this unfamiliar monster. She sensed that it had a gentle side and meant her no harm, but something troubled the beast. A power greater than itself was coming, and a feeling of utmost caution threaded through Ionuin's mind. The faint, but unmistakable tinkle of music edged her thoughts, lightly plucked strings, the hum of pipes; then the connection was gone.

Ionuin's eyes sprang wide open, she wondered what the vision meant, if indeed, it meant anything. There was also the music; this was new, nice, but unsettling. 'Am I going mad?' she laughed, pondering her meditation experience. She dismissed the notion. Only sane people ever questioned their sanity, allegedly. She put aside these unhelpful thoughts and decided to eat a cold meal of game with stone bread, which, despite its jaw-breaking hardness, is the favourite bread of travellers as it lasts virtually forever.

The meat was greasy, the bread crunchy and extra tough, but Ionuin enjoyed the food. By living the life of a hunter-gatherer, supplemented by a little farming, one became accustomed to plain, simple food. Nourishment was the important thing that could mean the difference between life and death, and Ionuin kept this fact in mind as she swallowed the last piece of bread.

After resting, hopefully snatching some light sleep, Ionuin intended to journey through the night. She thought the most effective plan would be simply surprising her quarry in the morning just as they awoke. She had considered taking their lives while they slept, but this method reeked of cowardice and besides, Ionuin wanted to witness the fear reflected in their eyes as she killed them, perhaps slowly, one by one. She was not a brutal person, but her father had suffered greatly and she meant for those responsible to pay their debt in full. Her father always said, 'The world is corrupt with injustices that have escaped correction and punishment.' Well, this injustice was one too many. Deserved punishment was on its way.

She strolled towards the nearby stream, intending to slake her thirst before bedding down, preserving her bagged water supply, then unexpectedly she pulled up short. A sudden burst of noise erupted inside her head and then slowly subsided as she raised protective mental barriers. There was no music this time, just the voice that continually haunted her, only now, it seemed louder and clearer, but still garbled.

Ionuin had always possessed some limited low-grade telepathic ability, but she had no idea how the energy should be channelled. Her father had never understood the voices and dismissed them as the result of an overactive imagination. He considered the concept of telepathy a childlike foolishness, encouraging Ionuin to concentrate on developing her physical skills. In her father's opinion, the application of the mind was to ponder things through and arrive at a logical conclusion by the use of homespun philosophy. Or to sleep on a problem, allowing the workings of the dream world to take action, so that on awakening, the answer one sought would appear in the blink of an eye.

To expand further and indulge in the mysticism and magic of life brought problems for Tharl and he had always discouraged Ionuin from the path of enchantment. 'Magic' he claimed, 'had its uses', but Ionuin was aware that there was much to know and understand before such power could be used properly and made to be of advantage. From visiting travelling carnivals and fairs, she knew many relied on magic to some degree, hurling curses, wishing for riches, forecasting the future, but it stood to reason that nobody ever got anything for nothing. Everything had its price, and sometimes, the price could be very high indeed, her father had claimed. Also; magic did not always work.

The travelling wizard had allegedly warned that without the correct method, using magic was sheer madness, and Tharl had taken him at his word. This was not a difficult decision for her father, as he would rather rely on the trusted physical solution to problems than something so elusive and unreliable. According to Tharl, the methods of magic and the way of mages were oblique mysterious things in which ordinary mortals should never dabble.

Her father had also claimed that he had seen men - hard men - go mental, ape-faced bonkers, while gazing at the stars trying to fathom some portentous meaning from the bright points of flickering light. Some had foolishly sold their souls for personal success, without even knowing what their soul was or even why they had a soul! They soon found out though, immediately after death in most cases. On cold nights, when the wind ripped through the sky, legend held that you could hear these selfish soul sellers screaming in eternal despair.

Ionuin smiled, for even though she doubted such a thing as a soul even existed, her father was always determined that such a fate would not befall his little girl and it had not been easy. She had often exasperated him, as she had displayed such an enquiring mind and raised questions to which Tharl had never even considered answers. However, he had done his best and no man could have done more; of this she was certain.

With her thirst quenched from the stream, Ionuin settled down on her bearskin and still feeling restless, applied herself to sharpening Fyrdraca in readiness for the bloodletting. It was going to be a long night, and when morning came, either her vengeance would be satisfied or she herself would be slain. She hardly cared about the outcome, such was her desolation at losing her only relative. This was a mission where the taking part was what counted. Victory would simply be an added bonus.

With the large rock behind her and hemmed by the curve of the trickling stream, she felt safe from sudden attack. So, she wondered, why such nervousness? There was something amiss, but she could not quite put her finger on the problem. She took several deep breaths, held her hands to the heavens and flexed her mind, sending her thoughts out into the night, but even though she touched nothing, the unsettling feeling twanging her nerve-endings persisted. She withdrew her thoughts, looked about her and feeling under threat, got to her feet.

For what seemed the longest time she peered into the deepening darkness where instinct told her something lurked unseen. The night pressed on her senses like a physical living thing, but there was nothing out there but darkness.

On the verge of ceasing the search, she focused on one point amidst a scattering of rocks. A hazy shadow shifted, and cold fear uncoiled in Ionuin's gut, making her knees feel weak and her mouth oddly dry: she knew it was the watcher. The movement was so slow and indistinct to the naked eye that it was hard to spot, but Ionuin had sensed, rather than seen, that something was definitely out there.

She sniffed the air, catching a whiff of brimstone, but not the smell from smoking mountains, this was something dark and sinister with an underlying taint of decomposed meat. She stared hard, trying to focus on the presence and to her horror, lingering in the far shadows where nothing had been before, she saw two tiny flame-red eyes.

The game had been slow and cautious. Both players had made a few strategic attacks, nothing serious or spectacular, and the defensive positions were evenly matched. Taj began sandbagging, moving pieces around behind the pawns but not intending anything that might be considered aggressive, then Bollfur made the crucial error he had been waiting for. Without a good move on offer, he had castled on the short side, solidifying his defence, something Taj had been trying to lure him into doing for the last five moves.

Taj instantly switched his point of attack, pushing his pawns into blocking positions, practically dividing the board in two with a diagonal defensive line. Bollfur began to look pensive, he snorted down his long nose, and once again the fetid stink of rotten meat wafted across the board. He tried to bring his knights across, but they became bogged down in the centre. Taj pushed down the short side with his bishops, sacrificing one, then the other, giving himself room for his own knights. Bollfur saw the danger but it was too late. Taj checked him with his knight, forcing the king into the corner, then slid his queen down the length of the board.

'Checkmate!' he shouted, leaping up and punching the air.

Bollfur let go of a deep throated growl. 'Why, you irascible scamp!' he grunted good-humouredly. 'How about best of three, eh?'

'Yeah right! You think that I'd be fool enough to gamble away a win I already got for nothing? Please!' Taj laughed, clapping his hands excitedly. 'Remember the wager, Bollfur, the name is Taj from now on, got it?'

'Oh yes, I got it all right.' Quicker than the eye he reached out and grabbed Taj behind the neck, dragging him across the chess table so they were eye to eye. 'And it is Lord Bollfur to you, Little Taj, and don't forget it!' he scowled, his big blue eyes bulging.'

'I won't,' snapped Taj, slipping out of Bollfur's grip with a neat twist of his neck. 'One more thing though, Lord Bollfur. Clean your gnashers! Your breath stinks like the rotted, flea-infested arse of a dead buffalo!'

The cavern erupted with laughter as Bollfur tried to make another grab for the boy, but Taj was snake-quick as he dived beneath the table, slipping through Bollfur's legs. Bollfur spun, tried to trap Taj, but his huge clawed foot caught on the edge of the chessboard, scattering pieces in all directions and nearly toppling him onto his ample behind. He lunged forward but others blocked his way as Taj scampered off to the safety of the smaller, higher caves dotting the cavern walls. He leapt onto a rocky platform, using nimble agility as he expertly scaled a steep rock-face, pulling himself onto a narrow ledge.

Bollfur eventually pushed his way through the crowd, shouting curses until he stood below the boy, looking up. 'You may be out of my reach now, Taj, but when I get hold of you-'

'Hey, Bollfur,' Taj Interrupted. 'You're a poor loser, must be your heritage!'

Nexus stood beside Bollfur and guffawed with laughter, slapping his old friend on the back. 'You have to admit, he does have a point, and let's face it, Bollfur, if you can't be bothered to hunt fresh meat, consistently satisfying your hunger with carrion, it's no wonder your breath stinks like a dead buffalo's bum!'

The cavern again erupted with laughter. Bollfur looked at all the familiar faces, glanced up at Taj and began laughing too. 'I'm an old fool,' he said, shaking his head. 'I know the boy is only funning. All right, Taj, you got me good and you won the game fairly. Come on down, I shall not harm you. Just to prove everyone wrong, we'll go hunting at first light and we shall all feast on fresh meat at tomorrow's supper.'

'Agreed!' shouted Taj, leaping off the ledge. Bollfur caught him and gave him a rough slap across his shoulders.

'To my chambers first, young Taj,' said Lord Nexus. 'I would have words with you.'

'Yes, your Majesty,' said Taj, obediently following Nexus, running to keep up, smiling to himself at his victory as they wound down the torchlit passageway towards the throne room.

Chapter Eight

Ionuin staggered back until she butted up against the rock. Whatever it was, it knew she was here, so there was no advantage in concealment. She swallowed her fear and tried to calm her racing heart; it felt as though it was trying to burst from her chest. She drew Fyrdraca and her short bladed boot-knife. The instant they were in her hands the weapons gave her strength. She weighed her options. Fleeing through the dark night was out of the question. She might trip and break a bone, making her easy prey. Rushing into battle against an enemy that could possess unknown strengths was also unwise, while just standing her ground at least gave her time; thinking time. Her father had taught her that useful thinking should always precede useful action, and she could not agree more.

Again, she pushed out her thoughts, mentally questing, trying to gauge the danger of this flame-eyed creature. She hit an incorporeal wall that made her recoil and gasp for breath. The creature's thoughts were unlike anything she had ever encountered before and it had potent mind defences, shielding a keen intelligence capable of blocking intrusion. She tried to probe again, but it was ready for her and stabbed at her thoughts with gnashing fangs.

'Ouch,' she yelped, snatching her head backwards, cracking her skull. Stars danced behind her eyes. 'What are you?' she murmured, utter disbelief racing through her mind, sending a decidedly icy chill tiptoeing along her spine. She knew there were plenty of monsters on Merm, of the mutant variety, but she had rarely seen any on her hunting trips. Still, what else could it be? She tried to swallow, but her mouth felt as dry as the Desert Sea. The shadows shifted again, seeming to unfurl and rise up, then flow down like a nebulous mass, shredding her nerves. The most heart-stopping aspect though, without a doubt, had to be the eyes; piercing red orbs that she felt could see right into her mind, into her very being. She recalled the strange animal markings around the cottage that she could not discern; then the eyes moved, coming closer.

'I see you, beast,' she whispered, more to herself than to the watcher, her shoulders pressing into the unyielding rock. Without realising what she was doing, she shouted. 'I offer you combat!' Her voice echoed hollowly, sounding weak and afraid. 'Why did I do that?' she wondered aloud. Issuing the challenge had, however, given her courage, and with limited options available she dug down to her reserves, summoning the nerve to throw out a threat. 'I said; I offer you combat, come now and fight, or beg for mercy when I thrust my sword to the hilt into your stinking guts: beast!'

No reply was forthcoming, but Ionuin hardly expected one. Whatever was skulking out there did not respond to threats, and why should it? She was a slip of a girl, an innocent of fifteen summers alone in the dark of the night. Admittedly, she had a sword and a knife, but such weapons were useless against phantoms, and phantoms are what Ionuin suspected were watching her.

'Stop it!' she told herself, her thoughts skirting the slippery edges of panic. Perhaps they were simply phantoms of her own mind, unwittingly conjured from her underlying fear. She fought down her growing anxiety. Mutant beasts were real, and could be killed, while phantoms were only childish illusions. 'Get a grip, Ionuin,' she warned herself. This watching enemy is real and also cautious. This suddenly struck her as strange. Was the beast afraid too? If it could be killed, it would be reasonable to assume it feared death and it had not exactly gone on the offensive, had it?

'Be brave Ionuin,' she murmured, 'seize the initiative and you may yet survive.' She cleared her throat. 'So be it!' she wailed, injecting venom and confidence into her voice, masking the quiver that would expose her nervousness. 'I gave you every chance to leave!' The pinpoints of light were eerily luminous, glowing like tiny stars, but they were definitely eyes. Eyes the like of which Ionuin had never seen before. 'Snap out of it,' she yelled, her tone reproachful and scolding. 'Just the night playing tricks, nothing to be afraid of. Just lychyaena, or a wolf,' she murmured. 'An overgrown mutant wolf with strange infected eyes, that's all,' she told herself.

She took a tentative pace forward, then another. The eyes blinked, wavered, then vanished, leaving Ionuin wondering if they were ever there at all. 'What the . . .?' She pushed her thoughts out and sensed nothing, the mental block had also vanished, or had she imagined it? Now was definitely not the time to become spooked by imaginary monsters lurking in the dark. She did not investigate further, but stepped back to the shelter of the large rock, sliding down to rest on her haunches.

She realised that she was panting heavily, sucking in deep breaths, her hands trembling. She knew she was lying to herself. There had been something out there and she was sure it was something more savage, more menacing, than a mountain wolf, even a mutant one. She calmed herself and began breathing more slowly, allowing her fear to slip away. She sniffed the air and the brimstone odour had seemingly vanished, so, still cautious, she scanned the area mentally. Nothing seemed untoward at all. The only life she sensed in her immediate surroundings were a few innocuous night gnats.

She tried to place herself in a state of full relaxation. Soon she would be facing adversaries of flesh and blood and the last thing she needed was added distractions. If she was religious, she supposed she would have prayed, but like her father, she believed destiny rested in her own hands and the only god in which she could ever find solace was the sun. It gave warmth and light, made life, all life, possible. She drew Fyrdraca, seated herself back on her bear-hide and closed her eyes, her weapon resting across her lap where it was to hand if required. Sleep would be a short, shallow affair this night, but sleep she must.

Nexus plonked himself down on his serpentine throne, which was aglow with green gems. 'Now, my boy, how is our secret mission progressing? Have you made contact yet?'

Taj shuffled his feet uneasily. He was always nervous in the presence of Lord Nexus, the golden ruler of all he surveyed. Their secret mission was so frightening that it scared him witless just thinking about it, as the risk involved

43

was enormous. Nexus had assured him that should he succeed, the rewards would be so overwhelmingly great, that it was unthinkable not to try. Besides, he had added, there was only Taj that he could fully trust so there was no choice in the matter. Nexus had lost so much over the years; first the death of his sister, Saturnine. Then his breeding-mate, Nadine, had mysteriously vanished, and Shogun, his father, and his son, Spuddle, had both died.

'Let's have it, Taj, have you been successful?' Lord Nexus asked, his voice brimming with encouragement.

Taj did not want to reply and shuffled his feet nervously. Whilst he had not exactly failed, neither had he met with astounding success. His struggle at this moment was finding some common ground between the two extremes that would not show him in an unfavourable light.

'Come on, boy, I need to know!' Nexus said, his voice rising, his talons tapping agitatedly on the arms of his throne. 'I have not got all night, and contrary to popular belief, I am extremely busy.'

Taj took a deep breath. 'Well, I've not been exactly successful,' he confessed, 'but, I have secured a permanent link with a target that promises interesting results.'

'You have? Well, splendid! You should have said, my boy!'

Taj smiled at the positive reaction and gained courage. 'It's, it's as if I have broken through a shield that has somehow lost its potency. I know my connections with the target can be heard, but unfortunately, much to my disappointment, I still haven't received a definite response.'

Nexus rubbed at his jaw. 'Hmm, well, at least we have a target. So this means the changes have begun.'

'Changes?' Taj asked.

'None of your concern, just yet,' Nexus said. 'The changes are already foretold and I suspected they were happening as there have been attempts to penetrate the protection of the cavern. Nothing too predatory; just probes testing our defences. Tell me; are you any closer to a possible location?'

Taj swallowed hard and cleared his throat. He knew more was expected of him, but he was doing his best and applying himself as rigorously as possible. 'I assumed that I had, but then, something unusual happened to me and that's why I never showed yesterday, for which I apologise, my Lord.'

Nexus waved his huge taloned foreleg dismissively. 'Think nothing of it, boy, but, what do you mean, by *something unusual happened*?'

Taj shuffled his feet restlessly. 'I'm, not sure, I was trying to connect with a lucid dream I had experienced, when something blocked my search.' Taj tried exploring his memory for what had occurred in Beulah's chamber. He felt confused and scared, but racked his brain, and as he did, dread assaulted his mind and fractured images tumbled into place. He recalled the girl being chased, the nebulous cloud hovering nearby and the capture of his soul. He collapsed to his knees. 'Oh no! It, was, it was the Dark Dragon, my Lord!'

Nexus leapt to his feet. 'The Dark Dragon is here now? The Dark Dragon will be the one testing our defences. So, the Dreadnoughts are stirring, are they? Hmm, and you say it actually attacked you, Taj?'

Taj nodded, but was unable to speak. Imagery skittered through his thoughts, fragmented pictures in disarray rippling through the fissures of his mind. Nothing made sense! The only thing he knew for certain was that he was scared half to death. Just the mention of the Dreadnoughts, the ancient enemy of the Light, was enough to stir fear in the stoutest of hearts. If the Dark Dragon was indeed a Dreadnought, then he had danced with death and escaped with his very life.

'What are you thinking about? What scares you, Taj?' Nexus asked.

'I-I, was wondering if the Dark Dragon is an actual Dreadnought?' he said, unsure if he should be raising such matters.

Nexus nodded. 'Yes, Taj, I suspect it could be. Or at the very least, an emissary of the Dreadnoughts.' He reached forth and pulled Taj to his feet, then re-seated himself on his throne. 'Be calm, Taj. Marshall your thoughts, then tell me exactly what happened, and leave nothing out; understood?'

Taj nodded. 'Somehow, it pierced my mind. It just smashed through all my barriers and ran amok among my personal thoughts!'

'Did it indeed? So, Dark Dragon now knows we have a sensitive,' said Nexus. 'What was the experience of touching that Dark mind like, exactly?'

Taj balked at dredging up the memory, but he had to reveal what he knew. 'Well, my Lord, the pain was incredible. Akin to, to hot spikes of sizzling metal sliding deep inside my ears. The heat built up so fast that it tried to surge out of my face. At one point, I thought my eyes were going to pop like squashed berries. And my head! Sheez, my head felt as if it would split like an overripe melon!'

'Hmm, strong imagery there, Taj.' Nexus said, thrusting out his chin, obviously in deep contemplation. 'Anything else?'

Taj cast his mind back even further. 'Yes, before that, there was a girl! A young girl being chased, but I don't know why. Then there was a dark-skinned lady; she helped me.'

'Interesting,' Nexus said.

'Yes, she was,' Taj said, trying to hide his smile. 'She said my soul was being shredded, but I can't fix any of it in my mind. It's all jumbled up, somehow.'

Nexus sat for quite awhile, silently watching.

'Any idea what this means, my Lord?' Taj finally asked, his impatience getting the better of him.

Nexus grinned. 'It means, my boy, that you have had your mind probed by the enemy.' He then leant forward and lifted Taj's chin with one talon and stared deep into his eyes. *Is there more locked inside your mind?* He asked telepathically.

I'm not sure. Taj mentally replied as he felt his inner-self swim free and drift into the golden eyes of his Lord and master where he found resplendent calmness.

Relax, my boy, be at peace; allow me to soothe your thoughts. Forget the invasion of the sanctity of your id, concentrate on the girl, not the dark-skinned lady of whom you seem overly fond, but the girl who was being chased, What of she? Ah, very good, now I understand.

Taj felt Nexus release him, his mind coming together, becoming whole once more. He coughed, rubbed at his eyes, trying to remove an itch that lingered beneath his eyeballs. The mind swab that Nexus had performed had eased him, but the after effects were annoying. 'I'm pleased you understand, my Lord. It's all a mystery to me.'

'All will be revealed in time, Taj. Tell me what you know about the girl?' Nexus asked, his talons again tapping on the arms of his throne with impatience, the points absently circling the myriad green gems embedded there.

'The girl?' Taj replied, now looking up to face Nexus, his confidence returning with every passing breath as a new explanation took shape. 'Yes of course, the girl! Not only is she the target with which I have been trying to link, but the real target of the Dark Dragon! It does not really want me at all! I just got in the way.'

'Well done,' Nexus said, praisingly. 'So, it is important that you establish a firm link with this girl.'

Taj nodded his agreement. 'I-I have tried but, I cannot quite connect with her. She sort of . . . shuts me out; denies me.' Taj blanched as the tapping of Nexus' talons increased slightly. 'Honestly, I have tried my best, Lord. I really have,' he said, unable to hide his exasperation. 'It seems improbable, but somehow, she is as strong as I am, maybe even stronger. How can this be?'

'Your guess is as good as mine,' Nexus said.

Taj thought that Nexus was, once again, being deliberately vague, keeping him in the dark when it concerned information that could possibly clarify things for him, but he said nothing. The untrusting attitude of Nexus only made him more determined to sort things out for himself, in his own way. 'I have nothing else to report, my Lord,' he said, wanting this audience to come to a swift end.

'Hmm, yes, no doubt, Taj. Only, taking everything into consideration, you have made no real progress at all; have you?'

Taj shook his head. He knew that progress had been made, but they were still no closer to having any firm answers. 'Um, not really, I suppose,' he said wanting to be away. Wanting to be by himself so that he could try and find the girl once more. She was the key, he knew it now, but what could he do about it? What could he do about her and how much danger was she in if his conclusions were correct and the Dark Dragon really was after her? He decided to push Nexus for more clues. 'I do know for certain that this girl is close. Definitely in the northern hemisphere, but only just. Maybe we should try and locate her by having dragons scout-'

'No!' Nexus snapped. 'Too risky.'

Taj was disappointed but kept his face blank. 'I am guessing now, calculating rather, but, I would say she is on the move and also on our timeline. Maybe even coming our way!'

46

Nexus got to his feet. 'Really! You were that close? My boy, this is real progress after all! You have excelled yourself; you should have told me earlier! You must try to link with her again.'

Taj was feeling very pensive at this sudden change of attitude and wondered if Nexus had been reading his thoughts all along. 'Um, what? You mean . . . you mean now, my Lord?'

Nexus grinned. 'Why, of course I mean now, no time like the very present, eh? Don't want you wandering off alone and trying to make contact by yourself! You do realise that if you left the safety of Fire Mountain, anything could happen? No, a mind link is the only way and I want it done now.'

This was not what Taj wanted to hear. He wanted to tiptoe around, search for the girl at a gentle non-committal pace, not go charging ahead with a full out quest with Nexus on his tail. Nexus was right about one thing; it was very dangerous out there now. He was not sure he really wanted to do this at all, not this way. Besides, had he not done enough?

'Anything wrong, Taj?' Nexus asked.

The mind-salve Nexus had previously applied began dissipating and thoughts of the Dark Dragon roared through his head, exploding his earlier confidence into shards of broken chaos. Slack-jawed, he fell to his knees.

'Taj? What is it?' Nexus asked, lowering his great, scaled head, genuine concern edging his words.

'Please, Lord. I can't! Please don't make me,' he begged. 'I-I do want to search for the girl, but if the Dark Dragon snares my thoughts again, snakes its way into my head, then my brains will surely be dissolved or blown apart!'

'Nonsense,' said Nexus. 'The Dark Dragon is tricking you with illusion.'

Taj shook his head. 'Illusion or not, it's so strong, my Lord, so terrible! I hardly dare say it, but I'm so afraid.'

'Of course you're afraid,' Nexus said, his voice cajoling. 'Being afraid is natural when facing an uncertain enemy.'

'Master, you don't understand. I-I can't take it. I just can't!' His resolve broke as thoughts of what had happened to him clamoured for attention within his mind. He collapsed forward as he broke like a bursting dam, the tears flooding forth in an unstoppable rush. 'The Dark Dragon is, is wicked! Pure evil, Dreadnought or not, it is not of this galaxy, this universe, it can't be! I can sense the cruel malevolence of its alien nature. Its thoughts flow with Dark energy, even Darker matter,' he sobbed, trying to regain some self-control.

Nexus patted his shoulder. 'It's all right my boy. No shame in being afraid; no shame in becoming upset. Gather yourself together while I have a think.'

Taj sobbed, dried his eyes on his sleeve. How could his world change so fast? There was no rhyme or reason to it, but change it had. He suspected the changes were not yet finished with and what was to come scared him. In truth, he wanted things to go back the way they were, but in his heart, he knew that was not going to happen, not now, not ever. It was time to grow up.

Ionuin stirred in her sleep and sat upright, her hand locked firmly around the handle of Fyrdraca. She had dreamt of a boy, a boy in distress, a boy in danger. He felt familiar, was he the one trying to peer inside her mind? If so, what did he want? Was he a danger to her? She had no answers to any of these questions and she found this most disturbing. What, she wondered, was she going to do about him? She had no idea, but one thing was for certain, the upheaval she was experiencing in her life had only just begun.

She sheathed Fyrdraca, rolled up her bear-hide, secured it with twine, and prepared to move. What to do about the strange boy could wait, for now. She had more immediate issues to deal with and those issues were out there, sleeping in the darkness, unaware that she was coming their way with violent menace in mind.

Lord Nexus paced the chamber as Taj lay weeping on the floor. The poor boy had totally come undone and who could blame him? He had been under intense strain and pressure since puberty. He was so gifted, yet, he continually failed to attain the best results with his gifts. If only his mother had lived, had been here to see him mature, she would know exactly what to do.

He crouched by the boy, gently stroking his dark, shoulder length hair. 'Feeling better, Taj? You have done well, you know, but never fear, I have strengthened our protections. The Dark Dragon could never penetrate your mind again, not here, not in my chamber. You must trust me, Taj. Our mission has to succeed. Our clan, unbeknown even to themselves, is dependent upon your success and more of our brothers and sisters are arriving everyday. The army builds, Taj. Soon there will be a battle. A battle we must win if we are to have any chance at all in the Clysm War.'

'Clysm War?' Taj asked his muffled sobs now abating.

'A topic for another day, Taj,' Nexus answered. 'For now, we must focus on the immediate future and the army that is gathering on Merm.'

Taj lifted his tear-streaked face off the floor. 'The dragon numbers are increasing with every passing day, master, and I know even more are coming. I can sense them drawing closer. Sometimes, when there are many, the portal hums with power, but why are such strong creatures depending upon an insignificant weakling like me?'

'Weakling?' Nexus said.

'Yes weakling. What difference can I possibly make? A simple boy who cannot even compete with the feeblest of the clan: why will the clan die if I fail?' A quavering sob left him with a shudder and he shakily got to his feet. 'Please explain this to me, Lord Nexus; for if I could fully understand our mission, I could perhaps be more helpful.'

'Impossible,' said Lord Nexus, sitting back on his huge throne. 'What we do, we do in secret, and believe me, Taj; it is for the greater good that I ask of you what I do. I wish I could tell you more. If there were any other way to solve our problems, to complete our mission, I would take it. Your birth line has given such special gifts, granting you a unique talent, a talent we must use to its best advantage. Even though the clan are aware of your ability, they have no inkling how far you have developed your skill. They still foolishly believe I protect you out of pity, simply because you appear to be so weak, but this is not true, Taj. I protect you because I have sworn to do so and I do need you and your natural ability. Believe me, you still have further hidden powers that you have not yet even touched upon. What you do not know cannot hurt you, but if you know too much, there are others who would think nothing of hurting you to learn that information.'

Taj wiped his eyes. 'I'm sorry for my emotional display, please forgive me, it won't happen again. I do appreciate your protection and I do respect your need for secrecy.'

'Taj, I know you do,' replied Nexus. 'Don't ever doubt my word, things will change. As you grow, your mental agility will develop and improve beyond all imagining. All you need is more confidence and the strength of mind to believe in yourself, then you will be able to access your true capabilities.' He placed a bony knuckle beneath Taj's chin, lifting his face so he could look deep into the boy's lavender coloured eyes. 'I do need your help, Taj. Say yes, and you will not regret your decision.'

Taj sighed. 'All right,' he said, his quavering voice barely masking his fear. 'I will do as you request.'

Chapter Nine

Ionuin shivered as the blustery dawn wind sighed, but managed to stop her teeth from chattering as it rushed along the sheer walls of the dry-bed canyon. A canyon, according to her father, that had been carved by a relentless stream of rushing water over millions of years.

It was now barren and dead; the ancient river that had once fed it had dried up, changed course, or, most likely, plunged underground, where it would probably remain forever frozen, until Merm broke apart. Clouds, tattered by the gently moaning wind, drifted high into the dawn sky. Pale colours of gold and pink mingled, interchanging as the sun peeped above the eastern horizon, creating an ever-shifting work of art crafted by nature herself. How beautiful, Ionuin thought, as her imagination formed palaces and citadels, towers leaning at impossible angles and whisper-thin bridges spanning incredible distances.

The light sleep that she had managed to have before making her move was just enough to ease the worst of her tiredness, and now, she travelled quickly through the night towards the campfire that guided her like a welcome beacon. The watcher from the rocks had bothered her no more, but she could not shake off the unwanted sensation of being followed. The hunter hardly wanted to become the hunted. Such an alarming shift in the scheme of things would only complicate matters and could be dangerous. Ionuin had halted several times on her nocturnal journey, listening to the sounds of the night, but she heard nothing untoward, and despite her gut instinct warning that all was not as it should be, she continued on her way. She decided to deal with the killers, then somehow, confront the ominous stranger who had shown such an interest in her and her quest for retribution.

The morning was bitterly cold and the flesh on Ionuin's arms puckered as she manoeuvred herself into an observational position. With Fyrdraca drawn, she moved quickly, but silently, skirting the last outcrop of prickly gorse that had provided her with cover as she crept towards the sleeping camp. A mule, an old haggard beast with protruding angular bones pushing at its mottled hide, gave her a cursory glance with its wide glaring eyes, snorted noisily, then went back to chewing the straggly piece of rope tethering it to a petrified stump.

Ionuin moved even closer, crawling behind boulders around the edge of the camp, halting suddenly as an unfamiliar noise assaulted her ears. With her senses on full alert she scanned the surrounding camp, but detected no other presence apart from the inhabitants. Assuring herself that the time had come to attack, and satisfied that the three sleeping forms had not stirred, she slipped behind a pair of the mule's wicker-pack baskets.

As she crouched, the early morning sunlight hit the top of the canyon's western wall; then the noise came again, an animal noise, low and mewling, sounding distressed as if in pain or great discomfort. Surely not the watcher from the rocks, thought Ionuin, but something else entirely. She peered over the rims of the battered old baskets, her eyes searching for the source of the strange noise in the half-light of daybreak.

At first, she spotted nothing unusual, then, she saw, nestling beneath the shade of several giant-cacti, a dark square shape. Ionuin peered hard at the shape, which at first she thought was an angular boulder, then realised it was a cage built from rough slats of old timber. Something was in the cage; she could sense it, a living creature of some description, but she could not yet discern the nature of the beast. It whined again, a pitiful moaning, tugging at Ionuin's somewhat hardened heartstrings, raising her curiosity along with a lively spark of lingering girlish interest in all things animal. Shadows shifted within the cage, and Ionuin fancied she spotted the movement of an oddly shaped head, complete with roving eye, but it was gone in an instant, retreating into darkness.

Ionuin wanted to get closer to the cage, to investigate the beast within, to try and see what these men, these killers, had trapped. She reasoned the contents of the cage were either valuable, dangerous, or both. She eased around the basket, watching her footing, being careful not to disturb the loose pebbles littering the canyon floor: then disaster struck. One of the sleeping forms sprang into action, hurling a knife at Ionuin's exposed torso, screeching a warning cry to his two slumbering companions. Ionuin twisted sideways as the knife flew towards her, spinning end over end in what seemed like deathly slow motion, forcing her to yelp as the blade sliced through the skin covering her lower ribs, drawing a line of crimson before sticking into the mule basket directly behind her.

She staggered backwards, grimacing in pain, clutching her hand to the cut, staring in horrified disbelief as blood, warm and sticky, squeezed between her clenched fingers. She had only ever been involved in one real fight, just a few days previous, and even though she knew about wounds, she never expected it to hurt so much! The killer who had surprised her with the sudden knife attack, a stumpy, aging, craggy-faced, balding man, with shifty muddy eyes, was up on his feet and bawling at his companions, but Ionuin's readily drawn sword caused him some indecision. Instead of leaping upon her and finishing the job he had started, he ambled steadily sideways, snatching up his own sword.

'Grog, Sterner, on yer feet lads! We're attacked!' he shouted. 'To arms I say! To arms!'

Watching his every move, Ionuin quickly glanced down at her midriff. The gash looked bad, but she knew it would not kill her, not yet, and she raised her sword in preparation for the battle to come. She had never before faced more than two opponents at a time; this was something of a journey into the unknown. Confidence was still running high though; she had endured many hours of tutoring from her father and knew exactly what to expect, or so she thought. She was also a good swordswoman when using Fyrdraca, her own sword, which looked quite different from any other she had ever seen. Its handle was long and could be gripped by both hands, and the blade was slightly curved. Fyrdraca was held across the body, while most swords were held straight out in front. It was a strange fighting stance, amateurish almost, but Ionuin liked it, it felt comfortable.

51

Nexus paced his chamber. Taj had tried all night to make contact via the link he swore he had established, but he could not break through. He claimed he was being blocked and ignored, but Nexus suspected it was his own fear that was stopping him from trying too hard. The Dark Dragon had seized his courage and squeezed him dry. Taj now lay curled on the huge serpentine throne, sleeping. Nexus had thrown a heavy drape over him, a tapestry the boy's mother had made depicting a scene from ancient legend when the wizard Catalin had visited their world and addressed the assembled Lords, warning them of the coming threat.

No-one had believed the old mage at the time, or any of the times since when he had again visited and issued dire warnings. Catalin had been a frequent traveller to this world, but he had not returned since Taj was orphaned, and the pact had been made giving over custody of the boy, along with his future welfare. Nexus cast his mind back to Catalin's penultimate visit, wondering how he had known about Dark Energy, Dark Matter and Dark Flow. Dreadful, unforgiving enemies; enemies that could never be reasoned with. No truce could be drawn, no surrender ever possible. Only the total annihilation of all matter, the building blocks of life, would satisfy the Darkness that loathed the blossoming chaos borne of Light.

He smiled, recalling the old mage standing proudly on the lintels of the outer circle at the stones, giving a rousing, rallying speech to the assembled lords. His white robes billowed in the dusty wind, his flowing beard and thin wisps of white hair fluttered freely, forming a fuzzy haze about his face. He had been laughed at, even mocked. The great clan could not conceive their future vulnerability. Catalin had known, had been trying to prepare them, but they would not listen, so he had stormed off into the wilderness with only jeers for company. He had returned years later in secrecy, but only a select few knew of his return as it was feared, even then, that there were traitors in the ranks.

'I believe his warnings now,' Nexus growled under his breath, sliding the throne effortlessly to one side, revealing a hidden subterranean passage in the floor. He grabbed a light globe from the wall, his body warmth making it pulse brightly as the mixture of gas inside responded to the heat.

He stepped down the winding stone stairs, entering his private study where the histories were kept. Most of the original documents dated from before the first part of the cataclysm and had long since crumbled to dust, but Nexus and his father before him, Lord Shogun, had made verbatim copies.

There was only one original set of documents remaining, and that was Herald Knell, a book of prophecy with several authors. It was bound with a hard cover, seemingly made of hair and treated with a hardening resin, while the rune script was printed with indelible gold ink on blue silk parchment. The book seemed to be protected by an incantation of some sort, a magic spell that one could actually feel, as if it were alive. He lifted the prophecy book down off the top shelf of a large overflowing bookcase; it was far larger than the other books and well read by successive generations who had been the keepers of the histories. He flicked to the page currently concerning him, one hundred and twelve, and began reading aloud.

'The old one gone, sacrificed for a greater good, power reversing through time, the fabled megalopolis shall fall. Minstrels celebrate summer equinox, within the stones, birth shall rise from death, becoming of one, heralding joining of two; ended line, re-emerging, future seeds blown asunder. Dead sentinel holding sway, preserving past for future. Beware Dark Dragon, dancing piper's tune, making all worlds suffer, Light losing sacred children chasing shadows, Dark reigning hither, forevermore. Pursue courage, embrace the Light, the Blackbird shall fly away, never to be broken again.'

The only part that makes perfect sense, thought Nexus, is the part about the Dark Dragon, as it is now here on this world, somewhere. The end of the line, he suspected, was his own direct family line that ended with himself, which was more than his father had deciphered. Lord Shogun had supposed the whole passage to be nothing more than cryptic nonsense, just one of the many 'red herrings' entered in the book to mislead unwanted eyes.

'Lord Nexus?'

Nexus whipped around to see Taj standing on the bottom step. Taj knew of the secret library and the histories; after all, he would be the hereditary custodian, one day. 'What is it, boy?'

'It's the link, my Lord; it's been pulsing like crazy, even in my dreams. There has been death, bloody death through conflict. More conflict is taking place at this very moment, and there is something else.' Taj hesitated; his eyes wide and glaring with uncertainty.

'Well, out with it boy!' snapped Nexus, unable to hide his impatience.

'I don't know how, or why,' said Taj, his voice barely above a whisper, 'but I can sense your son. He's, well, hmm . . . incredible as it may seem, he's alive!'

The words; *and birth shall rise from death*, raced through Nexus' thoughts, but it could not be true; could it? His son was dead, he had died with Lord Shogun. What trickery was this? He looked at Taj and anger, raw and menacing, burned in his golden eyes.

Chapter Ten

'Grog, Sterner! Come on, come on, you pair of lazy maggots! We have ourselves an uninvited guest,' bawled the balding killer who gave the impression of leadership - or so Ionuin thought. Although, he was not much of a leader; his feet stumbled over unseen stones, he moved with the gait of an inherently clumsy person and looked decidedly awkward. His eyes darted around, trying to see everything, but taking in nothing of any significance or importance. 'Rise and shine,' shouted the man with growing impatience. 'We got ourselves a visitor!'

'W-what's that you say, Crudder?' mumbled one of the others, knees popping loudly as he scrambled to his feet, eyeing Ionuin with confusion creasing his ruddy features. 'A visitor; did you say? Ooh, a woman! A real woman!'

This one seemed younger than the balding Crudder, early middle age at a guess with a large swollen paunch where his stomach should be, and slabs of wobbling fat on either side of his face, making his features appear squashed and unhappy. This man, his face hemmed in by a bushy red beard matted with dirt and what appeared to be bits of food that had somehow missed the intended target, belched loudly.

Ionuin already despised him just from his appearance and the stink of his unwashed body. The stench of stale sweat wafting in the air had Ionuin fighting the gag reflex, and his filthy, food-strewn face and beard disgusted her. She wondered how anyone could miss such a slavering, gaping maw of a mouth. *Slovenly stupidity* sprang to mind as a possible answer, but it was inconsequential, as he was about to die.

The third man, a scrawny youth, rubbed sleep from his eyes, blinking profusely as he sat upright. 'Wass-up? Well of all things, if it isn't a woman!' he hollered. 'Or a girl, hmm no, tis a woman for sure, yes; a woman visitor, eh?'

Despite his apparent uncertainty, he looked sharp and dangerous and Ionuin noticed that his left hand was heavily bandaged. Ionuin glared at him through slitted eyes.

'Yes, a real young female,' continued the youth, his eyes agog. 'Why, I'd almost forgotten what one looked like. A pretty one too!' he added, grabbing a sword from beneath his blanket. He passed an appraising eye over Ionuin. 'With real bodily parts! Is it my birthday?' he leered, springing to his feet, circling around the dead ashes of the previous night's fire. 'Can I have her, Sterner?' he asked, his tongue lolling stupidly from his thin-lipped mouth, his eyes bulging as they surveyed Ionuin's beautiful bleeding body. 'Can I, Sterner? Can I?'

'Grog, you would not get past her belly button, a pup like you,' replied the red-haired paunchy one called Sterner.

'You should have asked me, Grog!' exclaimed the short bald foul-smelling one with the overfed face, a spear and a sword now clasped firmly in his hands. 'I'm in charge here, not Sterner, you yellow Desert Sea coward!'

Grog snarled. 'Yellow coward? Me? Sterner, if you don't tell stinking, stumpy Crudder to shut his stupid face, I'm-'

'Silence, Grog!' Sterner bellowed. 'You couldn't even handle a woman like this. Crudder is messing with yah. Of course you can't have her, and besides, you wouldn't know what to do with her and I dare say there be plenty here for all of us, eh, Crudder?'

'Plenty,' Crudder laughed agreeably, his jowls wobbling up and down as if they had an independent life of their own. 'Enough to last us for months if we feed her right.'

Ionuin suspected Crudder was the leader here and should therefore be the first to die, or at least put out of action to make the other two more manageable.

'But I want her for myself,' Grog protested petulantly, stamping his foot on the ground. 'It's not fair! I've done what you asked and you've not paid me yet: I want her!' He stamped his foot again, harder.

The action raised a swirl of dust, making Ionuin jump a little, causing her to tense her sword arm. Not a good start, she thought, looking from one man to the next. I'm over-nervous. Too stressed, she told herself. I need to relax, take it easy: allow the fight within to flow through me and into my blade.

'I've never had a real girl,' Grog continued. 'Once though, some years ago, one did speak to me in Desert City! She said, 'Out of my way boy'. Her harsh words made me very happy, for a day. I almost slapped her and that would have been real contact with her flesh but-'

'Shut it Grog,' mouthed the bearded Sterner.

'Yeah, shut it Grog,' Crudder repeated, 'or I will shut it for you; got it?'

Grog sighed, his bottom lip trembling. For an instant Ionuin thought he was going to burst into tears, but he simply shrugged in acceptance of the threat. Ionuin realized that despite bullying Crudder claiming he was in charge, she had assumed wrongly; Sterner was definitely the real leader. Was this her first error in judgment? If so, it did not bode well for what was about to follow. Self-doubt crept in at the edges of her confidence, undermining belief in her ability to deal with these murderers. Perhaps I should have killed them while they slept, she thought, but wouldn't such action make me as bad as them? She calmed herself and fully assessed the situation. Now was not the time for questions; now was the time for justice.

The men spread out, young Grog still mumbling under his breath, his left eye twitching slightly, but none made a direct move towards her. They seemed perfectly happy to gawk at her for now, as if she were a sideshow attraction at a carnival. Ionuin mentally examined how the situation must appear with her simply standing idly by, perhaps she seemed frightened with indecision, nursing her wound, looking more than a little helpless, which is exactly what she wanted them to think, as nothing could be further from the truth.

After a brief spasm of doubt, Ionuin knew exactly what to do. She could not have them rushing her. If they did, she might kill one, perhaps injure two if she got lucky, but she would surely be overpowered in the struggle, then all would be lost. They badly wanted her alive to enjoy her body, so best to keep them thinking they had the upper hand, allow their advantage of favourable numbers and the fact that she was injured to play its full part. This would give her the element of surprise, but she did want them to know who she was. It would never do to dispatch these murderers and allow them to die in ignorance of the identity of their slayer.

She looked the one called Sterner right in the eye. 'I am Ionuin, daughter of Tharl,' she said, hefting her sword, attempting to intimidate them a little, just to keep them at bay for a few more moments. 'Tharl was the man you murdered in the small valley near the edge of the foothills.'

Grog started gabbling. 'So there was a fem-'

'Shut it Grog!' Crudder snapped, 'I won't tell you again.'

'Tharl! Yes, we know of him,' Sterner answered, tugging at his scraggy beard as if deep in thought. 'Nothing but a useless old man, he couldn't even see anymore; we'd been looking for him for long enough. We'd been told by a friend of ours that he had a young attractive daughter. Of course we didn't believe such nonsense.'

'I did,' Grog said, sulkily, 'and here she is. I was right. I knew the Dark-'

'For the last time; shut it Grog!' Sterner cut in. 'Or I will let Crudder beat you to death and laugh while he's doing it, you pathetic imbecile.'

'We did the blind old fool a favour,' Crudder slobbered, cautiously approaching, his gimlet eyes drinking in Ionuin's half-exposed breasts and shapely legs. 'We taught him a thing or two about pain before he died though, and now-'

Crudder moved, quickly closing on her, sword before him, spear held high. Ionuin's natural instincts surged forth, adrenalin coursing through her veins. She reacted instantly, releasing a short, sharp battle cry whilst springing into action. Everything happened so fast that Sterner and Grog were stunned, becoming hopelessly immobilised as swords clattered briefly and Crudder pulled up short, his weapons dropping to the ground.

'She's quick,' Grog muttered, his eyes visibly widening at the sight of a length of bloodied curved steel protruding from Crudder's back.

With a savage slicing twist and a muffled grunt, Ionuin yanked Fyrdraca free. Crudder gasped and tumbled into the remains of the dead fire, his hands trying to hold his innards in place while expelled gas burbled noisily from his abdomen.

'In my family, we believe favours should always be returned,' Ionuin remarked, before swiftly rounding on Sterner who appeared mesmerised, but still looked the most dangerous of the two still standing.

As with Crudder, she lunged quickly, forcing Sterner back, the tip of his sword parrying her strikes as metal rang on metal. Several quick blows were exchanged and Ionuin lunged again, making Sterner leap sideways with such speed that he nearly toppled over his own feet. Ionuin followed him, easily parrying two hesitant swipes before replying with a lunge to his face that Sterner only just dodged.

She risked a backward glance; Grog was following the fight but seemed reluctant to join the fray. Sterner attacked during the momentary distraction, forcing Ionuin to duck low while spinning away from the clumsy charge. Then she darted back in, skewering the hapless leader through his right knee. He shrieked to the heavens as she twisted the blade in an attempt to pull it free; his face stretched in agony, but the sword, festooned with trailing ligaments, was partly jammed, locked between bones. Sterner dropped to the floor, his body contorting with what looked like mind blitzing pain.

Aware that Grog was behind her, Ionuin drew her boot-knife, twisting to see his attack, but surprisingly, he had not advanced. His wide-eyed expression revealed that fear had exploded his mind, blowing away all reasoning, leaving him trapped in indecision. Ionuin had felt Grog's beady eyes crawling all over her and she knew he desperately wanted her to satisfy his lust, but he still retreated a few paces.

'I'm going to have you, bitch!' he said, taking further paces backwards. Even though he had seemed eager to make Ionuin's acquaintance at the outset, he now appeared reluctant. 'You'll have to sleep sometime and when-'

'You're the one who's going to sleep!' Ionuin snapped. 'Forever!'

Grog continued to retreat and she realised that Crudder had spoken the truth when he had called the youngster a yellow coward. Sterner continued writhing on the ground, pleading for help, but Grog did not want to know and turned to flee.

Grog's warning that he would return while she was sleeping still rang in Ionuin's ears. She snatched up Crudder's discarded spear, took aim at the fleeing target, relaxed and allowed her mind to focus. Her arm filled with power and she could actually feel the muscle pulsing from the energy rush. Emitting a guttural snarl, she hurled the weapon. The spear flew swift and silent towards its target, piercing Grog just below his left scapula, instantly rupturing his heart, ripping through his shattered ribcage with a resounding wet crunch. The only sounds Grog made were a loud farting raspberry sound and a low whistling squeal that ended abruptly when his body crashed amongst the loose boulders of the canyon floor, sending up clouds of dust that danced merrily in a passing breeze.

'Nice,' she murmured, dusting imaginary dirt from her hands. 'Little too much to the left, but very nice all the same.' She looked down at Crudder whose eyes were open and staring blankly ahead, his face frozen in a silent death mask cast with an expression of utter surprise. 'Nice weapon you had there, Crudder. I thank you most sincerely, as manners cost nothing.'

'You're flurking crazy!' Sterner wailed, still floundering on the ground.

'Yes, you might be correct,' Ionuin replied, turning her full attention back to Sterner. 'Two dead, one to go,' she said, as Sterner began edging away, dragging himself along the floor, gripping the sword protruding from his knee. Ionuin followed him, checking her wound. 'Hmm, no pain,' she mumbled. Her fingers came away sticky, but it appeared that the laceration had already closed and stopped bleeding, which Ionuin thought strange, but reasoned the slash could not have been too deep after all. She caught up with Sterner, who had ceased in his shuffling escape attempt. She tutted loudly, crouched and wiped her hands on his britches, never losing eye contact. 'I would have hurled my boot-knife at Grog, but I have another use for it,' she told him, a smile flickering around the corners of her mouth, receiving lots of satisfaction from the anguished glance he returned.

'Please, please One-knowing, don't kill me,' Sterner begged, his voice barely above a whisper. 'Please, I don't want to die. I'm only fifty-two and I'm sorry I called you crazy, truly sorry.'

'You're sorry?' Ionuin said, standing up straight, her face feigning a look of outright shock. 'And the name is I-on-u-in! One-knowing? Sheez, now I am beginning to think you're the crazy one, Sterner.'

'Ah, yes, a good name. So sorry I got it wrong, and you, you're right, I am crazy. Yep, that's me, Crazy Sterner!'

Ionuin giggled. 'An interesting word *sorry*. I'm not exactly sure what it means,' she said, waving her knife before her as she sauntered casually around the injured man. 'You killed my father. Tortured him by the look of the mess you made of his poor body, but do not worry. I'm not vindictive. Sorry or not, your death will be quick by comparison.'

'But, but I'm in pain and severely wounded,' Sterner protested, still clutching his knee with one hand while the other tried to remove the sword. 'I'm going to be a cripple, I am a cripple! You wouldn't kill a poor cripple, would you? Not a nice girl like you!'

Ionuin smiled. 'Now, Sterner, first you pronounce my name wrongly, then you call me crazy, now you accuse me of being nice! Some slight inconsistency in your assessments of me. So, Sterner the learner, tell me, why do you now assume I am nice; hmm?'

Taj stood stock still, watching as Nexus tried to grasp the news that his son was actually alive. His master did not look that pleased. Spuddle had been missing for over two full turns of the seasons, and even though the whole clan had searched the surrounding area of Fire Mountain, the settlements of the Desert Sea, the Valley of Caves and myriad gullies and canyons beyond, not a trace of the missing youngster could be found. As their leader, and an elemental, Nexus possessed some strange and wonderful abilities, being able to shield the mountain from intruders by setting up magical wards made from crossed lengths of ironstone rods, and sentinels formed of arranged crystals that would sound if they came under attack.

Taj had only heard the sentinels once, and that was when the Dark Dragon had appeared briefly the previous summer. The whole mountain had hummed with a deep tone, the resonance of which had set his teeth on edge. The Dragon had not entered the sacred caves; just its arrival and presence had been enough to sound a warning and the wards and sentinels all had to be reset and retuned. As well as approaching danger, Nexus could also sense the whereabouts of others. He claimed it was more of a feeling, an intuition, but when his son vanished, he felt nothing, even though he had roared out loud in tortured anguish when he sensed his father had died. Now, Taj expected him to be elated as it was not every day one learned that a son had returned from the dead.

'My son!' Lord Nexus exclaimed, looking pensive. 'You are standing there and telling me that you can sense my son?'

Nexus closed his eyes and Taj watched as concentration furrowed his brow and actually felt his master as he contracted his thoughts, searching for the aura of his son.

Nexus issued a long whistle of breath from his nose and opened his eyes. 'Strange, I sense nothing, not a glimmer. How can this be? Oh yes,' he shouted, stamping his taloned foot on the library floor. 'I remember now, my son died when my father took him for his transformation, his becoming, and no one has seen, heard, or even sensed Spuddle, even in the slightest capacity, since that fateful day! Is this not true?'

Taj was shocked by the rising ferocity in the timbre of Nexus' voice, but he stood his ground. 'It is true, my Lord, very true. At least, it was thought to be true, but-'

'Thought to be true?' Nexus queried, inclining his head, peering at Taj from beneath quizzical brows. 'Whatever do you mean, *thought to be true*? A thing is either true, or it is a lie! Explain yourself, boy!'

Taj looked deep into the glowing golden eyes of Lord Nexus, the leader of all the Dragon Clans, and found he was being scrutinised with a stern intensity that made him consciously have to control his bladder lest he should embarrass himself. 'There has been a mistake,' he blurted out, trying to control the tremor in his voice.

'A mistake!' Nexus roared. 'An actual mistake! Why, this is absolutely incredible! Taj, I am amazed, truly!'

Taj cleared his throat. 'Yes, well, my-'

'Be quiet!' Nexus roared, leaping forward so he stood directly before Taj, towering over him. 'Let me get this right. You're now saying, that I, Lord of all the dragon clans, made a mistake about the death of my only son?'

Taj rocked from foot to foot and kept his gaze fixed firmly on the floor, unsure what to say.

'Taj, I have to ask you this,' Nexus continued, 'just in case; have you gone completely mad? Has your contact with the Dark Dragon made you basket-case barmy? Are your brains so stupefyingly addled, that your pathetic human senses have warped your feeble mind to such an alarming degree that coherent reasoning is beyond your limited capabilities?'

Taj fidgeted with his fingers, wringing his hands. 'Please, my Lord, just hear me out. I am not blaming you for anything, and I don't know how I can sense your son, especially as you cannot. Neither do I know why! All I know with any certainty, is that Spuddle is alive, and that is the truth.'

'You know this for a certainty!' Nexus roared.

Taj flinched from the anger of Nexus, taking a few involuntary steps backwards. 'My Lord, as you said yourself at the time, it was strange that you had not sensed Spuddle dying. It was very odd how he just sort of vanished. My belief is that he did not die, but that he did mysteriously vanish, and miraculously, he has now reappeared.'

'Reappeared?' Nexus said in a hushed whisper that sounded more menacing than his roar. 'Is that the best you can do, Taj? My son has miraculously reappeared?'

Taj dropped to one knee. 'I swear it, my Lord. This is the truth; I would never utter a falsehood to you, especially about your own son. You have to believe me: you do believe me, don't you, my Lord?'

Nexus growled in reply and Taj blanched at the thought of what might happen next.

Chapter Eleven

Ionuin laughed at the confused expression on Sterner's face, and the sound was hard and cold, unreal, not like her usual good-natured laugh at all. 'I asked you a question, Sterner, what makes you think I'm nice, hmm? I just killed your miserable companions, are you blind? Oh no, of course not, you're the one who kills blind people, aren't you?' She could see that he was badly hurt and desperately wanted to live, but she was in no way inclined to be merciful, not anymore, and especially not when dispatching justice. She crouched down, absently picking at her fingernails with her knife, watching Sterner closely from beneath lowered brows. 'You see, you misunderstand the situation,' she said, rocking forward, kneeling by his side, but remaining alert. 'Like you, I think I might be crazy, but crazy or not, I am a killer for sure. You, Sterner, kill for the wrong reasons, but tell me, who is this friend of yours that told you about our hidden valley?'

Sterner shook his head. 'No, no, I can't. Oh god, don't you see my agony? I'm going to lose my leg! Bleeding-demons; isn't that enough? Haven't you done enough?'

Ionuin simply raised her eyebrows, as if considering his fate.

Sterner rolled his head to one side, then back again, squeezing his eyes tightly closed. 'Please, don't torture me. I can't take anymore hurt: I just can't!'

Ionuin shook her head, mimicking Sterner's body language, smiling as she saw his eyes flutter open then widen in terror. He thinks I'm completely mad, she thought, and perhaps I am!

'I'm begging you, begging you for my life!' Sterner cried.

Ionuin shrugged her shoulders and sighed. 'Beg all you want, but like your, bald, fat friend said, you were doing my father a favour. Now, at the risk of boring you and repeating myself, I'm returning the favour.'

Snake-quick, she stabbed Sterner in his upper thigh, not deep, just enough to let him know she meant business.

'Busted Bollock!' he cursed, and began howling like a baby, clapping his hand over the wound.

Ionuin kept thoughts of her father's battered body in the forefront of her mind, knowing she could not show any weakness. 'However, first, not only will you will tell me who your friend is, you will also tell me where I can find this friend.' With a quick flick of her wrist, she rapped his filthy fingers with the hilt of her knife, making him pull them away, then jabbed her thumb down, pressing hard on the stab wound, watching as a fountain of blood spurted onto the sandy canyon floor. Sterner yowled and tried to knock her hand away, but Ionuin was immovable. 'Wow, look at that, Sterner. Isn't it pretty? Like the clouds this morning, only a different kind of pretty. I like the colour red; it's my favourite. Do you like red, Sterner? Now, who is your informative friend?'

Tears burst from Sterner's eyes. 'The Dark Dragon!' he cried, 'it's everywhere, it sees everything. That's all I know, please, no more pain.'

Ionuin flicked her knife, tapping Fyrdraca's handle. It sang with a musical ring, the tremulous vibration travelling down the length of the sword through Sterner's blood drenched knee, making him shriek for mercy.

'Calm down,' Ionuin said placatingly. 'It's nearly over for you, then you can rest, you can have a long, long sleep.'

'Oh, god, no, no, no,' he pleaded, one hand clutching his knee the other pushing at Ionuin's arm. 'I don't want to die, I can't take it, I just can't! I'm telling you the truth, it's the Dark Dragon! Please, please let me go.'

Dark Dragon? Ionuin thought as she knocked away Sterner's grasping hand and removed her thumb from the thigh wound, truly surprised at the hole she had made. Who on Merm was the Dark Dragon? 'Ooh, looks messy,' she murmured, a look of apparently genuine concern arching her brows. 'You might need a stitch or two there, Sterner.'

'It, it is so painful,' Sterner moaned, his breath now coming is short gasps. 'Please, no more pain, I will tell you anything, anything at all, I promise! And, and I'm sorry for what I done, truly sorry.'

'Really?' said Ionuin, uncaringly. 'Hmm, all right, you're sorry. So what? Forget about being sorry, what I really need to know, who, for crying out loud, is the Dark Dragon?' She was shouting now, and was aware that her temper was escaping her control. She thought 'Dark Dragon' was probably a title some brigand had adopted, and half-expected Sterner to give the real name of another crony like himself, someone she could hunt down and kill. She placed the point of her knife on the edge of Sterner's nostril. 'I will ask you once again, who, beneath our glorious sun, is the Dark Dragon, and what do you mean; it's everywhere and sees everything? Is it perhaps, a magical Dragon?' she asked, mockingly.

Sterner swallowed and peered down at the blade, going cross-eyed. 'It . . . well, it came to us, one night, told us where the cottage was, said there was a girl.'

'Go on,' Ionuin urged, her intrigue increasing, wondering at the use of the word 'it' instead of 'he or she,' not knowing where this conversation was going.

'It said we could have the girl. It said we could use her as we wished.' He winced, the agony from his wounds causing obvious pain.

'How disgusting,' Ionuin said.

'I agree,' Sterner said, 'the Dragon is dis-'

'Shut it!' Ionuin snapped. 'Even though you're a despicable, murdering grunt, it seems you do have something of an imagination and we may be able to compromise a little after all.'

Sterner established eye contact and did not flinch. 'Well, it said that the secret valley of Tharl was protected by a magic ward, one that it could not break by itself.' He inhaled deeply, sucking in breath through gaps in his yellow-stained teeth. 'It gave us a cantrip. One that had to be uttered by an innocent, that's why we brought Grog along, he's a virgin and had never killed anyone; that is, until he killed Tharl.'

Ionuin slowly slid the knife up Sterner's nose, watching his eyes widen as its sharpened edges pressed against the sides of his nostril. 'Stop mentioning my father's name,' she spat. 'Your tongue is not worthy of uttering the word.' She withdrew the knife, but let the tip rest on Sterner's cheek, just below his eye. 'Go on; then what happened?'

'When we stood where the Dragon had ordered and Grog spoke the words, 'Flee Zariba', what had been a cacti-ridden valley, humming with insects and crawling with red scorpions, instantly transformed into the legendary valley of, of your father. I mean, we'd heard of the place, who hasn't? But to see it open up like that in a wavy blur: well, we were stunned!'

Ionuin tapped the tip of the knife against Sterner's cheek while she thought things through. Most of what the man had said made sense and fitted with her father's claims of a wandering wizard and a magical ward, but this Dark Dragon . . . now, that just sounded like a made up creature, a fabricated nonsense to protect his accomplices. She rested the edge of the knife on Sterner's eyelid, just enough so he could feel the sharpness without drawing blood. 'You know what I think, Sterner? I think you're mostly telling the truth, apart from the bit about the Dark Dragon. I believe this silly creature is a cunning lie, a lie to hide your friend's identity.'

Sterner looked to her as if he were about to shake his head in denial.

She pressed the blade's edge into his lower lid, drawing a bead of blood. 'Now then, stupid; don't even think about shaking your head, in confirmation or denial. You may give yourself a nasty cut. Don't want any unpleasant accidents, now do we? But, please, do tell me about your real friends, and, um, well, I might let you keep your eye,' she said, giving Sterner her best smile.

Nexus ran a long talon down the length of his golden snout and turned to pace the room. 'I see. You say you are sure this is not just some trickery of the Dark Dragon? After all, as I pointed out, so eloquently I might add, I cannot sense anything of Spuddle at all! Why do you suppose this is, Taj? Could it be that the Dark Dragon is perhaps playing tricks on you? Trying to unhinge you, if he hasn't done so already, and unbalance us all before the approaching solstice?'

Taj's jaw dropped. Nexus distrusted him, distrusted his skills as a sensitive. 'I, I don't know, my Lord.' He had not expected this reaction at all. He had been elated at finding Spuddle, and had expected high praise from Nexus.

'You don't know!' Nexus stood, accidentally knocking over the library table, sending Herald Knell tumbling to the floor. 'Last night, you could not even sense our intended target because of your fear of the Dark Dragon, could you?'

Taj felt stunned, bewildered. What if Nexus was right? 'I admit, I admit I was fearful but-'

'Don't 'but' me, Taj,' Nexus roared. 'I know the aura of my own son and I tell you he is gone from Merm. Dead, vanished, call it what you will: he is no more! Before you came rushing in here with your supposed good news, did you even consider the possibility that you could have been played for a fool by our enemy? Let's face it, your thoughts were snatched from thin air and you were scared witless last time you successfully projected your mind. What is to say that it is not the Dark Dragon playing with your emotions?'

'But I don't-'

'No!' Nexus snapped. 'Hear me, boy and consider that the Dark Dragon may have allowed you to believe what you want to believe, laying out a false trail of hope with the intention of luring us from our stronghold, from our guarded lands, then taking us by surprise with his fearsome misshapen army of beasts. Get a grip, Taj! Spuddle is dead and this is just trickery leading you into danger, a malicious trap. I'm surprised at your naivety; can you not sense the wrongness here?'

Taj hardly knew what to say. Nexus must be wrong, because he knew in his heart that Spuddle was not dead. He knew he was right and he had not been tricked, but how to convince Lord Nexus? How could it be proven?

'Answer me, boy!' Nexus bawled, his golden eyes flaring amber with anger. 'Do you not see through this, this, cheap masquerade of shameful deceit?'

The raw power contained in the voice of Nexus made Taj feel like bursting into tears, but he knew that he was right and Nexus was wrong. What could he do? Nexus was the law, and none defied the law and expected to live. He had to somehow escape and find Spuddle himself.

His course of action decided, he rose to his feet and bowed, giving Nexus a sign of formal respect. 'Your gracious Majesty, you told me yourself that you had strengthened our wards and sentinels so that not even the least thought of the Dark Dragon could pierce Fire Mountain. You also told me that you trusted my ability as a sensitive. I cannot offer proof of what I know, but do not fear; I shall find Spuddle myself. I apologise if I have upset you, my Lord. I assure you, upset was not my intention. I think you forget, sometimes, that I loved Spuddle too.' He turned and ran up the stairs as tears brimmed from his eyes.

Taj was fully aware of the dangers he would face by leaving the confines of Fire Mountain, but in his mind, this was the only way to prove that Spuddle lived, and prove it he would, or die trying.

Chapter Twelve

Sweat burst out on Sterner's forehead. He had turned deathly pale and his eyes were clenched tightly closed. 'I, I, yes, yes, I remember now. It was erm, Mad Travis, yeah, Mad Travis and, and Fat Shinny! Yeah, they erm, they gave us directions. I've tried to protect them, but you - you've given me no choice. I swear, it was them. They are responsible for your father's death, and it was Grog who did the killing, wanted to prove himself a man. Crudder goaded him along, but I never did anything. I was forced to accompany them because Mad Travis had threatened me! Yes, I remember now. That Dark Dragon lark, it was just a, a figment of my imagination! I've not been well, you know and, well, I was trying to cover for my mates, you see-'

'Shut it, you squirming lickspittle!' Ionuin snarled. 'The lies stink as you spit them from your festering mouth!' She wondered if he was, in fact, lying. His words sounded more plausible than the mythical Dark Dragon, but could both answers be lies? 'I think you are still lying,' she said, pressing on the blade some more, 'For arguments sake, let us say you are telling the truth. Where exactly can I find this Mad Travis and . . . ?'

'Fat Shinny!' Sterner supplied, licking his lips, his eyeballs rolling around nervously.

'Yes, Fat Shinny,' said Ionuin, removing the knife from his eyelid.

Sterner opened his eyes, slowly. He was breathing deeply, almost panting, and wincing with obvious pain. 'The Badlands,' he murmured. 'In a place called Huskers Mount. Everyone in the Badlands knows who they are. You'll have no trouble finding them, I promise!'

Ionuin giggled to herself, a smile stretching across her face. 'You promise? What a crock of donkey crap!' Her face turned dark and angry. 'I'll let you into a little secret, you dirty, miserable wretch. I don't believe in promises! Don't you dare promise me anything!'

Sterner gave out an exasperated sigh. 'But, you're one of the fairer sex,' he gasped. 'You're supposed to be gentle, caring, and fond of promises. They're supposed to mean something to the likes of you!'

'Likes of me? Hah!' Ionuin grinned. 'You should get out more. The 'likes of me' are few and far between. You have a seriously misguided knowledge of females, Sterner. I bet you haven't known many, have you?'

Sterner shook his head.

'Thought not. You probably think they're too difficult to fathom, which of course, they are, but I'll try to be gentle and caring,' she said, placing the knife blade against his red-bristled throat. 'Although, I don't see why I should; you killed my father, and what did he ever do to you?'

Sterner rolled his head from side to side, trying to pull away from the blade. 'No, no, no, this is not happening! I can't die like this,' he wailed. 'Not from the likes of you! A silly girl! A heartless, cruel gag-bag!' He mustered his saliva and spat into Ionuin's face, managing a manic grin as the bubbly spittle dribbled off her chin. 'There! How do you like that you, you torturing cow? Now, I demand that you let me go! Pull this steel from my leg and let me go. I've told you all I know, I have done nothing wrong! You said you'd let me live!'

'Um, no, I didn't,' Ionuin replied. 'I said that we might compromise, and that I would let you keep your eye. Anyway, I don't believe that you didn't take part in the killing. My father had more than one wound. Thank you for gozzing in my face, though, you inbred shit-pot,' she said, grinning, wiping away the spit. 'I was actually considering letting you live,' she lied, observing Sterner's changing features. 'Now, I don't see how I can possibly allow such a thing, do you?'

'You cold-hearted whore!' Sterner grabbed for the knife but missed, collecting a gash on his palm in the process, yelping as he shook his hand.

'Too slow,' Ionuin murmured, returning her knife to his throat, simmering anger making her want to whip the blade across his exposed windpipe. Just one quick swipe and it would be over. 'You helped murder my father, so you do deserve to die.' She thought she saw the glimmer of a smile insinuate itself upon Sterner's spittle-splashed lips, but that could not be right: could it?

Now Sterner did smile, or rather, grin. Ionuin could hardly believe it, the fool must think he had somehow won! She noticed that his left hand was no longer clutching his knee, it was sliding down the side of his body. She kept her gaze firmly fixed on his eyes. He was saying something, trying to cause a distraction, but Ionuin heard only a distant murmur. Sterner made his move, snatching the hilt of the hidden dagger he kept in his boot, but Ionuin was ready for him. Moving in a flash, she grabbed his wrist with her hand in a steely grip. With determined menace in his eyes, Sterner tried to turn the blade upwards, to push it into Ionuin's ribs. She allowed the momentum to drive the weapon forward, then with all the energy she could manage, angled the blade into his throat.

'Now look what you've done, you silly man,' she muttered, dodging sideways as gouts of bubbling blood shot forth. Sterner's body convulsed. His eyelids fluttered briefly, then closed forever as the rising sun peeped from behind breaking clouds, throwing warming rays into the ancient canyon. 'Death at dawn,' Ionuin muttered, wiping her blade on Sterner's tunic. 'For what it's worth, vengeance is mine.' She had expected to feel elated, but she did not, she felt oddly numb, detached, not satisfied at all. She did not enjoy killing, never had, but having being brought up around the desolate plains she saw killing take place nearly every day and knew that it was the natural way of things. For nature, death was a way of life: the only way, for without death there could be no life. Ionuin applied the same rules to her own existence. If she encountered a problem that the world would be better off without, if at all possible, she eradicated that problem. Guided by a strong moral code and possessing a trustworthy conscience, she could not envisage herself living any other way. The only thing that saddened her about this mercenary way of life was that there were not more like her.

Now, she had a new problem. She had to visit the Badlands and find out if this doubtful duo, Mad Travis and Fat Shinny, really existed, then kill them. 'Flee Zariba,' she murmured. She had heard the word 'Zariba' before, but could not remember its meaning. She glanced up at the dark square shape beside the giant cacti. 'Now,' she said, sheathing her knife before removing Fyrdraca from Sterner's knee with a fearsome yank, 'let's see what we have in the cage.'

'Taj!' Nexus roared. 'Come back here! Where do you think you're going, boy? You have been corrupted by the Dark! It's setting a trap for you, can you not feel it?'

Taj regained some composure and from the top step, looked at Nexus over his shoulder. 'If Lord Bollfur calls to take me on the hunt, tell him I have gone to find your supposedly dead son.'

'Why you insolent little tyke! I'll skin you!' Nexus shouted, making for the stairs.

Taj dashed across the throne room and out of the door, running as fast as his legs could carry him along the tunnel linking the throne room to the main cavern. Just before entering the cavern, he turned and climbed a set of narrow stairs leading to the higher levels. He knew that Nexus could not chase him by this route and the wide cave detour would take him so long that Taj could find his way back down to the lower levels. He had not entered these narrow passages since Spuddle and Glitch, prince of the Red Dragons, had played hunt and prey with him, many moons ago, but he knew the caverns like the back of his hand. He would not only prove Nexus wrong, he would prove his own bravery by leaving the guarded lands and finding Spuddle.

'I'll be a hero!' he panted, nearly breaking into fits of laughter. Of course, he would need help, so his first task would be to find Glitch. Luckily, he knew exactly where the youngster would be. He reached the lower annex, a chamber twenty spans across and thirty high. There were six openings besides the large tunnel leading up to the main chamber, from which he expected Nexus to come charging down at any moment. Taj dashed across to the smallest exit. He could already hear shouts and bellows from the upper reaches of the mountain complex, accompanied by almost deafening roars from the main feasting chamber, but they were too late.

There were no dragons small enough to follow him down this narrow service tunnel, created for human use when they served the dragons during an earlier era. From here, he could take any direction he chose. Taj knew Nexus would be trying to locate him by scent and when he lost the trail, by aura recognition, an ability that the dragon species had developed from their extra sensory perception skills. Dragon magic was limited, but their super senses more than made up for the deficiency.

Taj headed for a slim crack in the tunnel wall, one in which he used to hide from Glitch and Spuddle when they had played around this remote area of the mountain. He squeezed through and caught his breath. By now, he guessed that Nexus knew he had escaped down the service tunnel, which meant he would be trying to get a fix on his whereabouts using his sensory-location powers.

Taj reached into the pouch at his belt, which he was never without, and withdrew two crystals; a small blue connecting crystal and a larger red guiding piece of quartz. He warmed them with his hands, allowing some of his own limited elemental magic to connect his thoughts, his mind swimming within the swirling colours. The crystal he used for communicating; he placed in his mouth, his teeth closed around it, flattening his tongue. The large red one, as big as his fist, he held between both hands until it became heated. Pulses of energy were soon swimming away from him, penetrating solid rock, flowing through the whole mountain, disguising his path and confusing his trail.

He walked forward as his eyes became accustomed to the gloom. These smaller tunnels were never lit now, and had remained dark for eons, but the glow from his guiding crystal gave out enough light so he could find his way. He closed his mind to everything and concentrated.

Last night, he had not been able to use his communication crystal at all, and Nexus was correct about one thing; he had been scared of the Dark Dragon. His fear had inhibited his ability, but things were different now. This was not a secret mission; one that he did not really believe was anything more than an exercise in subterfuge set by Nexus to test his powers. Spuddle's life was at stake.

Glitch? He projected telepathically. *Glitch, I need you now, and my need is urgent.* As he walked, Taj waited for an answer.

Chapter Thirteen

Ionuin decided to deal with the remains of her father's killers afterwards, for now, she needed to satisfy her burning curiosity. With her knife sheathed, her sword at the ready, and the slash across her ribs apparently fully healed, she approached the cage. On her first fleeting inspection it had appeared dilapidated and flimsy. As she drew closer, she saw that the wooden slats were held together by thick metal binding straps, making the cage stronger than she had initially imagined.

She halted as something inside the cage moved, a shadow shifting within darker shadows, edging away, trying to hide. A haunting noise, akin to the soft cries of a weeping child, resonated through the air. Ionuin moved closer as it suddenly dawned on her what the animal might be. Such creatures were childish fantasies, though, weren't they? She reasoned that such animals must exist, but if so, why were they never seen? Even ghosts could be seen if they were inclined to be, but if her suspicions were correct, then this mewling, incarcerated animal before her was even rarer than ghosts. Her mind began to push at her scant knowledge concerning such things, trying to fathom the complex laws of nature. If she believed even half of her father's extraordinary tales, then what she was facing here was a creature of myth and legend. Could it really be a fully grown pig?

Crouching at what she considered to be a safe distance, Ionuin peered into the gloomy interior of the cage, trying to get a good view of the creature inside.

'What on Merm is it?' she murmured, rising slowly, fingering the hilt of her sword with some uncertainty.

Dissatisfied with the view, she circled around and with one swipe of Fyrdraca, lopped down the giant multi-limbed cactus that had been blocking out the light. Then at last, she saw, and was amazed, more than amazed, absolutely stunned. 'No,' she murmured, shaking her head in denial, retreating a little. 'It, it cannot be real; are you real?'

Something buzzed inside her head, passing right through her skull, like a shrill whine, as if an animal had screeched. 'Ach,' she said, clapping her hands over her ears; then the noise stopped as abruptly as it had started. Gulping loudly, she stepped closer to the cage, making sure she was not mistaken. A fully-grown pig would have been remarkable, but this creature, a baby dragon cowering in the corner of the cage, was beyond remarkable, it was absolutely incredulous.

The animal grunted, startling her, making her jump back. Without knowing why, Ionuin laughed aloud, her face splitting into an enormous smile. 'Just, unbelievable!' she gasped. 'Totally unreal! An actual, living dragon!'

Even though only a baby, Ionuin guessed it was the same size as a half-grown pig and probably twice as dangerous. Not that she could ever remember seeing a half-grown pig. On Merm, pigs rarely survived long enough to reach such a size. She replaced Fyrdraca in its scabbard and continued walking around the cage. The dragon was in an awful state. From what Ionuin could see, it had been used and abused as a living larder by the murderers she had just dispatched. Its forelegs and one rear leg were missing entirely. Its other rear leg, newly grown, was tiny in size compared to the remainder of its body. Its ears, if indeed they were actually ears, were merely shortened, grizzled stumps.

Ionuin wondered how long they had held this helpless creature captive, hacking off its limbs and feeding from it before allowing new limbs to grow, then eating those as well. She supposed the meat would have been tender and succulent, if the creature was kept on a diet of vegetation. This explained the strange meat she had scented on the killer's sweat and faeces out on the floodplains. The dragon did not look at all healthy. Its yellowish skin appeared mottled and discoloured, flaking away in hand-sized strips. A metal muzzle bound the dragon's jaws, rendering it defenceless, which explained why it did not roar, as dragons allegedly did, occasionally.

The creature watched Ionuin as she tried to unfasten the cage door, its green-slit yellow eyes flaring, teeth gnashing noisily together inside the muzzle. It tried shifting its bulk, probably in an attempt to attain a position from which to launch a strike, or so Ionuin supposed.

'A gutsy one, aren't you?' said Ionuin, drawing her knife and grunting with effort, trying to prise open the latch holding the door. She wondered if she was doing the right thing, or behaving like an idiot, putting her own life in mortal danger. As the door loosened the dragon instantly tried to attack. 'All right,' muttered Ionuin, stepping back slightly. 'Take it easy, I won't hurt you.' She was rocked by a sudden rushing wave of dizziness; her head swimming with strange reptilian thoughts. The sensation passed as quickly as it had occurred, but Ionuin was not alarmed. She knew exactly what had happened. How she knew was beyond her, but she knew. She pointed at the dragon, her finger waving uncertainly. 'Was that, was that . . . you, dragon?'

The dragon simply sat there; it did not appear to understand.

Ionuin rubbed at her temple. 'It, it was you, wasn't it? And before, with that high pitched whine, you, you were sending out thoughts: no! Not sending them out, blasting them out!'

Still, the young dragon did not move.

'Come on,' said Ionuin, leaning closer to the cage door. 'Admit it. You tried to see inside my head, didn't you?'

The dragon cocked its head on one side.

Ionuin wondered if it understood the common speech that was the universal language on this desert world. According to her late father, and the few books she had read that featured dragons, they were supposed to be elevated from most animals as far as intellect was concerned. This was only a baby dragon, though, and she doubted it understood language at all. In addition, given what it had recently been through, what sort of state would its mind be in? It did not bear consideration. However, she had to try and communicate somehow; then an idea struck her.

She concentrated, flexed her mind and tried latching onto the dragon's thoughts with images and emotions. She encountered hatred; utter hopelessness coupled with a strong yearning for death. The thoughts were jumbled, indistinct, but Ionuin got the message. She projected a feeling of warmth, mercy, forming an image of herself and the dragon actually hugging; picturing a big smile on her face. She then watched as the dragon reacted, appearing to reassess the situation.

'Come on,' said Ionuin, tentatively placing her hand inside the cage, beckoning with her fingers, encouraging it to come forward. 'I mean you no harm and you know this is true.' Again, she felt a strange swimming dizziness rifling her mind. 'Yes, that's it, I agree, don't trust anyone, but you need to trust me. I can get you out of here.' She looked into the young dragon's mind, searching for its birth name. She sensed that the creature was male; the name, 'Spuddle,' springing into her thoughts. 'Spuddle! Is that your name? Spuddle?'

The dragon's eyes opened wide at the sound.

'It is Spuddle; isn't it?' Ionuin said, tilting her head to one side as she examined Spuddle further. She had definitely seen him react to the sound of his name. 'And maybe you do understand common speech after all. Spuddle, Spuddle, all in a muddle!' The dragon frowned. 'Sorry, sorry,' said Ionuin. 'Bad joke, please forgive me.'

The dragon did not appear to be listening anymore as it shuffled forward, resting on the edge of the cage. With one hard yank Ionuin removed the door and let it fall to the ground. 'There you go, Spuddle, freedom.' The dragon eyed her, suspiciously, so Ionuin thought, and for some odd reason beyond her immediate reckoning, appeared reluctant to leave. Then it glanced at Ionuin and began whimpering.

Nexus watched Taj exit the subterranean cavern and run into the throne room. 'Curse that boy,' he mumbled under his breath as he stooped to retrieve the book of prophecy from the floor. He knew that the impetuous side of Taj's human nature now controlled his decisions, not even giving a second thought to their enemy. He had always warned Saturnine that no good would come from dallying with humans, but she would not listen. She so enjoyed transforming herself from dragon to human, to walk among them, fooling them, and then what does she do? Goes and falls in love with one, and now he had this almighty mess to deal with.

He placed the ancient prophecy book back on the shelf, righted the library table and then went after Taj. If he made it out of the catacombs he could be in danger, especially as he thought he was doing the right thing. He just hoped Taj's previous mental encounter with the Dark Dragon had scared him enough to make him at least a little aware of the danger.

As he walked down the main tunnel connecting the large chamber to the throne room, Taj's scent unexpectedly vanished. Nexus backtracked and as soon as he came to the disused service stairwell, he knew the boy had eluded him and could not be stopped. He mapped out the area in his head, attempting to visualise where the boy might be going, and realised that if he hurried, he could still cut him off. He ran down the tunnel, charging into the main chamber, almost colliding with Lord Bollfur, leader of the blue dragon brood.

71

'Your majesty, what's the big hurry?' Lord Bollfur cried, steadying himself. 'I was just coming to find Taj, to take him on the hunt.'

'He's skedaddled,' Nexus replied.

'Skedaddled? You mean, you mean he's run away?'

'Exactly,' Nexus sighed. 'Come on, we can catch him at the tunnel intersection. I'll tell you about it on the way.'

The trek through the service tunnels had been easy for Taj. Using his sensitive skills he followed a direct route leading south to where human villages had once stood at the base of Fire Mountain. All that remained now were crumbling low walls and partial foundations. By the time he neared his destination, a long forgotten southern entrance, night had fallen.

He had sent many telepathic calls to Glitch, but he had only received one reply, informing him that he would definitely be met. He wondered if his augmenter crystal was working properly. He had only recently mastered the use of the augmenter for long-range links, another secret kept between himself and Nexus, and his ability was relatively untested. Apart from his secret mission; seeking other humans that displayed any degree of talent, his use of crystals remained limited. Nexus had assured him there were other humans who were also sensitive, but he had found none so far and wondered about the true purpose of the mission.

With his mind distracted, he almost stumbled into the ancient stone wall that had once blocked the tunnel from outsiders. There were two ironwood rods crossed at the tunnel entrance, placed there to detect any unwanted intruders, but Taj knew he could pass them without sounding the alarm. Even though he was human, he was still part of the Fire Mountain Dragon Clan and able to come and go as he pleased. He stepped carefully over the rods, not wishing to touch them, just in case Nexus did detect the movement. Even a friendly passing of the rods might alert patrols of his whereabouts.

Once past the wards, he peered over a small gap in the wall where a stone had come loose and fallen out, but he could see nothing. He waited, listening, aware that he was now beyond the safety and relative security offered by Fire Mountain; thoughts of the Dark Dragon suddenly blasted through his mind.

Chapter Fourteen

'Aw, come on now, Spuddle,' Ionuin cajoled. 'There's no need for those distressing noises. I do want to help you and I won't harm you. Are you going to try trusting me, hmm? What have you got to lose?' She unfastened the muzzle on his snout, tossing it aside before aiding him as he struggled from the cage. 'There, see? Doesn't that prove I trust you not to bite me? Now, you must trust me not to hurt you.' Images of the men she had just killed assaulted her mind. 'Oh, I see.' She gestured towards the dead bodies scattered around the camp. 'Yes, I am human, like them, but I'm not cruel like them. Not inside, not inside my, my heart.' Such talk about the *heart* sounded soppy to Ionuin. It seemed to work though, as she watched Spuddle's eyes latch onto the nearest dead body. 'Are you hungry, Spuddle?' she quizzed. 'Have these bad men not been feeding you properly? Do you actually eat people? My father told me that your kind do, on a regular basis. Is it true?'

She received no reply either telepathically or via body language, and she did not doubt Spuddle's mental capabilities, although his messages were conveyed by hazy images rather than literal communication.

'Go ahead, Spuddle,' she told the dragon bluntly while pointing to the nearest dead murderer. 'I don't mind a bit! Not to my taste, you see, and as they have fed on you for so long, I suppose you have every right.' Spuddle looked her right in the eye. 'Don't look at me like that. I told you, I don't care if you eat them or not. It'll save burying them.'

Spuddle, drool dripping from his maw, edged over to the still warm corpse of Crudder and severed the man's head with a wickedly loud snap, so lightning fast that it made Ionuin jump.

'Wow!' she exclaimed, watching Spuddle grip the head in his teeth before hurling it into the air, catching it, and crunching the skull between powerful jaws. Blobs of brain dribbled through gnashing teeth, his incredibly long red tongue lapping up everything, not missing a drop. 'Who's a hungry boy?' she said, walking over, dragging back the body of Sterner.

As she turned around, Spuddle was covered in blood as he gorged on Crudder's torso. In the time it took for her to retrieve the speared form of Grog from the rocks, only Crudder's arms and legs remained. The dragon belched loudly, before stripping free thigh muscles and gulping them down whole.

'Steady on, Spuddle,' Ionuin warned, wondering if too much food all at once might make the starved creature sick. 'How about saving some for later?' She tossed Grog's body beside the carcass of Sterner. Spuddle looked at her uncomprehendingly, shuffled over and bit off Sterner's foot with a crunch and a crack, splintering bones.

'Suit yourself,' Ionuin said, shrugging and walking over to the underfed mule, checking its saddlebags for supplies. She removed a strip of salted pork, guessing that it had been taken from the cottage after they killed her father. She waved it at

Spuddle, smiling. 'You see, Spuddle; I eat human food.' She bit into the pork. 'Not humans.'

Spuddle appeared to nod before biting off Sterner's other foot, slivers of tendon dangling from his mouth. Ionuin continued rummaging around in the saddlebags, her searching fingers finally connecting with a soft leather pouch, the feel of which made her heart leap.

'My bracelets!' she exclaimed, quickly removing the pouch, tipping the contents into her hands. The two chunky gold bands were unmistakable as they were engraved with strange, distinctive rune markings. 'Father,' she murmured to herself, trying to suppress her rising sadness. 'You never did tell me the true tale of these.' She slipped a bracelet over each hand. 'They fit perfectly now that I'm grown.' They seemed to mould themselves to the shape of her wrists. 'Spuddle, look,' she said, holding out her arms, the sun glinting off the gold. 'Aren't they just beautiful?'

The dragon nodded his apparent approval between bites of splintered forearm.

She gazed at the bracelets, wondering at their origin, their purpose. All she knew about them was that they were a birth-gift from a stranger, a travelling minstrel who supposedly hailed from foreign lands.

The remainder of the day passed quietly, with Spuddle feeding while Ionuin made what use she could from the dead men's belongings. Using the discarded rubbish, she lit a campfire and piled all tradable items beside the mule. She intended to spend the night there and probably move on in the morning. What she was going to do about Spuddle, she had no idea. She just hoped he didn't grow peckish during the night.

She placed wood, smashed from the cage that had held Spuddle, onto the fire, enough so that it would burn well into the night, and settled down on her bear-hide. While she roasted pieces of cacti, Spuddle rested across from her and appeared to be dozing. She glanced around, trying not to stare into the fire, peering into shadows, more out of habit than anything else. Apart from Spuddle and the mule, she sensed no other life-forms of any significance. Even so, it felt eerie in this strange valley, as if there actually were others, perhaps lurking not far away, watching and waiting. She gave a little shudder, checked that she was not burning the cacti and continued to listen. The night felt alien, scary, even though the only sounds to be heard were the soft snores of the dragon and the crackle of flames from the fire.

Ionuin smiled as Spuddle released a gentle snort. She knew she had nothing to fear from the young dragon; his company felt right. She allowed her mind to wander over her situation and turned her thoughts to the future, then realised, with some despondency, that she had no future. Her whole world had revolved around her father and life at their lonesome cottage. She considered returning, but there was nothing to go back to if she did return. Without her father, it would soon become lonely, and whilst some solitude can be beneficial, too much could unbalance the cleverest of minds and Ionuin did not consider herself clever in the slightest.

Going back was not an option. Then, there was the matter of Fat Travis and Mad Shinny to be decided. Or was it Mad Travis and Fat Shinny? She could not remember, but even though they had not taken a direct part in the slaying of her father, they were still involved somehow: or were they? On consideration, she realised she actually had no proof, only the babblings of Sterner, and they could hardly be relied upon. Still, she reasoned, she had nothing better planned. It looked as if she was in for a long walk down the Valley of Caves and into the unwelcoming badlands.

As she pondered what might happen after arriving at Cavesend, the first big town at the end of the valley, subtle noises of something stirring in the night caught her attention. Then came the unmistakable sound of a creature roaring, a large creature, and it was drawing closer. Ionuin sprang to her feet, her ears straining to decipher the odd animal sounds, trying to picture what kind of beast it could possibly be. Wolf? Bear? Lychyaena?

Despite the noise, Spuddle remained asleep as she moved out of the glow of the fire. Cautiously, she crept forward, hiding behind the cactus she had felled earlier, trying to see from where any danger might spring, but her position gave a poor view. Unsatisfied, she leapt the cactus and at a running crouch, moved towards some boulders, concealing herself behind them. Her nerves were twanging, her heart hammering in her chest, her breathing short and shallow, but at least she could now survey the valley and easily see anything approaching the camp.

For a while, nothing happened. On the verge of returning to her bear-hide, thinking she had imagined the whole thing, something large and black dropped out of the sky and knocked her to the floor. Screaming, Ionuin tried to roll clear and to thrust her sword upwards into her attacker, but she hit nothing. Dust stung her eyes, filled her nose and mouth as she tried to roll away from danger. This was no wolf, bear or lychyaena, but something else entirely. Something with two massive legs that stamped around, making the ground shudder, and no matter where she rolled, she remained trapped beneath the creature.

It was matching her every move and appeared to know exactly what she was going to do next. The feet, scuffling by her head, had wickedly hooked claws that could gut her in an instant, and with fear mounting, Ionuin again thrashed wildly with her sword. In sheer desperation, she lunged at the nearest leg, her blade slicing through flesh, spraying her face with hot sticky blood. At least I've left my mark before I die, she thought, preparing to strike again. Then teeth and jaws clamped around her middle, making her scream for all she was worth! Was this the end of her very short life? Pain screeched through every nerve fibre and a part of her wanted and welcomed death, just to be free of the tearing, shredding agony ripping through her stomach, but then, instead of being bitten in two, she was somehow dragged free.

Ionuin ceased flailing and screaming and looked up. She had intended raising Fyrdraca, but she had no sword in her hand! Even more curiously, Spuddle hovered over her. Had he rescued her, or was he actually her attacker? Then she saw, far above Spuddle, the hovering head of another huge dragon, looking straight at her. Its luminous crimson eyes bored directly into her inner self; the same crimson eyes that she had spied among the rocks during the previous night on the floodplains. It was pitch black, and difficult to see anything with accuracy. With only firelight flickering off its shimmering body, the beast looked odd. It appeared to be absorbing light, instead of reflecting it. Then it roared and swooped down its massive jaws, making Ionuin shy away. She was about to scream, but instead of having her head bitten off, something warm and leathery licked her face.

Ionuin opened her eyes and saw in wonderment that she hadn't been attacked at all. Spuddle was crouched over her, his long red tongue lolling between slightly open jaws. Over by the fire, now burnt low, she saw chunks of scorched cacti. They were frazzled to a crisp. She realised she must have fallen asleep while cooking supper.

'A nightmare,' she murmured, clasping her hand to her chest where her heart was still hammering away. 'Just a damnable nightmare and a false awakening, to add to the terror.' She reached for Fyrdraca as a natural reaction, but her sword had gone. 'Spuddle? M-my sword? Where's my sword?'

Spuddle cocked his head and looked at her in a confused way, that despite the strange circumstances, Ionuin thought rather comical.

She leapt to her feet. 'I had it when I bedded down, I know I did.' She looked around, but Fyrdraca was nowhere to be seen. Ionuin extended the search to the outskirts of the camp, and by the boulders against which she dreamt she had been attacked, she found Fyrdraca, but that was not all. The ground was trampled and disturbed by animal prints, big ones, and Fyrdraca had sticky brown blood along the edge of its blade.

'What is happening here? This can't be, can it? It-it was a dream: wasn't it?' She glanced up at Spuddle. 'It was a dream, how weird is this? I don't get this at all, I just, just don't!' Spuddle eyed her with some curiosity, before waddling slowly back to the campfire. If I was dreaming, thought Ionuin, truly dreaming, then Fyrdraca should not have been by the rocks and there should be no animal prints in the dust. She remembered cutting the dragon, being splashed with blood, but her face had been licked clean by Spuddle. How had he known? Was he in her dream, or was she in his? Had there been a dream at all? Nothing made sense. Now Ionuin eyed Spuddle with some curiosity and knew that sleep, once again, would be a light affair.

Taj gasped as repressed memories reared up, making him tremble, images of a cruel darkness ripping through his mental barriers, slashing wantonly at his inner core. His knees felt weak, his hands were shaking, but he fought back, squeezing his eyes so tightly closed that stars appeared to dance inside his head.

'They are only memories,' he hissed, pushing away the unwanted pictures of his body being devoured by gnashing teeth. 'Just mental tricks, nothing more, they have no power over me, no power!' he whispered, calming himself, leaning against the cold stone at the side of the disused tunnel, catching his breath. Then a face appeared in his thoughts, a dark face with a bright smile, a female, a woman who he thought he knew, but could not name. She mouthed something, and even though her voice was inaudible, Taj still got the message.

'Aztalan,' he murmured. 'Just think of Aztalan and all will be well.' He saw a starless sky, a sunless sea with gentle waves breaking on the shores of a black beach, and peace filtered through his entire being. Taj sighed and opened his eyes. He was unsure what exactly had happened, but he knew the danger was passed; or was it?

What if he was wrong, and the images were not memories, but an assault on his mind? What if the dreaded Dark Dragon had tricked him out of the safety of Fire Mountain and intended to capture him, or worse, kill him?

'Stop it!' he told himself as his heartbeat again began to rise. 'They were memories of the missing dream experience, that's all,' he assured himself, again peering over the stone-wall and into the darkness of the Merm night.

He took a deep breath and reasoned that while he remained within sight of the mountain he would be safe from attack. Dragon patrols regularly circled the Desert Sea, picking up stray humans that had wandered too close, and dealing with them. He pushed all thoughts of the Dark Dragon out of his mind and turned his attention to the reason why he was at the edge of Fire Mountain in the first place: Spuddle.

Chapter Fifteen

Taj began to wonder how and why Spuddle still lived. The words of Nexus concerning trickery, calling him a fool for thinking such a thing, echoed loudly in his thoughts. He dismissed the words of Nexus, he was convinced that he was right, he had to be right! Spuddle was alive. He had glimpsed his unmistakable aura, and if that was not enough, he had sensed Spuddle's thoughts and occasionally, even thought he had heard him roar, the eerie sound rolling around inside his skull. He thought Spuddle was a long way to the south, but exactly where still eluded him.

As he pushed at the dry-stone wall, trying to make a bigger gap to climb through, he half expected Nexus, or a dragon from the patrols, to be waiting for him. It seemed unlikely, as Fire Mountain was honeycombed with tunnels that possessed far more exits than there were dragons available to monitor them. Besides, would Nexus even bother going to such extremes? Especially for one headstrong, runaway boy who was prone to acting rashly at the best of times.

'Probably thought I'd lose my faith or lack courage and return,' he mused, smiling at his own clever insight. 'No chance,' he murmured, lowering his voice, just in case he was not so clever after all and Nexus was indeed waiting to snare him.

As he looked over the dry rocks, he could see that Merm was dying. The planet was winding down, coming to an end as a useful place for comfortable habitation, and it was a good thing that preparations were underway for great changes. Nexus had assured him that the secret missions they had tried carrying out, disappointingly unsuccessful so far, were an integral part of the regeneration process that would soon be underway. Only, he could not see how, and Nexus, being the overly secretive sort, was reluctant to share more information than he deemed necessary.

"You know all you need to know, my boy!" said Taj, mimicking the authoritative voice of Nexus. Not seeing anyone about, he pushed a few more stones off the blocking wall until there was enough room for him to squirm through, but before he left the safety of the tunnel, he again stood, listening, making doubly sure no nasty surprises were afoot. Hearing nothing untoward, he leant against the wall and projected his senses, undertaking one last scan, just to be absolutely certain that there was no danger whatsoever.

'Risk free,' he muttered, climbing through the hole. He dropped to the other side, accidentally caught his leg on the edge of the wall and sprawled on the sandy floor, twisting over onto his back. 'Damn,' he cursed, clasping his scraped shin as he rocked forward, not seeing the dragon approach from a nearby pile of boulders.

'Must be more care-' his words ceased as he was clutched from behind in an iron grip. Looking down, he saw that a dragon's talons had a firm hold on him, and he opened his mouth to scream in fear and panic. The sound was instantly muffled as he found his whole head thrust inside a dragon's mouth. A lashing

78

tongue splashed across his lips, sharp teeth pressed against his throat and neck, his knees trembled at the horror of what was going to happen next. He knew there were worse deaths than decapitation, but at this moment, with panic seizing his ability to even breathe properly, he found no comfort in that fact; none at all.

The sun climbed above the eastern ridges, casting long shadows across the canyon floor where Ionuin and Spuddle stretched away the lingering vestiges of sleep. Spuddle had already begun breakfast, eating the head of Grog while Ionuin looked away. She knew the men had deserved to die, but watching this young dragon devour them was another matter. She looked at the sun-bathed western ridge, plotting a path that would lead her to what she thought could be a goat track. From there, she would exit the canyon and come out on the great-western plateau, stretching away until it met the untamed desert lands, pocked with craters and ruled by dust storms.

The plateau itself was alive with small game, and had become Ionuin's favourite hunting ground. Here she would while away the days lying perfectly still until an animal - rodents were her favourite - came scurrying by. She considered what she was going to do with her life now that her father was dead. Initially, she had set out to avenge his death; with this task completed, she had no immediate plans, apart from tracking down Mad Travis and Fat Shinny, Sterner's alleged associates.

Thinking of those two made her consider her recent nightmare. Its shadowy residue hovered in the back of her mind, plaguing her thoughts. She tried to make contact with Spuddle by projecting her will and accessing his mind, but this morning, the task seemed beyond her ability. If only I could get inside the dragon's head, she thought, I may get some answers. She desperately needed those answers, mainly because she didn't understand what had happened, but also because Spuddle had somehow appeared and rescued her. She began wondering about Spuddle; where had he come from? What was he doing here? How had he become captured and made prisoner? Were there others like him? Most importantly, where were his father and mother? Did he even have parents?

'Nothing but questions,' she mumbled.

Spuddle cocked his head, appearing to examine her, perhaps wondering about her just as much as she was wondering about him. She considered how deeply connected he actually was to the nightmare creature which had attacked her. That he was indeed connected to the creature was something of which she was certain.

'No, not creature,' she sighed, correcting her self-delusion. The creature was a dragon. A real big one, and it was . . . Dark! Sterner's words concerning the Dark Dragon echoed back to her. What if he had been telling the truth all along? There was no doubt in her mind that Sterner was a habitual liar, but even liars told the truth sometimes. So, could she really dismiss the Huskers Mount duo in the Badlands as sheer fabrication? After all, she had threatened him with her knife. She supposed under such circumstances, he would have been willing to tell her anything she wished to hear, anything at all, just to save his skin.

She drank a little water from her small animal hide canteen and nibbled at some rock bread, trying to fathom what had really happened during the night. After drawing no firm conclusions, she checked her meagre ration of salt pork and realised that, whatever she was going to do, she needed more sustenance than a few strips of dried meat and stone-bread could provide. After rummaging through the murderers' possessions, she had found nothing that could really be described as food, apart from a few stale biscuits and a handful of dried fruit that smelled very fusty. She had the cacti, of course, but it was hardly nourishment; merely a roasted pulp or, when eaten fresh, a thirst quencher when water rations were low.

With the pressing need for something to do, just to take her mind from her dream-experience and to stop thinking about her dear departed father, she made an instant decision. 'Spuddle, I'm going hunting,' she told the dragon, who was busy dismembering the remains of Grog's body and stacking the parts, rather haphazardly, in a pile.

He gave her a cursory glance, growled rather loudly, startling her a little, then began licking the heap of body parts, lapping at dark trickles of dried blood.

'I'll um, I'll return at sundown with fresh food,' she told him, backing away, trying to avoid watching his snaking tongue slipping over the pasty lumps of dead flesh.

The dragon glanced at her again, but gave no indication that he understood. With what appeared to be a shrug of his shoulders, he shuffled around, blocking her view of his actions. Ionuin flexed her mind, pushing out her intentions in picture form. The dragon growled deeply in his throat, the noise reverberating through the air. Ionuin flinched as dragon thoughts skirted around her mind, unclear images dancing teasingly in vivid colour. Fleeting glimpses of her walking, smiling, with sunshine playing along her bare arms. The hazy pictures made her feel good; they were obviously how Spuddle saw her, but she had no idea what they truly meant. She picked up her sword, collected a bow and a full quiver from the back of the mule and headed for the goat trail. Her survival instincts warned her that it might be a good idea if she never returned.

What a bloody fool that boy is, thought Nexus, strolling from one side of the throne room to the other. He knew Taj had much to learn about responsibility and the chain of command, and his impetuous nature had endangered them all. Even if he was right about Spuddle being alive, which he did not believe for a heartbeat, was charging out after him the wisest thing to do? Was leaving the safety of the impregnable Fire Mountain and the guarded lands wise? 'No' was the clear answer. Not even for the sake of his son, who, considering how his father had died, was most certainly deceased. He stopped his pacing: but what if Taj was right?

At least he knew where his mate Nadine had gone when she disappeared. Admittedly, apart from Catalin, he was the only one who did know, but Spuddle was a different matter. Most of the clan had assumed that Spuddle had died and become a meal for scavengers, while the wishful thinkers among them claimed he had gone the same way as his mother: vanished into thin air. As some believed they actually shared a parallel world, such occurrences might just happen occasionally. Others thought that the World Splitter might be involved somehow. Incredulous as it might seem for a dragon to simply vanish, it was unilaterally accepted that such things were indeed possible, and therefore, seen as quite normal. Most also thought that there was every reason to suppose that Spuddle might return again some day, as might his mother. As far as the 'parallel world' theory went, if they knew the actual truth, they would be more than surprised, they would be shocked to their very core.

Nexus had fully acknowledged that having two vanishings in the same millennium was unusual, but not beyond the realms of conceivable possibility, or so he had claimed at the time. In truth, he had no idea what had happened to Spuddle, but to cover the tracks of his mate Nadine, he had not pursued the matter. Considering what was at stake, behaving as if his son were dead had seemed to be the only option. Eventually, the whole clan had fully accepted this assumption. Over the passage of time, Nexus had come to accept it himself, until now.

'What are we to do?' Lord Bollfur asked, watching Nexus pacing the throne room.

Nexus sighed. 'You know, Bollfur, I'm not sure. I can't believe we missed Taj at the intersection. I suppose he knows the service tunnels better than we do and probably took a disused, long forgotten shortcut. You know his temperament; he's unthinkingly hasty and possesses an impulsive nature over which he has no control. Perhaps he'll return during the night.'

'Yes, yes he might,' admitted Lord Bollfur, 'but what if he doesn't?'

'Like I said, I don't know. We don't have enough dragons to cover every exit from Fire Mountain. The service tunnels are too narrow to accommodate our bulk, so we can't go after him. All we can do, I suppose, is double our patrols of the guarded lands, try to make sure he doesn't fall foul of the Dark Dragon.'

'Well, yes, I agree with you there, your Majesty. Of course, it will mean temporarily pulling some dragons away from the stone circle, but it can't be helped. More dragons are arriving all the time, so the circle will only be vulnerable for a short while. If Taj is as important as you claim he is, we must protect him as best we can.'

Nexus laughed. 'That's what I've been doing for the past fifteen years or so, protecting him, helping him to develop his curious talents. Maybe I should have given him more information about his status. Should I, perhaps, have instilled more confidence in his hidden abilities? We're all clever in hindsight, Bollfur.'

'True, true,' said Lord Bollfur, nodding his head in acknowledgement. 'Although, I still don't understand why you hold him in such high regard. I know you say he is important, but why? Is it because he is the last human on this world with any extra-sensory ability?'

Nexus eyed Bollfur curiously. The blue dragon's crest was undulating slightly, as if he were trying to suppress the colour changes that could indicate ulterior motives to his questions. The Blues were the only dragon species that lacked bodily control over colour changes to their skin, one of the reasons why they were considered inherently inferior. 'Partly so,' said Nexus, cautiously, wondering what Bollfur suspected. 'If Taj knew how vital he was to our final task, how his presence could turn certain defeat into probable victory, he would not have run away like a frightened goose!'

'Let's hope the Dark Dragon is not waiting for him when he exits Fire Mountain,' said Bollfur, his facial features unreadable. 'Or he might just end up a frightened goose, served as lunch.'

'Yes,' replied Nexus, caution edging his voice. 'Let us hope not, eh?'

Taj wanted to scream. How could he have been so stupid? Why hadn't he listened? It seemed that Nexus had been right all along. In a few moments, the sharp pointy teeth of the Dark Dragon would shear into his neck, slicing off his head in one cruel bite. He forced back the tears threatening to envelop him, clenched his fists and choked the rising sobs in his throat. He did not want to die, not like this, not yet. He had so much to do! So much to give, and there was Spuddle to consider. Who on Merm would save Spuddle if he died now? He considered pleading for mercy, but suspected such pleas would be pointless, given that the Dark Dragon was a merciless alien entity from beyond the void, and he therefore resigned himself to his fate. He also wanted to urinate, but that would have to wait. He was determined to check out with at least some dignity intact.

Chapter Sixteen

Ionuin reached the plateau by mid-morning and set off across what was once grassland, a vast savannah, but now resembled a parched wasteland. She never usually ventured this close to the Valley of Caves during food gathering trips, but for a skilled hunter with patience, game was still plentiful, even in this extra arid region. By early evening she had a dozen assorted small animals hanging from her belt. With curiosity overriding her earlier warnings, she returned to the canyon.

Spuddle was no replacement for her father as far as companionship went, even so, being with the dragon was preferable to remaining alone and she was confident that she could handle any danger which might arise. If last night's dreams were anything to go by, she felt the dragon might even be an ally rather than a possible foe. On peering over the ridge, Spuddle instantly turned his head. Again, Ionuin felt something slip inside her mind, indistinct images of herself, but clear interpretation proved impossible.

By the onset of dusk she had negotiated her way down the goat trail and arrived back at the makeshift campsite. Using flint and tinder, as taught by her father, she soon had a fire going. As she cleaned the assorted game, Spuddle ate all the unwanted bits of offal and skin with eager relish, his large jaws chopping noisily and his throat gulping loudly as he consumed the food. While Ionuin roasted a meaty carcass on the point of one of the killers' old swords, she noticed the young dragon's newly forming rear leg had taken on full shape. It was fattening out incredibly fast. The skin was very pale in comparison to the rest of him. In the light of the fire, it looked to be a kind of sickly cream colour with subtle undertones of light-green dappled by dark blemishes.

She had to admit, in general appearance, he looked far healthier than he had the previous day when she had first released him from the cage. What had been a saggy, flaky, yellow-scaly mess was slowly turning green and glossy. His eyes glowed brightly, taking on an amber colour that was almost luminescent, apparently watching everything. Survival instinct reared its head, making her heart race. Spuddle's eyes seemed to pulse in the approaching darkness, the green slit pupils widening, predator-like in their intensity.

She fought down her rising fear, not wanting to feel the urgent danger, turning her attention to the cooking; telling herself that Spuddle was fine, he meant her no harm and that she was safer with him than without him. She smiled at that thought, having her own reptilian bodyguard, as she hacked a portion of sizzling meat in two, throwing a piece to Spuddle that he caught in his mouth. To her alarm, he proceeded to shake the meat about wildly, as if it were still alive and he was trying to kill it, then he gulped it down. Yes, she thought, calming her jangling nerves, he looks much improved, comfortable even, but how was he really coping with the new changes?

'Spuddle, are you feeling better?' she asked, between bites of crisped flesh, picking bits of splintered vertebra from her teeth, thinking how natural it felt to be talking to a dragon; the most feared and fabled creature on Merm.

Spuddle mewled and waggled his tiny forelegs.

Ionuin could not help herself; she laughed. Something she thought she would never do again only a few days ago. Whatever trepidation had been lingering in the back of her mind vanished in an instant. Her curiosity concerning Spuddle was overwhelming. 'Spuddle, do you, well, um, do you actually understand me?'

Without warning, the dragon stretched upwards until he was standing as tall as Ionuin. His strengthening limbs wobbled slightly under the weight. He roared into the falling night, the noise challenging, awesome in its reverberating intensity. A cold shiver rippled through Ionuin at the majesty of the scene. Spuddle roared again and this time Ionuin felt the heat of his breath. Something queasy uncoiled in her stomach, trip-hammering her heart into overdrive, making her mouth dry. The rising fear she had vanquished suddenly returned.

She swallowed, tried to wet her lips with her tongue and fought down the uneasiness that had given her goose-bumps. 'Hey there, easy boy,' she croaked, uncertainly, the words tumbling out of her mouth in a choked rush. She coughed to clear her throat, suddenly feeling very hot and clammy. The odd sensation passed as quickly as it had arrived and Ionuin put it down to a piece of undercooked rat. 'Another display of that calibre and you'll have the canyon walls quaking,' she joked, stabbing at a piece of partially cooked meat, holding it over the flames again, making certain it was heated all the way through.

Spuddle slumped back down and began scratching his body, groaning and moaning at the apparent pleasure of removing the unwanted itch as flakes of old skin sloughed away. Ionuin watched him from lowered eyes and unconsciously pushed out her thoughts, telling him to be quiet. His head suddenly snapped up. He stopped his scratching, tilting his head, eyeing her through slitted lids.

'Ah, caught that did you?' Ionuin said, introducing tranquillity to her thoughts, chasing away unwanted uneasiness. Spuddle looked dangerous and sounded ferocious, but she sensed that fate had brought them together, and she intended to keep his company, at least for the time being. Some company was better than no company and she did not feel that she was ready to be alone; not just yet. The image of her father came into her mind and she fought back tears, held them in check, she was not ready to mourn, not yet, it was still too raw, too painful. In truth, the acceptance of what had happened was a barrier, one she could not break through just now. She smiled, pushed away thoughts of her father and looked at her dining companion, wondered if she could soon be on the menu instead of half-cooked rat. She thought not, but she knew she would have to remain vigilant in case Spuddle decided to invite her to lunch and serve her up as the main course.

All her senses told her such fears were unfounded and she felt no threat whatsoever coming from the young dragon. She cleared her throat. 'Well, I didn't mean to complain about the noise, Spuddle, just testing a communication theory, but, here are some more thoughts; suggestions really, you ready?' Spuddle actually appeared to be nodding which made Ionuin smile, although it could be coincidence. 'All right, here goes.'

She took a deep breath, focused her mind and tried to think in vivid imagery. Fire Mountain had always interested her, ever since she was a youngster and with a dragon for a companion, why not make a visit? Her inherent desire for adventure gave her a feeling of excitement and it was not as if she had much else to do, not now her father was dead. She concentrated with all her mental power, picturing the two of them leaving the canyon, travelling the full length of the Valley of Caves, exiting at its northern end. She knew this should bring them out near the town of Cavesend which bordered the Desert Sea. She allowed the images to flicker through her mind, taking them across the Desert Sea where the worst of the Badlands began and where the last remnants of human society survived in scattered settlements. Here, the land began climbing in great barren steppes until it reached the mountainous peaks where the legendry home of the dragons - home of the Gods, some folk actually thought - was situated.

As she allowed the hazy image of Fire Mountain to slip away, Ionuin released the pent-up breath that she had not even realised she had been holding. 'There, a long journey, but, well um, what do you think, Spuddle?'

Spuddle appeared to nod in some sort of agreement.

Great, thought Ionuin, maybe I've actually established a reliable mental link, or was he just nodding for the sake of it? She wondered what else she could communicate to Spuddle. Biting her lower lip, she pondered what really bothered her. Then, without having to use any projecting force, an image of the Dark Dragon flipped through her imagination, bouncing directly across into Spuddle's head before rebounding back into her own mind. Ionuin witnessed the exchange as if the imagery were a rubber ball leaping from head to head. Spuddle suddenly leapt into the air and Ionuin, startled half out of her wits, opened her mouth, an unborn scream aching to be released as he came down with a resounding crash, scattering hot embers from the fire, gnashing his teeth in anger.

Now Ionuin feared for her life. She wondered how she could have been so damn stupid as to sit with a wild animal as if it were a favourite pet, thinking no harm would come to her, Ionuin shuffled backwards on her bear-hide, haphazardly knocking burning chunks of wood from the scorched fur while scrambling for Fyrdraca. She then became suddenly still as a wave of warm gentleness swept through her head, melting away all her fear.

She looked round to see Spuddle eyeing her curiously. 'Spuddle, you, you soothed me; you actually soothed me and chased away any thoughts of danger.'

Spuddle nodded and it this time was a definite nod, thought Ionuin. She conjured up a fleeting image of the Dark Dragon and Spuddle growled in his throat, a simmering burble of power rumbling into the night air.

'Yes, all right,' she said, 'I get it, I really do.' She hurled calming thoughts back towards him, images of them both hugging. 'I was just curious, that's all, but it seems you don't like the monster either.' She now knew that Spuddle definitely remembered last night, and even though he was a dragon, she wondered if the dream had scared him as much as it had scared her. He had displayed a definite reaction to the image and although his anger was directed at the Dark Dragon, he had thrown more than a bit of a scare into her as she had barely held on to the contents of her bladder.

She stood and picked bits of ash off the bear-hide and gave it a shake and even though she now felt relatively safe, she decided she would sleep with Fyrdraca to hand again tonight, just as a precaution.

After returning from the shadows where she had relieved herself, not wanting to pee in front of the dragon, her sudden shyness and appropriate attitude making her smile, she settled down and prepared to sleep. She sighed loudly as hazy images of her father slipped into her mind, his face, caring and smiling. 'Dad,' she murmured, 'please, dad, not now. I cannot deal with the hurt, not yet, I'm not ready: maybe I will never be ready.' She pushed the thoughts away, gritted her teeth as she held back the pressing tears and choked off the sob rising in her throat. 'Soon, dad, soon I will mourn you.' His image faded as she drew in a shuddering breath, wrapped her arms around herself and embraced some much needed rest.

'Hmm,' mused Bollfur, his blue-flecked talons drawing circles on his scaled belly. 'Goose! Now there's a treat I haven't sampled in eons, a whole flock of plump geese!'

Nice change of tack, thought Nexus, but too slow. I must know what you're truly suspicious of. Then a plan occurred to him. 'Bollfur, do you never stop thinking about food? We might not sample goose ever again if we don't get Taj back here before the Solstice.'

'Oh, we'll get him back, my Lord. I don't doubt it.'

'Maybe so, maybe so,' conceded Nexus, before adding, 'what bothers me most about all this is, well, what if Taj is right?'

Bollfur gave Nexus a quizzical glance. 'How do you mean? Surely you don't think Spuddle is still alive! If he was, we would have found him before now! Also, I'm pretty sure you would be the first to sense him, wouldn't you?'

'Difficult to say,' said Nexus, plonking himself down on his throne, trying to appear dismayed. 'I have read the book of prophecy, you see, and it mentions the end of my line, so I just accepted his loss without question and I haven't thought about him since,' This was a lie. Nexus could feel his emotions bubbling to the surface; thoughts of Spuddle crossed his mind many times a day. Am I exposed, he wondered? Does Bollfur know anything he shouldn't? 'You see, Lord Bollfur, I confide in you and I expect you to understand, as you have offspring of your own, but it hurts too much to think about him. Spuddle was my only son, my heir, and in truth, I just could not take his loss. We all knew my father was going to die, he went out to die the dragon way, battling talon and tooth against the stupid obstinate stinking humans still existing on this baking vermin ridden dust ball.'

'Ah, well,' said Lord Bollfur. 'Don't forget, before you go condemning a whole species, just because you've tripped over your own tail at the final task, Taj is human too. Although, I'll tell you what interests me, this prophecy you keep going on about. I know it's a big secret and you were warned that, 'only those who need to know should know', but, would it hurt to allow a fresh pair of eyes to take a look at this juncture? What possible harm could it do? The Solstice is almost upon us and I might even prove to be of some help.'

'I suppose you might at that,' said Nexus, getting to his feet, wondering if his suspicions about Lord Bollfur were unfounded, and he just wanted to satisfy his burning curiosity. 'Although, I've read the paragraph referring to the events of this period over a thousand times, if not more, and it's as much a riddle now as it was when I first set eyes on it. Damnable prophets and prophecies, I often think they are more trouble than they are worth!'

'Yes, so I've heard,' said Lord Bollfur.

Nexus slid the throne to one side and reached for a light globe. 'I just hope Taj is safe, or we're all doomed.'

Taj relaxed, trying to calm his fears. The dreaded slice of teeth into soft flesh did not seem to be coming after all. He tried to fathom what was happening. I definitely have my head in the mouth of a dragon, he thought, but which dragon? Certainly not the Dark Dragon or he would be dead by now, wouldn't he? Or was this just wishful thinking? Summoning up all his courage, he cast out his thoughts. *Hello?*

Taj did not dare move; then thoughts slipped inside his mind.

Don't fret my friend, it is only I, Glitch, but you must be quiet, there is something dark and sinister not far away and I don't want to attract its attention. I think it may be looking for you.

Taj flexed his mind. *Looking for me,* he replied. *Why should it be looking for me?*

Because, since you sang out your request for my aid, you have been blaring mental communications at regular intervals throughout the night. I came as soon as I heard your call, but I only gave you the one reply as I think I was followed, at least to the edge of the guarded lands. There's also a dragon patrol not far away and this is just a guess, but I assume you don't want their attention either.

Taj gasped a sigh of relief as Glitch opened his mouth so he could slip his head free. 'You bloody fool!' Taj hissed as he looked up into the dark green eyes of his dearest friend, Prince Glitch of the Red Dragon brood. 'Until you spoke to me, I thought I was dead for sure!'

'You will be if you don't shut up,' Glitch warned in hushed tones. 'Come with me, and I know it can be difficult for a gobby little blabber-mouth like you, but please, do try to keep quiet. Dawn is not far off so the stirrings of other animals will provide some cover, but it is important that we are not detected: got it?'

'Yes, yes, I got it!' Taj hissed impatiently as he fell in behind the red dragon.

Glitch was far older than Taj, but at sixty-three, he was very young in dragon years as they could live for thousands of years, or so he had been led to believe. Still, he had the wisdom of sixty-three years and Taj held him in high regard. He could not wait to tell him about Spuddle. Glitch would believe him; he also knew he would help him find the lost prince of Nexus and Nadine, heir to the throne of the Green Dragons who would, if he survived long enough, one day become a Great Golden male.

Taj listened as Glitch cast thoughts into his mind while they moved stealthily towards a nearby pile of rocks that offered cover. Taj always found Glitch to be observant, if only because he enjoyed finding troublesome humans to play with before he ate them. He claimed their flesh was the most tender to be had on Merm, and even though it was outlawed to eat the cunning little things as they scurried about hither and dither, Glitch could just not help himself.

Even though Taj was human, Glitch never hesitated in sharing tales of his dining experiences with other humans, especially those where they were armed and had put up a fight. He used to laugh as he explained how 'there was nothing to be compared to one's food showing a bit of resistance just before sinking ones teeth into the tasty morsel, if only they weren't so salty'. Taj often shook his head at these times, saying things like, 'yeah, all that salt, must be awful for you' and 'well, just like humans, eh? To show no consideration at all for those who might want to eat them!'

Of course, Taj knew that he was different from other humans on this dusty old world; he had special gifts and as such, came under the protection of Lord Nexus. Any dragon that laid a talon on him risked their very lives, as Nexus was not only leader of all the clans, he was the most ferocious dragon alive. Glitch was also Taj's closest friend, the only one he had since poor Spuddle's demise. Hopefully, this was a situation that would soon be rectified.

Taj glanced up at the sky and thoughts of the Dark Dragon pierced his mind, making him shudder. This was bad, very bad, and he knew that his very life was in imminent danger.

Chapter Seventeen

Before the sun appeared in the sky, Ionuin had cooked up the remaining meat and Spuddle had eaten the leftovers. He had consumed the three dead bodies during the night, Ionuin had heard bones crunching and flesh ripping, but had kept her eyes firmly closed. She knew all about dragons from her father, but until she had encountered Spuddle, she had not believed they actually existed. As for eating people, she thought her father was simply trying to amuse her with wildly exaggerated scary stories. An ordinary child would probably have been frightened, but not Ionuin. Nothing much had ever frightened her, even as a child, and fear, real fear, apart from in her dreams, was still a relative stranger. She wondered what other stories that her father had told her were true.

Admittedly, she had off-handedly dismissed most of what he had said of the old days as jumbled memories. Memories that he mostly kept locked away, only breathing life into them on rare occasions, usually when seated by the hearth at Ducat, staring into the fire, mellow from wild-root brandy and in the mood to reminisce. Half the time, Ionuin had not really listened. The stories, for that's what she thought they were, had all seemed very familiar, but now, she could not recall any of them, not clearly. They seemed muddled, blurred at the edges and slightly out of focus.

'Just stories,' she mumbled, more to herself than to Spuddle, now wishing she had paid more attention to her father's ramblings. She heard Spuddle growl deep in his throat and wondered, not for the first time, if this was really happening. She sat up and looked around. Yep, she was in the dreaded Valley of Caves with a dragon seated on the far side of the fire. Not a dream, not going insane, her father was really dead, she had avenged him, and now her future was as uncertain as tumbleweed rolling over the parched grasslands.

Spuddle snorted and, as he had last night, stood upright, stretching to the lightening sky, balancing on his strongest leg. Ionuin thought he seemed a lot bigger than before and as he turned, she noticed tiny wings sprouting out of his broadening back.

He looks so impressive, Ionuin thought. 'Wow, you'll soon be fully formed, Spuddle. Then I suppose you, you'll fly away!'

Spuddle edged towards her and with genuine affection, stroked one heavy talon gently under her chin. She sensed no threat and felt unafraid, but somewhere deep inside, hot feelings flared, making her skin tingle and her nerves jangle.

She shivered slightly, wondering at the strange sensation rushing through her, making her tingle in parts of her body that were most definitely private. 'Time to go, Spuddle,' she said, leaping to her feet, changing the train of thought that was rioting in her mind, making her feel hot and bothered. She yawned while stepping around her newfound companion, covering her mouth with her hand, smelling her own breath and resolving to keep an eye out for some mint plants with which she could scrub her teeth.

She piled what useful small trade items she could on the mule, stashed what weapons there were away to claim another day, and set off along the canyon. Travelling would be easiest in the morning, and to avoid the blistering heat of direct sunshine, she kept to the shadowed eastern-side. Spuddle ambled along behind, favouring his good leg, the newly formed one not yet fully mobile, but able to support a little weight. Every once in a while he gave a bellowing roar, scaring Ionuin half out of her wits.

'Spuddle! If this mule upends the baskets and spills the load, you'll be in big trouble, do you hear?' she said, wondering how she could punish a dragon. 'Well, um, okay, not big trouble exactly but, but I'll be really angry and-'

Spuddle waggled his newly grown ears, flared his eyes and stared back, nonchalantly. Ionuin noticed his newly sprouted forelegs had increased in size and were now the length of her own arms. She wondered if he had consumed enough food to fully regenerate and if not, how much more food would he need? As she exchanged studious glances with Spuddle she again caught herself balanced on the edge of indecision. Her hunter's instincts cried out a warning of danger, which she supposed was understandable as she was, after all, in the presence of a monstrous carnivore. Her female intuition, to which she was more inclined to listen, advised her that there was nothing to worry about. Spuddle would not harm her, and if anything, he owed her allegiance and she suspected, in an odd unexplainable way, that he even cared about her, to some degree.

Her last thought surprised her, why would she think that Spuddle cared about her? She was nothing to him, she had saved his life, but they had no close connection, had they? What's more, could a dragon actually care? Caring was just a human thing, wasn't it? Or was that just plain stupid and arrogant, assuming that only humans had the capacity to care?

She was brought out of her deliberations by Spuddle as he sidled over to a huge flat rock and rubbed his back over the rough surface, the obvious pleasure he gained reflecting in his half-closed eyes. When he stepped away, there were lumps of dead skin left behind and his back looked fresh and shiny. The regeneration process did not strike Ionuin as odd. Once, when practising swordplay while her father was away hunting, something he had forbidden her to do, she had accidentally sliced off the end of her little finger. It had hurt, really hurt, and for the only time she could ever recall, up until her father's death, she had shed tears. The bleeding stopped almost instantly and by nightfall the finger looked as good as new. As with the knife slash across her midriff, not even a scar remained and she had completely re-grown the end of her finger. She wondered, as a child is apt to do, what would happen if she chopped off her leg? Of course, she did not inflict deliberate harm upon herself, but all the same, her curiosity needed satisfying.

On her father's return she had asked why he did not grow himself a new eye to replace the one he had lost in some long-ago fight. He had looked at her in such a strange way that she did not dare pursue the matter further. He questioned her with an intensity that she did not much care for, but she did not reveal her

90

experience. She never spoke of such things again and to her father's credit, he never asked.

'I miss you, dad,' she muttered, absently picking at her finger nails, she then jumped as Spuddle snorted and capered around the canyon floor, tossing his head from side to side, leaping back and forth as if play-fighting. Ionuin smiled as she watched him, pushed thoughts of her father away, not wanting to think about what she could not face.

After a few moments, Spuddle calmed down and they began walking again. Ionuin, happily wandering out of the shadows now and again to soak up the morning sunshine, stumbled when Spuddle nudged her in the back, almost making her fall flat on her face.

'Hey! Watch it, you clumsy oaf,' she scolded, catching her balance, passing Spuddle a warning look. 'You nearly had me on my arse there. Whatever has gotten into you?'

Spuddle roared and gestured wildly with his head and Ionuin caught hazy images of them both travelling very quickly indeed.

'What? You want me to pick up the pace? Is that it? You're tired of dawdling along and would like to travel faster?'

Spuddle made a soft whining noise then rushed by her, showing her how fast he could travel now that his legs were almost fully-grown.

'Oh, all right, fine by me, Spuddle-in-a-muddle, we'll get a move on,' said Ionuin, striding out with some urgency. 'I was taking my time for your benefit, baby dragon, but we'll see about travelling fast if that's what you want. Nudge me in the back again though and we'll do more than pick up the pace, we'll be having a little chat up close, understand?' She wondered how such a chat would develop and realised her words were empty threats. 'Well, maybe not a chat, but, I won't be best pleased; all right?' Spuddle gave no indication he had heard a word and continued leading the way. 'Fine, be like that,' she mumbled, quickening her steps.

The mule whinnied as if to say that it too had received the message, and the trio began covering some real distance. Within herself, and considering what she had gone through, Ionuin felt relatively good. She knew she would feel even better if images of the Dark Dragon were not continually rearing up and shattering any happy thoughts that dared to surface. She absently wondered if her father would approve of her actions, but pushed the thoughts away. What he would have thought mattered not one whit. He was gone forever and would never be returning.

Nexus yawned and stretched his huge wings. He and Bollfur had spent all night studying Herald Knell, the Ancient Book of Prophecy, and dawn had come and gone.

'Interesting,' said Bollfur as he closed the large book, examining the cover, scratching a talon over the rigid surface. 'Hair coated with resin! Of all the things to bind a book with. The whole book feels strange, don't you think? Any idea of its origins?'

Nexus nodded. 'I believe it is protected by magic. Perhaps the hair is special in some unusual way of which we are unaware. It was written by the ancients; I was told that Cai and Sireena had a hand in its creation.'

'The Numina?' Bollfur gasped. 'Impressive! So, the knowledge contained may well be grounded in truth, unlike some books I've come across in my time. I read somewhere that because of invented memories, they should burn all the books!'

Nexus grinned. 'I see some validity in the statement, not much, but some. When dealing with prophecies, especially those as convoluted as these, we have to remember, at best, they are simply cautionary tales. Prophecies act as a simple guide, they don't actually reveal the consequences of any action we might take; and while I understand your point, books should never be burned. Even story books full of fanciful imaginings have value, and I don't doubt there is truth in Herald Knell,'

'It is finding that truth that counts,' Bollfur said, smiling widely, as if he had discovered some great unwritten fact.

Nexus patted him on the shoulder. 'The most impressive lie is one slipped between two truths,'

'When you speak of the ancients, I suppose you mean Xanthippe, Shogun, Nubian and others of their ilk?' Bollfur enquired.

Nexus nodded. 'Yes, they had some input. If you flick to the middle there are some pictures of them, but Catalin also wrote quite a lot and I believe a female human prophet on Deburon called Tenja added a piece or two, as did Lyondell the bard.'

'Lyondell, bard and teller, the mysterious one, long time since I heard her name mentioned,' said Bollfur, reopening the book to the page they had pored over many times, sighing loudly before reading.

'The Golden Horn

When the Wizard blew his horn, on a bare and desolate world, its pitch and resonance so shrill, for so long, the whole planet rang like a bell, to the heart of Herald Knell. Mountains shook, ocean floors cracked, chasms yawned, fiery vents spewed forth gas and liquid rock. Vast continents trembled and moved, beginning a journey that would last for millennia. Comet showers sang, their thunderous wailing piercing the atmosphere, hurling down atomic packages of magical elements. Clouds, roiled, billowed and unfurled in an artistic aerial ballet. Storms lit up the sky with blazing streaks of energy as lightning forked, singeing the air, blasting rocks, boiling the waters of the churning seas and life, precious chaotic life, surged in globules of primordial, protoplasmic soup, when the Wizard blew his horn.'

'You like that passage, don't you?' said Nexus, stifling another yawn, wondering if boredom could actually split open the soul.

'Yes, I do; he was rather a poetic fellow this Catalin,' said Lord Bollfur as he reached the bottom of the page.

Magic Horn

The wizard's horn,
Of golden form,
An age of stars,
In tune are born,
A rejoicing Light,
Of Darkest scorn,
Clysm challenged,
Once gold is shorn,
Becoming again,
The wizard's horn.

Bollfur smiled at the quaint rhyme. 'Perhaps Catalin was a little bit full of himself.'

'I think Magic Horn was written by Lyondell,' replied Nexus.

'Ah, you may be right,' said Bollfur. 'Still, the poem is about Catalin and as one of the Chosen I suppose he had every right to blow his own trumpet; or horn, as in this instance.' He grinned at his attempted mirth.

'Yes, I suppose so,' said Nexus, not amused in the slightest. 'So, you never actually met Catalin, did you?' he asked, already knowing the answer.

'No,' Bollfur replied, shaking his head. 'I and my family hadn't arrived here until after the legendary meeting of the Dragon Lords at the stones, but naturally I heard all about it when I heeded the call to battle broadcast over the sub-ether network.'

'Ah, yes, the call to battle,' said Nexus. 'Almost fifteen summers ago now. You know, on a subconscious level, I can still hear Catalin blowing out that eerie range of sonorous notes, his face red from the effort. Even the Chosen have their limitations, and I would willingly wager that the sound hasn't even reached a quarter of the way across our galaxy yet. Of course, it was a different sound to the one that sparked life onto Merm.'

'Yes, well, I wasn't about then either,' said Bollfur, flicking back to the first page.

'Well, of course not,' laughed Nexus. 'None of us were. It happened three billion years ago, give or take a couple of hundred million or so.'

'Interesting fellow, this Catalin,' said Bollfur. 'I'd like to have met him. He seems very clever, in a quaint mystical way.'

'Quaint; yes, he's now gone from our physical dimensions,' said Nexus, 'and I agree, an interesting chap. Merely incorporeal these days, as you know, but that passage concerning the creation of life is merely the introduction. Look to page one hundred and twelve. There's an intriguing prophecy relating specifically to this period of time; the here and now.'

'Indeed,' said Bollfur, flicking back through the book.

'Herald casts worlds adrift. Old one gone, sacrificed for greater good, power reversing through time, fabled megalopolis fallen from newly shaped clapper. Minstrels celebrate summer equinox in stone ring, birth rising from death, becoming of one from joining of two, ended line, re-emerging so future seeds blown asunder.

Dead sentinel must hold sway, preserving past for future. Beware Dark Dragon, dancing piper's tune so all worlds suffer, Light losing sacred children, chasing shadows, Dark reigning hither, forevermore. Rue the Clysm, when heart-bell tolls, three shall blend when all worlds turn as one, and Cleave hast struck a second mighty blow, rendering Herald cleft a shattered peace, until ice shall cover the land.'

Nexus observed Bollfur, who remained silent, apparently absorbing the text. 'Well?' he eventually asked, his impatience getting the better of him. 'What is your erudite opinion?'

Bollfur shook his head dismissively. 'My dear friend, it seems that you have made a terrible mistake, a grievous error!'

'I have?'

'Oh yes, I'm certain of it. This coming equinox, only a few days away now, is the equinox to which this prophecy refers. Do you agree?'

Nexus shrugged his massive golden shoulders, the light reflecting from his iridescent scales bouncing around the small library. 'Of course I agree, I said as much myself earlier.'

'Yes, I forgot, of course you did,' said Bollfur. 'And we are also in agreement that the coming of the one refers to Taj, yes?'

'Perhaps,' said Nexus, edging his words with caution, but 'the one' might also mean the Dark Dragon.'

'Definitely not,' said Bollfur shaking his head. 'The Dark Dragon is mentioned by name in the fifth sentence, so why not in the second?'

Nexus took the book from Bollfur, reading through the prophecy again. 'Whiskers of Catalin's chin, you are correct!' he said, handing the book back to Bollfur. 'This aspect of the prophecy is the thing that has been disturbing me and the answer was there all along.'

'As I advised,' said Lord Bollfur, his talons sliding over the raised lettering, 'a fresh pair of eyes can often see what another might miss. We know the stone ring is at the edge of the guarded lands, but does the ended line refer to your family linage? And if it does, then this is your mistake.'

'You're not making sense,' said Nexus.

'No, no, I suppose I'm not. Just thinking aloud, really; forget I said anything, but by losing Taj, you may have helped the Dark Dragon, especially if it finds the boy before we do.'

'Now that *does* make sense.'

'I'm not accusing you of betraying the clan or deliberately helping the enemy, but you must see that you have played the Dark Dragon's game just as it would wish?' Bollfur stated.

'I know you're not accusing me of anything, my friend.' You would not dare, thought Nexus. 'I do admit, inadvertently, I have given Dark Dragon an advantage. One upon which it has yet to capitalize, I might add.'

'Yes, yes, point taken, all is not yet lost,' said Bollfur rather resignedly. 'One more thing though, I'm not sure about, *future seeds blown asunder*. Whatever does that mean?'

'I do not have the foggiest idea,' Nexus lied, expertly controlling his crest; it wanted to fluctuate wildly at his spoken untruth. 'What do you make of the first line referring to power reversing and the falling of the fabled megalopolis?' he asked, covering his lie.

'Probably just bunkum to disguise the real message,' said Bollfur, reading through the prophecy again. 'Neither do I know what the joining of the two heralds means either, or the dead sentinel. Any ideas?'

'I have a few,' said Nexus. He did, in fact, know the true meaning of Herald, which Bollfur had mistaken for heralds, perhaps on purpose, as he too must know; the clue was in the title of the prophecy book, Herald Knell. Taking the book from Bollfur, he snapped it closed. 'Speculation only,' he said, placing the book back on the shelf. Which was true, as he thought his speculation was correct, as a speculation that the sun would rise tomorrow would probably be correct.

'We should put more effort in locating Taj,' said Lord Bollfur, not meeting the eyes of Nexus.

'Oh, I agree,' said Nexus. 'Come, Lord Bollfur, we have much still to do if we are to be fully prepared for what is coming; and it is coming.'

'Without doubt,' said Bollfur, turning on his heel.

Taj tapped Glitch on his arm. 'I have some ex-'

'Shush,' said Glitch. He pointed to the horizon. 'Look below the faint edge of the fading blue nebula near the star of Iris,' he whispered. 'Keep watching, then tell me what you see, I'll be interested to know what you think.'

Taj peered into the night, but saw nothing. 'What do you think is out there?' he asked.

Glitch hunkered down. 'Well, I was scanning for humans, just to play with, you understand, when I noticed a distant speck in the sky that kept approaching the guarded lands, then flying away, only to return again and again.'

'A speck?' Taj questioned. 'I know where this is going,' he said, nodding his head knowingly.

Glitch cocked his head on one side. 'Anyway, I had seen this speck before, but just dismissed it as a high flying dragon coming from a neighbouring world to prepare for the coming battle everyone is talking about, even though it is supposed to be some sort of secret. Then I heard your desperate voice in my mind and the thoughts of another latched onto me.'

Taj swallowed hard. 'Really?'

'Yes really. Searching thoughts flashed through my mind, Dark and ominous, as if it too had heard your words. Since then, every time I look around, the high-flying intruder, as I now think of it, is there. I'm sure it's following me and I'm sure it's because of my connection to you and before you say it, I'm not going mad.'

'I know you're not going mad,' agreed Taj, now looking into the night.

'I mean, I thought I was,' continued Glitch. 'I know I'm thought of as the daftest dragon since Daft Des ate his own foot seven thousand years ago and-'

'I know you're not going mad,' repeated Taj.

'-I concede they do have a valid . . . you mean, you agree with me?' Glitch said, a note of disbelief in his growling voice.

'Yes,' said Taj, searching the night with his eyes and his mind, fear washing against his resistance to thoughts of the Dark Dragon. 'I agree with you, Glitch, I really do. I believe the Dark Dragon wants to devour me whole.'

Chapter Eighteen

The day passed slowly as Ionuin and Spuddle trekked towards Cavesend. It was perhaps a hundred leagues away, if Ionuin had calculated correctly from the few maps she had seen. Admittedly, most of the maps were hand-drawn guesswork, undertaken by her father during his extensive travels, and even though he was no *Master Cartographer*, he had assured her that to his knowledge, they were fairly accurate.

The canyon had widened considerably and dropped away on the eastern side to become gently sloping hills of sand-covered rock stretching away to the higher ridges at the very edge of the valley. Even though they had less shade, the oppressive heat did not boil their brains, as it could escape on the intermittent breezes eddying and swirling through the hills. During the hottest part of the afternoon, with the sun blazing directly overhead, they had tethered the mule beside them and rested beneath the shade of a clump of giant cacti. The mule was a little skittish at first, for even though it was used to Spuddle's scent, it was not overly keen on being tied up within such close range of the dragon. However, as Spuddle settled down and dozed, the mule eventually became calmer.

Ionuin watched the sky. It hadn't always been the clear watery-pink that is now was. The few clouds that now only appeared in greater volume during winter and wept until the ground became drenched, were once a common sight. Little rain had fallen on this drought-ridden land these last few years, and there was no sign that things were about to improve.

Her father had once told her an ancient tale of a star that had suddenly become so bright that one could see as clearly at night as during the day. This intense illumination had lasted for an age, and when the star eventually grew dim again, it left an amazingly bright blue and red web-like pattern across the heavens. The pattern eventually faded, along with the star, but its intense brightness had scorched the sky. Most of the plants and animals, and even people, had died from a strange unknown sickness that swept across all known lands. Civilisations on all continents crumbled and fell, some vanishing without trace, and society, as it had existed for countless generations, slid into ruin.

This was not the worst of the horror, as some people did survive the 'Death Star', as it became known, only to suffer an even worse fate, and untold suffering. Legend told of hoards of dragons suddenly appearing as if by magic, sweeping across the skies, swooping down and gobbling up men, women and children by the dozen. Ionuin had dismissed her father's account of historic events as just another one of his fanciful stories. After all, if hundreds of thousands of people had once inhabited Merm, would it not have been absolute chaos?

She could well imagine a few hundred, perhaps even a few thousand people living happily side-by-side, but not the hundreds of millions her father claimed had once lived here. Surely, such huge numbers could only mean trouble. Now that Spuddle had appeared, though, she wondered about the dragons. If hoards of dragons had eaten the people, it would certainly explain why almost everyone had disappeared, but then, apart from Spuddle, where had all the dragons gone? Was he the only one of his kind left on Merm?

Spuddle nudged her foot, snapping her out of her daydreams.

She yawned. 'What? What is it?'

Spuddle snorted down his long nose, his breath smelling hot and rank, and nudged her foot again, using much more force.

'Hey, back off, Spuddle,' warned Ionuin, growing agitated, drawing her knees up to her chest, pulling her feet away from the dragon. 'What have I told you about nudging me, hmm?'

Spuddle didn't even acknowledge that she had spoken, he just sat, unmoving. Ionuin projected her thoughts and stared deep into the dragon's glowing eyes. Without warning, his thoughts caught hers and she gasped at the sudden surge of power. She tried to stretch her mind away, but reeled as images flooded into her brain, bright, vivid scenes of many, many dragons in brilliant vibrant colour, flying across the sky in complicated wheeled formations. Again she tried to pull her thoughts free, but Spuddle's mental grip held fast as more imagery was forced through her mind, broken, flickering pictures of many men and women surrounding a huge old dragon. They were crazed with excitement, waving spears, firing arrows, cutting and slashing with swords and axes.

One woman in particular was very brave, a blue-haired girl with elfin-like features, determination stretching a wicked grin on her heart-shaped face. She wailed while leaping high into the air, smashing a two-headed axe into the dragon's head before falling away as a burst of light erupted in a dazzling flash. An instant later, others rushed forward, whooping and wailing, and the carnage inflicted on the old beast as it died was savage and bloody. Ionuin had seen all she wanted to see and tried to pull free, tried to break the hold Spuddle had on her thoughts, but he was too strong.

'Enough!' she screamed, desperate to wrench herself free from the sight of the slaughter. Spuddle released her with a feeling of gentle warmth, easing his thoughts from hers with great dexterity, but with Ionuin straining for release the parting of minds came with an unexpected mental jolt and Ionuin promptly fainted, her consciousness sinking into a well of inky blackness where she floated bereft of all worries and cares.

'So, what happens next?' Bollfur asked.

'We must have an all-out search for Taj,' Nexus answered. 'He must be found, or I fear for the future of life, not just on Merm, but all life.'

'Really!' exclaimed Bollfur. 'If you think he is that important then you have deduced far more than I, but then, deep thought never was my greatest strength.'

So true, thought Nexus, saying nothing as they ran up the steps and departed the throne room in great haste. The only strength Bollfur and the blue dragons possessed, he mused, was brute strength, and even that was limited to an initial surge, after which their abilities paled alongside those of any average dragon.

'Are you prepared to enlighten me and share the rest of the prophecy as you see it?' Bollfur asked as they approached a huge copper gong that hung in pride of place on a raised dais at the head of the Great Cavern. 'Perhaps I could be of further assistance?'

'No,' said Nexus as he picked up the ironwood hammer. 'I'm sorry, Lord Bollfur, I've already shown you too much and it is imperative that the last few secrets remain with me.' Nexus wondered if he would have to kill Lord Bollfur before this business was over. 'Our heritage, our history, and even ourselves, depends upon the information contained in the prophecy remaining untold. For the sake of us all, I am sure I can rely upon your discretion with what you already know.'

Bollfur nodded his agreement and Nexus pulled back the hammer. With a huge swing, he sounded the gong. The ringing echo reverberated off the walls, making all dragons present in the Great Cavern turn their heads. The gong was only ever rung when bad news was to be shared or in times of ominous danger. This particular sounding heralded both.

'One more thing,' whispered Bollfur as the dragons gathered around the dais. 'What happened to Catalin's golden horn?'

'Lost!' Nexus snapped, a little too quickly for comfort. 'At least, it is thought to be lost. Nothing has been seen of it since Catalin made his last summoning.'

Bollfur nodded, his eyes half-closed in concentration. 'Things that are lost often turn up when least expected, just as they are most needed. Maybe the ho-'

'Probably,' Nexus hissed, interrupting Bollfur, before turning his attention to the assembled dragons, clicking his talons to attract their undivided attention. 'The time has come. The foretold doom is upon us,' he said, his voice ringing out as he surveyed the Great Cavern. He estimated that there must be at least ninety adult dragons present, quadruple the number of the previous day, but still not enough. 'I have called you here to fight, because freedom is not a right, it has to be fought for and defended. Much depends on how we conduct ourselves in the coming battle, not only for our freedom; the freedom of future generations also rests with our actions.'

All the dragons cheered as one.

Nexus grinned, and gnashed his teeth. 'Brothers, sisters, we all know the Dark is powerful, we all know that some of us will not survive the coming conflict, but we give our lives willingly for a just cause, and those who fall will be remembered as heroes for evermore!' More cheers rang out across the cavern. Nexus then noticed, huddled in one corner, almost beyond view, Lord Bollfur's own two youngsters, Bolden and Blucher. He then began wondering how much Bollfur really knew about the prophecy and the actual whereabouts of the horn, and if he would have to kill his pale blue children as well as his devious confidante. 'So, my comrades in arms, feast at will, make merry, indulge in all pleasures! Whether the battle be lost or won, we do our best, prepared to do or die, and no more can ever be asked!'

The dragons roared their approval and Nexus left the dais, knowing, in his heart, that if Taj was lost to them, then no matter how brave they fought, all was lost.

'Taj?' Glitch hissed. 'Are you all right?'

Taj looked to his friend and realised that he must have been staring off into space while considering what course of action to take. 'Ahem, yes, yes, I'm fine, just thinking really.'

'Hmm, I always try to avoid thinking too much,' Glitch confessed. 'It only makes things more complicated in my esteemed view. There was once a . . . .'

Taj let the words of Glitch fade and allowed himself to admit the possibility that he had truly been tricked by the Dark Dragon. Snatches of conversation with Nexus flitted through his thoughts, and of course, the secret mission he had been working on since the passing of his twelfth summer must be important. Nexus would not simply allow him to go around wasting his time, such a notion was completely implausible. Admittedly, he had laboured to be positive about Nexus' insistence that he cast his mind out into the human population to touch the minds of the few that still lived on this desolate dust ball. All he ever found, and reported, was savagery and greed. Most of the people he touched were mindless morons not even worth bothering with. But now, he had established a link, and things had changed, dramatically changed. What he could still not fathom was with whom he was linking. He had protested that if he knew exactly what he was looking for, he might be more successful, but Nexus, as always, remained tight-lipped.

'. . . . don't you agree?' said Glitch.

Taj looked at his friend and realised he had not heard a word that had been said. 'What? Have you been talking to me?'

Glitch shrugged his red-scaled shoulders and glanced around. 'Well, Taj, who else would I be talking to?'

'Oh, yes, quite,' said Taj, his mind still distracted by thoughts of the deceptive Darkness wanting to swamp this world.

'Do you agree or not? Glitch asked.

'What? Oh yes, yes, I agree,' Taj said, patting Glitch on his chest. He was unsure to what exactly he was agreeing, but as Glitch was grinning it seemed to be the right choice. 'Thing is, Glitch, and this is very important, I have to return to Fire Mountain.'

'Return to Fire Mountain?' Glitch asked, his eyes opening very wide. 'Why?'

'Well, after what you have said, I have a sneaking suspicion that it's not safe for me out here anymore.' Then he saw it: A black speck that wheeled and turned, and he knew it had seen him. He felt it rifle his thoughts before he could erect his mental defences, and it was hungry, very hungry. 'Donkey dung for dinner,' he murmured. 'I take it back, I no longer think I'm not safe, I know I'm not safe and you, Glitch, my faithful friend, you are more right than you could know.' He pointed into the sky. 'There, look, there is your mysterious speck. It's the Dark Dragon and it wants me.'

'It is? It does? What are we going to do?' Glitch whispered; talons scratching at his head.

Taj stood up from behind the rocks. 'Well, I think running away is a most excellent idea to start with, followed by the outstanding idea of continuing to run away.'

'Me too,' said Glitch. Together they dashed from the rocks towards the dry stonewall that partially covered the hole that led back into Fire Mountain, looking over their shoulders to see the Dark Dragon bank and dive out of sight.

'We have a big problem though,' said Taj. 'One only you can help me with, if you are brave enough and willing.'

'Brave? Hmm, I'm ever cautious around that word, but I'll help you if I can,' Glitch said, nudging stones free with his huge snout so he could squeeze into the hole.

'It's Spuddle,' said Taj.

Glitch instantly froze and gave Taj a most curious look. 'Spuddle?'

'Yes, Spuddle. Now, I know it's hard to believe, you'll just have to trust me; Spuddle is out there and needs our help.'

Glitch's eyes narrowed and he shook his head dismissively. 'Taj, have you lost your senses? Spuddle is dead! He has been for some time, now. You haven't banged your head have you? Are you ill, perhaps?'

'Glitch, stop it.' Taj snapped. 'There is nothing wrong with me, just listen; Spuddle is alive, I sensed him and you're going to find him.'

'I am?' Glitch said; his face a picture of puzzlement.

'Yes, you are. Believe me, Spuddle is alive and only you can save him,' Taj replied, determination threading his words.

Ionuin roused herself and absently rubbed at her temples. The sun was sinking low on the western horizon, its rays casting long shadows across the floor, turning the red-pink rocks into dark, malevolent shapes. 'What, whatever happened?' Only, she knew exactly what had happened. Spuddle had captured her thoughts and spliced them with his own, before unintentionally dispatching her with a mental clip that had put her out cold. How he had achieved this was a mystery that would have to wait for an answer.

Presently, another mystery held her attention. Spuddle was seated beside her and watching the far side of the canyon with a sharp alertness, that with a single glance, Ionuin took to mean danger. She recalled the night by the stream when she had thought someone, or something, was spying on her. The same something that had entered her world of dreams, infiltrated her mental defences with subtle ease. Had the Dark Dragon, which had tried to stomp her into the dust and snuff out her life, finally decided to make its move? Was confrontation with pure evil only a breath away?

Spuddle grunted and shifted his bulk from one leg to the other, getting awkwardly to his feet. Ionuin stared across the canyon floor and there, a shadow seemed to move. If she had not known better, she would have said the rocks were coming alive, but rocks could not come alive, could they? At this moment in time, she felt uncertain. Just about anything seemed possible. After what she had recently experienced, rocks coming to life actually seemed almost plausible!

Until she had met Spuddle, she would have dismissed sightings of dragons as sheer fantasy, no matter how reliable the witnesses were, or how persistently they made their claims. Some deep instinct warned her that this particular shadowy creature was not the Dark Dragon, but some other deadly beast. She cast the web of her thoughts into the shadows and caught an emotional impression of something dangerous, something that felt strangely corrupted, different from anything she had ever encountered before. Her imagination skittered around the edges of numerous possibilities, but she could think of nothing that could possibly be a match for what she had sensed. Unless…?

'Ahem, what is it, Spuddle? What do you suspect is out there?' She jumped to her feet. 'Can you sense malevolent danger too? Is it another dragon, Spuddle? It-it's not, not the Dark-'

Spuddle's thoughts suddenly slammed into her brain, a whirl of sharpened claws and slavering teeth; the mental barrage knocked her sideways, tumbling her back down to the floor. She tried to stand, but her legs disobeyed and she keeled over and began retching. 'Spuddle? Spuddle, what have you done to me? I can't . . .' the world momentarily swam out of focus and drifted slowly back again '. . . I, I can't even think straight!' Spuddle hooked a talon through her belt and lifted her clear of the ground, bringing her face close to his. Oddly, he appeared to be smiling at her.

She looked deep into his eyes, which had taken on the texture and fluidity of a syrupy golden liquid. A clear wave of undulating thought eased into her mind, its soothing gentleness subduing all anxiety, flushing away fatigue until her dizziness dispersed. A surge of light energy followed, building, building, building; until her whole body quaked with sudden power. 'Oh, wow, what a head rush! How did you do that, Spuddle?' She felt so good; sharp, alive and super-alert. She had Fyrdraca clasped tightly in her hand and she became fused to the blade, mind, body and soul. 'I-I believe I could split rocks apart!' she stammered. 'I feel absolutely fantastic!'

A savage roar suddenly erupted, echoing off the canyon walls, reverberating through the dusty air. Even though she felt better than she had ever felt in her whole life, an uncontrollable shiver rippled along her spine as Spuddle lowered her to the floor.

Spuddle growled in return, the sound deep and powerful.

'What in the name of . . . ?' The cadence of Ionuin's voice trailed to nothingness as the shadow, which she thought she may have seen move, suddenly burst into life. Only, it had more substance than any shadow. It had more substance than Ionuin had ever seen before in any living, breathing animal. If indeed it was an animal, for this beast had two mismatched heads.

With deceptive speed, it charged towards them. Ionuin slinked sideways, moving away from Spuddle, dividing the creature's intended target, her flowing movements fleet and nimble as she brought Fyrdraca around in a swishing arc. She stood poised for battle, her senses on overdrive, courage filling her heart until it pounded with a rhythmic pulse that streamed through her from head to toe. 'I am invincible!' she screamed, a wild excitement dancing manically in her eyes. 'I am woman . . . GIRL POWER! No, woman power! I am indestructible!' She glanced back at Spuddle and laughed; he looked puzzled, his head full of frown lines.

The monstrous creature kept coming straight towards her, roaring, and even though Ionuin felt juiced to the hilt with raw primal strength, there was an unsettling, underlying sensation fighting to break free and she recognised it for what it was: fear! It was trying to warn her of the lethal life threatening danger pounding her way, but Ionuin was not listening anymore. She had the incredible energy of reptilian bloodlust surging through her spirit and she wanted to fight, to kill, to rip apart! She wanted to taste the blood of unadulterated violence! Savour and revel in the insatiable glory of wielding death!

'I am dragon!' she yelled, raising her arms to the sky, her eyes wide with pleasure, a beaming smile glowing on her upturned face. 'I am dragon and I live to fight!'

Chapter Nineteen

The creature was now only a few spans distant, and Ionuin recognised it for what it was; a brown kodiak bear. Not an ordinary bear, but an odd looking, massive monster with three front legs and two heads. It was a descendant of the legendary star-creatures that began appearing after the heavens had brightened; creatures that were born grotesquely deformed and acted crazily. Her father had claimed that some humans were also born this way for many generations, but they had been taken into the wastelands and left to die, starved to death by their parents or devoured by whatever beast happened along. In the wild though, things were different. In the wild, nature ran rampant and creatures such as this survived and thrived.

The bear jumped across a low barrier of rounded boulders with an incredible leap and seemed to hang in the air, both sets of jaws gaping, dripping with saliva, ready to tear open its next meal. Ionuin tensed, held her ground and prepared to thrust Fyrdraca deep into the beast's heavily muscled, fur matted chest.

Even though she willed the bear to approach, to feel her wrath, a subconscious voice screamed a warning that she would instantly be crushed. This was Ionuin's last coherent thought as Spuddle sprang forward, bravely intercepting the bear's charging leap, crashing into the giant teeth-gnashing fur-ball, causing them both to go tumbling in a thrashing melee of flailing limbs and crunching jaws.

Ionuin jumped onto a nearby rock, laughing manically at the sight of the ferocious hostility unfolding before her, her mind wild with battle fever. The two creatures strained for supremacy as the fight escalated to savage proportions. Spuddle was brave, but the bear was strong and vicious. Teeth tore at flesh. Claws and talons gouged huge rents in fur and scaled skin. Copious amounts of blood streamed from open wounds, spattering the surrounding rocks, splattering Ionuin as she searched for an opening to strike home a decisive killing thrust.

The advantage of the bear, with two heads and an extra limb, was telling, and even though Spuddle fought valiantly and appeared to be giving as good as he got, he was staggering under the onslaught. Taking a chance, Ionuin screamed an angry battle cry and leapt into the fray.

She slashed down with her sword in a looping arc, then flicked up the tip so that the blade sliced deep into the bear's underbelly. Both its heads ceased their assault on Spuddle as it staggered sideways and roared in agony. Blood and entrails splashed across the dusty floor as the severely injured animal lurched wildly from side to side. Ionuin launched herself into the air with a twisting motion and struck again, her sword almost lopping off the smaller of the bear's two heads; it flopped forward and dangled from sinews and skin. In a reverse scything action, Ionuin swept Fyrdraca upwards in a flashing blur, the blade completing the task, the head thumping to the floor, a look of almost comic surprise in its slowly glazing eyes. Ionuin staggered backwards, taken aback at the lethal blows she had delivered. Fyrdraca was super-sharp, but no way should two strikes have sliced clean through the bear's neck with such ease. Spuddle edged her aside as he leapt in, finishing the kill, clamping his jaws around the remaining head, shaking it wildly as he had done the cooked rat, his teeth shearing through the animal's neck until it too was decapitated. The beast slumped over onto its side, blood gushing from its wounds in a dark red flood.

Ionuin dismissed the seemingly magical power that came from her sword; perhaps it was normal, after all. With battle fever still coursing through her veins, she yelled her victory to the skies, but her wailing was quickly curtailed, as from the corner of her eye she saw another kodiak bear emerge from the shadowy rocks and come bounding towards them. This one only had one head, but looked twice the size of the one they had just slaughtered.

'Uh-oh!' Ionuin said, tapping Spuddle on his shoulder, 'Here comes mummy bear, and I have a teensy inkling she might be a tad upset.'

Spuddle growled and turned his attention to the approaching danger.

As Ionuin prepared herself to fight again, she noticed that the previous battle fever that had consumed her and energised her had begun to diminish considerably, and she knew that this fight would be different. Unlike the one against the two-headed bear, this one they were in danger of losing. She looked to Spuddle, who was already circling away. She wanted eye contact; she wanted to be saturated with the power again and feel the vigour of pure dragon adrenalin fuelling her fight. As these thoughts circled through her mind, the oncoming bear dodged Spuddle's attempted interception and was upon her.

'Dollop of dung!' she cursed under her breath, backing up a pace. With urgent, limber speed, wielding Fyrdraca before her, she just missed the huge bear's nose before skilfully rolling clear of its deathly charge. The creature crashed into the giant cacti that had sheltered them from the afternoon sun, felling the tall, multi-limbed, thorn-studded pole and scattering the mule baskets and their contents. The mule brayed wildly and kicked out with its back legs, hitting the bear in its shoulder. The bear retaliated with a thumping swipe, crushing the mule's spine as gouging claws ripped out its back, exposing ribs and intestines, instantly killing the poor animal.

Infuriated at the loss of the innocent mule, Ionuin dashed forward and attacked the bear while its back was turned, slicing open one of its rear legs. The bear roared, arching its back as Spuddle joined her in the offensive, rushing past her, leaping high and coming down with all his weight. The bear met his charge and both beasts tumbled into the dust.

The clash of the two giants was fast and ferocious as they rolled and thrashed at each other, talons and claws causing untold damage as their jaws locked in a trial of teeth and strength. Ionuin dared not join the attack in case she accidentally hurt Spuddle. The bear rolled backwards, pulling Spuddle on top before ramming the paw of its uninjured rear leg into Spuddle's gut, propelling him over its head. Spuddle came crashing down onto his back with a crunching thump, flattening the dead mule's remains in a messy splurge.

Their jaws untangled, and with the animals separated, Ionuin attacked before the bear could fully regain its feet. She slashed back and forth trying to deliver a killing blow, a quick zigzag of her blade opening up a line of crimson on the bear's heaving chest. It roared, sending spittle flying in all directions. Blood poured from the wounds inflicted by Spuddle and Fyrdraca, turning its previous glossy brown coat into a gory matted red mess of tattered fur as it returned Ionuin's assault.

It lunged as Ionuin circled away, forcing her to leap back, ducking beneath its great encircling front legs that could crush the life from her in an instant. Her feet betrayed her, skidding on loose pebbles she fell to her knees. Sheer panic screeched in her mind as she scrabbled backwards, rolling to one side, just avoiding the bear's dive as it slammed beside her, landing between herself and Spuddle. She scrambled to her feet and rushed up the side of the bear as it turned to swipe at her, jabbing Fyrdraca deep between its shoulders trying to sever its spine before leaping clear, landing on the far side of Spuddle. The bear howled and Spuddle had recovered enough to raise his back legs and push it away, tumbling it to the floor. It was badly hurt, sucking in great heaving breaths and Ionuin knew now was the time to kill before it could sufficiently recover.

Spuddle struggled to his feet and stood wobbling as Ionuin rushed around him, intending to thrust her sword into the bear's throat to inflict a telling wound. As she drew close she realised the bear had tricked her, feigning the severity of its injuries. Ionuin was too close, and before she could drive Fyrdraca home, the bear lashed out with deceptive speed, one of its forepaws catching her with a savage glancing blow to the side of her head. Fyrdraca flew from her grasp and arced away, its blood-smeared blade glittering in the setting sunlight as she spun around. She briefly saw her sword dancing in mid-air; seemingly trapped in an expanded moment of time, and the world felt altogether wrong as the ground reared up and smacked her in the face, sending up a cloud of swirling dust.

After discussing what Taj insisted was the truth about Spuddle, he and Glitch had reached no firm conclusion, and settled down to spend the day sleeping within the shadows of overhanging rocks near the entrance to the lower caves of Fire Mountain. Glitch had been the first to awaken as the sun arced towards the western horizon. Taj appeared to be having a bad dream of some kind, and he reached across and shook him awake; 'Taj, snap out of it! You're having a, a day-mare!' he said, vigorously shaking Taj's shoulder.

Taj sat bolt upright. 'Spuddle!' he wailed. 'Spuddle and the dream-girl, they are together and in danger: great danger!'

'Shush!' Glitch hissed. 'Always noisy, bloody humans. Do try to be quiet. Dragon patrols might still be searching for you and what's all this about a tasty dream-girl?'

Taj rubbed at his eyes, the remnants of his dream dissipating at a speed equal to his ability to recall them. 'Crapping gnat bites!' he cursed. 'They're gone, but I saw Spuddle and the girl! They, they were in trouble and, and some hulking mass of fur was fighting with them!'

'Spuddle and a tasty girl fighting with fur?' Glitch said, scratching at his head. 'I don't really understand? Are you testing me with a puzzle?'

Taj jumped to his feet and nibbled the edge of his tongue to generate some saliva. 'Glitch, there is no puzzle and you don't need to understand. I need you to believe that Spuddle lives and I never said anything about the girl being tasty.'

'All right; you didn't exactly say *tasty,* not in so many words, but do tell me more about this creature.'

'The girl is human and not a creature to eat!' Taj protested.

Glitch nodded. 'Yes, but I like girls, softer flesh than the males, juicier, more scrumptious!' he said, saliva dripping from his mouth. 'Long time since I ate a yummy young girl, I can almost taste her. Is she skinny or meaty? I do like plump girls best. Not too much hair though, and I don't like-'

'Glitch!' Taj snapped. 'You cannot eat the girl! It matters not if she is fat or thin, understood?'

Glitch pouted, as much as a dragon could pout. 'I was only asking, you know, just curious.'

Taj sighed. 'Curious or not, what she looks like does not matter. It should never matter, not under any circumstances. A girl is a girl and should be accepted as such, and trust me, along with Spuddle, I also need the girl; got it?'

Glitch nodded his head despondently. 'Just saying, I like girls, all girls, and most of them are very tasty.'

'Look, Glitch, just forget the tasty girl.'

'So, she is tasty?'

Taj frowned. 'What? No! Look, forget I mentioned her, she is not the priority. I'm more concerned with Spuddle.' he snapped. 'You said that once we had rested you'd think on my words, and we have rested, over-rested. So, will you help me find him or not?'

Glitch did not respond.

Taj sighed. 'Glitch, did you hear me? Spuddle is alive and you are going to find him!'

'Are you sure Spuddle is alive?

'Yes!' Taj exclaimed. 'I am positive and you shall be the one to rescue him.'

'Erm, I will?' Glitch hissed, uncertainty edging his words. 'And what of this girl? I know you 'need her', funny way of putting it, but when you have tired of *needing her,* can she be my reward? That is, if she is plump and juicy not got much hair. It gets stuck in my tee-'

Taj leapt forward and pushed his nose into the end of Glitch's snout. 'Listen, my friend, and listen well. You will find Spuddle and the girl and bring them here to me. You will not harm the girl. I need her, I am not sure how or why, but she is special, no hidden salacious agenda, just special: understood?'

Glitch glanced around him, trying not to meet Taj's glaring eyes.

'I said; is this understood?' Taj demanded, folding his arms across his chest, trying to look defiant and stubborn.

Glitch sighed. 'Oh, all right, if you insist, but don't I get a reward?'

Taj patted the red dragon on his neck and scratched beneath his chin. 'Glitch, the reward is in the deed itself, but yes, there will be other benefits, and I do need your help with this, I cannot do it alone. Trust me, this is very important.'

Glitch glanced around again, shuffled his feet. 'Um, well, yes, I suppose if you really are sure that Spuddle is alive, then of course I will help.'

'Good, thank you,' said Taj, hugging Glitch with as much force as he could muster, pleased that he had not had to resort to begging, which he would have been prepared to do if necessary.

'All right,' Glitch said, stepping out of Taj's embrace. 'No need for theatricals.'

Taj smiled. 'I'm just happy you are willing to aid me.'

Glitch harrumphed. 'I did not have much option, really.'

'Always an option,' Taj said, before moving on quickly. 'It is still daylight and no time like the present, is there?'

Glitch grimaced. 'What about the Dark Dragon?' he said, pointing a sharpened talon to where the speck had been hovering in the sky that very morning.

Taj was ready for this objection. 'Glitch, for reasons I've not yet fathomed, the Dark Dragon is only interested in me. He only showed an interest in you when you were connected to my thoughts, yes?'

'Hmm, you really think so?' Glitch asked. 'I'm not so sure.'

Taj flapped his hands at Glitch dismissively. 'Of course I think so! Glitch, you worry too much. You'll be fine. I would never put you in danger and anyhow, what possible danger could you be in?'

Glitch stared back, his face aghast. 'That's easy for you to say, Taj. You'll be safe inside the Mountain, won't you?'

Taj began fidgeting, clenching and unclenching his fists, feeling uneasy at the thought of returning to face Nexus. 'Yes, well, I've got to face Lord Nexus yet, but look, the Dark Dragon has been flying around the guarded lands for days; nothing untoward has happened yet, has it?'

'Um, I suppose not, not yet,' Glitch conceded. 'but suppose-'

'Never mind, *supposing*,' Taj interrupted. 'There is no 'suppose' about it, tell me, where were you going before I called to you?'

Glitch shrugged his shoulders. 'No secret, as it happens. I was out, just flying around and-'

'You were hunting humans: yes?'

'Hunting! Me? Hunting humans?' Glitch said, a note of surprise edging his voice. 'Bah! I wouldn't have called it hunting! Not really, just, having some fun with humans, you know.'

'It's all right, Glitch, there's no shame,' said Taj, reaching out and clasping Glitch's talons. 'My point is, you were indeed having fun. You were in no danger whatsoever, now were you?'

'Ahem, not really,' Glitch admitted, 'unless you consider what my parents might say if they actually caught me hunting . . . having fun with humans. Now, Dad would say nothing, but Mum would be-'

'Never mind your parents,' cut in Taj. 'They'll never know, so listen. What I want you to do for me is what you were actually doing before I called to you! Only, go and hunt - sorry! I mean, have fun, in the Valley of Caves.'

'The Valley of Caves?' Glitch said, his brow creasing with questioning thought.

'Yes,' said Taj. 'That's where I last sensed Spuddle. Can you do that for me, for Spuddle?'

Glitch seemed to consider how to answer. 'What if, well, what if I don't find him?'

'Then I'm wrong,' said Taj, 'but I know you will find him. He is alive, Glitch, I'm not mistaken. I would know Spud's mind anywhere - once encountered, never forgotten.'

'True,' said Glitch, nodding his head knowingly. 'Right, I'll go take a look. I have heard there are humans living along that valley. Why, is beyond me! I mean, there is nothing of interest down there! Apart from the old tombs, but who would want to go mooching around in the halls of the dead?'

'Who indeed!' said Taj, agreeably, climbing over the rough wall at the entrance of the Mountain. 'Oh, and um, good luck!'

'Good Luck? Will I need good luck?' Glitch gulped. 'Taj, you said I'd be safe!'

Taj turned and saw that Glitch looked very uncertain. He smiled. 'I meant, good luck with finding Spuddle. Of course you'll be safe.' He touched Glitch on the end of nose with tactile affection. 'Trust me, Spuddle is out there and waiting for rescue. You'll be a hero, Glitch.'

'I will?' he said, smiling, his teeth glistening, a faraway look dancing in his eyes. 'Why yes! I will, won't I?' He stretched his wings. 'Glitch of Glead Hall; a true, living hero! Now that is a proper reward! Much better than tormenting and eating a delicious girl, not that I do that sort of thing, you understand.'

Taj waved bye to Glitch as he took to the air then turned and ran back through the narrow tunnels, trying not to think about what he was going to say to Lord Nexus. It would take Glitch, an excellent flyer, most of the night to reach The Valley of Caves, and only then would Nexus know the truth; Spuddle lived. He was aware that until Glitch returned with Spuddle, he would have to suffer his master's wrath, but that was nothing. When the truth was confirmed, he would be forgiven, even rewarded, perhaps handsomely, but more importantly, Spuddle would be safe and returned to the clan, and the mystery surrounding the girl could be solved. Why she was so special, he did not know, but he knew he was going to find out if it was the last thing he ever did. He just hoped it wasn't the last thing he ever did.

Ionuin's senses were still reeling as she felt herself lifted aloft and carried. Her face felt wet, cold and tingly, and there was so much pain. She began wondering if this was the end for her. Is this what her life had come to, a quick feast for a mutant Kodiak bear? She tried to reach down to her boot where she kept her knife. If she was going to die, then she was determined to go out fighting. As her hand touched the hilt, thoughts of comfort washed over and through her.

'What the...? Spuddle?' she murmured, recognising the reptilian touch of his thoughts. She then opened her eyes to see the underside of the dragon's blood-smeared jaw. 'Spuddle, it is you!' He glanced down and hot breath enveloped her face. It was still rank with the scent of dead flesh, but, fetid though it was, she welcomed the smell. 'Spuddle, did you kill the bear?' Deep within her mind, she received a muted image of herself being pulled from the bear's grasp, then the bear limping amongst the rocks, dragging the mutilated carcass of the mule. 'It took the mule, then, then went away?'

She swam in and out of consciousness. The next time she opened her eyes, she could see they were in the entrance of a cave: or was it just an overhang of rock? Spuddle placed her on the ground, gently resting her head on soft sand, and she heard the bear welcome the night with a gigantic roar, and knew they were far from safe. The bear, the terrible monstrous bear, had not gone away, but was waiting, probably hiding, thought Ionuin, intending to come and finish the job it started. She began to lose heart, then Spuddle roared in return, echoing her own defiance and determination not to yield.

'Not dead yet,' she mumbled, her hand clasping her knife.

Chapter Twenty

Ionuin tried to keep awake - she did not want to die in her sleep - but Spuddle cradled her to his body, giving her warmth and projecting feelings and images of comfort and reassurance via their mind-link. When she eventually gave way to the need for sleep, visions of the Dark Dragon slithered inside her head and attacked her slumbering thoughts. It tore through her resistance and clawed her helpless body, tearing open huge rents in her skin, gouging out whole chunks of flesh dripping with blood.

The night closed in, and as the pale sun sank out of sight, darkness crept down the valley. Sleep did not come easy for Ionuin. Along with the darkness came other creatures; small nocturnal feeders that shied away from the sunshine, scavengers existing on the waste left by other life forms, and of course, evil beasts from the Dark dimensions. No Darkness would ever be complete without the wispy, curling essence of these little black monsters.

They skulked in the shadows, formless and shapeless, patiently watching and waiting, always prepared to take advantage of the unwary. They fed on the primeval fear that existed within all sentient creatures since the dawn of time, an inherent distrust of the night and the unseen demons that inhabit it. Pickings for these Dark phantoms were scarce on this dying world, but they did not starve. Slipping through open imaginations, creeping into dreams, infiltrating the minds of those unfortunates that left themselves unguarded through need of rest, stalking their victims like vampires. These Darkling waifs would be no real threat this night; the real threat skulked outside, licking its wounds, feasting on dead mule.

Ionuin stirred, screamed, half-awoke, and the dream phantoms skittered away, their cravings satisfied, their appetite sated, their lust for the horror of the mind fulfilled.

'The Dark Dragon is coming, Spuddle,' Ionuin murmured as the warm blanket of sleep cosseted her body. 'It wants me, it wants my life.' Unseen by Ionuin, Spuddle nodded his agreement as he urged her back to sleep, and she began drifting into a deep, untroubled slumber. 'It wants my life,' she repeated, then snored, softly.

Taj came to a lava tube, smooth and glassy, and shinnied up its curving length. The tubes in the lower passages were barely wide enough for him these days, some were a very tight squeeze, but they connected all levels and were useful short cuts. He exited the tube into a wide curving tunnel lit by green wall crystals, and set off running. He then realised, in his haste, that he was going the wrong way, and doubled back on himself.

He seemed to have been running forever when he saw a faint yellow glow up ahead, the start of the dragon home proper; the lower chambers at any rate, and there was noise coming towards him; voices. Glitch had mentioned patrols out searching for him and he guessed this must be one of them. After all, they had no idea where he was, and every passage would be searched thoroughly as well as the lands surrounding the great mountain.

Taj slowed to a steady trot, then a walk as he emerged into a small cavern with only two entrances: the narrow service one he had just exited and a large one that led to the main access route to the lower sleep chambers. The dimly lit cavern had once served as quarters for the old helpers, but were now disused. There were stone tables in the centre and bunks hollowed out of the wall on one side. Stone benches circumnavigated the whole chamber. Taj found himself staring at two blue dragons, both of whom were sniffing the floor. He instantly recognised them as Bollfur's sons, Blucher and Bolden. They had not yet noticed his arrival, which did not surprise Taj as they were both idiots, especially the younger one, Bolden.

'I tell you, I can smell him,' said Bolden. 'Yes, yes, he was here all right,' he added, his nose snuffling along the ground. 'Oh my, I have a good scent of him now! I tell you, bro, he came this way, for sure. I know he did, I just know it.'

'I don't trust your nose as much as you do,' Blucher replied, who was much bigger and heavy with fat, especially his drooping gut. 'Although, hang on, yes! I too can smell him now!' They both shuffled around excitedly, their noses finally leading them to where Taj stood.

'Hello there!' Taj yelled. 'Having fun are we?'

Both dragons leapt back in surprise, teeth bared, sharpened talons unsheathed.

'What the . . . ?' wailed Bolden, clasping his chest.

'You, you silly little tit!' Blucher harrumphed. 'You scared the living crap out of us!'

'Sorry!' Taj said, stepping into the chamber. 'Looking for someone, are you? Can I be of assistance, perhaps?'

'Assistance?' Bolden queried.

'He means help,' said Blucher, cuffing his young brother across the ear. 'We were looking for you, Taj, as you must know, half the gathered clans are searching for your scrawny little carcass! Tell me, exactly, just where have you been?'

'Yeah, where you been?' asked Bolden.

'Out,' said Taj, pushing between the two dragons. They immediately closed ranks and held him tight. 'Hey!' he said, wriggling free and stepping back. 'What's wrong with you two? You found me, all right, so let's go! Nexus will be pleased with your success; you might even get to sit at the grownup table at the feast tonight.'

Bolden circled around him, blocking off the service exit, and Blucher crowded him. 'I asked, where you been, Little Squeaker?'

The night passed slowly and as dawn approached, the giant mutant bear still roamed outside the cave where Ionuin and Spuddle sheltered. It had bellowed continuously throughout the night, leaving them both wondering if an attack was imminent.

Touching her face, Ionuin could feel four raised welts where she knew open wounds should be. Her miraculous healing powers had been at work again, and Spuddle, who had been covered in greenish-orange, sticky dragon blood, looked unharmed. She observed him as he watched through the cave entrance; his ears now stood erect, pointed and proud. A dark green crest had begun forming on top of his head and now ran down the full length of his spine. His newly formed wings, which had been knobbly vestigial stubs, now sprouted from his shoulders, hanging down his back, silver tipped, shimmering and glistening. His legs looked firm and strong and his extended forelegs looked like capable limbs. His tail, which had been a limp, pathetic appendage, now swished back and forth with vigour. Ionuin could hardly believe it, but Spuddle was now, clearly, a fully formed adult dragon.

She flexed her mind and Spuddle welcomed her thoughts inside his huge green head. There was no longer a hazy indistinct mess, but clear patterns she could understand. Through strange communications beyond her fathoming, she could relate to his thinking, and his mind swam with a heady fusion of fear and survival instinct, driven by adrenaline. She also sensed concern, both for her own and his safety. There was something else too; a desperate sorrow linked to a lifetime of yearning for some elusive need that lurked deep within. A yearning so deep, her thoughts could not penetrate. She realised that there was more to Spuddle than she had ever imagined. She had assumed, just from his sheer size; that he was no more than a baby, but now, it was apparent that he was far more than that. It occurred to her that the changes could mean danger, so why did she feel so safe?

'Spuddle, you, you're not a baby dragon at all, are you?'

Spuddle appeared to grin, his thin red lips peeling back, exposing rows of sharp pointed teeth that interlocked with each other perfectly. Ionuin rocked back on her heels as his mind slammed into hers.

Dragon! screamed inside her head, a jumbled mixture of flickering images that only just made sense.

Ionuin wrapped her own thoughts around those of Spuddle. *I . . . understand.*

Spuddle tilted his head, frown lines creased his face. Ionuin took this to mean confusion. Of course, he had no real command of language: or had he?

Again she flexed her mind. *Yes, yes, you are dragon.*

Spuddle still looked confused and she realised she needed to think in pictures, not words. She brought to mind the image of the bear and Spuddle roared. She then thought of her sword and how it could hurt the bear and Spuddle roared again. Then she saw Spuddle flying, with herself riding on his back; this was Spuddle's thought and she tried to convey signs of agreement. Any means of escape would suffice, so long as it helped them avoid the clutches of the ferocious, wounded bear prowling around outside. Although, taking into account the changes that had come over Spuddle, Ionuin hoped she would not simply be exchanging one death scenario for another.

'I do need my sword, Spuddle,' she said, trying to inject some urgency into her voice.

Spuddle nodded and drew back his lips in a wide grin that showed off his teeth. Ionuin's breath caught in her throat at the sight, and a tingle crept up her spine. Again, taking into account the changes to Spuddle, she wondered about her safety. A choice of being eaten by dragon, or bear! Wonderful, she thought, her hands flapping dismissively before her. She cast her mind into Spuddle's and his thoughts suggested that she would be safe, and not to worry, which was fine for him; he was not the one currently on the menu! Dragons were notorious eaters of people. Not only that, but Spuddle was becoming huge, no longer a baby that she could cajole and encourage, even castigate, but a flesh devouring creature of terrifying reputation.

Her hand dropped to her side as she watched him creep stealthily towards the cave entrance, swishing his lengthy, muscular tail behind him in long, lazy strokes. Resigned to accepting the circumstances in which she now found herself, Ionuin followed. The mutant bear, outlined in the pearly light of pre-dawn, was crouched on some rocks in the middle of the canyon. It looked extremely threatening and fearsome, and as Ionuin and Spuddle appeared, it roared and scrambled from the rocks. Spuddle stretched up to his full height and inhaled, his huge, green-scaled chest ballooning out. With a mighty roar, he let forth a great breath that exploded in a ball of flame. Ionuin jumped back in surprise as the illuminating fire seared across the canyon, striking an outcrop of brushwood directly in front of the bear. The bear howled as the brushwood turned into a raging inferno and, turning tail, retreated to the rocks, dragging its injured leg.

'Wow,' mouthed Ionuin, silently. This was certainly an improvement in her situation. The bear could not possibly stand a chance now that Spuddle could breathe fire! She envisaged herself retrieving Fyrdraca while Spuddle held the bear at bay. Controlling her growing excitement at the sudden change in fortune, she cast the images into Spuddle's head. Spuddle glared menacingly after the bear as they gingerly emerged from the cave and started across the canyon. The bear retreated as fast as it could, roaring its angry defiance.

On rounding a slight bend, the sun just peeping above the horizon, they arrived back to where the bears had first attacked. There was little left of the mule, apart from some blood-smeared rocks and red stained sand, and even the bear they had killed had great chunks taken out of its belly. Ionuin looked up as a high-pitched screech filled her ears. Winged carrion eaters, birds and flying lizards, were circling high above. A fresh kill never passed unnoticed for long, and Ionuin knew that they could soon expect more animals along, wolves, lychyaenas and maybe more bears.

Spuddle found Fyrdraca amongst the rocks and kicked it towards Ionuin, the blade skittering along the pebbled ground as Spuddle continued watching the bear. Ionuin snatched up her sword, releasing a huge sigh as she clenched her fist round the handle, feeling more secure for having her weapon to hand. After quickly salvaging her small pack of possessions, watching the bear warily, she drank deeply from her deerskin water-bottle, quenching her thirst, the contents warm and brackish, but still very welcome.

'Much better,' she gasped, wiping water droplets from her chin as she caught a mental image of herself walking away, alone. She glanced at Spuddle who was looking down the canyon. Ionuin followed his gaze and saw a dust cloud slowly rising in the early morning heat. More animals were coming. Things were looking dangerous. Ionuin realised that here in this valley, she was well out of her depth. Out on the plains she was the alpha predator, while here, she was well down the pecking order, more prey than hunter. Spuddle nuzzled his nose into her neck. It tickled. 'Spuddle, what are you doing? This is no time for playing around!'

'Go.'

The word was hushed, like a whisper travelling on the wind. Ionuin was amazed. 'Spuddle? You can talk? You can actually talk?'

'Go!' he repeated, his voice soft and delicate. 'Danger coming.'

Ionuin could hardly believe it. Spuddle was one surprise after another, but she would not leave him. She felt somehow responsible, which was ridiculous, as he now towered over her and was well equipped to defend himself, but she was determined. She sent forth a mental image of herself riding on his back and them both flying away. 'Spuddle, you must come too!' she pleaded. He roared loudly in reply, startling Ionuin, as he looked terribly angry. In the fine mesh of her thoughts he showed a picture of her running down the valley, alone. Ionuin caught hazy images of Spuddle going in the opposite direction, pursuing the bear, roasting it with his flaming breath.

'Can you really do that whenever you like?' she asked, backing up a few steps.

Spuddle nodded his head in confirmation. 'Go. Go now,' he urged, gently pushing her shoulder.

'Okay, Spuddle, I get the message,' Ionuin said, staggering backwards.

She turned and walked away, glancing back every twenty paces or so. The bear had ceased roaring and Ionuin feared nothing from it anymore, but Spuddle had changed and she was not sure she was entirely happy about this sudden transformation.

'He's not a baby anymore,' she told herself. There was a world of difference between a helpless baby dragon and a fire-breathing beast with huge talons and gnashing teeth. As a baby, he had been food for men, now, the roles were completely reversed. She did not think Spuddle would attack her; he had saved her: hadn't he? It had all happened so fast, but in her mind's eye, she thought they had actually saved each other. Surely this counted for something? The canyon rounded another bend up ahead and when Ionuin looked back for the last time, Spuddle was feeding on the remains of the dead two-headed bear they had killed the previous day.

'Eat well, Spuddle,' she mumbled under her breath, her own stomach rumbling, not looking forward to the cooked rat she had stashed in her backpack, but knowing she needed the nourishment, as it looked like she was going to have to suffer yet another hot, punishing day in the Valley of Caves. Only now, she was going to be all alone. After a lifetime of enjoying and relishing her own company, she was already missing the companionship of Spuddle.

115

Chapter Twenty One

'Come on, Little Squeaker,' said Blucher. 'I asked, where you been?'

Taj bridled at the use of the nickname he loathed, but remained calm. 'I told you, I've been out.'

Blucher smirked, showing a fine array of gleaming teeth. 'Yes, I heard you, but *out* is not an answer; is it?'

Taj shrugged. 'It's the only answer I have for you.'

Bolden giggled, but both Taj and Blucher ignored him, the palpable tension in the group rendering them cautious and edgy.

'Thing is,' Blucher continued, 'our glorious father, Lord Bollfur wants to know exactly what you've been up to.'

Taj grinned. 'Not having a good day then, is he?' he replied mockingly.

'I think his day will improve, Taj.' Blucher said, matching Taj's mocking tone. 'He wants to chat with you, in his own chambers, up close and extremely personal.'

'Yeah, his own chambers,' echoed Bolden. 'Up close, and . . . close!'

Taj became slightly concerned as he realised that these two were not searching him out on the orders of Nexus, they were here for other reasons entirely; to capture him. Silence bloomed in the small room as alarm bells chimed discordantly through Taj's mind, and he sensed much danger afoot. Uninterpretable looks passed between Blucher and Bolden. Taj glanced from one to the other, keeping his expression vacant to disguise the sudden fear that had spiked his thoughts.

'So where you been?' Bolden asked, turning his full attention back to Taj.

Taj decided to ignore the younger brother. If he was going to escape from this unexpected messy encounter, then Blucher was the one with whom he must negotiate. He concentrated his thoughts on the fatter, older dragon with keen intensity, trying to bore into his reptilian mind with his piercing eyes, which were now glowing violet. After what felt like an eternity, he got no discernable reaction and gave up the mind games, finally accepting that he could be in serious trouble.

'Hah!' said Taj, suddenly changing tactics, poking Blucher in his great big chest, startling him. 'I bet your dad wants another game of chess, doesn't he?' Taj watched as Blucher's eyes widened just a little. 'Come on, you can tell me,' whispered Taj, conspiratorially, trying to wrong-foot the dragon even more. 'Was he really angry when he lost earlier; eh? I bet he was more than just angry, I bet he was fuming! Probably furious, as I know that when Lord Bollfur loses at anything, he can be quite irritable. More than irritable; a grumpy old bumpkin!'

Bolden growled. 'Bumpkin? Our dad is-'

'Shut it, Bolden!' Blucher snapped, his face pulsing with hidden anger.

'I mean, I'm willing to play him again,' said Taj, now picking absently at his fingernails, pushing the chess angle for all it was worth, noting that Blucher was eyeing him with a curious intensity that made the hairs stand up on the back of his neck. 'A rematch would be fun, methinks,' he added, just for good measure.

Bolden snarled. 'Our dad wants to rip-'

'Yes!' Blucher laughed, interrupting his brother, not fooling anyone with his forced merriment. 'He does want to play you again, he asked us to bring you to him, as soon as possible, in fact! Says he's looking forward to giving you a damn good thrashing.'

'I bet he did,' Taj said, looking from one brother to the other. 'A good thrashing, indeed.'

Bolden's face brightened. 'Oh, yes, yes he did!' he said, chiming in, as if this were all fun and games. 'He asked us to bring you to him, very quickly. Just can't wait to play you again, up close, wants to beat you so badly.'

Indeed, I don't doubt that he would thoroughly enjoy beating me, thought Taj, knowing that this was the unembroidered truth, although he was not sure why Lord Bollfur would wish to cause him harm. For no obvious reason he could discern, he had never really liked fat old Bollfur, or his moronic sons. Even though they usually minded their own business, they always gave him the general impression that they were lowly and untrustworthy. Always cheating at games, then jesting about it, always greedy at feast time, but justifying a good appetite, and always bullying younger smaller dragons, then claiming it would toughen them up, prepare them for life. Taj's overall assessment was that they were just not nice, lacked common decency, and now, without any real proof whatsoever, Taj believed his very life was in imminent danger. His nerves were twanging, his stomach was flipping over and he did not need proof when he felt like this; but what could he do? Then he had the answer, and it was tactfully beautiful.

He assumed an air of nonchalance, picking rock-dust from beneath his fingernails. 'Blucher, old friend, coming back to your earlier question, about what I have been doing. Truth is, I was looking for Glitch.'

'Glitch?' Bolden snapped, looking around him, as if Glitch would magically appear just by saying his name.

'Earlier question?' Blucher asked, scratching his long snout.

Unbelievable, thought Taj. 'Yes, you asked me where I had been, when I first arrived here, remember?'

'Ah,' said Blucher, 'you were looking for Glitch.'

'Yes, Glitch,' said Taj, admiring his nails while trying to think. 'You see, I had challenged him! Yes, that's it, I have challenged Glitch!'

'What?' Blucher snarled. 'You're not making sense! What do you mean, you challenged Glitch?'

'Um, yes,' said Bolden. 'What is it you have challenged Glitch to do?'

'Arm-wrestling!' Taj laughed, even surprising himself with his false enthusiasm. 'I challenged him to an arm-wrestling contest in this very chamber!'

'So, where is he?' Bolden asked, again looking around.

'Oh, well, he never showed,' said Taj, shaking his head. 'While waiting I fell asleep just along the old service tunnel back there,' he said, thumbing over his shoulder at the small entrance. 'When I heard you two yattering, I thought it was my soon-to-be-defeated friend, finally arriving.'

Taj looked around as Bolden guffawed, holding his stomach. 'What a joke! A pitiful thing like you, besting a dragon at a feat of strength? You expect us to believe that? Why, I would gladly wrestle you now, Squeaker! I will tear off your ugly face and use it as an arse-wipe! Do you accept my challenge?'

Blucher wasn't quite so taken in, thought Taj, as he watched the older brother shift his weight from foot to foot, his face conveying a certain amount of mistrust.

'Nah,' said Taj, dismissively. 'I wouldn't want to hurt a youngling like you, Bolden. Besides, I said *arm-wrestle*, not wrestle. There is a huge difference between the two, but, tell you what I'll do, I'll challenge you, Blucher; what do you say, old friend?'

Blucher even took a step back. 'You, you would challenge me?'

'Sure,' said Taj, walking over to the stone table. He knelt down and waved Blucher to sit opposite him. 'Right, this is how a human arm-wrestles a dragon.' He gently took Blucher's arm, held it down flat on the table so his talons were facing upwards, and grabbed hold of two side talons. 'Obviously, as you're much bigger than I, we can't lock arms as two dragons would, and to compensate for my disadvantage, I also get to use two arms: agreed?'

'Hah, agreed,' said Blucher, now fully taken in by what would in all likelihood be an easy victory. 'Even with two arms, I will snap your skinny wrists as if they were dried twigs!'

'Do him, Bro,' Bolden chuckled, his eyes wide with excitement, his talons scratching at the crown of his big blue head.

Ionuin seemed to have been walking for the longest time and the day had grown sticky and uncomfortable. The sun hurled down unrelenting waves of blanketing heat from a clear, pink sky, unforgiving and merciless in its intensity, but Ionuin kept going. Spuddle was somewhere behind her and she was not sure she wanted to be reunited with what she had come to think of as a dangerous unknown quantity.

Which was somewhat strange, as she also felt close to him. A kind of mutually acknowledged friendship had grown between them. A strong, dependant friendship too, as they had certainly aided each other, saved each other really, but he was a ferocious dragon while she was just a human. Such mixed emotions as these were new to Ionuin, as Tharl had not considered emotions to be high on his agenda when it came to preparing her for the world. Where people were concerned, for both her and her father, things had always been relatively clear.

Admittedly, when it came to people, she only really knew her father, but when she had dealt with traders on the occasions she accompanied Tharl to various settlements across the dry plains, they appeared to fall in to one of two categories. Honest and reliable, which were the rarest kind, or untrustworthy and unscrupulous, which was almost everyone. Beyond the traders, she did like Mr and Mrs Mumble who owned the tea stall at the edge of the Plains Market. Her father, much to her delight, always insisted they stop at the Mumbles for refreshments before heading home. Until now, all situations concerning people were decidedly one thing or another with little room for grey areas in-between, thought Ionuin. She stopped in her tracks. Could she actually consider Spuddle as she would another person?

'He's a dragon,' she murmured, under her breath, knowing she needed to think this situation through properly. 'Spuddle is not a person at all, but a dragon, so get used to it and adapt.'

She smiled as she acknowledged she had acquired her father's habit of talking aloud when working things through. Now though, being alone, things were different; much different, and talking to herself would probably be the least of her worries. Living a secluded life in their little valley, her father had been the only true friend she had ever known during her whole life. Therefore, she understood little of real friendship, but had read lots of books, and some of them touched upon the subject. However, it was not until she had met Spuddle that she grasped what it meant to trust another beyond your own family circle. It was not easy, you had to believe that most people, person or dragon, in her scenario, felt the same way. If the circumstances and their experiences were anything to go by, then yes, she trusted Spuddle. Why then, she wondered, was she now walking away from him?

She also wondered how far she would have to travel before she found an animal trail that would lead her up the sheer cliff face that flanked the west side of the valley. Then she could return to the familiar plains on which she regularly hunted, where there would be relative safety. She looked east, over the craggy hills, and wondered what lay in that direction. She knew there were scattered settlements, but even her father had not ventured that way for years, so she did not know if they would be friendly, or what wildlife hunted those strange lands.

Feeling tired and thirsty, she drank from her water bottle as she walked towards a small cave opening in the cliff face. After climbing over several large rocks, she scampered up a slope of loose scree and crawled into the shade provided by the cave entrance. She checked around for signs of life, animal prints, bones and the smell of urine marking out territory. She did not want to relax before the den of a wolf or bear and have it sneak up on her from behind. The cave appeared to be unoccupied, so she seated herself and dug into her pack, pulling out what was left of the game she had killed a few days ago. Was it one or two days, she wondered? So much had happened, she could hardly remember, but what did it matter? After smelling the meat, she bit down into the cooked flesh. It did not taste great, a little greasy and chewy, but it had not yet turned bad. It would not last another day though, she thought, and decided to eat all she had.

As she sat gazing out into the hills that ran along the eastern side of the valley, it occurred to her that once again her life had taken a strange twist. There was no longer any point visiting Cavesend, it would only mean meeting people, and she had no desire to meet anyone. The fanciful story of Shinny and Travis was just too ridiculous to be believed, and anyway, it could be looked into another time. She considered taking time out to see the Mumbles, and she should really inform them that her father was dead. She convinced herself that it was the right thing to do, but it only meant further complications, complications that she felt she could do without at present. She did not want to spend time explaining what had happened, reliving the pain. All she really wanted to do was pay a visit to Fire Mountain.

'The Mumbles can wait,' she muttered, spitting out a piece of gristle that tasted rank. If anything, the urge to seek out the legendary home of the dragons seemed even greater now than at any other time in her life. She supposed her meeting with Spuddle had a lot to do with this urge, but she could not help herself. Her curiosity had become roused and needed satisfying, and she knew the Mumbles would understand.

'I'll tell them when I return,' she murmured as she rummaged in her pack. She put to one side the few tradable items she had taken from her father's killers, except for a folding knife, a compass and two light globes. The globes sprang to life as she touched them. One was a deep yellow and the other a pale blue. Even in the bright sunshine of late afternoon they looked beautiful. Her father had reliably informed her that there were few people left who could actually make a light globe, as it was a specialist skill, awakening the power from within the precious crystal.

They used to have one in the cottage, a green one, but her father never used it. He preferred candles or lamplight whenever they had oil. Ionuin had kept the globe as a plaything, using it to read at night, though it cast an eerie light. Ionuin believed her father did not like the globe as he could hardly make it light up at all, while she could make it blaze brightly with the merest touch. 'Gifted, like your mother,' he would always say, but never revealing what he meant by 'gifted'. Even when she questioned him about her mother he would completely ignore her, and if she pressed too hard, he could turn angry. Occasionally, he would shout at her and storm off, only to return later, apologetic and inconsolable.

As she looked at the crystal in the fading light of the day, she saw something move among the low hills across the valley. Lychyaena, a whole pack of them. She quickly returned the globes to her pack and chided herself for being so stupid. If they haven't seen me I'll be fine, she thought, but if they have, then I'm trapped. On looking around, she could see the cave entrance was not a bad place to defend. She had Fyrdraca, but would be happier if she had her bow, only it had been broken to pieces when Spuddle was hurled onto the mule baskets.

She watched as the lychyaena, more ferocious than hyenas and bigger than wolves, scented the air. There were too many to count, but what did it matter? From within the concealment of the cave, she thought she would be safe. While they did not exactly fear mankind, they were wary, as they were also wary of kodiak bears, although they could scent weakness, as she could herself. A sick animal gave off a particular scent. Even a bad tooth could mean an easy meal. If an animal had not been feeding properly, because of a mouth infection, it would not be as strong as its herd members, and that was the one to single out and hunt down.

She sat, stock-still, as the lychyaena scanned the valley. She could smell them, but could they smell her? The wind was minimal, although it was coming from the east. She thought they had probably come here after spotting the carrion birds earlier and were on their way to investigate. Any meal was welcome, and out on the plains during desperate times, she had even seen a wolf play dead to entice carrion birds closer, then rear up and kill the would-be feeder. Such tactics were risky and the wolf was not guaranteed victory, as some of the birds were enormous and they were always vicious, armed as they were with talons and a hooked beak. However, such cunning had to be respected, and Ionuin knew that the lychyaena were just as wily.

Chapter Twenty Two

Bolden jumped around the chamber, giggling. 'Taj, even if you use two arms, my bro is going to rip your shoulders apart!'

'Sounds very unpleasant,' Taj replied, trying to ignore the dragon as he focussed his thoughts on the plan.

'More than unpleasant!' Bolden snarled. 'You're going to have your muscles and ligaments stretched and mashed! The pain will be incredible! I can't wait! Honestly, I just can't wait!'

Taj smiled, pushed away the bloody images infiltrating his mind and concentrated on Blucher. 'Now, what you do,' he instructed, keeping his voice as calm as possible, 'is try and raise your arm off the table slowly, increasing power as I resist your movement. If you can slowly bring your arm to the upright position, then you are the winner: understand?'

'Snap his bones, bro!' Bolden yelled, leaping in the air with excitement, actually head-butting the wall. 'I was going to enjoy busting up his skinny legs, but-'

'Shut up, brother!' Blucher snapped. 'Also, do try to calm down; you're going to do yourself an injury if you don't take care.'

'Yes, shut your silly, fat mouth, and stop clowning around, you stupid jerk!' Taj snapped, holding his unflinching nerve as Bolden sprang forward, pushing his long blue snout into Taj's face.

'Why, you, you dare to speak to me so?' Bolden snarled, saliva dribbling from his lips. 'It'll be my turn to hurt you soon, you little piece of-'

'Back off, bro!' Blucher warned. 'Give us some room, will you? If I have to tell you again you'll be the one getting hurt!'

'Yes, please behave yourself, little dragon,' said Taj in hushed tones, full of smiles. 'Listen to your big bro; he's the brains and the brawn.'

'I'm going to eat your warm liver, little boy,' snarled Bolden, who then, for no apparent reason that Taj could discern, punched his own face. 'Then, then I will gobble up your kidneys, and your heart!'

'Good for you,' said Taj, dismissing the threats with a wave of his hand.

Bolden nodded his head, and raked his talons across his chest with enough force to leave raised welts spotted with beads of bright orange blood. 'Yes, yes, good for me. Then, then I'll rip off your skinny arse in one big mouthful, yummy, yum, yum!'

'Is your brother all right in the head?' Taj asked Blucher.

Blucher ignored Taj's question, but gave Bolden a most severe glance and the younger dragon backed off and began pacing the chamber, muttering and cursing under his breath, his jaws snapping wildly at the air every few paces, as if he were trying to bite off his own snout.

'Right, I'm ready,' said Taj, eyeing Bolden warily while clenching his fingers tightly around Blucher's massive talons, then leaning back so his full weight could be used. He focussed his mind; he had seen Glitch play this same stunt on

Spuddle many years ago, but in a playful manner. He knew that this time, the trick would be far from playful. He felt Blucher gradually take up the strain, then saw him grin. He already thinks he's won, Taj realised. He dug down for latent reserves of strength and actually surprised himself. Blood pumped through his heart as he forced Blucher's talons downwards. His muscles began to throb in a way he'd never experienced before. He gritted his teeth, tightened his jaw muscles until he thought his face might explode with the effort, and applied all his power and pressure to holding down the dragon's arm, but slowly, very slowly, Blucher began lifting.

Taj, heaved back on the talons, and heard Blucher grunt with effort, the strain was beginning to tell on them both. Blucher looked slightly shocked as he heaved upwards and failed to raise his arm any further. Taj saw lilac stars dance before his eyes. I'm holding him, he thought, hardly able to believe it himself as his pulse hammered in his brain, making his whole body tremble. Taj heard Bolden screaming, and from the corner of his eye he saw him ramming his head into the wall with adrenalin fuelled excitement. Blucher reached for more leverage and Taj sensed him reassessing the situation as he held the dragon's talons with secure firmness. Blucher grunted, his eyes rolling wildly, the shame and disgust at not winning with ease written on his face as he strove to lift his arm with all the power he could muster. With perfect timing, Taj simply released the talons and watched as they sprang forward in a blur of speed, arcing upwards, the big middle one sinking deep into the sensitive end of Blucher's own snout.

The dragon jumped up and yowled as greenish-orange blood sprayed out in a gushing fountain. Taj suppressed a burst of chaotic laughter and sprang forward, rolled over the stone-table as Blucher slammed down on his behind, knocking a surprised Bolden to one side, a deep growling yell echoing round the small chamber. Peels of merriment bubbled up in Taj's throat as he burst from the room and charged along the tunnel. Muffled giggles began escaping when he replayed the scene in his mind, the look of shock on Blucher's face as his own talon split skin and dug deep into muscle, muscle crisscrossed with twitching nerves. Then he heard the roars of indignation behind him and the giggles ceased as he concentrated on his escape.

After the glow of the crystal lit chamber the tunnel was pretty dim in comparison, and Taj struggled to keep his footing as he negotiated the twists and turns. What was even more worrying was that he could hear the pounding feet of Blucher and Bolden, and they were rapidly gaining on him. He knew the tunnel split in two just ahead, the left side leading down to old servant quarters that was a dead end, right and upwards the only viable option. He just hoped that he had not miscalculated the distance and that he could outrun his pursuers and reach safety. He saw a sudden brightness flare along the walls and knew they were blowing fire. He risked a quick glance behind; Bolden was in the lead and he shot out another burst of flame, the licking tongue of heat falling short by about twenty spans.

Taj had thought to run at a conservative pace, saving energy, but they were gaining too fast, so he accelerated some more. He could barely recall how far it was to the sleep chambers, probably too far, he thought, knowing that he desperately needed help or they were going to catch him. Another blast of flame blazed around him and this time, he actually felt the heat warming the back of his neck.

'Roast his ass, bro,' he heard Blucher bellow, and fear gave Taj another burst of speed, but would it be enough?

The pack of lychyaena trotted down into the valley, sniffing along the rocky floor. The lead beast, which to Ionuin looked like a large female, had found her scent, and she knew there was definitely going to be a fight. Ionuin instinctively touched her hand to the hilt of Fyrdraca as she looked around for sizable stones, nicely rounded ones that fitted snugly into her palm and flew with the best accuracy; she could see at least ten that were suitable from where she sat. When she looked up again, the big female was staring back, her yellow eyes luminous even in the bright daylight. The rest of the pack followed their leader's gaze until Ionuin was the focus of at least twenty pairs of eyes, probably nearer thirty, she thought, as some of the pack began milling around excitedly.

Ionuin did what she always did whenever hunting, flexed her mind and cast out her thoughts. Her mental feelers spread before her like a quivering yellow net, ideal for short-range detection when prey was hiding close by. Within this net, she could sense any life in her immediate vicinity. It made a kind of shimmer along the threads, a faint blue aura glimmering around a lumpish knot; which meant life of some kind was present. Discerning what kind of life was still beyond her developing talents, although as she touched upon the minds of the lychyaena they showed up in her projected net as a pulsating, tangled, shimmer of dark blue nodules. This was different to hunting a single animal; the lychyaena showed as a hazy blur, too indistinguishable to separate into individuals, as if they were one collective mind. Probably mind-linked and working as a team, was Ionuin's first thought, as she had observed their behaviour on other occasions, but always avoided them whenever possible.

When she had been only eleven summers old and her talent for extending her mind and using mental energy was still undeveloped and raw, her father had decided he was confident enough in her ability for her to go out on daily hunting trips unaccompanied, so long as she did not stray too far beyond their valley home. On her very first outing she had encountered a small lychyaena pack wandering warily across the open plains. She had observed them from the cover of a felled cactus, the skittish animals running westward, travelling alongside the Valley of Caves until they reached Flathead Mountain. They were not far from her home valley, and finding such packs so close to the cottage was a rarity. Even though she had been armed with her bow and Fyrdraca, Ionuin remembered she had still turned and ran for home, finally losing the pack on the trail that led down to Ducat.

As she had made her escape, she had convinced herself that the pack was actually hunting her, and that they had scented her out on the plains and wanted a quick meal. Her father had laughed uproariously when she told him of her cowardice. 'Not cowardice,' he had said, 'but pure common sense. Facing a lone lychyaena is scary enough, but battling a hungry, hunting pack is sheer folly, and extremely dangerous.' Since then, she had always avoided what few there were. Now, it would seem, she found herself in a situation where the best option was to offer battle.

The leader - definitely a female, thought Ionuin - lay down, her paws stretched out before her. She howled. The sound was eerie in its lonesomeness and it threw more than a bit of a scare into Ionuin, making the hairs spring up on the nape of her neck. Hearing lychyaena from a distance was unnerving enough, having one baying just fifteen spans away was absolutely terrifying. Ionuin bit gently into her tongue, trying to generate some saliva in an attempt to conquer the dry mouth brought on by her sudden fear. She then got to her haunches and crept forward, picking out the choicest throwing stones and dropping them by her feet, never once taking her eyes from the vicious looking leader. The rest of the pack began howling. Some of the larger ones lay down beside the big female and began licking her fur, nuzzling her sides. To Ionuin, it looked like they were offering her encouragement and support in a testy situation which appeared to be turning into a standoff.

She withdrew her mental net and, focussing with her mind, cast out a gentler web of fine meshing. The web operated differently from the cruder net as it could detect emotional content, but it was much more difficult to project with any accuracy and Ionuin had hardly ever used the skill. By sensing the state of their minds, she could tell that they wanted to eat her, but many of them did not want to fight unnecessarily. It was the large males, now crowding the female leader, who were most keen on tasting her flesh, at any price. Ionuin knew that if a fight came, they would be the one's forcing the attack. The leader, surprisingly, thought Ionuin, seemed reluctant to assault the cave; it was if she sensed that there may be unknown dangers from the intended prey.

'I don't want to fight either, if I can avoid it,' Ionuin murmured, withdrawing her web, wondering if she could actually trust the information she had just gathered. She had been able to cast the hunting net since she turned ten summers, while the sensory web was relatively new to her; the idea of it had come into her mind by way of a dream not long ago. It seemed to work as she had originally envisioned, but could it be trusted? She sensed growing restlessness spreading throughout the pack, so flexed her thoughts and went on the attack, plucking at the tangled web of the pack.

They had no mental defences, not like she or her father, or Spuddle for that matter. In the centre, at the heart of the pack, she saw the biggest of the blue pulsing knots and knew this had to be the lead female. Visualising her sword, she hacked down with her mind and the big female actually yelped. 'Got you,' hissed Ionuin. She hacked down again, imagining she held three flashing versions of Fyrdraca, slicing at other big knots that flashed red when hit. The whole pack stirred, some leapt about growling their discontent while others mewled and scraped at their ears with the insides of their legs. Ionuin knew the mental assault was having the desired effect, and so moved into phase two of her plan, throwing her choice stones, sending them crashing amongst the pack. Uncertainty began to build; minor members of the pack were snapping at each other, the big female was unsure how to proceed. Ionuin grew more confident and even though the stones were not thrown hard enough to cause any serious physical damage, they were also having an effect. Lychyaena were leaping around, some chasing their tails, and when Ionuin added the mental sword strikes into the mix, the blades slicing into their unprotected minds, total chaos soon erupted.

Some of the younger lychyaena bolted, and others, spooked by the sudden unexpected departure of a third of the pack, soon followed. Ionuin cheered inwardly and gave further quick jabs with her mental blades. The female lychyaena danced on her hind-legs and howled. The web of knots hummed, changed through various colours, and Ionuin felt a severe pain in her temples as teeth seemed to gnash into her brain. They were fighting back, and although they were newcomers to mental warfare, they were many, and unexpectedly strong.

Ionuin grew desperate and began slashing wildly, severing the now pulsing glowing knots, shredding the webbing of the pack. Some of the creatures slumped over, their tongues lolling between giant yellowish teeth, while others grew brave and charged the cave entrance, leaping over the lead female who was now turning round in circles, whining and wagging her head. The first beast through the cave entrance leapt at Ionuin's throat, huge dirty claws stretched out, growling, slavering, maw gaping wide open. Ionuin spun, ducking low, and with incredible speed, brought Fyrdraca round in a forceful, slicing arc, the deep cut she delivered almost lopping off the savage creature's head as it tumbled to the floor and lay still.

The second one faltered as she slashed harder at the knots with her mind, getting lucky, hitting the one preparing to launch itself at her. It yowled its defiance, shuffled backwards, shaking its head, sending globs of spittle in all directions, then turned and ran. A third crept in low and snapped at her legs; Ionuin stabbed its nose with her sword and it also turned tail and ran. The lead female convulsed as Ionuin drove her mental blade deep into the large blue knot that was now flying apart. The big lychyaena female staggered sideways, going to her knees, howling in agony, then she leapt away, yelping and baying as the remainder of the pack followed in her wake. Ionuin sank to the floor, totally exhausted. The only drawback with fighting mentally and so energetically, was the tiredness that rushed in immediately afterwards, sapping whatever strength remained.

'Done it,' she muttered, between heaving breaths, her body already feeling weak and floppy. 'Barking banshees,' she gasped, 'that was harder than fighting in the physical world, much harder.' She slumped sideways, actually sprawling across the warm belly of the lychyaena, that sadly, she had been forced to kill. Ragged breaths puffed from her slack-jawed mouth as sleep, light and refreshing, began claiming her mind and body. Her drifting thoughts subsiding, slipping free, floating away on a sea of wavering, inky blackness.

Chapter Twenty Three

Taj ran on and on. His breathing became laboured, but he did not feel tired, he just could not run fast enough. The thump, thump, thump of the blue dragons' footsteps pounded closer and closer. They're definitely gaining, thought Taj; then the tunnel brightened and he felt his hair frazzle, and heard Bolden laugh.

'See that!' Bolden roared. 'I got him, I got Little Squeaker!'

The flames came again. Taj heard them roar and ducked, just in time, as fire arced over his head. They rounded a bend in the wall. Taj leaned into the curve, actually running a few paces along the wall, keeping his momentum going. Bolden was travelling so fast that Taj heard him crash into the rock wall with a grunt. Far up ahead, Taj knew there were lava tubes, several of them, if only he could reach them in time.

Footsteps continued to pound behind him and Taj risked a glance back at his pursuers. This time, it was Blucher in the lead, a savage grin leering across his face. Fear gave Taj more strength as, even in this dim, blue crystal light, the dragon's eyes were glowing with malicious ferocity. Taj saw Blucher's chest puff out and dodged sideways as he belched a gout of searing flame that filled the tunnel, but he was not quick enough. His hair burst into flame and his neck and ear were severely burned. He could not help it; a squeal erupted between his clenched teeth as he slapped out the fire.

Blucher bellowed laughter. 'Listen to Squeaker squeal!' he yelled.

'Bring him down, bro,' panted Bolden, 'go for his legs!'

Taj's mind tumbled into turmoil; what could he do? There was no escape. The lava tubes were getting closer with every stride, but now, he could feel hot breath on his back, never mind the fire they were belching out at regular intervals. He heard a roar and leapt high in the air as the ground he had just occupied was scorched, accompanied by guffawing dragon laughs. He knew they were playing with him, and he skipped again as flames lit up the tunnel, pain ravaging his legs as his ankles seared with sizzling heat. He closed his mind to the agony and ran all the harder; he could not give in, not now! Up ahead, light reflected from the edge of two glassy tubes, side by side, their ridged lips protruding into the tunnel. Cold air whipped across the top of his head and he realised Blucher had taken a swipe at him and only just missed, but he could not understand why did he not just fry him. Had the big oaf burnt himself out? Taj took heart from this small hope as the tubes drew closer, but how was he going to dive inside them? It would mean stopping, turning, taking aim; then they would have him.

'Roast him, bro,' he heard Bolden pant.

'No fire,' gasped Blucher.

Taj felt another whoosh of air across his shoulders as Blucher tried to grab him and missed.

'Out my way, bro,' yelled Bolden. 'I got plenty o' fire!'

The lava tubes were only ten paces away, now five. He passed them as the tunnel blazed with fire. Leaping to the left, Taj dived to the floor and rolled. He sprang onto his feet as both dragons blundered by him, almost crashing into each other. Bolden's outstretched talons whipped past his nose, as he dashed back the way they had come. Lining his body up with the wider of the two tubes, he dived.

Pain seared through his body as his legs were engulfed in a blast of heat so intense that he screamed, and kept on screaming as he slid down the slippery tube. On and on it went, Taj's wails only subsiding as he crashed out of the other end and rolled across a wide tunnel floor, smacking up against the rock wall on the opposite side. He groaned, his body wracked with agony. He thought he might have broken his ribs in the fall, his legs were raw; skin had peeled off his calves and shins from the fire and his feet were still smoking. His knees and thighs were a mass of blisters that were popping and oozing. Again, he used his mind to block out the worst of the pain, trying to remain calm and focussed. He had escaped, but at what price? Then he heard footsteps, someone was coming. He looked down the tunnel and saw that it was Nexus. Taj closed his eyes in relief and fought hard to contain his shredded emotions.

He raised his arm. 'Here, my Lord,' he said, his voice feeble and barely audible. 'I'm here, I'm hurt.' He struggled to control his trembling body as he tried to sit upright. 'It was Blucher and Bolden, they, they tried to kill me, my Lord.' He looked towards Nexus, only now the big dragon had drawn closer, he realised that his need for it to be Nexus was purely wishful thinking; this great hulking shape looming over him was not Nexus at all.

'Blucher and Bolden, you say?' Lord Bollfur muttered, scratching at his chin. 'Boisterous, high spirited boys, both of them,' he said reprovingly. 'Probably just having a bit of fun; lively sport, that's all.'

Taj opened his mouth to shout, but Bollfur clipped him on the chin with a flick of his talon and Taj rocked sideways, instantly sinking into the welcome abyss of oblivion.

Ionuin had no idea how long she had slept. Sunlight filtered into the small cave as she unstoppered her water skin and slaked her thirst. 'I think an animal crapped in my mouth during the night,' she said, wiping away water droplets, the image causing muffled giggles to escape as she gained her feet. As the memory of the lychyaena surfaced, the threat of laughter subsided. She wrinkled her nose at the smell of the poor dead beast beside her and stepped cautiously outside, scanning the canyon with her eyes and her mind, but seeing nothing of interest. Some small mole-like creatures were scurrying along tunnels just beneath the topsoil, otherwise, she was the only thing alive as far as the eye could see in both directions. Deciding to forego breakfast, she made for the shadowed side of the canyon and set off walking towards Cavesend; her intended destination, Fire Mountain.

Coming to terms with the changes that had wreaked havoc in her life over the last few days was proving difficult. She had not even had a chance to mourn her father. Truth be-known, she did not want to face such awful sadness.

'Cowardice shows its ugly face, yet again!' she said to herself, suddenly halting, taking deep breaths; her chest heaving up and down. She sniffled, snorted snot up her nose and spat it out; passing her forearm beneath her nostrils, absently wiping away a trail of thin mucus before walking on, shaking her head in disgust at herself. 'Dad, what would you think of me, hmm? What would you really think?'

In the depths of her mind, something told her that he would laugh at her for being so daft. 'It's like, it's like you're not really dead,' she muttered, her feet scuffing up small stones as she sauntered along. 'Not really.' She imagined him still alive, living back at their cottage, drinking tea, sitting in his over-stuffed chair, awaiting her return. She smiled; he would look up when he sensed her coming down the track, pieces of game attached to her belt. She would pretend she hadn't noticed his observation and try to sneak up on him, acting surprised when he leapt out and took up a defensive position, maybe grabbing her arm if she was close enough.

'Gotcha!' he would exclaim and laugh. 'Too slow girl, much too slow.'

'Dad, you're just too quick for me,' she would reply, 'much too quick,' and she would feign wonder at his canniness for an old blind man, although they both knew it was a game they were playing. She stopped in her tracks, realising he was not the first thing she had thought about on awakening. Or, perhaps it was yesterday when that first happened? She shook her head dismissively and wondered if she was losing her mind. So much had happened over the last few days that she knew she was struggling to cope. She began breathing deeply again and crouched down, her fingers reaching for some loose pebbles that she threw carelessly at a small cactus. She noticed moisture droplets on the sandy floor and felt wetness on her face.

'I, I'm crying!' she murmured, rocking forward, kneeling in the dust. She wiped away the tears, but they kept flowing. 'Dad,' she sobbed, 'what am I going to do?' She had thought that taking revenge on his killers would make things better, but it had not. Then a smile appeared as she remembered her father once telling her, revenge was for fools who knew no better. 'Not revenge,' she said, picking up another handful of pebbles. 'Retribution, that's what I took out on that scummy band of worthless wasters.' She wiped her face along her arm, sniffling as she gained her feet, letting the pebbles drop to the floor where they bounced among her drying tears. 'Retribution, that's what it was,' she told herself and began walking. Her short bout of grieving was done with, for today at least.

'Aw, has the little girlie been crying, then?' said a voice behind her.

Ionuin spun around, drawing Fyrdraca in the same fluid movement to find she was facing four men, two of whom, armed with spears and knives, she instantly recognised as Edan and Jord from the slaver caravan she had encountered a few days ago. She groaned and involuntarily stepped backwards.

Taj felt himself burning, consumed by fire. He held out his hands as flames writhed through his outstretched fingers, but strangely, it did not hurt. Then he remembered Blucher and Bolden chasing him, trying to roast him alive, and Lord Bollfur actually hitting him. A scream became trapped in his throat, straining for release as his eyes sprang open. He was covered with animal skins and resting on a stone bench in a dimly lit chamber, pale blue light casting grotesque shadows around the room. Gasping for breath, he wiped his hand across his forehead, which was drenched in sweat.

'Ah, awake at last,' said a voice behind him.

Taj twisted his head around to see Lord Bollfur sitting on a great wooden chair made from the long dead trunks of large trees. 'You!' he hissed.

'Yes, me!' said Bollfur, excitement dancing in his eyes. 'It's been a wonderful experience, Taj. Sat here, watching you sleep. Fascinating really, and what I have witnessed has made me very curious, but the most curious aspect of it all is the fact that I doubt you have any idea about yourself, do you, Taj?'

Taj sat up. He expected to hurt all over, especially his legs, but he felt no pain, apart from a faint tingling in his jaw that he nursed with the palm of his hand. 'You, you struck me! You, you fat blue freak!'

'Oh, Taj, name calling is so juvenile,' said Bollfur, grinning. 'And yes, I did hit you, but for your own good, dear boy. You see, you were verging on delirium, spouting all sorts of nonsense! Most of it was improbable rubbish about my wonderful sons.'

Taj felt his anger rising. 'It is not rubbish, Bollfur! Your sons, the gruesome-twosome, were hunting me, and when they found me, inadvertently I might add, they chased me down, burned me, hurt me, and also tried to strike me!'

'Yes, well, when you put it like that, it does sound pretty bad,' Bollfur admitted.

'Pretty bad!' exclaimed Taj. 'It's more than 'pretty bloody bad' it's an outrage!'

'Be quiet, Taj,' Bollfur snarled, his voice filled with menace, 'I am sure my boys, gruesome or not, meant no real harm and neither did I, Taj. You must know that your welfare is our concern too.'

Taj was shocked at the outright duplicity. 'I'm, I'm going to tell Nexus about this; all of this, this charade!'

Bollfur leaned forward, pushing his nose into Taj's face. 'Really? What exactly will you tell him? Surely not the ludicrous, unrepeatable piffling drivel you were spouting earlier about my boys? If so, I suppose I would argue that you had become temporarily unhinged, perhaps through fear of the Dark Dragon.'

Taj felt suddenly wrong-footed at the mention of the Dark Dragon.

'Yes,' continued Bollfur, 'you don't like the Dark Dragon, do you, Taj? Don't even like hearing the name, do you? Scares you, doesn't it? I would simply claim that thoughts of the Dark Dragon had clearly frightened you witless, and my boys and I found you whimpering and alone.'

'Then, that would mean you are a liar!' hissed Taj, finding some courage.

'Am I a liar? Deary me,' said Bollfur, looking hurt. 'That will never do, *Lord Bollfur the liar*, how awful, and what a terrible accusation! As for striking you, I gave you a little clip to aid your rest, nothing more. Anyway, it matters not; none of what you claim can ever be proven.'

Taj gasped. 'Are you mad? Of course I can prove it!'

Bollfur flapped one great taloned foreleg at Taj. 'How can you prove it when you were never really hurt?'

Taj, still covered with furs, swung his legs to the floor. 'Never really hurt? What absolute nonsense!' he yelled. 'Of course I can prove that what I say is true, as you well know you, you glutinous, galumphing oaf!'

Bollfur clicked his tongue. 'Name calling again, Taj. It does not become you, you know. Now, don't let me have to warn you again, little boy!'

With an angry flourish, Taj yanked away the animal skin that was covering him and pointed to his legs. 'You call this nonsense, eh?' he yelled, his frustration rising as he locked stares with Bollfur. He pointed to his legs. 'If this is not proof, then I am an idiot!' His jaw dropped as he glanced down and saw there was no actual damage to his legs: none whatsoever. 'But, that cannot be right! I was, burned and, and what the . . . ?'

Bollfur reached over and patted Taj's legs. 'Something wrong, idiot? Really, Taj; to declare that you are an idiot is a bit harsh, even by your low standards. Although, I don't want to disagree or argue, you must know yourself best, I suppose.'

Taj was completely dumfounded, he did not understand, could not understand. It was not a dream, not even a vivid one, it had all happened, it had! So . . . where was the damage? 'I, I was badly injured, badly burned and the pain was incredible! I was, I was hurting so much,' he said, vividly recalling his recent agony. Tears pricked at the corners of his eyes. 'It, it can't be nonsense, it just can't be.'

'Yes, it can,' Bollfur said, patronizingly. 'The exact same stuff and nonsense you were complaining of earlier. Wailing like a baby when I found you, silly boy. I don't know what has gotten into you, but for what it's worth, I don't think you're losing your mind, not quite.'

Taj placed his hands on his temples, trying to remember. 'It did happen, it did!'

'You're mistaken, that's all,' Bollfur said, placatingly. 'Happens to the best of us. Perhaps you fell asleep in the tunnel and had one of your bad dreams? Or, as you are an idiot, maybe you tried to walk through a solid rock wall? Is that it, Taj, did you try to walk through solid rock?'

Taj ignored Bollfur's taunts and gingerly felt his neck, his ear, his hair; all perfectly all right and pain free, but the area of hair he thought had been burned was a little shorter than the rest of his dark wavy locks. 'I, I don't understand,' he mumbled, rubbing his hands over his legs. They looked fine, if a little blotchy, it was hard to tell if there had ever been anything wrong. He stood, swayed a little, before sitting down again.

'Tell me, Taj,' asked Bollfur, 'where have you been since leaving Lord Nexus yesterday, hmm?'

'Yesterday? You mean . . . just how long have I been here, Bollfur?'

'Not important,' replied Bollfur. 'Please answer my question, and do respect my correct style and title or I will have to correct you, and that could prove very unpleasant for one of us.'

131

'Don't you dare threaten me, Bollfur, and where I have been is none of your business,' said Taj forcing defiance into his voice. 'I only answer to my master and that is not you, *Bollfur,* and never will be.'

Bollfur smiled. 'Now, now, let's not fight.' He flicked out his talons and Taj lurched backwards. Lord Bollfur's attempted swipe missed his nose by a whisker. 'Yes,' said Bollfur, his eyes flaring a deep penetrating blue. 'Remember what happened in the tunnel, Taj. It could happen again, you know, only with more severity. Now, I want you to do us both a favour and be cooperative by answering all my questions, little boy.'

Taj shrank back against the wall of the chamber as Lord Bollfur leaned over him, the large dragon's teeth glistening behind grinning lips. He knew he was in trouble, and he had no idea how he was going to escape.

Chapter Twenty Four

'You two!' Ionuin hissed, cuffing tears from her face. Edan had his leg heavily bandaged, and Jord sported what appeared to be a handkerchief strapped around his wrist.

'Oh, she remembers us, young Jord,' said Edan, a fake smile stretched across his face. 'Well, bless my soul, we must have made a worthy impression upon the wee lassie.'

Jord shifted apprehensively from foot to foot. 'We should not have come here,' he said, looking around fearfully. 'She be more trouble than she's worth.'

'Oh, I dunno, Jord, me boy,' said the bigger of the other two men. He was easily a head taller than Edan, who was a big man. 'She looks to be a fine catch to me, so she does. More than fine; pretty face, nice shape, what's not to like?'

'She is dangerous,' Jord murmured. 'I can feel the threat coming off her in waves.'

Thom chortled. 'I tell you what I feel, it is almost inconceivable that bone and flesh could be wrought like that and yet I don't get to enjoy it. I imagine she will be very feisty.'

'Feisty for sure,' said Edan, tapping his knife against the shaft of his spear. 'She be very feisty indeed, Thom.'

'Oh, I like feisty, so I do,' said the one called Thom, who was dressed in a long plain white robe which failed to hide his ample gut. 'The feistier the better,' he said, slamming the head of a spiked club onto the sandy floor. 'It all adds to the pleasure mix.'

'Forget feisty and pleasure, I think we should leave her be,' said Jord, glancing around. 'I don't like it here, in this valley. It's teeming with ghosts. My Mama says so, and she should know, she sees dead people all the time.'

'Of course your mama sees dead people!' Edan snapped. 'She's the carnival embalmer, you dolt!'

'Other dead people, the un-dead, my mama knows strange things,' Jord protested.

'Your Mama knows nothing,' said the fourth man, who looked to be the leader. He was the oldest of the group by far, and was dressed in fine silk robes. 'She's a superstitious old crone, Jord, and you know she talks rubbish. Now this little baby,' he said, uncoiling a whip from a hook on his belt as he stepped before the other three men. 'Why, she talks the most sense I have ever known.' He held his open palm towards Ionuin, walking forward until he was only ten paces away, then he halted.

'My name is Deck, my dear, and I have heard all about you. I have journeyed across the wastes to make your acquaintance. We almost gave up on you, but Edan insisted we had to be fairly close.'

'I knew she wouldn't be far away,' said Edan, looking pleased with himself.

'Little fool left a trail a babe could follow,' added Thom.

Ionuin did not reply; she knew they were both right. While tracking her father's murderers, she had never seriously considered that others might be tracking her. There had been moments when she had suspected that others were actually on her back-trail, but had offhandedly dismissed such a notion. She looked at the outstretched hand Deck proffered and thought of dashing forward and chopping it off at the wrist, but she would just be venting her frustration at having been caught so easily.

She cleared her throat. 'If you have heard all about me, Deck, then you'll know I'm not to be messed with,' she said, looking Deck straight in the eye. Even though he was greying at the temples, he was not an unattractive man; rugged, muscular, but there was a hint of slyness lurking behind his eyes that warned of danger.

Deck laughed and looked around to his three companions before turning back and meeting her gaze. 'What I heard, young lady, is that you can fight, but cannot kill, it takes you all your time to wound.'

'Do not kill, if you need only maim, do not maim, if you need only wound,' said Ionuin, repeating the words of her father.

Deck laughed again. 'Oh wise words indeed, very erudite, very . . . philosophical. Hmm, brains as well as beauty, an appealing combination not lost on one such as I, my dear.'

Ionuin hated the term, *my dear*, and did not reply, but she noticed a small metal star affixed to the end of the whip that Deck was slapping against his leg. A star that could do a lot of damage, thought Ionuin, if it connected with speed and struck bare flesh.

'Listen up now, Missy,' said Deck, his boots kicking at loose stones. 'There is no need for any unpleasantness. Why don't you just slip that fancy blade back in its scabbard and come with us, peacefully, eh? Nobody will harm you. Such a pretty little thing, I might even take you to wife myself.'

Thom groaned loudly, drawing a harsh stare from Deck.

'Thom has other plans,' Ionuin said, nodding at the big man, offering him a generous smile, wondering if she could split him apart from the others. 'Are you big all over, Thom?' she asked, pouting slightly, a playful teasing look flitting across her face, as bright as summer lightning in a clear sky.

'Thom will do as I say,' Deck said, not even raising his voice. 'My other three wives are getting on a little now and some young blood around the camp would wake them up a mite, so, what do you say, girl?'

Disappointingly, Thom had not reacted, so Ionuin continued to look the group over, assessing their strengths, searching for weaknesses. They outnumbered her four to one, but Jord was not up for the fight and Edan was barely capable. Big, fat Thom bothered her, but not too much. He would not want to kill her, not while there was any hope of her showing a voluntary interest in him, no matter how vague. Deck, however, accompanied by his oiled whip with its menacing metal star, was another prospect entirely. She reasoned that Deck had deliberately walked to within striking distance with his weapon, and she also reasoned that he would know how to use it to maximum effect. Her future freedom was at stake,

134

so even though the odds were stacked against her, there was definitely going to be unpleasantness. She wished Spuddle were still with her; that would alter things radically. The idea of these four facing a fire-breathing dragon brought a fleeting smile to her lips.

'Something funny?' Edan asked, stepping up beside Deck.

'Nothing a lunking dunder-head like you would find amusing, Edan,' Ionuin replied, moving slightly to the right with careful, slow steps so that the whip would be impeded by Edan if Deck decided to suddenly lash out.

Deck sighed. 'Well, what is it to be, girl? We don't have all day, so are you coming with us peaceably, or do we have to get a little rough, hmm?'

Ionuin spat on the floor. 'Go boil your skinny-arse, Deck, that's what I say, and I give you fair warning, things have changed since I met your two friends. You might find that killing is not a problem for me anymore. Not a problem at all.'

'She's bluffing,' said Edan, coming forward, going into a crouch. 'Come on, why are we waiting? There are four of us, we're fully armed, let's take her down!'

Ionuin pretended to ignore Edan and walked casually to the right, putting Deck further away from her. Edan continued forward and Thom also made a move, circling to his left, trying to trap her in an attempted pincer movement. Jord simply stood by Deck, looking ready to wet himself while Deck observed his two men.

Ionuin stopped suddenly and squared up to Edan. 'I told, you, didn't I? Next time we meet, it would be your throat I'd slice open.'

'You don't have what it takes, wench!' Edan snarled. 'I owe you, I owe you good and I'm gonna make you pay, you lit-'

Ionuin leapt forward, releasing a small cry, whirling Fyrdraca underarm with alarming speed, slipping the blade neatly inside Edan's guard so the tip slid deeply into his solar plexus. Edan looked stunned as his jaw opened wide, but no scream came out as Ionuin whipped her boot-knife across his wind-pipe, striking hard and fast. Edan released a pitiful croak as his legs gave out and he dropped on his face.

Ionuin sensed, rather than saw, Thom looming up behind her, and dropped to her haunches. Rolling onto her back, she punched upward with both feet, hitting the big man in his lower belly, knocking him backwards where he lost his footing and crashed to the floor. As she scrambled to her feet she saw Deck was making his move, uncoiling his whip, while Jord remained motionless.

Thom moved surprisingly quick for a big man who had just had the wind knocked from him, and was already on his knees and raising his spiked club. Ionuin spun on one heel, Fyrdraca outstretched as it zipped through the air, slicing into the side of his neck, decapitating him in an instant, his head spinning end over end as it arced away in a fountain of blood.

Ionuin yelped as she felt pain in her shoulder and heard a crack splitting the air. She touched her palm to where agony rioted in her flesh, and it came away sticky with blood as she whirled to see Deck levering back his arm to lash her again. The whip was so fast she never saw it coming, and Fyrdraca dropped from her grasp as she felt more pain shoot through her hand. She shook her fingers to see drops of blood dripping to the floor.

'At her, Jord!' Deck snapped as he pulled the whip back for another strike.

'Not me,' said Jord, backing away. 'I told you I didn't want to come. I told you this is a bad place. She's a gwrack, look what she done to Edan and Thom!'

Deck lashed at her again but Ionuin danced beyond range, the metal star flashing before her eyes.

Deck growled and grabbed Jord by the arm and pushed him forward. 'Stop being such a pussy, Jord. She's unarmed isn't she? Go get her, boy, go on!'

'She has a knife!' Jord protested, still coming forward. 'Whip her knife hand, Deck, then I might stand a chance.'

Deck mumbled something under his breath as he charged past Jord, his whip arm flicking back, then forth. Ionuin half guessed where he was aiming and again danced out of range, only this time she lined up Deck and hurled the knife with all the force she could muster.

Deck stopped still. Dropping the whip, his hands flew to his throat where blood bubbled and gurgled around the hilt of the knife as he tried to speak.

Jord stepped in front of him. 'I told you d-didn't I, Deck? I, I w-w-warned you, so I did.'

Deck did not reply. His eyes rolled to the top of his head as he fell over backwards, sending up sprays of sand when he crashed to the floor.

Ionuin charged forward, snatching Fyrdraca off the ground with the intention of splitting Jord in two, but the boy threw down his weapons and dropped to his knees, his hands clasped before him as if praying.

'Please, please, d-don't kill me,' he pleaded; his eyes wide with fear. 'I would never have hurt you, truly! I didn't even want to come, but they made me. They said I'd become a man, I was forced, can't you understand? I had no choice, I had to come.'

'There are always choices,' said Ionuin, stooping and yanking her knife from the throat of Deck. She wiped the blade clean on his silk robes before slipping it into the sheath on the side of her boot, never taking her eyes off Jord.

'I, I d-don't even know your name,' said Jord. 'I, I admire you so much, and-'

Ionuin placed the tip of her sword on Jord's chin, instantly silencing him. 'You what? You admire me? What kind of crazy talk is that? Only moments ago you were part of a gang who would have snatched away my freedom. You would have probably used and abused me along with the others, so don't go talking crap about admiration, or I'll make your death slow and painful, Jord!'

'I'm, I'm, s-sorry,' cried Jord. 'So sorry, p-please, I beg for mercy, please!' he broke down, his chest heaving with sobs, his chin trembling so much that he cut himself on Fyrdraca's sharpened tip.

Ionuin pulled her blade back to see a thin red split in his skin from lower lip to the point of his chin. He looked pathetic, kneeling there, crying like a baby, pleading for his life, but she knew she would let him live. She was a killer, but not a murderer.

'I am called Ionuin,' she said, slamming Fyrdraca into its scabbard, taking a deep breath, calming her jangling nerves. She instinctively licked her thumb and pressed it to the accidental wound on Jord's chin, and was surprised to see it stop bleeding almost instantly, leaving behind an indented groove. 'How strange,' she murmured.

'S-strange?' Jord repeated, haltingly, his eyes narrowed in puzzlement.

Ionuin shook her head dismissively. 'Nothing,' she mumbled as she watched Jord's skin knit together, forming a shallow cleft, pink and shiny. As far as strangeness went, this hardly bore any comparison to recent events.

Jord gulped noisily, seemingly unaware of the injury to his chin or the sudden healing. 'Y-yes, yes I am strange. I always have been, but my moth-'

'Oh be quiet, you dull-witted moron,' snapped Ionuin, her impatience getting the better of her. 'Today, I am merciful, but don't test me or - never mind, just go, will you?'

'Oh, yes, yes I will go,' said Jord, his eyes wide with disbelief. 'Er, what is your name again?'

'Ionuin!' snapped Ionuin, her fists clenching and unclenching. 'Now please, you must leave before I do something I might regret. Go on! Get out of my sight!'

Jord wiped his tears away. 'I-on-u-in,' he murmured slowly under his breath. 'Ionuin, I shall sing your name to the heavens, every single night, for the rest of my life. I shall tell all who I meet that you are the greatest swordswoman that ever lived. I shall-'

'For the last time, just go!' Ionuin snapped, already tired of him, 'or I might change my mind and trust me, you won't like me at all if that happens.'

'Oh, yes, y-yes I do trust you,' Jord blurted out, his voice wheedling and croaky.

Ionuin sighed with exasperation. 'And one more thing, get clear of this valley. Dragons roam hereabouts, they might not be so merciful, or patient.'

'D-dragons?' Jord gasped, getting to his feet and staggering backwards.

Ionuin sensed sudden horror pour from Jord in an emotional flood. 'Well, one dragon, really, one I happen to know on a personal level,' she said, forcing an air of nonchalance into her voice. 'Thing is, I'm on my way to Fire Mountain, where there is one dragon. There may be more; dragons are said to live inside Fire Mountain and for what it's worth, Jord, I fully expect the dragon to be following me, not you.'

Jord was now pacing slowly backwards, looking around nervously. 'A d-dragon? Here in this valley? Unreal, truly unreal and, and, you already know one personally, and you're going to F-Fire Mountain to look for more?'

Ionuin picked up Jord's discarded spear and hefted it in her hands, testing its balance. 'Why not? I have no family, no parents to care about what happens to me and I've always been curious about Fire Mountain. Some say it is the home of the Gods, did you know that, Jord?'

137

Jord shook his head, still walking backwards; almost stumbling over Thom's bloated body. 'No, no I didn't. I, I'll be going now, I-on-u-in. I, I meant what I said about singing your praises.'

'Just go,' said Ionuin, as she continued to pick over the dead men, looking for anything useful. When she looked up, Jord was scrabbling along an animal trail that curved up the side of the valley. She hoped she had not made a mistake allowing him to live, but reasoned that she had not really had a choice in the matter once he crumbled before her. Her own words to Jord, that there are always choices, echoed back to her.

She flicked a fly away from the wound on her shoulder, which was already healing, and stabbed Jord's spear into the ground. It was going to be a hot day, again, she mused, and she hardly needed to be carrying extra weight. She heard Jord shouting something about worshipping as she walked away from the carnage she had wrought. She did not glance back, but simply waved her hand at him dismissively. She considered him one of life's many fools; he would be lucky if he reached full adulthood. The mercy she had shown was probably only a temporary reprieve for him.

The remainder of the morning passed without incident and as the day wore on, the canyon began changing shape, flattening out slightly. The walls, which had towered high above, diminished as the floor rose, and in the distance, she saw something very unusual. At first she had no idea what it could be, but as she drew near, she realised what it was, but could not believe what she was actually seeing.

'No, no, it can't be,' she murmured. For the longest time she simply stood and stared, unable to comprehend what lay before her. She squinted, shook her head, but nothing changed. This was no mirage, and the enormity of the implications of her discovery were utterly staggering.

Chapter Twenty Five

'It, it can't be! It's . . . just not possible!' Ionuin exclaimed, although her tired eyes told her otherwise. She began to laugh, then to cry as she stumbled forward, before halting in her tracks, checking out her immediate surroundings. 'This, this is crazy!' she mouthed, her hands resting on her head as she moved closer to the giant structure stretching across the canyon floor. It looked so imperial and imposing, dominating the landscape. A huge arc; the biggest skeleton Ionuin had ever seen. It was at least ten times bigger than Spuddle, perhaps even twenty times bigger. The girth of its spinal column was thicker than the thickest tree. Not that Ionuin had seen that many trees. Apart from the skinny pines around the cottage she had called home; she had only come across the odd one or two. Her father had claimed that in aeons past, trees had covered most of the land. She hadn't believed him, of course. Such a notion seemed ridiculous when their accessible surroundings comprised of rocks and barren red deserts with scatterings of meagre plant life. Now, as she observed the massive ribs curving away from the spine, forming a great arched tunnel through which she could walk, she knew she had been wrong about many things. She travelled the length of the weathered bones, looking in wonderment at the spectacle of what could only be the remains of a dead dragon.

At last, she arrived at the skull. She could have stood inside what would have been a monstrous head and gazed out through eye sockets that were bigger than her face, but she didn't. Instead, out of some deep respect that she could not fathom, she walked around the broken cranium. The jawbones were long, but almost all the teeth had been stripped out. Here and there, a few broken stumps jutted precariously upwards in apparent defiance.

Tentatively, Ionuin reached out and touched the skull. It felt smooth and unbelievably, it seemed to vibrate beneath her touch. Surely she was imagining things? She quickly removed her hand, took a deep breath then slowly, using great care, placed her sensitive fingertips on the skull and concentrated. She knew then that she had not imagined it, there were definite vibrations, and they seemed to be calling to her. How was this even possible?

She felt overwhelmed with curiosity at the slight tremors, and tuned her mind to the odd, trembling sensation. The vibrations suddenly pulsed through her mind in a powerful rush, allowing her to sense a flood of emotions. Sadness prevailed. She picked up underlying nuances of trepidation towards impending certain doom, and there was something else; the same feelings that she sensed in Spuddle, but could not interpret. The vibrations ceased and Ionuin broke contact. It was too much of a coincidence that she should find Spuddle and in the very same canyon - admittedly some distance away - discover the skeleton of what must have once been a magnificent dragon.

Ionuin envisioned how this spectacular creature would have looked, in the flesh. How it would have commanded the respect of all in its presence. The sheer majesty of such a beast left her feeling in awe of a power greater than herself. A supreme power that ruled all and yet, this once incredible beast had met its end here, in this canyon. A canyon that her father had claimed stretched half way round the world, from the great Fire Mountain to the salt plains across the once humid lands in the far South.

When she was still only a little girl, Ionuin had once seen Fire Mountain from a fairly close distance. It had been a long journey over sparse grasslands to the west of this great chasm in which she now stood. It wasn't much of a spectacle, as far as she was concerned, just a big pile of rock reaching into the pale, pink sky. It had three smaller sisters at its shoulders, but compared to Fire Mountain, they were nothing. She could remember asking, 'where was the fire?' Her father had told her that it had died when the heavens brightened, but dragons lived there still. He had claimed that at night, they could still be seen, circling Fire Mountain, looking for people to eat. The thought of real dragons had excited rather than frightened her and this apparently fearless attitude pleased her father. He told her that her lack of fear showed great strength of character, and this was very good, as life was tough and only the strongest ever survive.

Stepping away from the Cathedral of bones, she found other bones. The bones of men: lots and lots of them. She had become so engrossed in the skeleton of the dragon that they had gone unnoticed, until now. Some were broken and scattered. Others appeared to be blackened and charred as if consumed by great heat. Lots had their heads missing, and the ground was littered with broken weapons of all descriptions.

'A battle,' murmured Ionuin, 'between men and a great dragon.' She continued looking around, trying to count the skulls. 'There must have been an army of men,' she concluded. She realised it would have taken an army of men to subdue such an incredible beast. She never imagined so many people existed, but here was the evidence all around her. Memories of her father's tales again reared up and flashed across her thoughts. He had often spoken of scattered colonies living all over this dry, harsh world, communities of survivors who stuck together and supported each other. Those people were supposedly very different from the brigands and murderers they usually encountered this far north. But what did it mean? And how did Spuddle fit into all this? Was he the last survivor of a dying dragon race, hunted and persecuted by men?

A long drawn out screech, high pitched and keening, echoed through the air, jolting Ionuin out of her thoughts and back to full awareness. She looked upwards, and there, in the far distance, silhouetted against the sun, something sailed majestically across the sky. At the sight of the flying creature, fear, cold and sickening, slithered into the pit of her stomach. At last, the horror that haunted her dreams was finally coming for her. The Dark Dragon was finally showing itself, and Ionuin had to consciously control the trembling in her legs to stop her knees from knocking.

'Not so much *dying race* as *thriving race*,' she murmured, observing the dragon drawing ever closer as she searched for somewhere to hide.

140

Taj drew his knees under his chin as Bollfur got to his feet. 'I will have my answers, Little Squeaker. I know you are working for Nexus, I also know you are not who you think you are.'

'Not who I think I am? Of course I am,' countered Taj. 'Don't be daft! How can I not be? Now you're been ridiculous, Bollfur.'

'Am I?' said Bollfur. 'Um, so, you can explain your miraculous healing then, can you?'

Taj remained silent, now fully aware that he had not dreamt his recent encounter with Bolden and Blucher after all. He had been half-roasted by Bollfur's sons, but where was the evidence? Why was he now perfectly healthy? Very hungry too, he thought, his head swimming and his mouth watering at the thought of food. Bollfur was also correct in his assumptions; there was indeed something going on about which he knew nothing.

'I, I don't know what you mean,' Taj said, defiantly, trying to fathom what was happening. His remarkable healing was a mystery that he could not explain, but he knew who could and who would. Once he got out of this stinking, morbid chamber, he was going to demand answers from Nexus.

'I know what you are thinking, Little Squeaker,' said Bollfur, 'but you're not going anywhere. I do believe, though, that you have absolutely no idea why you have healed while you slept, have you?'

Taj did not reply. He refused to give Bollfur any satisfaction. Instead, he tried to work things out for himself. He needed to find a way to escape from the chamber; he would have no real answers and no way of finding the truth while he was held against his will.

'Hmm, no idea, have you? I thought not,' said Bollfur, sitting down beside him, invading his personal space. 'You should have seen it, Taj! The dead skin just flaked away! New skin formed in mere moments, knitting together, so neat and tidy, that there was barely any evidence of any injury at all. I watched as I carried you, and by the time I got you into my chamber, even your severely burned ear and neck were recovering nicely. I couldn't believe it myself, but there was no denying it; you are more than what you seem, Taj, much more. Now, please tell me,' he leaned in close and hissed in Taj's ear, 'where have you been?'

Taj shuffled away, but Bollfur wrapped his arm around his neck and began squeezing. Taj tried desperately to fight him off, but Bollfur was far too strong. 'No, no, no!' protested Taj. 'I won't tell you anything, you stinky-breath, crap-gorging, bulbous fool!'

'Let me hug you, Taj,' said Bollfur, squeezing even tighter. 'Everyone enjoys a hug, so let me hug you, until you feel you can tell me all your secrets, Little Squeaker.'

Ionuin wondered if this encounter would at last bring her death. She did not want to die, even though she had lost everything, she knew that death was never the answer. She watched closely as the flying creature drew ever closer, recalling how her father had once told her one of his favourite sayings, the words of a

141

famous warrior from ages past. 'If Death should smile at you, be unafraid, and smile in return. He may become curious and let you live a little longer.' Ionuin had forgotten the warrior's name and had never really understood this advice, until now. Wanting to live, not a little longer, but much longer, through mounting fear and with some reluctance, she smiled.

The Dark Dragon, if that's what it was, banked, dropped low and coasted towards her. Ionuin's forced smile fell of her face as she squealed under her breath and ran back to the great skeleton. It could just be Spuddle, she reasoned, but Spuddle had changed. Would he do her any harm? Would he remember how she had helped him? Or how he had helped her? Or was Spuddle himself actually the Dark Dragon?

'Impossible!' she whispered, scrambling over bones. Such a thing was unthinkable. Without a doubt, Spuddle had saved her from the mutant bear, but that was before the significant changes in his appearance had occurred. Instead of the abused, bumbling, relatively harmless creature she had first encountered, Spuddle was now a ferocious, fire-breathing winged fighter with attitude.

Standing between the giant arched rib-bones she watched the flying creature cross the canyon and heard it screech. It was a dragon all right, but it wasn't the Dark Dragon, of this she was certain, and neither was it Spuddle. This new beast was easily twice the size of Spuddle, and Ionuin could see its body was flame red. What's more, its wings seemed to be coated with a shining yellow metal in some places. Or perhaps that was that just the sun's reflection, she thought. To her acute alarm, she found that she was actually admiring the beast. It circled around, this time coming in lower, screeching again, the high pitched piercing sound making Ionuin clap her hands over her ears.

'Freaking pond-scum for dinner,' she hissed as the dragon - for she could now see clearly that it was unmistakably a dragon - continued circling. Only now, it was directly overhead. It cannot have seen me, Ionuin thought, casually drawing her sword. No way can I be seen, not hidden amongst these bones, surely?

The dragon veered away, slowed its circling to a gentle hover, before descending to the canyon floor, landing where Ionuin had stood only moments before. It sniffed the ground and snorted, then roared, shooting out billowing flames that licked the canyon walls, instantly firing dry scrub-brush and splitting ancient rocks. Ionuin, her heart pounding, terror coursing through her veins, stealthily backed away, slipping from between the ribs and taking shelter amongst a few scattered boulders against the east side of the canyon. Thinking she was undetected and safe, she released her breath slowly. She then knew instantly that she had thought wrong, as the alert red dragon glanced towards her.

'Oh, skippering-scallywags!' she murmured as the dragon flapped its leathery looking wings, becoming airborne, momentarily hovering, the movement forming swirling dust-clouds on the canyon floor. 'Fight or flee,' she whispered, instinctively choosing flight, but also wondering to where she could actually flee.

The dragon roared, startling Ionuin, making her gulp, almost swallowing her tongue. Her mind raced in desperation as the scaly monster glided towards her then swooped over the lifeless skeleton, landing on the boulders behind which she was sheltering. Ionuin screamed as the dragon peered down at her, its bulging yellow eyes, slit through with crimson pupils, pulsing malevolently. She jabbed upwards with Fyrdraca, but the dragon easily dodged the sword strikes. Her father once claimed to have killed a dragon. Looking at this monstrous beast peering at her from what appeared to be hungry eyes, she wondered how such a thing could ever be possible.

She cast out her thoughts, trying to attack mentally, but her mind assault rebounded and rocked the inside of her own head, making her feel dizzy and nauseous. Changing tack, fighting for balance and trying not to stagger, she once again thrust the blade upwards, and this time the dragon snapped its jaws, catching Fyrdraca. Ionuin yanked back hard, drawing the blade between clenched teeth with an ear-piercing squeal. The dragon snapped again, missing the top of Ionuin's head by a finger's breadth.

'Yow-ee!' yelled Ionuin, suddenly becoming enveloped by hot breath, ducking as the dragon lunged again, managing to roll clear of the rocks in which she had initially sought cover. This was very bad, she thought, her mind a whirling cacophony of indecision, trying to fathom the dreadful situation from which escape seemed to be the only route to survival. Fear, real fear, caused a rush of adrenaline to surge through her limbs, giving strength to her legs as she leapt to her feet, heading for the canyon wall and the welcome safety of the black-eyed caves. At least I'll have some cover if I can scramble inside a cave, she thought, her legs throbbing as she pounded between rocks and cacti, gaining speed with every stride.

With two thirds of the distance covered, she began to believe in herself again. All her life she had felt she was different, strong, invincible, almost. This feeling now flooded through her, providing much needed energy as her legs moved rhythmically; she was almost there. The first Ionuin knew of the dragon's pursuit was when she fell into shadow from the beating wings flapping above her head. She glanced around mid-stride, and raised her sword, her eyes wide with terror as a huge talon flicked at her wrist, sending sharp pains rioting down her arm and Fyrdraca clattering away to the rock-strewn canyon floor.

Ionuin uttered a frightened shriek as her legs became tangled. She lost her balance and tumbled, but never hit the ground. With one huge gulp the dragon snatched her up in its gnashing jaws and soared high into the air. As the dust settled, the only sign that Ionuin had ever been there at all were a few scuffmarks in the red dirt and Fyrdraca, twinkling in the dying rays of the setting sun.

Chapter Twenty Six

'You can squeeze all you like, Bollfur, I won't tell you anything!' Taj yelped.

'I am *Lord Bollfur* to the likes of you, Little Squeaker. Now, don't worry your silly little head, for in a moment, I will have connected my mind to yours and then I will know everything.'

'Not if I can stop you,' Taj protested, as he tried to break free of Bollfur's grip.

Bollfur growled loudly. 'Do stop this incessant wriggling, you fecking little fool, or I will be forced to break something.'

Struggling to breathe, Taj coughed. 'Break what you like, you twisted-turd, I won't tell you anything! I'll die first.'

'Persistent, personal and obnoxiously rude to the very last, eh? No need to die though, Taj. Not just yet, anyway; ah, I have you.' He relaxed his grip on Taj's throat, but Taj did not move; he sat, straining as he felt Bollfur's thoughts flickering through his head, replaying events in fast motion and more worryingly, in reverse.

'No! No, don't!' Taj muttered, his arms flapping around uselessly as he tried to think coherently, erecting mental walls around his mind. 'You cannot look inside my head, Bollfur, you, you cannot! You will not!' He flexed his mind, trying to force Bollfur from his thoughts, trying to erect formidable barriers.

'Hah! Trying to fight me, Taj? I do appreciate a challenge' said Bollfur, growling deeply. 'Well, foggy-brained fool, don't say I did not warn you!'

'Whatever,' Taj replied, strengthening the walls around his mind, then yelping as a mental punch sent sparks of light zigzagging through his skull. His hastily erected walls cracked and shattered as if they were made of crystal.

'Hah, how'd you like that, Squeaker?' Bollfur yelled in triumph, pushing his thoughts through Taj's head.

'No, no, no, you bed-pressing bell-end!' Taj wailed as his struggles were swept aside by the onslaught of Bollfur's mental attack.

'Now, Squeaker, let's see what we have. Oh yes, wonderful, I see everything now; how you hopped and dodged, but my boys are good with flame, don't you agree? That had to hurt, just a little bit, but, ooh, you like those lava tubes don't you, Little Squeaker? What's this? Arm-wrestling? Nasty trick you played on Blucher there. Let us go further back, shall we? Ah, and where were you before that?'

I must do something, thought Taj, reeling as if in a mental tailspin while Bollfur's thoughts skipped over his efforts at defence faster than he could get them in place. I need a diversion, a telling distraction.

The encounter with the dragon had forced Ionuin into a frenzied panic. She thought she had been eaten and then had somehow escaped, but how could this be? Night had fallen and she didn't care how it could be, she only wanted to feel safe again. She could hear dragons roaring, and ran towards the only visible light

144

on this cold, windswept night. The only thought in her frightened head: escape from the certain death that stalked her.

The flickering firelight she had seen from a distance seemed to beckon to her. Fighting for breath, weak with exhaustion, Ionuin drew close to what looked like a huge stone flanked circle. The standing stones, which looked weathered and ancient, were almost four times her height and linked by impressive stone lintels. Ionuin stepped between the stones and stiffened. The exposed skin on her hands and face puckered into tiny goose-pimples as an icy chill enveloped her. She knew she had made a mistake: a big one!

On approaching this place, she had thought it might provide refuge, sanctuary from the ravenous beast hunting her. She now realised that instead of fleeing from the dragon, she had inadvertently stumbled into its lair. As numbness spread over her trembling body, alien thoughts infiltrated her mind, thoughts of the beast: dragon thoughts. She tried to block the insistent probing; the mental pressure overwhelming, latching onto her quaking mind with strong determination. Dark burning eyes scythed into her vulnerable soul, forcing a small gasp from her as snake-like tendrils slithered into her thoughts.

Her acute senses understood that this power was so incredibly devastating, it would crush all opposition should it ever be unleashed in its entirety. She had to escape, had to break free from this unbearably suffocating force. Her first instinct was to fight, and she drew her sword, only it wasn't Fyrdraca that she held in her hand, but an unfamiliar weapon. She slashed the air where she sensed the invisible menace stood, but hit nothing. The blade then melted in her hand and dripped to the floor as if it were rapidly thawing ice: then the beast approached. Unarmed and totally defenceless, Ionuin attempted to scream, but only managed a hoarse inarticulate croak as pure fear constricted her throat. In the end, this same fear propelled her from the terrifying nightmare, allowing her release from the terror of the unknown, yet strangely familiar menace.

Her first explosive waking breath screamed out of her, eyes springing wide open to discover that she had merely exchanged one nightmare existence for another. Soft sponge-like tubes surrounded her body, slithered up her nose and bound her limbs to a warm throbbing wall of flesh. Then she remembered; a red dragon had indeed eaten her, swallowed her whole. She should be dead, shouldn't she?

She knew little of dragons except what she had learned from her father and her experiences with Spuddle, but eating people was definitely what dragons did. So if a dragon had actually eaten her, where was she now and why was she still very much alive?

Dragon thoughts again pushed into her mind, searching her out, trying to communicate. On a lower, subliminal level, there was that voice again, the same voice that had haunted her since she was a small child, only now it was much clearer. The voice seemed to be under some duress and in great distress. She could not make out the words, but the sounds were more distinct, and instead of being garbled, she detected the meaningful pattern of some kind of language. Ionuin struggled to free herself, but the tubes that resembled animal's entrails held her fast. As her eyes adjusted to the poor light she could see she was in a small chamber with rounded, soft walls that were apparently very much alive.

Falling skies, I'm in its stomach! Ionuin thought. An unfamiliar feeling - commonly recognized as rising terror - raced into her mind, slamming into a cool wall of reason where it instantly froze. I'm alive, but trapped in a dragon's stomach, awaiting digestion! Panic stamped all over reason and fear-fuelled adrenalin pumped through her body.

Again, she struggled against the soft spongy tubes holding her tightly, but if anything, they held her more firmly, perhaps because of her efforts to break free. Then the walls bulged inwards, crushing her, pushing her around. The tubes that had kept her immobile released her and slithered back into the pressing walls with wet, satisfying snaps. Ionuin continued to struggle, but the walls eased her on her way. She thought she might be slipping further into the pit of the dragon's stomach, but on glancing upwards, she saw, at the end of a long slippery tunnel, the welcome sight of daylight.

Then she was out, coughed up unceremoniously and spat onto the floor where she lay in a pool of sticky goo. She blinked several times to clear her eyes, then saw that three red dragons surrounded her, two of whom were very large, with tendrils of smoke slithering lazily from their nostrils. This does not look at all good, Ionuin thought, spitting out a strange tasting slime from her mouth, cuffing away strings of slaver and mucus that were dangling from her chin.

Chapter Twenty Seven

Taj tensed his neck muscles, then, in anguished desperation, threw his head forward with all his might, hitting Bollfur in the chin. Bollfur growled and grabbed him around the throat, but Taj had broken the connection, and he rapidly threw up solid mental walls, visualising towering structures of metal and stone to protect his mind, before crossing his arms in defiance.

'More resistance, Taj?' Bollfur snarled.

Taj grinned. 'Yeah, just a bit, only this time I'm ready for you, so go boil your grotesque, carbuncled arse, you flatulent, gruesome bozo!'

Bollfur smiled and shook his head. 'Little Squeaker, silly boy, you're just a freakoid. Do you honestly believe that your pathetic barrier will keep me out of your head?' he snapped.

'Certainly,' said Taj, raising his chin in the air. 'I have no doubt, because I have been taught mental defence techniques by Lord Nexus, and he is the best!'

'Oh, I agree,' replied Bollfur. 'Lord Nexus is the best, now the old guard are deceased. So, let us see just how much his star pupil has yet to learn, shall we?'

Taj flinched as he saw a giant hammer swinging towards his mental wall; the battle for control of his mind had truly begun in earnest.

'Come on you pathetic piss-wipe,' Taj snapped as Bollfur began hammering away inside his head. 'You can do better than that, can't you?' Bollfur roared and the hammer came again, twice as hard. Taj shuddered under the sudden impact and wondered if he was actually as good as he thought he was. 'Hah! You hit like a girl,' he taunted, bracing himself for another savage mental blow, knowing this would be a battle of pure willpower.

Ionuin knew she should be terrified as the dragons looked her over with cautious interest, but fear was absent from her thoughts; she was overwhelmed with curiosity and surprise. As she listened to the strange tongue of the dragons and their deep, growling speech, she found she could understand every single utterance.

'She is one of them,' murmured the largest of the three, who had shining black eyes that pulsed and glistened. 'The cleverest of the little monkey people.'

'Yes, I agree, dear Sheratz,' said the second dragon, snorting loudly. 'She is certainly one of them, most definitely, but how can this be?'

'Who could possibly know?' said the large one called Sheratz. 'Certainly not I. Any firm ideas, my darling Seraph?'

'Not particularly, but, well, someone must know how, mustn't they?' said Seraph, her lips pursing. 'I know the universe works in mysterious ways, but I strongly doubt one of these fabled monkey creatures can simply pop into existence of its own accord, it must have history.'

'Yes, a full history, obviously, my dearest. Why is it not recorded in the annals?' Sheratz asked.

'Perhaps someone wanted it kept quiet?' Seraph suggested.

147

Sheratz snorted loudly and blew air down his long red snout. 'Seems they succeeded, until now. Thing is, as King of our Brood, I should know of this creature, and furthermore, what is one of them doing loitering about, totally unwarded, in the Valley of Caves?'

The one called Seraph sighed. 'Would it seem unreasonable to suppose that we are faced with not only a dilemma, but an acute mystery, dearest?'

Ionuin stared at the one called Sheratz, who, if he were to be believed, was some kind of Brood King. She then glanced at the one she assumed to be the Queen, Seraph, unsure what to do or what to think. She did not feel threatened, but this lack of threat bothered her. Being surrounded by three red dragons was hardly usual and yet, she felt calm and relaxed: well, almost. She still had the dilemma of what to do next and how to react to the situation she now faced and emerge unscathed.

'She was hiding inside the skeleton of Shogun,' offered the third and smallest dragon, who Ionuin recognised as the one who swallowed her whole. She would never forget those searching, slit yellow eyes as long as she lived. The thought crossed her mind that that might not be very long at all.

'Hiding? Hmm, therefore, it thinks like us too,' said Sheratz, his eyes displaying no obvious emotion. 'Avoiding unwanted notice and attention. I wonder who her father could possibly be? Any ideas, Seraph?'

Seraph lowered her great head and sniffed at Ionuin. 'Perhaps,' she said, 'although, for the life of me, I cannot begin to imagine how such a thing could have actually happened, dearest. Unless of course, the rumours that abounded a few years ago are actually true! I did think it was simply malicious gossip at the time, but now, I'm beginning to wonder.'

'Rumours and gossip, my dear?' asked Sheratz.

Ionuin marshalled her thoughts, remained calm and tried to fathom not only what rumours they were talking about, but what significance their conversation had concerning her wellbeing. Who were these dragon-creatures and why was she here, standing before them? She decided to reveal nothing of herself, and focussed on the certainties. She knew for certain that the second dragon, Seraph, was a Queen, Sheratz was definitely the King and the other, much smaller dragon, had to be their Princekin.

She switched from deductive reasoning to gut feeling and perhaps it was nothing more than her feminine inclinations rushing to the fore, but Ionuin found herself greatly favouring Seraph. The Queen appeared gracious and possessed warm, friendly eyes; green like Spuddle's, with slit yellow pupils and the longest lashes she had ever seen. Ionuin took a step backwards as Seraph lowered her head so she was at eye-level. This might be where I find my gut reactions are false and I have my head bitten off, she thought, reaching for a sword that was no longer sheathed by her side.

'Do not be afraid, little one. I am Seraph, Queen of the Red Dragon Brood,' said Seraph, in common speech, pushing her nose towards Ionuin, her black forked tongue flicking out, swishing across Ionuin's face, cleaning away gunk and dirt with one easy sweep.

148

'Good idea, my dearest, addressing it in its own language,' said Sheratz. 'Do you think it can understand our own tongue?' he continued. 'It looks from one to the other as we speak. Has it spoken to you at all, Glitch?'

The one called Glitch shook his head.

Sheratz straightened his long neck, stretching high above Ionuin, and sighed. 'Very strange, very strange indeed. Perhaps it has some knowledge of the dragon tongue? Or maybe, just maybe, it is simply overly inquisitive!' he exclaimed.

'I understand,' said Ionuin, the words leaving her mouth before she could stop them. She gasped, sighed, and shook her head with dismay.

'How remarkable,' said Sheratz, nodding his great head.

'Hmm, remarkable indeed,' acknowledged Ionuin with a long sigh, 'and very surprising, even to myself.'

'What is life without surprises?' said Seraph, sniffing loudly at Ionuin.

Ionuin shrugged and resigned herself to whatever fate had in store. 'Yes, I suppose you are correct, Queen Seraph.'

'My mum usually is correct,' offered Glitch, looking at Ionuin inquisitively.

'No doubt,' Ionuin replied, extricating herself from the sticky mess pooled around her feet, 'and so much for my initial plan of not revealing too much of myself, eh?'

'There is not much can be hidden from the likes of us,' said Sheratz, snorting loudly. 'We are the proudest of the dragon races.'

'And the fastest,' chimed in Glitch.

'Do be quiet, Glitch,' Seraph scolded.

'So,' said Ionuin, looking at each dragon in turn, 'now you know I can understand everything you say in dragon tongue and common speech, what is to be done with me?'

The dragons exchanged surprised glances.

'Well, well,' said Sheratz, 'a decisive, bold little monkey; is it not?'

'Quite,' said Seraph, nodding knowingly. 'The thing is, it does have a valid point. Whatever shall we do with it?'

Despite being surrounded by three fearsome looking dragons, Ionuin's confidence and instinct for survival asserted itself and took complete control. She had never been one for fostering fear, and her survival instincts quelled all trepidation. 'I am not a monkey or an it,' she snapped, trying to blunt her annoyance, absently peeling away streaks of dried goo that had set all over her body like a second skin. 'I am a *she*. A human, with thoughts and feelings and my name,' she looked from one dragon face to the next and back again, trying to gauge how she was doing, 'my name, is Ionuin.'

Sheratz snorted very loudly, making Ionuin jump a little. 'Snort all you will,' said Ionuin defiantly. 'I speak the truth. As for my father, to answer your question, he is Tharl. Or rather, he was Tharl, before he was murdered.'

'Ah!' said the two big dragons in perfect unison.

Seraph actually chuckled. 'From the windblown seeds of disreputable rumour we finally harvest the fruits of acceptable truth.'

149

'Erm; whatever can you mean?' Ionuin asked, her curiosity piqued and running riot within her head.

'We know of Tharl,' said Sheratz.

'He once killed a dragon, didn't he?' said Glitch.

'Not any old dragon, Glitch,' said Seraph, 'but a young golden female by the name of Saturnine: sister to the Great Lord Nexus of Fire Mountain.'

Ionuin gulped at this news; maybe she should be afraid after all.

'And as for you being human,' said Sheratz. 'I think not, young lady.'

'What?' Ionuin gasped, pushing away rising concern. 'Not human?' She waved her arms mockingly above her head. 'Can you see me? Are you blind? Have you never seen a human before?' She then thought she may have overstepped the boundaries of courtesy, just a little, and looked down sheepishly.

'There is no call for stroppiness, child!' Sheratz scolded.

'Sorry,' Ionuin murmured, shuffling her feet.

'As you should be,' said Sheratz, forcefully nudging Ionuin's shoulder with his nose, making her stumble backwards.

Ionuin clasped her hands to her face, trying to focus. 'What am I thinking? What am I doing? Arguing with dragons!' She realised she had spoken aloud. 'Oops, again, so sorry, I seem to be speaking out of turn. Would you believe, I'm usually very quiet? In fact, I cannot ever recall speaking so much in my entire life.'

Seraph grinned, the action looking both fearsome and pleasant. 'I~on~u~in, try to relax, I think the short slumber you had inside the belly of my son is making you overwrought.'

Ionuin rubbed at her eyes and wondered if she had lost all her senses. She then realised that, despite a few concerns, she still had no real fear of the creatures before her, which just did not make sense. Unless, she reasoned, her encounter with Spuddle had changed her, somehow. 'Um, I, I don't mean to be stroppy,' she said, rubbing at her shoulder where Sheratz's nose had connected with her, feeling a small welt of raised skin where it seemed she had been nipped. 'I, I know I have attitude,' she admitted, jabbing a thumb at the marks Sheratz had made, 'but, is there any need to be so physical with me?' Ionuin looked at the dragons, saw their expressions change and instantly regretted her words of complaint.

'She is awfully troublesome,' said Sheratz, straightening his long neck, peering at Ionuin down his snout. 'I hardly touched her.'

'Agreed,' said Glitch. 'If nobody wants her, I have a good idea.'

'Be quiet, the pair of you,' hissed Seraph.

'She's probably a cry-baby,' said Sheratz, eyeing Ionuin with disdain. 'but what can one expect from such as *she*, whomever and whatever, *she* actually is?'

'And such impudence,' said Glitch.

'You would know all about impudence, Glitch,' said Sheratz.

Glitch grinned as if he had been complimented. 'Thing is, father, she sounds human and looks human, this is why I tried to eat, I mean, swallowed her.'

'Indeed,' said Seraph, turning her glaring eyes upon Glitch.

Glitch swayed uncertainly. 'I mean, I had wondered what a human could be doing so far north and I'd hoped she was one of the bad people, so I could rip her apart and eat her flesh. Might have known she'd be one of them. I mean, what are the chances?'

'My thoughts exactly,' said Sheratz, eyeing Ionuin quizzically. 'What are the chances?'

'I should have realised she was different when my system refused to digest her,' continued Glitch. 'It was when my body began applying the sleep chamber that I knew something was wrong. It was-'

'Yes, yes, Glitch,' interrupted Sheratz. 'Why do you always seek praise for doing the right thing? It should come naturally and not be a forced decision-'

'That's quite enough, Sheratz,' cut in Seraph.

Sheratz rounded on Seraph. 'I was only giving him instruction, dear!'

'I think that he has received the message, have you not, Glitch?'

'Of course I have, I'm not a fool,' said Glitch, recalling his chat with Taj about Daft Des. 'Did I do the right thing then?' he added.

Both Sheratz and Seraph sighed with some despondency.

'Yes, you did the right thing by bringing it back here,' said Sheratz.

'She!' Ionuin corrected them, looking from one to the other, confusion mounting as each spoke in turn. 'Can someone tell me what is going on?' she asked, peeling away the remaining remnants of dried goo while wondering what 'idea' Glitch had in mind. 'I've had some really weird dreams just lately, exceptionally lucid and to be honest, this feels just like an incredibly special weird dream.' She actually pinched herself and winced at the small sharp pain. 'No, not a dream, so what's happening? Why am I here?'

'All in good time,' said Seraph. 'Are you hungry?'

Ionuin was hungry. She could not remember the last time she had eaten a proper meal. Before she could answer, Seraph regurgitated a hunk of steaming flesh that plopped to the ground. It resembled the torso of a man, but Ionuin could not be sure what it actually was. 'Uh, really, thanks, but, I'm not that hungry,' she said, wondering if they expected her to just tuck in with eager relish. 'Besides, this is no time to be thinking about food. I want answers. I know you can help me, I also know you have more information than you are revealing, so do tell me, please! I just need some answers, is it too much to ask?'

None of the dragons spoke, they simply stared at her. Since the last moon had risen the life she had known had ceased to exist. She had lost her father. Discovered creatures she previously thought were figments of her father's imagination, been forced to take life, even save life, including her own, and these dragons possessed knowledge that she meant to have.

Glitch gestured towards the steaming meat with his quivering nose. 'Mother; can I have that? I have lost my potential meal.'

'What, oh, yes, Glitch,' replied Seraph, a little distractedly. 'I suppose so, but it is your fault that you have lost your dinner. I have told you time and time again to leave what humans are left on this world well alone.'

'Oh, I agree,' said Sheratz. 'Leave the humans alone, Glitch.'

Glitch eyed his father with a look that conveyed mistrust. 'Father, it was you who told me what fun can be had hunting people! You insisted that I should investigate the species!'

Seraph rounded on Sheratz. 'Hunting the remaining humanity is banned by common consensus amongst all dragon broods, with no exception!'

'I know, I know,' said Sheratz, 'but I saw no harm in a little fun. He would not have really eaten the creature, would you, Glitch?'

'Did you want to eat me, Glitch?' Ionuin asked.

'What? Um, oh no,' said Glitch. 'Oh no, perish the thought that I would ever do such thing, no not me. I just wanted to show how clever I am by catching a human. Father did say they are the trickiest of all the monkey creatures.'

Ionuin listened intently, but also concentrated mentally, and with a little effort she found she could actually tap into their thought waves. Why she had this skill, which had first become apparent on meeting Spuddle, remained unknown to her. She caught the exchanges of the two-way mental traffic, and the mystery surrounding her life vanished as the unspoken truth hit her in a telepathic avalanche that unhinged her at the knees. She staggered backwards, falling unsteadily against the flank of Glitch.

'No, no, it cannot be so!' she wailed, her breathing coming in such short, rapid, gasps that she began to hyperventilate. 'I don't believe it!' she shouted, swaying on her feet. 'I won't believe it: I won't! Not ever!'

'No, it's true,' said Glitch, 'you can relax; I don't want to eat you, not anymore.'

Chapter Twenty Eight

Bollfur continued hammering at the wall of Taj's mind, making him wince, but he held fast. The constant pressure on his thoughts was relentless, and he did not know how much longer he could hold out before he eventually caved. Bollfur might be a fat, lazy blow-hard who fed on offal and carrion, but he was far more proficient in the mental arts than Taj had expected. As he had easily whipped the blue giant at chess, he had imagined him to be more dull-witted than he actually was. This underestimation had cost him dearly; the acute strain on his defences was beginning to tell.

'Yes, Taj, I feel you weakening,' Bollfur snarled. 'Tiny cracks are opening up. I'll be back inside your head any moment now and then I will waste your tiny mind as if I were squishing a worm; do you hear me?'

'No chance, fatty,' Taj gasped, but he knew it was true. It was only a matter of time.

Bollfur leapt forward, grabbing Taj by the shoulders, shaking him violently. 'Come on, you wormy pip-squeak!' He squeezed Taj hard, both mentally and physically.

'Oh, no, no,' muttered Taj, snatching at Bollfur's talons, prising them apart just enough to slip free. An incredible slice of scything pain slashed open his mind, and he fell to his knees. It was excruciating, like being probed by the cold, numb psyche of the Dark Dragon, but with added ripping and tearing. Taj screamed and collapsed onto his knees, his mind and body wracked with agony, the stone and metal barriers with which he had encircled his thoughts crumbling away to powdery dust. He tried in vain to resurrect them, but giant hammers battered them down as soon as they were formed.

'Hah! Who's the daddy now, Taj?' harrumphed Bollfur. 'Not a chance of resisting me, you quivering slug!' He laughed, nastily. 'I was being gentle with you before. Now, you may suffer some really horrible mental damage. So sorry, but I have to know everything for the benefit of my master.'

Taj swayed back and forth, watching his own memories flicker back through his mind, one racing image chasing another. Bollfur had the truth, now; Glitch and Spuddle, and on it went, until Bollfur released him. Taj groaned and dropped onto his face, smashing his nose on the unyielding rock of the chamber floor.

'Hmm,' said Bollfur, 'you know that Spuddle is alive, but you know nothing of the other, do you? She is still a mystery. Should I tell you, I wonder?'

Taj rolled onto his back, blood pumping from his nose, dribbling into his gaping mouth, coating his teeth. Too much had occurred all at once for him to comprehend what it meant. Bollfur had a master? When did that happen? What did it mean?

'My master is nothing for you to be concerned about,' laughed Bollfur. 'You need not think about anything anymore, your life as you know it will cease to exist in a few more moments, my promise to squish your mind is almost here, just building up power, so be patient.'

Taj tried to speak, to resist, to erect defences, but Bollfur was too strong.

'Ten for effort, boy, I'll give you that,' Bollfur said, taunting him. 'It won't hurt much, just a white blast of heat, then no more worries. Actually, I may be wrong about the *not hurting* part. I imagine it will be excruciating agony, at first, but eventually, as you deteriorate into a gibbering heap of fleshy waste, it won't matter, not really.'

Taj was past caring, he had failed, and Bollfur knew everything. Not only that, he had already known that Spuddle lived! And who was this *she* to whom he was referring? Hot pain flared inside his skull, he could hardly think properly. He wanted to ask Bollfur why he was doing this and how he knew about Spuddle. Presently, though, concentrating on keeping breathing was about all he could manage. Then, the slab of rock covering the chamber entrance burst inwards and Blucher and Bolden were leaning over him. Great, thought Taj, as heat began searing his mind, what an incredible boon seeing these two again, and what a wonderful day I am having. He gathered his strength for one last effort, determined to die fighting and with dignity, with at the very least a witticism on his lips for them to remember him by.

Ionuin flung both her hands backwards, fetching Glitch a sharp slap.

'Say! Watch yourself, girly!' Glitch growled, steadying Ionuin by curling his tail around her waist, gripping her firmly, but not overly tight. 'You sure you're not hungry? You seem upset. If you want food, I suppose I'm willing to share, you know. Since I cannot eat you, I might as well eat with you.'

'It, it can't be true,' Ionuin murmured, paying no attention to the words of Glitch, trying to control her breathing and stop her body from trembling.

Glitch grinned. 'Well, I admit, I'm not known for outright generosity, but it is true, I am willing to share this meal, but only as I like you. Well . . . a little.'

'I want nothing from you,' Ionuin said, wriggling free of the muscular tail curled around her waist, pushing herself away from Glitch, his words hardly registering as she began focussing all her attention on Seraph.

'So touchy, but, suit yourself,' said Glitch, flicking his tail across his back, biting into the still steaming hunk of food.

Ionuin flexed her mind and reached into Seraph's brain with her own thoughts, trying to ignore the palpable tension between her and the large red female. *Tell me, Seraph; tell me what you were thinking. I only caught a glimpse and, and I need more, much more.* Seraph sighed. To Ionuin, she appeared unsurprised at the telepathic communication. She then realised that to a dragon, such a thing would probably be second nature. *Please, Seraph, I need to know, I must know!*

The words of Seraph bounced right into Ionuin's mind, loud and booming. *Are you ready for such knowledge, child? I mean, really ready, hmm?*

Ionuin was rocked by the forcefulness of Seraph's voice booming in her mind, but pressed on with her request. *Ready or not, I already suspect the truth, but suspecting a thing and having it confirmed is very different, and I desperately need confirmation.*

154

Seraph locked stares with her before giving her head a desultory shake. *Well, I'm just not sure, Ionuin. Your initial shock tells me that you are not yet ready, not for the knowledge I have to impart.*

Ionuin gave Seraph her most pleading look. *Please, Seraph, I am begging you. I need this like I have never needed anything before in my whole life. I assure you, I am ready, and what's more, I feel I have a right to know the truth about myself. You would want to know, would you not?*

Seraph sighed and glanced at Sheratz, who nodded his assent. *She is correct, Seraph, do as she requests.*

Seraph sighed with stoic resignation. *So be it. Well, child, there are some dragons who, when they are very young, can shape-change. There was once a dragon named 'Saturnine' who became an expert at shape-changing and used to perform the feat for pure amusement, even walking unnoticed amongst the humans whom she resembled. While out hunting, she encountered a certain man, a wild hunter, a warrior among his own kind, and Saturnine instantly shape-changed.*

Ionuin raised her hand. *The man? Was he-*

Seraph glared at her. *Shush, child. Have patience, listen and learn; then you may ask questions. Now where was I? Oh yes, Saturnine thought it would be fun to outwit the man-hunter and of course, to see the look upon his face when she changed back, for it would make for much merriment when it came to the telling of stories around the fire during feasting time in the Great Cavern. She easily tricked the man into thinking she was human, and told him she had been kept prisoner by a wicked dragon who had flown away. After a while, she became so intrigued by this man that she changed her mind about transforming herself back into a dragon and the two became firm friends. Men are easy prey for the charms of a woman, any woman, and he fell in love with Saturnine and she allowed him to seduce her.*

Is, is this all true? Ionuin interrupted, unable to help herself.

Until now, it was all merely speculation, but your appearance here today, my dear, is the proof that what was previously rumour is indeed the living, breathing, truth, Seraph confirmed. *They spent much time together and the man settled into a regular life and built a cottage, but Saturnine was coming of age.*

'I was a rumour?' said Ionuin. 'How can someone be a rumour?'

'You can be anything you like, if you have a good imagination,' suggested Glitch, between mouthfuls of food. 'I was once a tree for a whole afternoon!'

'Glitch!' Sheratz harrumphed. 'Eat your food and be quiet, we do not need your witless waffling here today.'

'Sorry, father,' Glitch apologised.

Sheratz turned his attention to Ionuin. 'Ionuin, you were not a rumour,' he said, his voice so low, Ionuin could hardly hear him. 'It was only your existence that was a rumour.'

The voice of Seraph once again echoed inside her mind. *Shall I continue?*

155

Ionuin started to speak, then concentrated and answered with her mind. *Yes, Seraph, please do. Forgive my interruptions; I am desperate to know more. Please continue.*

All right, child. Well, it seemed Saturnine could retain her human shape no longer, and rather than allow the man to know the truth, she fled to the Valley of Caves and transformed back into her true shape before returning to Fire Mountain. Lord Nexus, her brother, was furious with her for behaving with such folly. Even so, Saturnine allegedly refused to give the location of the man's cottage to her brother for fear of what he might do; after all, she was still in love with the man. Legend has it that she coerced one of the Chosen, known to the dragon clans as Catalin, to provide a safe sanctuary for the man in which he could abide and never be found.

'Our hidden valley,' Ionuin murmured, absently fingering her gold bracelets, wondering if Catalin and the provider of her jewellery were one and the same. She glanced up at Seraph. *Sorry, I was distracted, please continue.*

Seraph flexed her mind. *Yes, I know humankind are easily distracted.*

A simple shiny bauble is enough to make them goggle and flounder like mindless morons. Sheratz added.

True, added Seraph, *but I digress. As I was saying, in time, it was rumoured that Saturnine gave birth to two children, human in shape, but with all the skills of a dragon. When the children were born she was forbidden to leave her chambers inside Fire Mountain, but Saturnine was never one for following rules, or accepting punishment. After all, she was of royal blood, just like Nexus, so why should she not do as she pleased?*

Typical female, offered Sheratz.

Seraph scowled at Sheratz. *Typical female or not, she grew desperate to be with the man creature again and her love for him had grown stronger since their parting. While Nexus was out hunting, she took one of the children, the girl child as it happens, and flew back to the isolated cottage the man had built in his sanctuary. There he was, seated on a rock, sharpening his sword. In her yearning to be with him and excitement at seeing him, Saturnine swooped down and placed the child at his feet. She had taken him by surprise, and after one glance at the child, he launched a sudden attack. Saturnine retreated and attempted to tell him who she really was by flooding his brain with her thoughts, but the man became enraged and she could not break through to him.*

Typical behaviour of a human male, probably, suggested Sheratz.

Seraph sighed. *Ignore my mate, Ionuin. As I was telling you, Saturnine could not break though to him. In sheer desperation, she tried to change, to reveal her humanity, but such a thing demands lots of energy and she was no longer in the first spring of youth. As she tried to initiate the change, while fending off her true love, the man, being a skilled fighter, inflicted mortal wounds. Saturnine, taken by surprise, hardly resisted and in any case, she could not kill the one she loved. So badly injured was she, that to try and shape change would instantly mean her death, so she made her escape and returned to Fire Mountain. For Saturnine, it was too late. Her heart had been pierced and her rejuvenating powers had all but leaked away. She lived to tell the tale, made Nexus promise there would be no retribution for her death and Nexus, somewhat unwillingly, agreed. The man, as you have probably guessed, was Tharl, your father, which makes you, Ionuin, of royal dragon blood.*

Ionuin stood speechless for what seemed the longest time. She looked from dragon to dragon, finally locking stares once again with Seraph.

'You mean, you mean I am the child who Saturnine left with Tharl? I am the offspring of a union between a, a dragon and a human? But it, it can't be! It just can't be true, none of it can be true! I refuse to believe it; I won't believe it! Do you hear me? I won't believe it: not ever!'

Sheratz lowered his head. Ionuin noticed smoke curling from his nostrils. 'Shush, child. Do you not see? It matters not whether you believe anything Seraph has told you, it still remains the truth; do you not understand? Your belief in anything at all, strong as it may seem, right as it may feel, regardless of unshakeable faith, is immaterial when confronted with the bare facts.'

Ionuin felt tears well in her eyes, threatening to brim over. 'But, I don't want it to be true,' she sobbed, the strength leaking out of her legs as she squatted on the floor.

'Typical human,' said Glitch, gulping down the last of his meal. 'I heard that some of them believe in an invisible man in the sky who rewards and punishes them for their daily deeds without any proof whatsoever, and if anyone tries to inform them that the notion is ridiculous, they simply reply, 'One must have faith,' but I ask you, what use is faith when the truth is-'

'Glitch,' Seraph growled. 'What you know of humans is hardly worth bleating on about. Can you not see Ionuin is hurting? Do behave, and keep your silly mouth shut for once.'

'No, no please, what Glitch says is true,' Ionuin sobbed, cuffing tears from her eyes. 'Some humans are silly in what they say and do and how they think. I care nothing for such things, what worries me, is what would my father think if he knew about all of this?'

'He wouldn't think anything, he's dead,' said Glitch, before burping loudly.

'Glitch!' scolded Seraph, turning round, her tail thwacking Glitch in the head, knocking him off his feet, while at the same time reaching out and gently embracing Ionuin, pulling her to her feet into a comforting hug. 'Poor child, I knew it would be too much for you, and I am sure your father would understand.'

'I'm sorry for being so upset,' Ionuin cried. 'It's just, well, it's just a lot to accept, you know?'

'I know, child, I know,' said Seraph, patting Ionuin on the shoulder.

Ionuin felt a shudder pass through her body and somehow, the strange sensation offered relief. She sniffled, trying to stop her nose from running, and sighed. 'I think, perhaps, I'm feeling a little better,' she said, snorting cold snot up her nose.

'Of course you are, dear,' said Seraph. 'I'm allowing waves of calmness to pass through you, just to ease the shock away, just for a little while. You will feel champion in a few moments, trust me.'

157

Sheratz walked tentatively around the two hugging females. 'Glitch, you say you found her in the Valley of Caves?'

'Yes,' answered Glitch, shaking his head, getting to his feet. 'I was helping Taj by searching for Spuddle and-'

'Spuddle!' exclaimed Seraph and Sheratz in unison.

Ionuin quickly wiped at her eyes and nose, feeling a little ashamed at her undignified display of emotion, considering it a disgraceful weakness as she pulled away from Seraph. 'I know of Spuddle,' she said, annoyed at the slight tremble in her voice.

Seraph lowered her great head. 'You do? But, he's supposed to be dead, dear girl; are you sure?'

'Oh yes, quite sure,' said Ionuin, clearing her throat, absently wiping at her tear-streaked face. 'I rescued him from those who killed my father. They had him trapped in a cage and had been feeding from him for quite some time, or so it seemed to me.' All three dragons gasped. 'He's fine now,' said Ionuin. 'At least, he's got much better since we first met, bigger too. We killed a kodiak bear between us; I left him fighting another one by himself.'

'You left him fighting a kodiak bear!' said Sheratz, some alarm in his voice.

'By himself,' said Glitch, regurgitating a lump of meat before snatching it back up again and swallowing it whole. 'The big kodiak bears are quite tough.'

Ionuin swallowed her mounting fear and wondered if she had done something seriously wrong. 'Well, yes. I mean, I didn't run away, if that's what you're thinking. He insisted I leave, he asked me to go! Well, he commanded me really, and he looked pretty capable, he had the bear on the run.'

'Nexus must be told,' said Sheratz.

'Taj already told him,' offered Glitch. 'Old fool didn't believe him, and-'

'Have some respect for your betters, boy!' Sheratz yelled!

'Er, excuse me,' said Ionuin, 'what is going to happen to me now?'

Seraph glanced at Sheratz. Ionuin could tell mental traffic was passing between them but she caught none of it. She pushed out her thoughts, latching onto the conversation, catching snatches of words and imagery, then something inside her head shifted, she stumbled forwards feeling strangely weak.

Seraph caught Ionuin and gently steadied her. 'We have decided,' she said, looking quizzically into the girl's eyes, 'that as you are of royal blood, you must be taken to Fire Mountain. Lord Nexus, your uncle, and now the Dragon King, will want to see you for himself. Of course . . . .'

Seraph's words trailed away to nothingness. Ionuin slumped into the big female's arms, the thin membrane separating her human side from her dragon side disintegrating as reality came rushing in, swamping her mind with the cold, cruel, truth. Her whole life had been a lie: an unwitting deception. A total mockery of everything she had ever believed. She was half dragon. Half of her was the most feared creature on this desolate planet. What of her father? She had always thought he had been too quiet, too distant and unapproachable. Now she knew why. He had been in love and all his hunting trips, his travels far and wide,

158

had been desperate searches for Saturnine. He had killed the love of his life and he knew nothing about it.

Still in a daze, Ionuin felt nothing as Sheratz lifted her gently and eased her onto his back, settling her between his huge wings. 'Poor thing,' she heard him say, although it seemed as though the words were coming from a great distance. 'She couldn't take the truth, just too much for her mind. I do hope she's not permanently damaged.'

'I tried to calm her with sensory waves,' said Seraph, 'but they can only do so much. We must hurry; time is short and I suspect the arrival of this child is a portent of universal forces at work.'

'Yes, I sense she is the hunted one,' said Sheratz.

'Almost certainly,' agreed Seraph. 'I suspect that the Dark Dragon has sought us out and intends to destroy the Children of the Light, the gifted ones. It must not be allowed, Sheratz, or all that we have achieved since the dawning of our time will be lost. Try sending a message, dear, before we start our journey. Nexus will want to dispatch flyers to find his son.'

'Are we going to Fire Mountain, then?' Glitch asked.

'We're going to Fire Mountain now!' Sheratz replied. 'Tomorrow is the eve of the joining of the great stone circles and Ionuin may be important.'

'Cool!' said Glitch, shooting a bolt of orange flame into the sky, showing his approval.

All of this Ionuin saw and heard, but was unable to respond as she relaxed on Sheratz's back, her mind already tumbling within waves of coming sleep.

Chapter Twenty Nine

The raging fire inside Taj's mind, stoked and provoked by Bollfur, began to abate. He eyed Bollfur's two sons with caution as he gathered himself together. Blucher's nose was very swollen and gunk still oozed from the gash he had made with his own talon. Their presence did not bother him though, not in the slightest. He was just about done for, so what more could they do to him? 'Come in,' he said, his voice a lazy drawl, beckoning them forward with a languid flick of his hand. 'Your dad and I are having a going away party. It's me that's departing, and I won't be coming back!' He began to laugh, but stopped suddenly as Lord Nexus pushed the two blue dragons further into the chamber.

'Lord Bollfur,' said Nexus, his voice loud and authoritative. 'I have questioned Blucher and Bolden extremely thoroughly, and I am dismayed at what they have told me.'

Bollfur leapt to his feet. 'You have questioned my sons? What-'

Nexus surged forward, pushing his face into Bollfur's, so that they were eye to eye. 'When I say dismayed, I really mean, incredibly angry! More angry than you would ever believe!'

Bollfur snarled and pushed back, his face slamming into Nexus so they were snout to snout. 'Well, angry you may be, but don't go blowing your stack with me, old boy! You may find you have bitten off more than you can chew, if you know what I mean, my Lord.'

Nexus growled. 'Oh, I know what you mean, you turd-munching moron, and leave out the perfunctory pleasantries; we are way beyond honouring that level of respect for each other, don't you think?'

'Please, stop it!' said Taj, sitting up, shuffling out of the way. Even though Nexus was king of all the dragons, Bollfur was something of a giant himself, and Taj wondered what would happen if they began to fight. He struggled to remain upright, but with great effort, found his balance and the use of his legs, and slid onto the stone bed. He coughed, blood and phlegm dribbling down his chin, and tried to speak again, but Nexus demanded his silence with a single glance. Taj gulped. He was pleased for the intervention. It had almost certainly prevented his demise. Having previously accepted that potential outcome, he was now afraid of what might happen next.

'Dragon shall not kill dragon,' said a voice from the doorway. Taj looked and saw a host of dragons filling the tunnel outside Bollfur's chamber.

'I'm not going to kill him,' said Nexus, backing off. 'Not yet.'

'King you may be,' snapped Bollfur, 'but do not presume-'

'Be quiet!' Nexus snapped. He looked to Taj and pointed. 'Bollfur, I want an explanation. Why is my ward here, in your chambers?'

Taj wiped his nose. The blood had stopped flowing; his head was clearing. 'He was going to kill me,' he blurted out, almost choking with emotion. He pointed at Blucher and Bolden. 'Those two as well, my Lord! Pair of raving maniacs, they are! They chased me and set fire to my head and my legs.' He looked down at his legs. 'I seem to have got better, though.'

Nexus sighed, shook his great head, then strode over to Taj and picked him up in his arms. 'I know what happened, boy, but you need not worry, it's over now.' He turned to Bollfur and his sons. 'Execution springs to mind, but we shall decide what to do with you three after the battle. You will not be needed during the coming conflict. We cannot trust you anymore, so all three of you are confined to this chamber.' Bollfur began to protest, but four green dragons, not the brightest breed, but the biggest, and the usual choice for sentinels, blocked the doorway. 'If they try to leave,' Nexus ordered over his shoulder, 'feel free to roast them alive!'

Taj looked up into the golden orbs of Nexus. 'He knew about Spuddle,' said Taj, biting his lip.

'I know all about Spuddle,' said Nexus, grinning. 'The Red Dragon Brood have contacted me, we are fetching him home. You were correct, Taj, and I refused to believe you. For that, I am sorry, very sorry, truly.'

Taj smiled, and then recalled other things Bollfur had said. 'Also, Bollfur has a Master!'

Nexus stopped in his tracks, almost colliding with the troop of dragons that were following him. 'A Master? Hmm, what do you know of this so-called Master?' he asked.

'Well, nothing,' confessed Taj, 'he just mentioned him, and-'

'Him?' quizzed Nexus.

'Ah, yes, could be a female, I suppose,' Taj agreed, nodding his head thoughtfully. 'I never thought. Speaking of which, there's another person. 'The other one,' he said, and I think this 'other one' is definitely a female.'

Nexus grinned, his teeth gleaming in the yellow light of the wall crystals. 'You are about to meet the female in question,' he confided in a hushed voice, 'as am I. As for this master, be it a 'he' or a 'she', there will be plenty of time to deal with such things once the battle is concluded.'

'As long as we win,' Taj pointed out, uncertainly.

Nexus laughed. 'Yes, providing that we win, but do not doubt it, Taj. Loss is unthinkable, so we must win, we will win, and when we do, Bollfur and his brood shall face the joint council.' A large blue dragon stepped before them. It was Beulah, the blue dragon matriarch. 'Ah, Beulah,' said Nexus, 'just the Lady I wish to see.'

'Oh, Taj,' said Beulah, her face a picture of concern, tears moistening her lower lids. 'Are you all right, child?'

'I have known better days,' replied Taj, trying to sound manly. 'But yes, thank you for asking, Beulah. I am now as well as can be expected.'

'Oh, good, good,' said Beulah, smiling and gently running a talon down his cheek. 'I could not bear it if anything bad happened to you.'

'Beulah, I thank you for your concern,' said Nexus. 'There have been some changes, my Lady, and from now on, you are in full command of the blue dragon forces.'

'I am?' said Beulah, her eyes widening.

161

'Yes, yes you are,' said Nexus. 'Unfortunately, Lord Bollfur and his sons are indisposed and will not be leaving their chamber.'

'Indisposed? I don't understand.' Beulah said, her face creased with perplexity. 'Why can't they leave their chamber?'

'All three of them tried to pass through the narrow doorway at the same time and they became immovably wedged.' Nexus replied.

Beulah gasped and then laughed heartily. 'You are joking, my Lord?'

'Yes, yes, of course I am joking, they are just detained,' said Nexus. 'So, until all issues are resolved, you are in charge of the blue brood. Are you agreeable?'

'Oh, yes,' said Beulah, bowing so low that her nose touched the floor. 'I look forward to it with great pleasure, my Lord, great pleasure indeed.'

'Good,' said Nexus, edging round the great female. 'Please excuse me, Lady Beulah; I have to get Taj cleaned up and prepared to meet someone very special.'

'Oh yes,' said Beulah, bowing low once more, 'the special one. I'll be there, my Lord,' she added, before striding away, a swagger in her gait.

Taj was about to ask who this someone special could be, when Nexus rested a giant talon on his lips. 'You will see, my boy, no more questions, you will see soon enough.'

Ionuin roused herself from sleep, and opened her eyes to see wispy pink clouds whipping past at incredible speed. She was riding on Sheratz's back with Glitch and Seraph bringing up the rear. The encounter with the red dragons burst upon her conscious mind with such an incredible brain-shaking rush that she thought she must still be asleep. Although, this was no dream from which she would awaken and stretch away the remnants of slumber. Dragons not only existed, but were intricately linked with her own life, both now, in the past, via Saturnine, her mother, and ultimately, in the future. She undertook a hasty reappraisal of existence as she understood it, and found she knew hardly anything about the real world.

Ionuin felt totally drained as she watched the scenery fly past in a dizzying blur. Latching onto dragon thoughts, even in her sleep, was most taxing, and the earlier mental communications with Seraph had truly sapped her strength. She knew she was on her way to Fire Mountain to meet the dragon they called Lord Nexus, and she sensed great urgency. She was also aware that trouble was brewing in the air, threading through the night like an unwelcome stranger. Powerful forces were engaged in bringing about the destruction of life on Merm, and from what she could gather from the thoughts of Seraph and Sheratz, they really meant business.

Sitting upright, Ionuin forced herself to shake off the lethargy she felt. She could see early evening stars glistening like pinpricks of crystal light, and as she looked below, her stomach lurched at the thought of falling to the rocky ground. She fought the gag reflex, swaying gently, ignoring the queasiness uncoiling in her bowels, wondering if the dragons would allow her to walk the rest of the way. Surely it could not be all that far?

Sheratz's thoughts tripped through her mind. *Ah, so you're awake at last.*

Ionuin responded immediately. *Yes, yes, I'm awake! And alive!*

Glitch's young mind broke into her thoughts. *You seem surprised, Ionuin!*

She is more than surprised, laughed Sheratz, *and don't concern yourself with falling, dragons excrete a sticky resin from their scales which secure a rider by bonding with the skin.*

Ionuin tried lifting her leg and felt gentle resistance.

Sheratz again laughed. *You are not stuck tight, Ionuin, you can move, but you will never fall. You are not afraid, are you?*

Seraph joined in the telepathic conversation. *We had better slow down a little, Sheratz. We must allow her mind to adjust, or she may pass out again.*

Ionuin flexed her mind. *I'm, I'm not really afraid. I just don't understand what's happening.* A queer feeling made her shudder, and the world swam out of focus then drifted back, but settled out of its accustomed place. *All right, I suppose I am afraid, and slightly confused!*

Sheratz actually laughed, surprising everyone. *That's understandable, young Princess, after all you've been through.*

'Princess!' Ionuin wailed. 'I'm no princess, am I?' Her words were carried away on the swirling dust filled wind, but her thoughts got through.

You will see, all will become clear very soon, advised Seraph, her thoughts soft and embracing. *Just relax, Ionuin. We are almost there.*

Ionuin glanced around and saw they were indeed heading for Fire Mountain, legendary home of the dragons. Previously, her natural curiosity had drawn her to the mountain. Now, she was heading there for entirely different reasons. She had something she had thought she would never know again; she had purpose.

Sheratz swooped low, and Ionuin felt her stomach turn, forcing her to stifle a nervous giggle. Strangely, and unaccountably, her fear had all but evaporated. She felt slightly light-headed, but put this down to Seraph's presence in the back of her mind, offering calm reassurance and soothing comfort.

It seemed ludicrous that she should be here, winging across the land on the back of a huge red dragon, indulging in telepathic communications with creatures she had only recently met. So much had happened! There were sure to be even more surprises, and she wondered how it was all going to end. Who was she really? Was she a princess? And where was Spuddle?

Fire Mountain drew ever closer and soon it seemed that she could reach out and touch it. It was not long before the huge edifices of rock were looming above them.

'Wow! It's massive,' Ionuin gasped; her eyes wide with awe. *How do we get inside? Will there be many other dragons? Will Spuddle be there?*

Sheratz dipped beneath an overhanging shelf of craggy rock as his thoughts filtered through to Ionuin. *So many questions, child! Have some patience. As Seraph has already informed you, all will be revealed very shortly.*

I, I will try to relax, Ionuin assured Sheratz. He dived around two huge pinnacles of carved stone, his red scaled back arching as he made a death defying turn, flying through an elongated split in the mountain side. A split, so Ionuin thought, that resembled a cruelly twisted mouth complete with sharpened stone teeth; the mouth of a giant standing guard like the world's most formidable sentinel.

Darkness rushed in upon the three dragons and their passenger as they negotiated the tricky twists and turns. A scream rose and became trapped in Ionuin's throat, yearning for release, but it retreated, living to wail another day. Her eyes soon adjusted to the pitch black, turning it into a murky gloom where shadows flitted and danced against the rock walls, like excited marionettes from one of the rare travelling carnivals she had visited as a girl. On and on they flew, deep into the heart of the biggest mountain on Merm.

As they penetrated deep into the interior, Ionuin noticed a soft orange light that seemed to glow from large crystals embedded in the red walls. Up ahead, she saw a line of dragons standing upon a wide rocky ledge. It was far lighter here, and dimly flickering torchlight, filtering through enormous stone arches, illuminated the dragon's outlines. There were far too many to count; their numbers ran into dozens, and in the centre of the throng, so much larger than the others, stood a magnificent golden dragon. Even his eyes were orbs of pure glistening gold, and at his feet stood a boy.

Sheratz swished his tail and they slowed, almost to a standstill. Ionuin slid forward, butting up gently against the base of Sheratz's neck as the resin released its grip on her flesh, seeping back into the scales. This was it! This was the fabled 'Dragon Kingdom' about which she had often dreamed. It all came flooding back in heady waves of disjointed broken thought.

Seraph intercepted the sudden mental rush that might otherwise have blown Ionuin's mind. 'Take one careful step at a time, Ionuin. Compose yourself and relax. All will be revealed. The impatience you are experiencing is the human part of you that constantly thirsts for knowledge, knowledge which you are not yet capable of dealing with.'

'The human part of me?' Just saying it seems strange, she thought.

Seraph landed gracefully beside Sheratz. 'You are not really human, Ionuin. This much is true,' she said. 'Only part of you is human. The remainder is all dragon. How much dragon power you possess is yet to be determined and tested, but do not worry. Whatever the outcome, no one here will ever hurt you.'

Ionuin nodded. Each answer that she received only gave rise to more confusion, and she decided that there was no point in asking any further questions, or she feared her head might simply burst apart. 'I'll be patient,' she promised, crossing her fingers to show good faith, absently wondering if crossed fingers meant anything to dragons.

Sheratz rippled the muscles along his back, sending her sliding to the floor. She landed on the ledge and stood facing the boy, who was slightly taller than herself. He tried to speak to her, but words seemed to elude him for the present. They stared at each other as if transfixed by an immobility spell. Glitch careered onto the ledge, breaking the atmospheric magic, throwing up loose pebbles and dust.

'Whoa! Sorry about that, Your Gracious Majesty. I'm just a natural speed freak who doesn't know when to stop. I remember once when . . .' the other

164

dragons were staring '. . . I was, never mind.' Glitch hung his head in embarrassment.

Sheratz growled at his youngster's slipshod arrival and Seraph rolled her eyes towards the high, cavernous ceiling.

'There is no need to apologise, young Glitch,' said the large golden dragon, his voice deep and authoritative, 'but as you have seen fit to crash into these historic and auspicious proceedings, please consider yourself grounded until further notice.' He smiled and turned his attention to Ionuin, who was still fixated on the young male.

The boy was clean-shaven, his angular jaw reminding Ionuin of her father, and he also possessed similar darkly coloured hair to that which had once crowned Tharl's head in a mass of wayward curls. However, this young male wore his hair shorter, and he was also leaner than her father, not much more muscular than herself, really, but he looked strong.

'So, Sheratz,' continued the golden dragon, 'this is the one called Ionuin. I must say, she does resemble Saturnine's human form.'

Ionuin looked up into the eyes of the golden dragon. 'You are Nexus!'

Seraph pressed her thoughts into Ionuin's mind. *Ionuin! You must address Nexus as, Your Gracious Majesty or Lord Nexus, unless he deems otherwise.*

Seraph then vacated Ionuin's mind altogether and proceeded to scold Glitch with a mental tirade that had the other dragons present smiling and exchanging amused glances.

Nexus lowered his head until he was eye to eye with Ionuin. His face was huge, but very shapely, handsome even, and not frightening at all. His golden eyes conveyed a feeling of infinite wisdom and strength, and Ionuin knew she was in the presence of greatness.

'Your Gracious Majesty,' she began, 'I have many-'

'Very good; I am pleased you speak our tongue. As befits your status, you may address me as Lord Nexus and I must say, it's very clear that Saturnine did well with your first year of education, before she died.'

'Saturnine educated me? But-'

Seraph nodded. *Easy Ionuin, it is not how it seems; believe me.*

Ionuin turned back to Nexus. It was all too much. And who was this boy? His thoughts slipped into her mind. *Ionuin? It is I, Taj. Your brother: your twin brother!*

Chapter Thirty

Ionuin instantly recognised the voice that had been visiting her mind for as long as she could remember. She stepped closer to him, reaching out, touching his smooth face with the tips of her sensitive fingers. 'Taj? You! You are the voice inside my head!' She was beginning to understand, but was not entirely sure she really wanted to. 'And you say, you say that you are my brother, my twin brother?'

Taj clasped Ionuin's hand within his own and she felt his energy ripple along her arm, making her skin tingle. Imagery flashed through her mind, flashes of Taj's life. She saw him running along dimly lit tunnels as a small boy, being chased by two dragons, one red and another green. She saw him playing on a mountain slope, swinging a piece of wood as if it were a sword, shouting challenges to imaginary enemies. It seemed like an ordinary childhood to Ionuin, with the exception of the dragons accompanying him. Next, she saw Taj at a feast, surrounded by enormous dragons of various colour; some were play-fighting, some were singing, and all seemed very happy. Ionuin had never known this kind of happiness and merriment in her own life, and she snatched away her hand.

'It can't be true,' she scolded. 'None of this is real. I don't want it to be real, do you hear me? I don't want it! I don't want this life, any of it, it's false! I want, I want my father!'

Taj held Ionuin as she tried to pull away from him, stepping dangerously close to the edge of the ledge. *Ionuin, please; try to relax.*

Leave her to me, Taj. It was the voice of Nexus filling Ionuin's mind, his great talons reaching down with incredible gentleness, and lifting her into the air. 'Look into my eyes, child, before you reject your altered world. See it for what it is: not false, but the truth.'

Ionuin's mind reeled, but she gazed into the eyes of Nexus as he had asked her to, and his thoughts vaulted the mental block she had started to erect. *Ionuin, denial of these changes, of your new reality, will hurl you into a downward spiral of chaotic thought, one that will lead to madness, to vegetative oblivion, and we do not want that to happen, now do we?*

No, no, I suppose not, Ionuin conceded.

Nexus smiled. *So far, you have accommodated the changes very well, but you have much still to learn and understand. As for your father, your inability to grieve keeps him in the present, even though his life belongs in the past. Do you understand? You have to release your pain. You have to shake off the remnants of what once was, and accept what now is, acknowledging that your father has no part to play in your new future.*

Ionuin resisted. *I have grieved,* she thought, *I have shed tears.* Then her conscious thoughts swam free and entered the labyrinth of Nexus' brain where his tempered wisdom embraced her worries and soothed her anxiety. In a state of

166

relaxation, she found herself observing from a cliff-top. Down below, a man and a dragon, a golden dragon, were battling.

'My father,' she murmured. 'My father and Saturnine! My mother! No wonder my father became upset when I asked about my mother, he never knew who she was. When he said I was like my mother, he was simply easing my mind.'

Nexus' calming voice echoed inside her head. *Yes, Ionuin, he probably was, there is still so much that you have to understand, that you have not yet fathomed, but for now, see behind the rocks; there is a child. That child is you, Ionuin. You are just one year old.*

Saturnine reared and Tharl thrust forward, sinking his blade deep into her chest before diving low as a burst of flame exploded from her mouth. Saturnine keeled over and slumped to the floor. Tharl moved in for the kill, but a lazy passing sweep from Saturnine's outstretched wing sent him sprawling. He was soon on his feet again, but Saturnine roused herself and managed to take flight. Unsteadily, she hovered above the child and tried to pick her up, but Tharl leapt into action again, slashing and cutting with his sword, becoming drenched in orange-green blood. Saturnine abandoned her rescue attempt and, screeching, circled round before flying off, becoming nothing more than a speck in the distance.

Ionuin saw it all inside the head of Nexus and she knew that Seraph certainly had told the truth and left nothing out of the tale. A stray tear escaped her and she quickly wiped it away before it was spotted, but nothing escaped the attention of Nexus.

'Do not fret, little one. Saturnine was always mischievous and delighted in posing as a human. Alas, she went too far and fell in love with your father. From this love, both you and Taj were born.'

He reached down and hoisted Taj, embracing both him and Ionuin. Now the tears flowed freely as the reunited brother and sister hugged, and there was no shame in this emotional outpouring.

A hushed murmuring rippled through the gathered dragons.

'Way to go, Ionuin and Taj!' Glitch shouted, receiving a resounding thwack from his father's tail for his trouble.

Ionuin wiped away her tears. It was true. All of it was true. The eroding of her identity was complete. The life she had known existed no more. But who was she, really? Who had she become now that the transformation from childhood to adolescence had run its full course?

She turned her sad face towards Nexus. 'Who am I, Lord Nexus? Am I human, dragon, or just a freak like the mutant star people?'

'Freak? No, not a freak, you are one of us, child,' said Nexus, his voice brimming with comfort and care. 'From this day forward you will always be one of us, and like your mother, I sense that you possess a great spirit, a lively spirit that burns like a raging firestorm; one that can never be quelled.'

'Great spirit,' agreed Taj, 'and I also sense you are brimming with energy, Ionuin. This may mean that you possess special gifts, and you might also be able to wield great power.'

Ionuin remained unconvinced about special gifts. 'Great spirit, great power? It all sounds incredible, but it never did my parents any good, did it? If this spirit and power are so great, how come my father was able to kill my mother? If they truly loved each other, can't love surmount any obstacle? Surely my mother could have revealed her true nature and saved herself?'

There was much shuffling of feet and nervous clicking of talons at these words, and Ionuin thought she had touched upon a few raw nerves.

Taj placed his hands on her shoulders. 'In the chronicles of our library, we learn how love for a human and love for a dragon are two different things entirely. Humans experience only a brief lifespan, whereas a dragon's lifespan is virtually immortal by comparison. Love for a human could be swift and all consuming. For a dragon, it grows more slowly, but it has more permanence and lasts forever. That is, as we understand the concept of 'forever', for our understanding of such things is in constant flux.'

'The concept of forever is in constant flux?' Ionuin questioned.

Nexus lowered his head and stared Ionuin in the eye. 'That is enough of that kind of talk, Taj. You are only confusing her even more. Ionuin, what you need to know is that your mother was very brave,' he said, in a hushed voice. 'She managed to return here, to Fire Mountain, where, after telling her story, she died in my embrace.'

Tears welled in Ionuin's eyes again. 'And my father, my father died a lonely man, ignorant of the truth, spending his final years searching for a love that could never be found.'

Taj took her hand as Nexus lowered them back onto the ledge. 'Ionuin, you must rest. Then, you must tell me of Tharl, our father. All I know of him is what is told in dragon-lore. These revelations are new to me. Your existence is a miracle and now that I have family, a sister, to hear of a father figure, even a deceased one, is incredible and wonderful! But I want to know Tharl through you, my sister, for you knew him better than anyone.' He leaned over and kissed her on both cheeks, then on her forehead.

Ionuin felt Taj's warmth and affection. She cast aside her own feelings of loss and held him close for what seemed the longest time. Eventually, she turned to Nexus. 'I am overwhelmed by all the changes, but there is one change I haven't told you about. I am afraid the news is grave, Lord Nexus. In the Valley of the Caves, I met another dragon by the name of Spuddle. I suppose we came to each other's aid, if the truth be known, but I fear for his safety.'

'Be unafraid, Ionuin,' replied Nexus. 'We have at long last heard Spuddle call to us and dragons have been dispatched to assist him. Now, you must rest.'

Ionuin opened her mouth to protest, but Nexus hushed her to silence.

'Ionuin, I insist that you take rest and recuperation. You have experienced many revelations, enough to overwhelm you, but there are yet more to come and I too harbour fears. This is not over, and there are Cosmic forces speeding here even as I speak. I want you fully recovered and at your best, do you understand?'

'Erm, no,' said Ionuin. 'Not really. Cosmic forces?' she questioned. 'Do you mean, do you mean, the Dark Dragon?'

'Ah, so, you do know!' said Nexus.

'Well, I've never really seen the beast, apart from in my dreams when it invades my sleeping thoughts. I do sense it though, sometimes. It watches me, just, well, watches, as if it's waiting for me to do something.'

'Very interesting,' said Nexus. 'I believe it sees you as a weak link and desires to break you. While you were not in our company, you were very vulnerable. Perhaps if you had focussed on the Dark Dragon, or forced a confrontation, it could have latched onto you, increased its own presence and hurt you severely. Now that you are within the realm of Fire Mountain, you are safe, but you must rest, Ionuin. Rest is going to be so important if you are to be successful in what is to come.'

'Rest? I can't possibly rest!' Ionuin protested. 'Not now, I'm too excited, I'm buzzing, rampant with energy! My mind is whirling and, and . . . .'

Her eyes connected with those of Nexus and his hypnotic power instantly sapped her energy, her buzz fizzled out and strength seeped from her legs.

'That's better,' Nexus growled as Ionuin began collapsing into a sleepy dream state, Taj catching her in his arms.

'Sleep, sister,' he said, 'for there is so much yet to do.'

'Much to do,' Ionuin murmured, her mind beginning to float, the words of others echoing around her

'Take her to the chamber we have had prepared,' Nexus commanded. 'When Spuddle returns, I want to see him.'

'As you wish, Lord Nexus,' Taj replied.

As Ionuin closed her eyes and allowed sleep to claim her wandering mind, the dragons turned and filed one by one from the rocky ledge, entering the antechamber to the Great Cavern where a feast was being prepared to mark the end of an era and the birth of new beginnings.

Chapter Thirty One

Walking into a huge cavern, Ionuin felt warm, cosy, untroubled. Flames flickered all around her, great walls of raging fire, but she discerned no threat in the conflagration, none at all. On instinct, she reached down by her side and touched the comforting hilt of Fyrdraca. I have my sword, she thought, but how can this be? Before her, an enormous dragon suddenly appeared, emerging from the flames, its tail swaying lazily through the fire. Ionuin gasped, then as her eyes became focused on the creature, she realised it was not the dreaded Dark Dragon; this creature was golden in colour and exuded friendship.

'Nexus,' she mumbled, 'am I, am I dreaming?'

Nexus smiled and nodded. 'Yes, child, I needed to enter your mind, see you dream, know that you are truly safe from Dark forces, even in slumber.'

'But, I have my sword!' Ionuin said, her voice edged with surprise. 'Will I still have it on awakening?'

'Hardly,' Nexus answered. 'Dreaming a thing does not make it real, now does it?'

Ionuin frowned. 'No, no of course it doesn't.' She reached for the hilt of Fyrdraca, but it no longer hung on her hip. Glancing up she saw that Nexus had also vanished. 'Weird,' she mouthed as several sharp voices erupted around her. 'Hello?' she said, but on looking around, there was no one to be seen. She then came fully awake to the sound of muffled grunting interspersed with a loud sibilant hissing. Taj was standing over her and beside him loomed a concerned-looking green dragon.

'Now look what you've done,' Taj snapped. 'Your bumbling, grumbling voice has awoken her and it is not yet time for the feast to begin!'

'Spuddle?' mumbled Ionuin. 'Spuddle, is that you? It is you!' she shouted excitedly, trying to sit upright.

Of course it's me! Who else would it be? His thoughts fell into Ionuin's mind with gentle ease. *Relax, just rest. You've been through a lot, you know.*

Ionuin nodded her agreement, Spuddle was right, she had been through a lot, but she was so pleased to see him she felt a need to reach out and hug, perhaps be hugged in return. *Can you not communicate with me by word of mouth, like Nexus and the Red Dragons?* She asked, pushing her own mind into Spuddle's.

I've been away a long time. Five turns of the yearly cycle, at least, and in all that time I remained speechless and had not communicated with anyone or anything, until you came along. Now, I have to go and prepare for the fight.

'Fight?' Ionuin asked.

'Nexus will explain.' Taj interjected, having eavesdropped on the conversation.

Spuddle, perhaps sensing what she needed, leaned down and touched Ionuin on her forehead with great affection. *I have to go, Ionuin. I just wanted to see you, to make sure you were safe and let you know that I am safe. Father is so relieved to have me back and I, well, I am just glad to have finally come of age, thanks to you. I also need to thank you for saving my life. Those fools in the Valley of Caves would have fed from me until Merm turned to dust, which won't be long, if the prophecies are correct.*

Spuddle? You're talking in riddles. Whatever is all this about prophecies and the planet turning to dust?

It's only a prophecy, things could turn out differently. Look; I must go. There are preparations to be made, Taj will explain everything.

'I will not, Nexus will explain,' Taj said, adamantly.

'No, Taj,' said Ionuin, taking his hand. 'I have gone through so much and I feel so lost, that if I don't get some answers soon, I think I will turn as mad as the beasts that bark at the moon!'

Spuddle left the room and Taj seated himself beside his sister. 'Ionuin, it's all so complicated, I would not even know where to begin.'

Ionuin patted his hand. 'Complicated or not, there are things I need to know, yearn to know,' said Ionuin, looking into her brother's eyes, searching for some comfort. 'And, and I want to trust you and, well, giving trust is not easy, not for me!'

'Giving trust is only easy for the innocent and the gullible, Ionuin,' Taj replied, confidently. 'So do not worry on that score, and yes, I agree, you do need answers, but first, please Ionuin, I want to know more about you. I want to learn about your life and especially about father. I've seen the pictures through the mind of Nexus, but I know so little and you know so much; you've lived so much, Ionuin.'

Ionuin clasped Taj's hands and offered him her best smile. He had already elevated her life above his own to make her feel special and he had lived with dragons. She tried to peer inside his mind, to touch his thoughts, but hit a solid wall of resistance.

'Mind defence,' Taj said, 'comes automatically these days.'

'Ah,' replied Ionuin, then felt the wall before her dematerialise and she became embraced by affection and sincerity. This, she thought, was the warmest welcome she could ever have imagined. Feeling totally relaxed, she began telling Taj as much as she could about life with their father. Their minds swirled within each other as she revealed what Tharl was really like, his kind gentleness, his unusual sense of humour, his short temper coupled with instant forgiveness, his skill in the ways of the wild and his legendary bravery.

She shared all the good times they'd had, as well as the long lonely days when Tharl would slip into deep depression and hardly speak a word. She spoke of the adventures they'd embarked upon and also the times of isolation at their cottage. Taj listened to all that Ionuin had to say, asking questions when necessary, but listening in silence for most of the time, and when she had finished, there were tears in his eyes.

'I have missed out on such an important part of my life,' Taj said, his voice tinged with regret. 'The human part, and because our father is dead, there is nothing I can do to make amends.'

Ionuin gently squeezed his hand within her own. 'I can give you what you missed, Taj, or at least, I can try. In return, you must share with me the way of the dragon, for I too have missed out on much that I should know. Although, I must admit, my mind is besieged and reeling as a result of all the changes.'

'Changes,' murmured Taj, 'are the only constant we have, according to Nexus, and there have been many changes recently.'

'Um, I'll say,' Ionuin agreed. 'My life is not my own anymore and now that I think about it, I don't think it ever was, not really.'

Taj related to Ionuin's words and empathised with her identity struggle. He stood up and began pacing in a circle. 'Is anyone's life ever their own?' he asked, his voice sounding anxious. 'Seriously, it's the same for all of us, Ionuin. We mosey along, thinking we're in control, and then bang! Changes crash through our lives, uprooting all we have known in a chaotic rampage, showing us how destiny has us at its mercy!'

Ionuin was a little stunned at the passion in Taj's voice. 'Um, well, brother, I can tell that changes have certainly had a big impact on your life, at some time or other.'

Taj sighed and sat back down. 'I'm sorry, I did not mean to go off on a tangent. I'm not referring to the changes you have brought about, Ionuin. In a way, it's good that you're here, you have brought stability to my life and the timing could not be better. I think you're needed.'

'You really think so? I'm not so sure.'

'Time will tell,' said Taj, patting Ionuin's hand. 'But forgive me, I am so selfish sometimes, I'm forgetting how you have suffered and how you have lost all that you knew.'

Ionuin nodded her agreement. 'True, I have lost much. I mean, until father was murdered my life was just fine. Hunting, trapping, living at one with nature, and now, here I am, in a dragon kingdom that only a few days ago I did not even know existed.'

'I know; your old life has vanished, the family you had is no more, but, Ionuin,' he clasped her hands tightly, 'see it from my perspective. I had no human links at all, until you came along and the pressure I was under had become almost crushing.'

'Pressure, Taj? What pressure?' Ionuin asked, clasping his hands firmly within her own. 'What is it that I don't know? Why do I feel we are skirting round something here?'

'Hmm, well, not for me to say,' Taj sighed. 'You'll see, but don't worry. I'm sure your presence will make all the difference and now, at long last, we have some tangible hope that our enemies can be truly vanquished.'

Ionuin felt at a total loss, unsure what was going on, why there seemed to be a hidden agenda. 'Taj, whatever are you talking about?'

Taj smiled. 'Don't fret, trust me and you'll see, before your arrival I was beginning to fear the worst. So much seemed to depend upon me and my supposed ability.'

Ionuin shook her head dismissively. 'Taj, you're still not making sense. What enemies have to be vanquished? Also, why am I so important and why all the bloody silly riddles? Just tell me what is expected of me for crying out loud!' she said, her voice rising with exasperation.

'Ionuin, calm down,' Taj hissed. 'I'm supposed to be soothing you, keeping you confident and relaxed. If the dragons hear you shouting they may come running and I need more time alone with you.'

Ionuin leapt to her feet and paced the small chamber. 'If you want me calm and confident, then I need to know what is going on here.'

'Please, Ionuin, sit down,' Taj said, patting the bench beside him. 'It's no big deal, not really; only, it seems we are somehow linked to the end of days here on Merm.'

'End of days on Merm?' Ionuin said, sitting beside her brother 'What do you mean?'

'You don't know?' Taj said, looking at Ionuin in a manner she found uneasy. 'Surely Tharl told you the history of our world?'

'Um, sure, well, he told me some things. Most of which I thought was nonsense, like the bright star bursting and the all the people and animals becoming ill.'

'No nonsense there, Ionuin. I assure you, it's quite true; have you not seen the crazed creatures roaming around?'

Ionuin was instantly reminded of the two-headed bear. 'Yes, I've seen a few things, but, even so, I assumed there must be an alternative explanation to a bursting star! I mean, whoever heard or saw such a thing? And how can days come to an end?'

Taj laughed. 'Nothing lives forever, everything comes to an end, eventually, the dragons call it entropy, but you only have to glance skyward and the evidence is there, splashed across the heavens.'

Things began clicking into place for Ionuin. 'You mean; the hazy colours that often appear at night?'

'Exactly, the blue and red patterning that can be seen, well, that is the remnants of the explosion that decimated our world.'

'It is?'

'Truly. What else did Tharl tell you that you do not believe?'

Ionuin cast her mind through her memories, warm nights by the fire with her father, his voice loud with the effects of turnip wine, rambling about the world and its history. 'He told me about dragons swarming over the land and eating people by the hundred,' she said, nodding her head emphatically. 'He told me how everything began dying until existence here became limited to a few small areas. He told me how the natural state of things changed and the animals went mad, or bad, or both!'

'Er, yes, all true: well, kind of,' said Taj.

'Really!'

'Yes, really.'

'I've also been led to understand that Merm was once covered with forests and many, many, running rivers threading though luxurious grassy plains. All rubbish of course, tall stories, but my father had a wonderful imagination.'

'Our father,' corrected Taj, 'but these things you speak of are not stories. Before the Clysm, Merm was once as Tharl described it to you, but the bad things that happened-'

'Clysm?' Ionuin asked.

Taj sighed. 'Too much to explain, a story for another day, where was I?'

'Bad things happening,' Ionuin prompted him.

'Yes, the bad things that happened were the workings of the Dark. Allegedly, mostly our arch enemy; Dark Dragon, who has stalked the various dimensions of Merm for as long as anyone can remember, and trust me, dragon memories go back quite a long way.'

'I've seen that beast in my dreams.' Ionuin said, leaping to her feet. 'It's so dark that you can't really see it at all, not unless you sort of squint and look a little sideways. Does it live near a stone circle?'

'No,' said Taj, visibly shuddering. 'It doesn't live there, but it wants control of the circle. The circle is a space-time portal connecting our world to others that have similar portals. The Dark Dragon is not really here; not yet. What you have sensed so far is just its projected presence; a presence that it has somehow managed to slip into our world through the portal when it was unguarded.'

'Sounds too incredible to believe,' said Ionuin, absently running her fingers through her tousled hair. 'A bit like father's stories.'

'Incredible or not, Ionuin, it's true, believe me, it is all true,' Taj assured her, clenching and unclenching his fists.

'Taj, are you all right?' Ionuin asked him, again sitting down beside him and reaching for his hands.

Taj smiled. 'Yes, I'll be fine, just reliving an incident that sits in the back of my mind, but won't fully come forth. What was I saying? Oh yes, by passing through the portal you can travel across our galaxy, reach other worlds. Some claim you can even reach other galaxies in distant parts of the universe.'

'Other galaxies? Taj, your words are getting complicated. I don't think I can listen to much more and still understand what I'm supposed to know.'

Taj nodded his agreement. 'Well, to simplify things, those who control these stone circles, control just about everything. They are built by the forces of Light and-'

'The forces of Light?' Ionuin interrupted, her brows furrowing.

'Yes, Light. You see Ionuin-'

'Oh Taj, stop it, please, this is so frustrating, but it's all beyond my understanding. I know I wanted things explained, but you're just making it more difficult.'

'Sorry, I didn't mean to, but I've nearly finished.' He smiled as Ionuin sighed. 'You see, dragons and people, and every other living thing that ever existed, came from the hearts of stars.'

'What? You mean . . . ?'

'Yes, I mean everything and everyone are made of dust, stardust!'

'Dust? We are made of dust? You mean like the sand beneath our feet, the stinging grit that fills even the mildest wind?' Ionuin sat, eyes wide, trying to comprehend the words, trying to make sense of what Taj was saying. Could it really be true? Everything that existed or had ever existed came from the hearts of stars? 'We are stardust . . . so; we are truly Children of the Light.'

'Exactly!' Taj exclaimed. 'And I know what you're thinking, it just cannot be true, but it is true! Every single one of us, even the worlds, which are countless, are made of elements once forged inside of stars.'

'Are you sure?' Ionuin asked. 'I mean, this is open knowledge among dragons, right? Not just some imagined fantasy?'

'Quite sure,' said Taj. 'The worlds are bathed in rays of pure Light and the elements respond by giving birth to life. It is a long process, but it is gaining momentum, and through the life it creates, the power of Light is fighting to save the whole universe.'

Ionuin still felt confused. 'If this is so, I mean, we're all on the same side, then why would the dragons eat all the people?'

Taj laughed. 'Now that is just a gross misconception, Ionuin. The dragons were not eating the people, but saving them. Remember when you were rescued by Glitch?'

'Rescued?'

'Well, that's how Glitch tells it, but anyway. He didn't really eat you, did he?'

'No, he sort of swallowed me whole, but-'

'Exactly! You were unharmed, instantly put to sleep by the gases of his stomach, and the sleep chamber took care of you, didn't it?'

'Well, I'm here, so yes, in a way, I suppose so.'

'In ancient times, what the dragons were actually doing, after the nearby star exploded, was swallowing the people in order to transport them from this world to another, through the space-time continuum.'

Ionuin shook here head. 'I, I don't understand, another world? You mean a world beyond Merm?'

Taj again laughed. 'Sure, there are three other worlds that are inhabitable in our region of the galaxy; Deburon, Tarsier and Earth, and all can be reached through the stone circles.'

'I see,' said Ionuin, although she did not really see at all, the whole idea appeared somewhat bizarre. 'So, you're saying, 'travel by dragon, it's the only way to go!''

'Hmm, something akin to that; only this was before we built the stone circles, you understand. Now we have the circles, mankind can travel from world to world by himself. It's just that the obdurate people left on Merm choose not to do so; very frustrating.'

Ionuin looked thoughtful for a few moments. Her father had been keen on travel, but the idea of actually going to another world seemed preposterous. 'So, let's get this clear, these days the dragons simply point the way, like guides, yes?'

175

'Yes.' Taj replied. 'In my opinion, the dragons are no more than guards and guides, but Lord Nexus doesn't see it like that.'

'Well, he wouldn't, he's the dragon king.'

'I know, but to him, the relationship between dragons and humans is as important now as at any time in the past. Why he thinks like this is a mystery to me.'

'It's all a mystery to me, Taj, but surely Lord Nexus will explain his reasons, won't he?'

'He tells us some of the things he knows, but he possesses an awful lot more knowledge than he's prepared to reveal. What I am aware of, is that time was short when this world became flooded with poisonous radiation and the dragons had to save as many people as they could. A few, like our human ancestors, held out in small underground enclaves and sheltered villages. The dragons gave up on those as they felt it was pointless saving anyone who did not want to be saved.'

Ionuin thought about Taj's words. Some of it did seem to make sense, now. She needed time to apply her own kind of reasoning, but the questions kept coming and she still thirsted for answers, even if they were complicated. 'So, the dragons saved the people and did not eat them, but why? And how did such a relationship become possible between two species which are so obviously different? It still doesn't make sense.'

'The key to understanding is intelligence, Ionuin.'

'But, I don't understand and-' Ionuin again leapt to her feet. '-are you saying that I'm stupid?'

Taj raised his hands defensively. 'No, no, Ionuin. Not you. The key is intelligent life! According to Nexus, there is much life in the universe, thanks to the Light, but not all is yet intelligent.'

Ionuin did not look at all convinced. 'Well, yes,' she eventually conceded. 'I met some unintelligent life in the Valley of Caves.'

'I don't know all the history, but thousands of generations ago, people and dragons allegedly merged together and cohabited. Despite our physical appearances, genetically, the races are very much alike. This is why we can interbreed.'

Ionuin raised her eyebrows at Taj's last statement, but said nothing. After all, her mother was a dragon, allegedly.

'Not all dragons can shape-change, but the prophecies foretold of our coming and, maybe I shouldn't tell you this just yet, but, along with Glitch and Spuddle, you and I are apparently very special. Within us, lying dormant, there is supposed to be a great power. A sleeping energy that when released, will change the course of events between the battle of Dark and Light.'

Ionuin laughed. Tears rolled from her eyes, and she clasped Taj around his shoulders so that she did not slip to the floor. She had heard him say lots of things that sounded like rubbish, but this was beyond ridiculous. 'Now, I know you're joking, brother. What a load of cockamamie waffle! Tell me, oh please tell me that you're having a laugh. You are, aren't you? Dormant energy? Cosmic battles between higher powers? And we are somehow linked to this, this-'

'Ionuin, it is all true,' Taj, said, interrupting her outburst, 'I would not jest about such things. Not going to become hysterical are you?'

Ionuin stifled her giggles and looked into Taj's eyes to see he was solemn and quite serious, so she calmed herself. 'No Taj, I'm not becoming hysterical, but please, try to see things from my perspective and understand how ridiculous some of this sounds. You sure you're not teasing, not even a little bit?'

'Ionuin, dear sister, I really do wish that I was teasing, for what I am about to share with you will rock your world to its very foundations. I also wish you to know, before I reveal more, that I am truly sorry.'

Ionuin gulped as she scanned Taj's surface thoughts and her face blanched at the prospect of what was to come.

Chapter Thirty Two

Shaking her head in denial, Ionuin pulled away from her brother and felt his mental walls slam into place. 'I, I don't want to know,' she told him.

Taj grimaced. 'Ionuin, this is not something from which we can just run away.'

'Is this the 'special' to which you were referring?' Ionuin asked.

'Of course.'

'Taj, I thought you meant 'special' in a nice way? Not this, this-'

'Duty, Ionuin, we are special and it is our duty to see this through.'

Ionuin hung her head. 'I wish I had kept my silly mouth shut. The more answers you give the more questions I have, and to be honest, I half expect to awaken at any moment to discover this whole adventure is nothing more than a vivid dream! Do you ever suffer from false awakening?'

'Sometimes,' Taj admitted, 'but trust me, this is not false awakening, and if it was a dream, well, some dream, eh?' he laughed, trying to lighten the mood.

Ionuin sighed. 'I have only glimpsed what I suspect to be true, and I tell you now, it's all too much for me to accept. Go on, though. You might as well reveal everything.'

'Another time,' Taj said, failing to hide his disappointment. 'It's pointless me explaining any more if what I say seems so unbelievable and unacceptable to you. Besides, they are expecting us to attend the feast in the Great Cavern and it will be better to experience our duty first-hand rather than me telling you anything more.'

'Feast?' Ionuin quizzed, her mouth watering at the prospect of food. She could hardly recall when she last ate a proper meal. 'It, it will be proper food, won't it? Not just hunks of regurgitated flesh?'

Taj looked at her aghast. 'Of course it will be proper food, it is a feast!'

'Good,' Ionuin said, running fingers through her unkempt hair, 'I'm famished.'

'Come on, little sister.' Taj said, getting up and walking to the door. 'Time to meet our destiny. Don't worry, no harm will ever come to you, you have me by your side as protector.'

Ionuin stood up with alacrity. 'Oh well, in that case I suppose I'll have nothing to fear ever again!'

Taj glanced back at her, shook his head and smiled. 'Have you recovered enough to walk?'

'Oh, I can walk all right,' said Ionuin, returning his smile, 'but I'm not sure where I'm walking to, anymore,'

Taj laughed. 'Don't worry so much, please. Just follow me; we must not keep Nexus waiting if it can be avoided and I promise, all will be revealed.'

'Whatever,' murmured Ionuin, releasing a noisy sigh, blowing air between her lips, directing it upward so it flicked her fringe, throwing up her hands in exasperation as she followed her brother.

They walked down spacious dimly lit passages, hewn from the rock with hard-packed floors of small stones. She became quite transfixed by the huge, glowing, coloured crystals casting weird shadows on the rough walls; shadows that danced and moved as if alive. Warm air brushed her face, smelling of roasting flesh and smoke. As they drew near to the Great Cavern the noise of the feast became apparent. Large roars, hushed growls and the strains of high-pitched dragon laughter echoed along the passages.

They rounded a corner and stepped through one of the many entrances to the Great Cavern. It was huge! An underground amphitheatre with broad steps where countless dragons mingled in groups, enjoying themselves, making jokes, or busily engaging in conversations ranging from the impudence of young Glitch to the almost unfathomable workings of the ceaselessly expanding universe. All this, Ionuin soaked up in an instant through strange communications beyond her fathoming: she knew what she knew, how she gathered the information and understood what she saw, was not so clear. What was clear, what felt right, was that she actually belonged here, that her whole being was somehow tuned into her surroundings, as if she had been a part of the dragon world all her life.

'Amazing,' she murmured, allowing her mind to go with the flow, letting her sense of being adjust as she went along. 'Just, so wonderful!'

'Yes, isn't it?' Taj replied, staring around at the scene before them.

The walls were hung with tapestries depicting scenes from dragon history and every colour in the rainbow was on view, perhaps some, Ionuin thought, she had never seen before. Separating each of the twelve walls were columns of stone, forming towering archways, through which the largest dragons could walk two abreast. The archways were ornately carved in bas-relief and sunk-relief with more scenes from dragon history and they stretched to the vaulted roof where they merged into smoky darkness. In niches along the cavern walls were more carvings only these were done in high-relief so more of the figures could be seen and were ornately lit with crystals of various colours so the shadows accentuated the figures, actually making them seem alive, or so Ionuin thought. It would appear that the inside of Fire Mountain was just as impressive as the outside, if not more so, with all the dragons present. A table standing in the centre of the cavern appeared to be made of solid bronze and upon this table, amongst other roasted creatures, stood the charred carcass of a kodiak bear.

Ionuin brushed by Taj and walked right up to the table, placing her fingers on the bevelled edge, feeling vibrations tingle up her arm and into her mind. 'Wow! It's packed with memories, callings, signals for all dragons to attend the, the sealing of the Clysm?'

'It is a gong,' Taj informed her reaching out and taking her hand. 'We sound it to send out warnings, to call our armies to war, all sorts of things. It is also rung upon the death of a great one. The sound travels across the universe forever, mingling with the echo from the mighty crash that heralded the beginning of space-time.'

'Yes, but what is the Clysm?' Ionuin asked.

Taj shook his head. 'It is too difficult to explain just now. Besides, you need not worry about such things, they are in the future. First, we have to deal with the here and now. Do you understand?'

Ionuin nodded her agreement then turned her attention back to the table and the roasted delicacies waiting to be devoured. She guessed that Spuddle must be responsible for bringing the carcass of the bear to the feast, but that particular piece of meat looked to be a little too well-done for her liking. Taj snatched up what looked like a small bird, pulled it apart and handed some to Ionuin.

'It's chicken, I think,' Taj said around mouthfuls of white meat.

Ionuin bit down into what looked like a leg. 'Hmm, yes,' she said, chomping loudly, 'definitely chicken, I've eaten this many times, and goat.' While she ate she took in everything around her. Such marvellous scenes, and presiding over it all was Nexus sitting on a large serpentine throne encrusted with glittering green jewels. She smiled at the thought of such a large ferocious creature loving small, bright, shiny things.

'Come,' said Taj, grasping her by the hand, leading her to a table piled with platters of sliced food. 'Are you still hungry?'

'Yep, still ravenous, thank you,' Ionuin replied, her tummy rumbling as Taj piled slices of red meat slathered with pulped fruit onto a wooden board. He handed it to her with a slight bow. 'There you go, tuck in, when you've finished with the savouries, there are plenty of sweet delicacies on the next table.'

Ionuin ate her fill; slice after slice of hot meat and mashed apples, then she followed Taj and tore hunks from a massive slab of lemon sponge cake, something she had eaten only once before at a travelling fair when just a little girl.

'My favourite,' Taj said, sucking crumbs and sticky lemon syrup from his fingers. 'Dragons fetch the small yellow fruits from far off southern lands and the blue dragons cook them up a treat with a mixture of grain and cane products.'

'We call the yellow fruit, lemons,' Ionuin told him, rubbing her belly, which felt like it might burst.

'Lemons,' Taj repeated, belching loudly.

A shadow passed overhead and Ionuin instinctively ducked, reaching for her sword, which was not there, then going even lower to her boot-knife, but stopping short of drawing the weapon.

Taj patted her shoulder. 'Relax, there is no danger here.'

'Ionuin, so glad that you have recovered,' said a croaky voice above her head.

She glanced up and was relieved to see it was only Spuddle hovering, flapping his wings gently, his jaws greasy with food; then Glitch flew in and bumped him aside.

'Of course she has recovered,' Glitch chimed in, 'I saved her so she could fully recover. Isn't that right, Ionuin?'

'Yeah, course you did,' snapped Spuddle, butting Glitch in his stomach sending him crashing through a large archway where Sheratz dragged him away.

'I'm pleased you've found your voice, Spuddle,' Ionuin said, happy to see him looking so fit and healthy.

'Returning slowly and increasing in strength with every passing moment,' Spuddle replied, before gliding over to the up-turned gong, snapping a huge chunk of burnt meat from the crisped bear.

'So much improved!' Ionuin remarked.

'Yes, isn't he just?' Taj said, taking Ionuin by the hand, leading her across the chamber. 'Dragons heal rather quickly when nourished properly.'

Ionuin nodded knowingly, recalling how Spuddle had transformed himself on their trek along the Valley of Caves. She allowed a smile to play along her lips. She hardly dared to believe it, but she felt an unfamiliar, buoyant sense of happiness as she and Taj threaded their way through the party-throng under the gaze of all assembled, receiving gracious looks from appraising eyes.

'Do you feel the love in here, Ionuin?' Taj asked.

'Is that what the feeling is: love?'

'Of course; the love of life, the love of being, the sensation of belonging, becoming a part of something greater than the individual: group power!'

Ionuin thought about Taj's words and they made sense. Even though she had thought that she knew everything there was to know about survival and life, somehow, actual life, lived to the full, dragon life, held more mystery than she had ever thought possible. She scanned the room, picking up on latent vibrations that echoed down through thousands of layered years, mingling easily with the present sensation of casual wellbeing, cushioning her with blissful contentment. 'Hmm, yes, I do feel the love in here, if indeed, that's what it is.'

Taj laughed. 'Woman of little faith! Of course that's what it is! Think about it, without the love of life, what is the point of living?'

Ionuin did not immediately reply; the word 'woman' fell unkindly in her ear, as she had always thought of herself as a girl, until now. One of the men she had dispatched in the Valley of Caves had called her a woman: but for different reasons entirely. 'Taj, I don't think of myself as a woman. I'm, I'm just a girl really, and-'

'I know,' interrupted Taj. He placed his arm around Ionuin's shoulder, giving her a friendly squeeze. 'You worry too much, sister. Girl, woman, it's only a matter of perception. Take Spuddle for instance. He's just a big kid really, but he is also the son of Nexus and the king in waiting of the Green Dragon Brood, and if accepted, one day he will be a Great Golden Male like Nexus.'

'Really? Spuddle is actually a king?'

'In waiting,' Taj corrected her, 'but in the past, he stubbornly refused to come of age, so in desperation, his grandfather, Shogun, whose skeleton you were hiding inside when Glitch found you, took him out into the world and forced him into a situation where he would have to defend himself. We had thought Spuddle would enlighten us as to what really happened with his grandfather, but he has no memory of the event, so unfortunately, we are no wiser as to why things did not work out as planned.'

'The big dragon skeleton was the grandfather of Spuddle?' Ionuin said. 'So, if Spuddle is the son of Nexus, our uncle; then that means . . . ?'

181

'Yes, Shogun was our grandfather too, Spuddle is our cousin and thanks to you, he's now back with the clan.'

'How weird! Shogun lost his life in order to make Spuddle come of age? Is this the usual thing with dragons?'

'Well, no, not exactly. Shogun had already handed leadership over to Nexus as he felt the time was right. Dragons often act solely upon such instinct. It was this same instinct that made Shogun feel he had outlived his present incarnation. His time of parting had come and instead of just dying in a chamber and melding into the stone, some dragons often choose to go out with a bang. What better way than by battling with a few diehard humans too obstinate or stupid to leave a dying planet and at the same time, force Spuddle into fighting through his coming of age?'

Ionuin ignored the remark about humanity being obstinate and stupid; after all, it was fair comment. 'Taj, the danger! Spuddle could have been killed!'

'Yes, yes, he could,' Taj agreed, 'or he could have come of age and fought, but it took you to bring that out of him.'

'Hmm, must be my magic touch. What of Spuddle's mother?'

'Nadine. Yes, well, she's another mystery about which no one ever speaks. I think the Dark Dragon is involved in her disappearance, but only Nexus knows the truth and no one dare ask.'

'I see. Perhaps I should-'

'Don't even think about it, Ionuin. Nexus sees and hears almost everything and he likes to keep private things private.'

The Great Cavern fell into hushed murmurings as the two neared the throne of Nexus.

'Taj, Ionuin, my nephew and niece,' said Nexus. 'I am so proud of you both. Dragons! Clear the sacred gong,' he commanded.

Dragons swooped upon what remained of the half-eaten bear and the other roasts and everything was devoured within seconds. Spuddle and Glitch were left licking up juices from the tabletop. Nexus gestured for Taj and Ionuin to stand upon the bronze gong while Spuddle and Glitch, still licking their lips, reluctantly shuffled out of the way.

'Now,' said Nexus. 'We are foregoing the ceremony and ritual, it's not really required. So, when you are ready, I command you both to transform yourselves.'

'Transform?' Ionuin whispered to her brother. 'Does he mean what I think he means? Is this what I saw in your mind, Taj?'

Taj nodded his head, a look of concern registering in his eyes. 'Afraid so, dear sister; this is the duty from which there is no escape.'

'But, transform? I mean, I never . . . is it even possible for us to do such a thing?'

Taj sighed. 'Well, apparently, since we are half-dragon, we should be able to change our physical appearance in the blink of an eye.'

'You mean, we can turn dragon, like, like our mother turned human?'

Taj shrugged. 'Nexus told me before your arrival that it ought to be possible, well, not exactly true, he told me it is possible and it will be done.'

Ionuin snorted with laughter. 'Taj, tell me you jest?'

Taj shook his head, his features very solemn. 'I am not jesting, Ionuin. Neither would Nexus jest about such a thing. He rarely jokes about anything. Not only is he adamant that we will transform, it is expected and it is also crucial.'

Ionuin felt totally bewildered at this new turn of events but before she could protest further, Nexus was on his feet.

'Less of the chatter, you two,' he roared, his voice booming around the chamber. 'I commanded you both to change, so less talk about changing and more changing, if you don't mind.'

Ionuin flexed her mind and looked at Taj. *But how, Taj? How do we turn dragon?*

I suppose we simply think about transforming our physical shape, he sent back. *In truth, I don't know as I've never done it, not once.*

The voice of Nexus filled their heads. *Ignore Taj's negative approach; Ionuin, but he is correct about one aspect, transforming is simple, just think about becoming dragon. Your mother managed it with ease; so can you two. Now, one more time, I command you both to change.*

Ionuin and Taj exchanged uncertain glances and then gave it everything they had. They flexed their minds, thought of dragons and attempted to make their bodies alter shape. They strained and strained, but nothing happened.

'I can't do it,' gasped Taj despondently, with a release of pent up breath. 'I just can't do it!'

Ionuin fell to her knees, breathing hard. 'Neither can I! It is too hard, it is impossible!'

Nexus looked confused as he circled the low table. 'I don't understand. According to the prophecies of old, this should be child's play. Are you positive that you are both trying your very best?'

'Lord Nexus,' said Taj, 'I swear, I am trying my best. I feel Ionuin also doing her utmost. Perhaps the prophecies are wrong, or perhaps, we are not the chosen children that you-'

'What?' Nexus bellowed. 'Not the chosen children? Wrong prophecies! Are you insane, Taj? What you lack is self-belief, both of you. If you truly believe you are the Children of the Light then anything is possible, do you hear me? Anything! Now try again!'

'Children of the what?' Ionuin hissed, recalling how they are all made of stardust.

'Just a title,' Taj replied. 'It means nothing; it's how we're described in the prophecies. It means more than being made from stardust; it means we are the chosen ones.'

'Well I never did any choosing,' Ionuin stated.

'Well, why am I waiting?' Nexus bellowed, with obvious impatience. 'Are you going to continue kneeling there and jabbering or are you going to transform?'

'Nexus?' Ionuin said, getting back to her feet, the note of trepidation in her voice revealing her uncertainty. 'What if, if we just can't do it?'

183

'Can't do it! Can't do it?' Nexus bellowed, hot smoke bursting from his nostrils. 'Of course you can do it! Transformation is easy!'

Ionuin gulped, hardly able to believe that she was actually arguing with Nexus, the mighty Golden King. 'Well then, maybe it is the circumstances that are wrong,' she ventured. 'Maybe when the time is right, we will change.' She looked to her brother, who nodded his agreement.

'I think my sister is correct,' Taj said. 'Maybe the time is not yet right.'

'The time had better be right soon,' said Nexus. 'The enemy will try to break through at sunset and the fight for our existence will begin. Not only our fates rest upon the outcome, but the whole galaxy could be thrown out of kilter should we lose. Defeat is unthinkable.'

Sheratz moved out of the concealing shadows behind the throne. 'I think Ionuin has a valid point. Remember, Nexus, that Spuddle and Glitch are also included in the prophecy if we have deciphered the wording correctly. Being reasonable, Glitch hardly resembles anything special and Spuddle could never perform any dragon feats at all in his first flush of youth! Even Shogun, our former leader, could not achieve Spuddle's coming of age and he died trying! It was only when the time was right that Spuddle discovered the true power of his inner-self . . .' Spuddle snickered and rolled his eyes in an attempt to look amusing. '. . . well almost,' finished Sheratz, moving back into the shadows.

Nexus appeared to drift into deep thought and consider the matter. 'So be it!' he said. 'Perhaps the heat of battle will change things. Prepare to go to the stones, my loyal dragons. The time is fast approaching and we must be ready.'

'Nexus?' Ionuin said. 'Before Glitch snatched me from the skeleton of Shogun I had a sword that was given to me by my father. It is called Fyrdraca, and if I am to enter into battle, I will be needing it.'

'Yes, child, we know of Fyrdraca and its power,' Nexus said, 'only, it was a birth gift from the Catalin, first of the Chosen, not your father.'

'Fyrdraca came from Catalin?' Ionuin remembered the words of her father. 'Hmm, yes, my father mentioned this wizard-like fellow from time to time. I will still need my sword, that is, if there is to be a battle.'

'There is going to be a battle, don't doubt it. As for Fyrdraca, we sent a dozen dragons back to the Valley of Caves to find the sword, but it has been taken,' Nexus informed her.

'Taken?' Ionuin wailed.

'Yes, what is more, we suspect you have been trailed since your father's death. I have seen the dreams inside your mind. Forces have been trying to break you mentally, trying to make you afraid and cower, so you give up on yourself, and life. I suspect these forces have taken your sword to make you weak, so you lose hope, but I know you are strong. I know you and Taj will save us all.'

'I don't understand; how can I fight without my sword?'

'Dragons don't have swords,' Nexus told her, his voice firm and commanding, 'and you will become dragon, Ionuin: you will!'

Two green dragons flew into the Great Cavern from high arches near the ceiling. 'Lord Nexus,' shouted the first one to land. 'Sincere apologies, but Lord Bollfur and his sons, they have all escaped!'

'Escaped!' exclaimed Nexus. 'But, but how? There were four of you guarding the entrance.'

Ionuin nudged Taj as dragons began talking in subdued voices. 'Who is Lord Bollfur?'

'Shush! A lethal enemy,' Taj told her, his voice deathly quiet.

The green dragon prostrated himself on the floor. 'My Lord, they never came by us, but we found a hidden exit beneath the stone bed leading into old disused tunnels. We followed them, but there was no sign of Bollfur or his sons.'

'Well, that's just brilliant,' said Nexus. 'Whatever else can possibly go wrong?'

If they expect me to fight without Fyrdraca and turn into a dragon, just about everything can go wrong, Ionuin thought, biting her bottom lip, but she said nothing and quietly wondered if she would actually live to see another day dawning.

Chapter Thirty Three

Across the rock-strewn land they flew, skimming the jagged rims of giant craters, Ionuin and Taj astride the back of Nexus, Taj sharing the tale of his escape from Blucher and Bolden and the traitorous Lord Bollfur. In the far distance, ringing a circle formed from tall stones and capped with lintels, were hundreds and hundreds of dragons of many colours all bathed in a pale, pink glow from the darkening sky. Maybe more than hundreds, thought Ionuin, perhaps thousands. She had never had so many things to count before and it was hard to guess. What she was certain of though, was that the scene looked so beautiful, breathtaking almost, and yet, at the same time, unsettlingly eerie. The sun, sinking fast, had faded to a dull shimmering orange, its tinged light appearing to make the horizon shake. It was setting, bringing in the night, the day's end supposedly heralding the arrival of the Dark Dragon in its entirety.

Nexus flew downwards, circled once and landed gently within the stone ring. He rippled his great muscles and, free of resin, Ionuin and Taj slid to the floor. Other dragons watched through the gaps in the stones and murmurs rippled outwards until the whole congregation were indulging in quiet conversation. Taj stared directly ahead at the central altar stone, seemingly trying to concentrate, while Ionuin glanced around nervously, unsure what would happen next.

Glitch and Spuddle landed in the circle and took up positions opposite each other. Neither dragon flinched or showed any emotion, not even acknowledging the presence of the others. Both looked mature beyond their years and Ionuin thought it all seemed rather odd. The first stirrings of doubt flickered into life. What if this whole charade was nothing more than a cruel trick? What if she were just an unwitting sacrifice to some ancient mysterious ritual performed for the benefit of the dragons? When she thought about it, really thought about it, everything that had happened seemed to be beyond the realms of even the most extreme possibility. She was just a girl, wasn't she? Not a princess or a unique dragonet, just a girl. This whole thing, when examined properly, seemed outlandish and absurd in the extreme!

'Nothing to be afraid of, Ionuin,' Nexus said, his calm voice reassuring. 'Nothing here will harm you apart from those who are yet to come, and against these enemies we shall defend you with the last drop of our ancient blood.'

Well, that's comforting, Ionuin thought, but she simply acknowledged Nexus with a nod of her head, hardly daring herself to speak for fear of the words she might utter. She hoped he was right, but she knew that hope, blessed hope, even if it was the last bastion of deliverance, could also be cruel.

'Of course,' continued Nexus, 'the self-doubt you are now experiencing is part of the Dark Dragon's considerable armoury. A vast blotch of repulsive negativity planted in your mind to disrupt what you must do, must achieve.' Nexus lowered his head so that he was face-to-face with Ionuin. 'Don't defeat yourself, Ionuin. We are relying on your inner courage and conviction to do what is right: you do understand, don't you?'

Ionuin nodded; she knew that Nexus was right. She had simply spooked herself, that's all, nothing to be afraid of. She was not merely a girl, but a girl whose life had changed and had become part of a universal struggle against tyrannical forces that sought to eliminate the existence of life: all life! Whatever am I doing here, she wondered? Of course there is something to be afraid of! She felt like screaming. It was all too much to cope with. Transform herself into a dragon at will? Who was she kidding? 'I can't do it,' she murmured. 'It's sheer foolishness, it's nonsense; I'm not who you think I am. I'm not, I'm, not, I'm . . . I'm just a girl! A silly little orphaned girl, lost and afraid!'

'Ionuin, please be calm and try to relax,' Nexus said, offering reassurance. 'Take deep breaths, and remember, even little orphaned girls must be brave, must face life, but you are more than this; just trust your instincts, look deep within: you are dragon!'

Ionuin took a deep breath as instructed and looked around at the other dragons that were watching her. She glanced upwards, seeing the sky filled with even more dragons, and others were arriving all the time. It was not a dream, not an illusion, this was actually happening. She was going to face an enemy far greater than any she had ever before imagined, and Nexus wanted her to relax! Utter madness, she thought, chewing hard on her bottom lip, her hands trembling by her side as conflict assaulted her mind again. She swayed uncertainly, her head swimming with fuzzy imagery that spiralled away as she tried to draw it into focus. She stumbled, the gaze of Nexus pierced her eyes and she felt herself slip inside his mind where everything changed. Clarity burst through her in an instant as she sank beneath layers of dragon thought that lay centuries deep. Down, down, down she went, seemingly falling back through time until she found what appeared to be the real Nexus. A small green dragon, nothing more than a baby really, and he smiled so warmly. *Nothing to be afraid of Ionuin, is there?* The words whispered into her brain.

I don't know, is there? She replied. *One moment I am certain of everything, then nothing seems real, and I am not used to being scared. It, well, it scares me! Are you not afraid, Nexus?*

The tiny dragon embraced her. *Yes, Ionuin, I am afraid; only a fool would not be afraid. After all, we are about to face the Dark Dragon and its army and we may all be slaughtered like fattened cattle unless you and Taj can transform and then aid Glitch and Spuddle to become Children of the Light. I know you can do it, girl. You just have to believe in yourself. Do you trust me, Ionuin?*

Yes, answered Ionuin instantly. Then realised she meant it. *Yes, yes, I do trust you, you're right, I can do this.* Nexus released her and she floated up, up, up! *I can do this, she repeated, I know I can.*

She snapped back into her own head and looked at Nexus and smiled. 'Sorry,' she said, her fingers massaging her temples, 'I lost it there for a few moments. Just, lost it, and, well, thank you, my Lord.'

'You're welcome, Ionuin. There is no need for apologies, just keep your concentration. Remain focussed, and everything will be fine. You do realize that this is the last of our brood on this desolate planet, don't you?'

Ionuin nodded. 'I do now.'

'A great race, on a once great world,' Nexus continued, sadly, 'but nothing lasts forever, child. Not even the hardened rock from which we were initially forged. You, Ionuin, you and Taj are the future. Between you both, within this circle, you carry the duty and burden of responsibility.'

'I know. Taj spoke to me of duty. Forewarned, I suppose, is forearmed,' said Ionuin confidently, looking around. 'I've visited this place in my dreams and I admit, it is scary, twanging the nerve-endings as it does, but there's also a sort of comfort to be had.' She reached out and touched one of the great upright stones that formed part of the inner circle. It trembled slightly as it vibrated beneath her hand. 'I can feel something here, a presence. Nexus, who actually built this monument?'

'Men and dragons,' Taj answered, 'with the help of magic.'

'Magic?'

'Not important,' Taj assured her, as he reached for her hand. 'What is important, is the incredible power: can you feel it? It's the energy of us all, everything we are, linking to other worlds through time and space.'

Ionuin nodded and touched fingertips with her brother. A static charge rushed through them and they both tensed at the feeling.

Taj slipped his hand down the side of Ionuin's face, his fingers pushing her hair behind her ear. 'I have been here many times, sister, many times. I never fail to become uneasy, but, like Lord Nexus says, don't be afraid. It's just the power flooding the air, flowing through us, making us feel different. Forget about the responsibility; search out your confidence and allow it be your ultimate guide.'

'Do you sense the encroaching Darkness though, Taj?'

'Yes, I sense it, but I cancel it out by ignoring everything except the power from the stones.'

Ionuin hugged Taj then kissed him, on the forehead and on both cheeks. As she pulled away Taj clasped her shoulders and squeezed her, an unfamiliar look surfacing in his lavender eyes that she could not interpret. 'Taj?' she said, her hands reaching for his face.

'I, I love you sister,' he said, his cheeks flushing with colour.

Ionuin pinched his chin. 'I know; I feel your love, Taj. I love you too, brother,' she said, gently removing his hold on her, stepping back, not trusting herself to speak further.

Taj took a deep breath, his chest puffing out, then deflating as he exhaled with a sigh, a smile twitching at the corners of his mouth.

'Take your places. It is the time of reckoning,' said Nexus, rising into the air with one great beat of his broad wings. 'The enemy is coming and only the Children of the Light can secure victory. Prepare to utter the words!' he bellowed. 'Let them ring out through the night so the whole galaxy knows that the first true battle for our region of the universe has at last begun.'

Ionuin and Taj moved into position and faced each other across the circle, as did Spuddle and Glitch. The other dragons stirred. Nexus hovered above the proceedings and there was a loud flapping of wings as the whole brood took to the air in one heaving movement, flying around the stones in an unbroken circle. The words they chanted scorched the very air.

Universal energy: universal energy.
Resonating through the open mind.
Touching the heart, infiltrating the soul.
Give unto us, the raw power of Light.

The ground trembled as the last words died away. Nexus lowered himself onto the central stone ring. Ionuin heard the approach of the enemy before she saw them. A loud screeching, like metal scraping against metal, pierced the darkening sky. Ionuin felt dizzy and began to sway to a rhythmic beat that pounded within her, pulsing inside her temples, racing through her blood. Wailing notes pierced her mind, rising in pitch as if two different musical instruments were playing in unison. First one instrument seemed dominant, then the other rushed to the fore and became more prominent, then they blended together before drifting away entirely, leaving Ionuin with a susurrus trembling in the core of her soul.

This was it. She was changing, becoming dragon. Nothing could stop it now. With the music dispersed, the screeching of the yet unseen enemy was deafening and the dragons wheeled, gathering momentum, chanting 'Power is the Light. Power is the Light'.

The urge to change then suddenly lessened; she felt weak, sick and sleepy. Then the voice of Nexus penetrated her mind. *Gather together all that you are, child. Know yourself, look deep into your id, search out the beast that dwells within and then, and only then, will you become!*

I was wrong, she thought, *I cannot do this, I can't! I don't believe, Nexus!* Ionuin's mind screamed back at him as self-doubt again reared its ugly head. *I can't believe! I can't! None of this is happening! I am just a girl and I know I am not special! I can't be special!*

Nonsense, child! You live and breathe with the power of the Light from which you sprang, from which we all sprang. Just being alive makes you special, child: just being alive makes us all special, every single one of us, but you must find your way through the labyrinth of your inner-sanctum of thought, suppress your humanity and wrench the hidden dragon into life! Do not sabotage yourself! Once you be . . . .

Nexus's words faded into nothingness, becoming channelled out by something sinister. Inside Ionuin's mind the Dark Dragon appeared, its burning red eyes pinpoints of malign glee that pierced deep into her soul. It grinned, a chilling grin. Ionuin's breath caught in her throat, her screams struggled and died.

The Dark Dragon hissed. *I am the one whom you fear, Ionuin. I am your undoing. Servant of the Light, now you will witness my power! The power of the void, I am the Dreadnought condemned to be the monster of the abyss! The monster who seeks you out in your dreams.*

I deny you! Ionuin screamed.

The Dark Dragon sniggered. *Deny me all you like, all to no avail, weakling. Your attempt to become dragon is pathetic, little girl. You are an abomination, a freak of nature. an interference that, as a transmogrified agent of the Dark, I cannot, and will not, tolerate.*

Ionuin gasped inwardly and tried to break her thoughts free. She struggled and writhed, but was held so fast that her mind could barely function. *Get . . . out . . . of my head, you hideous-glob-of-putrid-phlegm!*

Bah! So childish, hurling powerless insults in the theatre of war where only grown-ups battle for supremacy. Do you not understand, human? The likes of you can never compete against the likes of me and mine! My Dreadnought savagery will rip your Light asunder, plunge your screaming soul upon the jagged spike of your own reality, where it will writhe for eternity in tormented anguish!

I, I deny you! I am not just a child, not just human, I am special! Ionuin wailed.

The Dark Dragon laughed. *Oh, yes, yes you are special. Especially stupid to think you could ever survive here, in this place, the realm where I rule all that I survey! I taught your brother not to venture into my Dark abyss of ruthless cruelty and now, child, I shall teach you!*

Ionuin extended her thoughts, pushed out her being as she did when dreaming and soared away from the macabre menace, taunts and laughter chasing her.

There is no escape, little Ionuin. You are doomed before you begin, for you know the truth and you fear the truth. You exist in the poverty-ridden shadows of poor-reality, beyond the void, or so you think. But the void is everywhere, Ionuin. It is even within you, lying dormant, waiting, hiding, yearning to rise and claim you! Allow me to awaken your darkness. You'll like it here, in the dark, alone with the cold emptiness stretching on beyond forever.

Ionuin continued to race away, her thoughts hurtling faster and faster, the voice of the Dark Dragon beginning to fade.

We'll meet again, Ionuin, in your world, and I shall seek you out and slice you from the self-delusion that has been your whole life. You are a lie, Ionuin. Your life has been a lie, a hollow shell of pitiful fabrication.

Ionuin could see light, she was almost there, almost free!

Laughter, deep and booming as if from a bottomless pit, echoed through her mind. *Come back, Ionuin. Stay for awhile, why not join me . . . and stay indefinitely!'*

The voice of Nexus blasted into her mind. *Ionuin! Deny it, just deny it and it is defeated!*

Ionuin rocked back on her heels. *I tried, but it had me, Nexus! The damn Dark Dragon broke into my mind; latched onto my soul!*

You are safe, push its words from your thoughts, it wants to crush you before you even begin.

Ionuin opened her eyes and bent into a crouch as a torrent of blackness streamed upwards from the centre circle, funnelling into the sky, a spiralling column so darkly opaque that it resembled a breach in reality. High clouds, faintly tinged with a blush of orange from the sinking sun, were swept aside as the column arced outwards. It filled the sky with an expanding cloak of pure darkness that fell back to the ground, like an unfurling umbrella, locking all the dragons inside an impenetrable black bubble.

The deafening screech vanished to be replaced by a deathly cold silence that covered the land. The Darkness took on shapes and forms, blood red eyes and gaping mouths, with razor-sharp teeth, appeared everywhere. Leathery black wings thrashed the air and scything claws hung at the ready. The Dark Dragon army numbered thousands upon thousands and still they poured through the circle that had become an open portal to the Dark side.

Ionuin knew she had to do something, or all was lost; she had to become, she had to transform, and like a yearning to quench a raging thirst, the urge to find her destiny blossomed outwards like a desert rose. She flexed her mind, but nothing happened. All communication, physical and mental, had become blocked. Gusts of wind blew her hair as the circling dragons of Fire Mountain built up speed and in the impenetrable blackness, Ionuin fought down her rising fear. Determination to do what was required quashed all doubts and she again flexed her mind, focussing on the stones around her that were now glowing in a fluctuating purple light.

'That's it, that's the way, Ionuin,' she heard Nexus shout, 'but more, you need more, much more!'

Ionuin concentrated and the glow increased as she realised that it was the power from within that gave the stones their light. Glitch and Spuddle also gave off a faint shine, as did Taj; she then caught a flicker of uncertainty in Taj's eyes and she hurled her thoughts across the circle. *We must become, Taj. Everything depends upon us. We must become!*

She hoped her encouragement reached him and helped, but, from the strain on his face, he was struggling and ultimately, she knew it was down to her. Stiffening every fibre of her being, she drew on the self-belief instilled in her by the words of Nexus. She remembered the teachings of her father, who had told her to always do her best and everything would be as it should, and she pictured her mother, sleek and golden, like Nexus, and knew what she must do.

The changes began in the pit of her quaking stomach. A dormant seed, splitting open, an intense heat growing, unfurling, spreading along her limbs in a quickening rush until her whole body throbbed and Ionuin thought she just might explode. Then, all pain ceased. All human thought stopped. Time itself appeared to stand still. A pleasant fire, warm and soothing, erupted deep within her body and it actually did feel like she was exploding, but she was becoming her other self: she was turning dragon! Limbs stretched, wings sprouted, facial features altered out of all proportion. Flesh changed in texture and colour, teeth and nails grew. Eyes widened as lilac-coloured light streamed away from her and blazed into the sky, touching the other dragons, until they too glowed.

Ionuin could see Taj had also transformed, his face was now elongated into a dragon snout complete with shiny white teeth and red lolling tongue. His eyes were huge, glowing purple and hooded as he looked over his new dragon-body,

191

the scales rippling as he flexed his muscles and he blazed with the same lilac colour.

The dragons circled at such speed, that they became a flashing blur of kaleidoscopic colour and Nexus, a streak of pure gold, flew slightly above them, like a guiding force. Ionuin, Taj, Glitch and Spuddle watched in fascination, then the Dark Dragon screeched and its army closed in for the attack.

Chapter Thirty Four

The enemy targeted Nexus first; waves of blackness poured from the nebulous mass and totally enveloped him in a writhing mound of lethal mayhem. Howls of pain and death skewered the air as black beast after black beast was flung aside by the strength and speed of the Golden Dragon King. A heady mixture of terror and excitement fused together as further streaks of the Dark Army lunged downward, smashing into the circling dragons of Fire Mountain.

Ionuin's ears rang with the devastating cries of the dying Fire Mountain dragons, wrenching at her heart. The wheeling circle began to slow from the repeated attacks. Combat broke out on the ground between groups of opposing forces and through sheer weight of numbers, the Dark Army began to secure the upper hand. Ionuin saw eyes gouged out, wings and limbs torn off, throats slit open. Walls of flame spewed forth in every direction, destroying countless numbers in a raging firestorm. Blood flowed freely, thick and orange with streaks of luminescent green, bubbling and hissing as it covered the area around the stones. The enemy disintegrated upon death, but as one fell, another two took its place and there seemed no limit to the carnage, no end to the killing.

Ionuin stumbled forward and, unused to her new body-shape, promptly fell over. 'What the . . . ?' She glanced over and saw Taj sway backwards, then drop to the floor. Feeling vulnerable, Ionuin scrambled to her feet and flexed her mind. *Taj, how can we use our dragon shapes to fight, if we can't even walk?*

Spuddle's voice broke into Ionuin's thoughts. *Pat yourself all over, feel your body's extremities; know where you are then focus your mind. You have not completed your becoming. You need to link brain and body, and hurry, you are as exposed as a newly fledged babe!*

A dark shape flew at Ionuin. Glitch snatched it from the air before it could reach her, his jaws clamping around its neck, shearing off its head, the body tumbling to the floor and rolling about as if still very much alive.

I, I have it! Taj exclaimed, getting to his feet, swishing his wings back and forth, scuffing the dusty floor with his talons. He pounced forward, his mouth snapping at the flailing wing of the beast Glitch had just decapitated, ripping free a sheet of leathery membrane. *I, I am no longer weak! No longer just Little Squeaker! I am dragon!*

Ionuin noticed that unlike Spuddle and Glitch, who had taloned forelegs and independent wings, her arms and hands were attached to a leathery membrane, as were Taj's. Her fingers were spread through the membranous wing itself, while her thumbs were transformed into wicked looking hooks.

She sent thoughts through her body, felt them travel all around her dragon-form and come bouncing back into her brain; her whole world changed in an instant. Suddenly, she was plunged into a depth of whirling sensation, previously unimaginable vitality coursing through her. Her tongue flicked out, tasting the air, sending information flowing through her mind, all her senses erupting into life, taste, smell, seeing, hearing, all incredibly enhanced beyond her wildest imaginings. Even her feet, planted firmly on the ground, relayed a heightened awareness of touch that was staggering to behold. She felt connected to everything around her, not only in the physical world, but in spiritual essence too. The vibrant pulse of life in all its glory filled her with wonder and awe to such a degree that she thought her very soul might simply burst with pleasure.

'Wow! Oh wow! I feel so alive! Is it like this for all dragons?' she asked of no-one in particular.

'You'll get used to it,' Glitch said, 'now come on, monkey-girl, in case you hadn't noticed, there's a bit of a scrap going on here.'

Ionuin swayed, took a step forward and found her sense of being and spatial awareness now worked perfectly. The suggestion to connect mind to body made by Spuddle had certainly worked a treat; she felt at home with being a dragon; so natural, so alive. She then ducked as an enemy swooped overhead, trying to kill her.

'Close one,' she murmured, before leaping at her would-be attacker with devastating precision, lashing out with sudden limber speed. The talon at the end of her wing scored a wicked slash in the creature's belly, sending it crashing into the upright lintels where its head crunched sideways on impact, killing it instantly.

Nice kill! Spuddle sent into her mind as he smashed another enemy out of the air, whereupon Taj rushed forward to take his first kill. *So, my method works well then, eh?*

Ionuin flapped her wings and mounted the altar stone. *Um, yes, it, it does; I feel, so good! It's like I've had this body all my life!*

In a funny kind of way, you have, Ionuin, offered Glitch.

But, Spuddle, Ionuin asked, dodging another attempted attack, butting her opponent in the face sending it staggering backwards where Spuddle decapitated it with one snap of his jaws, *how did you know what to do? How did you know what would work for us?*

Spuddle grinned. *It worked for me when I began regenerating, but later, Ionuin, time is also our enemy here.*

Taj released his grip on the dead beast at his feet, snatched another leathery creature from the air and scrunched it up into a mangled mess. 'Come, this is only the start. According to the instructions of Nexus we have to connect our thoughts and become a linked unit!'

In unison, the four youngsters interlocked their minds and began thinking as one entity, sharing thoughts, sharing strength, discovering their real power. Together, they spread their wings and joined the fray proper. Nexus was the first to benefit from their strength born of Light. Pinned helplessly beneath a churning mass of Dark bodies, the four dived to his aid.

Ionuin exhaled and fire roared from her mouth, the flames so hot that they burned a deep purple colour, consuming a dozen or more of the Dark creatures. Nexus struggled free.

'Oh wow!' wailed Ionuin. 'Yay! Did, did you see that, any of you? Did you see what I just did? Oh wow, wow, wow!' she squealed with unbridled delight.

'Well done, Ionuin,' Nexus said, patting her on the shoulder. 'But don't become isolated. You are only strong when working as a team, so catch up with your brother.'

Ionuin smiled and nodded, then saw that Taj, Glitch, and Spuddle had moved on. They were fighting as a compact group, cutting a swathe through the throng of tumbling bodies, ripping open stomachs and slicing off heads, hurling the surprised enemy in all directions. Ionuin joined them and other dragons formed a rear guard, forcing the tide of the battle to turn in their favour.

Dark dragons soon fell upon the knot of fighters and all the attackers were either blown apart in explosions of fire or hacked to pieces by talons and teeth. The Children of the Light had become and their strength passed through the dragon ranks with the speed of white lightning. The more Ionuin and Taj fought, the better they became at handling their new weapons of talons and teeth. When they made errors, Glitch or Spuddle leapt to their aid and their enthusiasm for the fight grew as confidence increased. Very soon, the enemy were shying away from the formidable pack of young fighters.

Then more dragons, Dark and demonic, some with many heads, some with giant heads, burst into the inner-circle, seemingly from thin air, and pounced on the four gallant youngsters. Ionuin shot gouts of flame, slashed and tore with ferocious glee at the hideous beasts, snarling, squealing, screeching as she fought. Spuddle hurled several skywards, where other dragons leapt upon them and tore them to shreds. Taj and Glitch fought back to back, laughing while wrestling with creatures twice their size and still more burst through to attack, each new arrival more repulsive in form than the last.

We are losing, thought Ionuin, staggering as she slew yet another slithering beast. She became crushed as a large giant-headed dragon pounced on her from behind, sending her crashing head-first into the altar stone, making stars dance before her eyes. A shuddering blow slammed into her head and she felt herself sinking into the abyss of oblivion, then a mighty roar filled her ears, bringing her mind rolling back to clear thought.

The weight of the giant-headed creature was thrust from her. Ionuin glanced around to see Taj tangled up with the massive dragon, his head actually inside the monster's enormous mouth, but he was not being eaten. Instead, he suddenly lurched backwards, with a huge wriggling tongue clenched in his teeth. The giant-headed dragon screeched and jumped forward, only to be met by Glitch and Spuddle, who slammed into it in mid-air, snapping back its wings. Taj spat out the tongue and dived in, taking the beast's life.

'Thank you,' Ionuin said, gratefully, getting to her feet, very dazed, but already recovering.

'Anytime,' said the trio as one, turning to face more attackers. Ionuin noticed that the large headed monsters had stopped appearing as she launched back into the fight to help finish the last of them, and she sensed they might even be winning.

Just as the Dark Dragon army appeared to teeter on the brink of defeat, the Dark Dragon launched a penetrating assault directly towards Ionuin. Several dragons charged, but were no match for the leader of the enemy and they were trampled underfoot. Others tried to halt its progress, but they were slain without mercy. Sheratz shot a burst of flame at the malevolent creature, but it would not burn; it absorbed everything Sheratz had to offer, then pounced and began ripping him apart.

Nexus roared and dived to save his friend, smashing into the Dark Dragon with a mighty crunching thump, knocking it to the ground. They tumbled over and over, each battling for supremacy, two giant powers unleashing their energy in a tirade of violence that was mesmerising to watch. They slashed and clawed at each other in a flailing whirlwind of gnashing-jaws and raking-talons, grunting with effort, growling with such ferocity that many stopped their own fights and turned to watch.

Brave and ferocious as Nexus was, the Dark Dragon fought like the raging demon it was, and Nexus reeled under an assault of scything blows that severed one of his legs and tore a gaping rent in his stomach. Power ebbed away from the Golden King, the light of life flickered in his eyes and as the wounds took their toll, he gave one massive swing with his right forearm that would surely have decapitated the Dark enemy, but it missed.

The Dark Dragon brought up its rear leg, crunching it into the jaw of Nexus, hurling him aside where he crashed into the stone circle, toppling uprights and lintels. The distraction caused by the attack of Nexus had given the four youngsters a slight advantage and time to get into good positions. The Dark Dragon roared and shot black flames into the sky. 'You are all finished!' it hissed. 'The reign of Light and its spreading chaos shall now be ended, as the prophesised Children it bore are about to die.' It swung around to gauge its enemies. 'Come to me, little ones, come, taste my Dark power.'

All four attacked at once, biting and gouging, but they were flung away in an instant. Spuddle rolled clear as the menacing giant pounded into the ground where he had lain a moment previous. Taj and Ionuin sprang into the air, breathing lilac fire that, unlike the ordinary fire of the other dragons, did have an effect, making the skin of the Dark monster smoke and sizzle. The Dark Dragon momentarily stopped, peeled away strips of its own flesh, laughed, then leapt at Ionuin and Taj, smashing them to the floor.

Still laughing with what seemed like manic pleasure, it came to pounce on Ionuin, but was taken unaware as Spuddle, in a speeding forward roll, bowled it off its feet, sending it crashing down in a flailing heap. Glitch leapt on top of the fallen enemy and began ripping chunks from its face, but was thrown aside as the Dark Dragon sat upright. Spuddle uncurled himself and rushed forward, only to be punched in the face. He staggered backwards, falling over; his feet becoming tangled in the remains of a sheared-off head.

'Wow!' mouthed Ionuin, getting to her feet, dragging Taj up with her, now realising how strong Nexus must have been to last as long as he did, for the Dark Dragon was awesomely powerful. It cackled as it leapt at Glitch, but Seraph and Buelah dived on the monster's back, both their jaws clamped around its neck as they wrestled it to the ground. Other dragons defended the two females, battling back any enemies who sought to come to their leader's aid. To Ionuin, the thrashing throng of battling bodies looked like a gigantic free-for-all where the gifts were pain and death.

'Join minds!' Taj shouted, leaning on his sister, linking the hooks on the end of their wings, pulling her into the air where they circled the heaving mass of battle. 'If we fight as one, like when we started, we can multiply our power.'

Glitch became airborne and joined them. 'Taj's right,' he agreed, as he watched his mother thrown skyward while Buelah became pinned with a giant taloned foot across her throat.

Spuddle joined the trio and together, they sought each other out mentally. As they hovered in the centre of the stones, reaching forth, stretching their minds; time slowed, slipped backwards, before staggering haltingly onward. One by one, the young dragons became connected to each other and it appeared they were suspended in an unfamiliar place, peaceful and quiet, colourless and still.

'Where are we?' Glitch asked, glancing round in astonishment.

'Between worlds,' Taj answered, knowingly. 'I've read about this place in the old manuscripts, it is called Aztalan, and it feels strangely familiar.'

'Have you been here before?' Ionuin asked, trying to take in her surroundings.

'Um, not sure,' Taj replied, glancing around. 'But it's unimportant. What is important is that if we really wanted, we could journey to another planet from here, escape and leave all this behind.'

'Escape!' Ionuin gasped.

'I think it's what Nexus would want of us,' Taj explained. 'After all, we are supposed to be the future; we could run and live to fight another day.'

Ionuin could hardly believe what she was hearing. 'Taj, you cannot be serious!'

Taj shook his head. 'No, you misunderstand, I'm not suggesting that we do escape; that is only one option, which would indeed be blatant cowardice. I'm just trying to explain where we are.'

'So, where are we?' Spuddle asked, looking confused.

'Well, we're on the cusp of a portal,' Taj answered. 'Sort of, on the brink of the event horizon that forms a kind of broken edge around space-time. I, I cannot make it any clearer.'

'Well, I sort of know what you mean,' said Ionuin, 'but I agree, it's not important. What we have here is some time to work out how we can destroy this thing. It is so incredibly powerful!'

'I don't understand any of it,' said Spuddle. 'But, I don't really care,' he sniffed. 'My dad is badly hurt, maybe worse than badly hurt.'

'True, but listen, Spuddle,' Taj said, trying to comfort his friend with a touch of his talon. 'Nexus is a lot tougher than any of us know and he was convinced that we are the Children of the Light and that our combined power is an unstoppable force. So let's see if his words are true, shall we?' They all nodded their agreement. 'Now, link minds, let's do this.'

Ionuin breathed deeply as they focused all they had on each other, and became one unique entity. There came a sudden deep pulse of binding energy that linked their thoughts, channelling their power. Ionuin felt invigorated, immensely strong, as she had when Spuddle had enthused her in readiness to fight the kodiak bear. She now knew, come what may, live or die, they would all give the fight their best effort.

Acting as one, they dived, leaving the void between worlds. The Dark Dragon turned to meet their assault, kicking the unconscious Buelah to one side like a discarded rag.

Taj attacked first, spewing out a purple fireball, engulfing the Dark Dragon. Spuddle swung his claws into action, aiming for the enemy's eyes, but was instantly felled with a savage blow. Glitch swooped down, gnashing his teeth, causing a distraction before arcing away, while Ionuin swung low and then punched upwards at the last moment, thumping hard and fast into the beast's underbelly, trying to rip it open with her claws. She scrabbled with determined ferocity, but the beast was so strong and tough that she made very little impression at all and in retaliation the Dark Dragon stamped down hard on her tail, halting her assault, making her yowl before slashing at her head, catching her with a glancing blow in the face, spinning her sideways. She staggered into a toppled lintel where she stood swaying, dazed and disorientated, her thoughts momentarily unhinged and floating free, disconnected from Taj, Glitch and Spuddle.

Taj's voice sought her out, blitzing through her mind, but it was an incoherent jumble of broken mumbling mixed with static that was beyond her befuddled comprehension. With a mighty yank she dragged her tail free, stumbling forward, ducking under another swipe from the Dark Dragon, by chance rather than design, and crunched her teeth into a thick, scaly leg, biting down hard, the action actually clearing her head as she tore and savaged at the scales that just would not yield. Mocking bellows came from the Dark Dragon, which Ionuin ignored. She found some clarity of mind, and pushed out her thoughts. *Taj? Spuddle? Glitch? I need to link with you all again.*

Spuddle was up and darting around the Dark Dragon while Taj spat small fire bombs that the Dark Dragon batted away. *We're here, Ionuin, send us your thoughts,* Taj and Spuddle replied in unison.

To me! To me! Glitch wailed. *Give your power to me!*

Ionuin saw Glitch in her mind's eye, diving directly for the Dark Dragon's head, then felt rather than saw Spuddle and Taj grant him energy through the established link.

Do it! Ionuin, wailed, latching onto the tenuous connection, then pouring vast amounts of herself along a twisting cord of undulating thought directly into Glitch's brain. She lurched at the impact as Glitch smashed in the Dark Dragon's skull and saw the beast's legs shudder and buckle. It had been hurt, maybe only slightly, but enough to give them an opening which Ionuin took, leaping forward, plunging her open jaws into the Dark Dragon's belly. This time the scales crackled, splintered, and began to split. Ionuin tore at them frantically, knowing this might be the only real chance they had to seize victory.

198

Glitch was squealing as the Dark Dragon ripped him free from the back of it's head and began scrunching him up into a tight ball. Ionuin felt Glitch's pain before Spuddle and Taj came to his aid and pulled him free. Ionuin bit all the harder, gnashing frenziedly, until at last, under severe pressure, a whole sheet of the Dark Dragon's stomach caved inwards and Ionuin was through, her mouth chomping away at its steaming innards. Mashing entrails and pulsing, wriggling organs in her slavering mouth, she burrowed deep into its body with urgent speed. All other fighting ceased abruptly as deafening howls of screeching agony rang out into the eerie dusk of early evening.

Taj leapt into the fight in earnest, avoided two punishing blows before lashing out, his claws severing the arteries in the Dark Dragon's throat. Blood, brown and sticky, splashed onto the floor. Glitch, still only half recovered, climbed quickly up the side of the creature, ripping and tearing at it's neck and back, scrabbling haphazardly with his feet, howling like a demented animal. Spuddle regained his feet, unleashing searing bolts of fire that now breached the monster's fire-proof defences, splitting open its eyes with loud boiling pops. The four fought together now, helping each other, forming a united power that was simply unstoppable. Blinded, semi-gutted, head lolling uselessly from loose tendrils of flesh, the Dark Dragon slumped to the floor and burst into a blazing, raging, black inferno as the new moon appeared from behind fat-bellied clouds.

'Ooh,' wailed Glitch, leaping clear as flames flickered around his legs. 'We've done it, we've actually done it.'

With their leader dead, the remaining army lost heart in the battle and escaped back through the portal of the stones, their wild screeches of departure warning that they would live to fight another day, but for this day, at least, the fight was over. Victory belonged to the Children of the Light and the dragons of Fire Mountain. Hundreds had perished in the fight and hundreds more were severely wounded, but the wounds would heal. Dragon recovery powers were legendary and as for the dead, they had not died in vain. The battle for control of the universe had begun in earnest in the sweeping spiral arm of a small insignificant galaxy, and the Darkness, which had become the dominant ruling power until now, and had successfully pushed back the frontiers of Light, suddenly had worthy challengers.

Without even noticing, Ionuin and Taj resumed their human shape. Beulah coughed and spluttered as she sat up. Other dragons, glad to be alive after expecting certain death, whooped and cheered. Dead dragons were incinerated where they had fallen, their ashes blowing in the wind, returning to the cycle of creation where their very atoms would perhaps help shape future generations of dragons.

'Is he dead?' Taj asked, as a group gathered around Nexus, who lay perfectly still.

'Father, wake up,' Spuddle said. 'You can't be dead, I've only been home a short while. I hardly know you, and, and I need you.'

He nudged his father's shoulder with such gentleness, that it brought a lump to Ionuin's throat. 'Spuddle,' she said, embracing him. 'You've got to be brave now: very brave.'

Spuddle turned to her. 'But, we won, we really won.' Dragon tears brimmed in his eyes and threatened to unleash an avalanche of emotion. 'Can you hear me, Lord?' He touched Nexus on his bony brow. 'You have to hear me, you just have to!'

'I don't believe it,' said Glitch. 'He, he, can't be dead, not, not Lord Nexus.'

'He saved my life,' said Sheratz, stumbling forward with the aid of Seraph, her broken wings hanging at an unnatural angle.

Ionuin cast her thoughts into the great dragon's head and found nothing but dormant darkness. *Nexus? Can you feel my thoughts? We won! We beat the Dark Dragon and its army has skedaddled. Nexus, you can't be dead, you can't be!*

Taj's thoughts slipped into Ionuin's mind. *He's gone, Ionuin. I can hardly believe it myself, but he really has gone!*

'He was so brave,' Seraph said, tears forming in her eyes, 'truly brave.'

'And a hero,' Buelah added.

Other dragons crowded around their dead king. Moans of anguish filtered into the air, rippling outwards as Spuddle fell sobbing to the floor beside his father and openly wept. Ionuin could not believe this was happening. She wanted to scream at the sky with frustration. To her, the death of Nexus was not acceptable, not expected, and she sobbed loudly as she watched Spuddle cradling the head of his dead father.

Chapter Thirty Five

Bleeding heavily from gaping wounds, Sheratz bent low and nuzzled his old friend. 'He's not dead, he can't be dead. Just recovering, that's all. Come on, move back, give him some air and allow him to breathe.'

'You are wrong, Sheratz,' Taj said. 'I've been inside his brain and there is nothing, not a flicker of life.'

'Really? And did you also look inside his soul?' Sheratz replied.

Ionuin had also tried to find a sign of life, but she had not delved into the soul of Nexus. Such a place, she felt, was very private and extremely sacred. She opened her mind and allowed her thoughts to drift into Nexus. Nothing stirred. She pushed further, deeper, remembering the depth to which she had plunged before the fight, where he had given her vital encouragement, where his inner-self dwelled, where the child inside everyone resides, penetrating the subconscious and beyond. There was nothing; then, within a previously concealed enclave, a flickering speck of ensorcelled light caught her attention. *Nexus? Nexus, is that you?*

No, it's a lychyaena waiting to eat you all up, silly girl. Who else would it be?

Ionuin was suddenly overwhelmed. *Oh Nexus! We thought, well we thought you were-*

Dead! Hah! It would take more than the likes of the Dark Dragon to kill an old campaigner like me. Out of my head, child. I'm coming round.

Nexus stirred, opened one eye, then the other. 'Well, don't just stand there looking useless, you lot! Help me to my feet for crying out loud! I have not got time to be lazing about here; there are things to do, important things!'

Spuddle hugged his father; then helped him to rise with a smile so wide, it was almost dazzling. 'Uh-oh, father; you, erm, you are missing half your leg,' he said, wiping away his tears.

Nexus glanced down, shook his leg, as if he could hardly believe his eyes. 'Ah, so I see, wondered why it felt so numb. Well, no matter. I suppose it will soon regenerate, my boy,' he replied, sitting down on his haunches and examining the ragged stump where the bottom half of his leg should be.

'My boy,' whispered Spuddle, repeating his father's words with awe and respect, nudging Ionuin. 'You hear that? He said *my boy*!'

Ionuin was still looking at Nexus, wondering what the 'important things to do' could possibly be. She turned to Spuddle. 'Yes, yes, Spuddle, I heard him, and I'm pleased for you.'

'I can't believe that this mayhem is over,' Glitch said, staring around at the carnage that had been wrought.

'I can't believe we won,' offered Spuddle.

'Me neither,' added Taj. 'Though I thought we deserved to win, we did fight bravely, did we not?'

'Yes, we did fight bravely, all of us,' replied Nexus. 'Only, it is not over and we have not won. This, my friends, is only the end of the beginning. The

Darkness desiring to swamp our galaxy with its insidious evil will stop at nothing to gain control and destroy the Light, all Light; although, we do have an excellent defensive weapon against the creatures dwelling between the stars and beyond the stars.'

'We do?' Spuddle asked, his face flushed with awe and wonder.

'Yes, we do,' said Nexus, 'you four special children standing here before me.'

Ionuin, Taj, Spuddle and Glitch exchanged puzzled glances.

'Don't appear so dumbstruck,' Nexus said, grinning. 'You four are Chosen.

'Chosen?' Taj asked.

'Fully fledged representatives of the Light,' Nexus informed them, looking from one awestruck face to the next.

'You mean, you actually mean us?' Ionuin said, half laughing, half dreading the way this conversation was going. 'We are Chosen? Chosen by whom? I, I don't understand, you mean-'

'You are Cosmic Warriors, all four of you,' Nexus assured them, his voice firm with command, obviously not brooking any argument concerning his statement. 'The prophecies told of your coming together in the time of the Light's greatest need. For the longest time I assumed it was all bunkum, then when Spuddle went missing and, no respect meant, but with Glitch being Glitch and Taj unable to even find his sister, never mind transform, I was fully convinced that the prophecies were wrong, had to be wrong. Only, I never breathed a word of my doubt, not even on the glummest of days. Then, one by one, all my reservations were laid to rest and with the final transformation, I knew the words in Herald Knell were indeed the undisputed truth. The Light, the powers of the Light, have selected you four to fight for the cause.'

'The cause?' Spuddle asked.

'The cause of the Light, the effort to throw back the edges of Darkness trying to swamp our very lives.' Nexus said, grinning happily. 'I tell you, till the very last I was unsure, but I am sure now.'

Taj laughed. 'You mean, you mean even at the very last moment before the battle began you were not sure what would happen?'

Nexus smiled, nodded his head. 'Something akin to that, I suppose.'

'Something akin to that?' Sheratz questioned, being held upright by Beulah and Seraph.

'Yes, all right,' said Nexus, good-humouredly. 'No denying it, I admit I doubted the prophecies, I really did, but I was wrong to doubt; so wrong.'

Taj suddenly spoke up. 'Nexus, I know you have faith in the prophecies and as with all things of faith, a little doubt is expected, but who wrote the prophecies? Was it perhaps the wizard Catalin? Also, even though this part turned out to be true, how do we know the remainder are to be trusted?'

'Taj, no one person wrote them,' snapped Nexus, rather too sharply. 'Not in the way you mean. They are an ongoing collective effort over millennia, the original authors lost in the swirling mists of time.'

'I, I don't understand,' said Spuddle, his talons fidgeting noisily.

'Not many do, my son,' said Nexus, placing a fatherly arm around Spuddle's shoulders. 'They are not so mysterious though, and as I say, they have many authors and yes, Taj, Catalin is among them, though enough said on this subject. One never knows who might be listening.'

'Hmm, thought as much,' Taj said, nodding his head agreeably, 'Catalin though, he seems to be involved in quite a lot of these secretive dealings.'

Nexus placed a talon beneath Taj's chin so he could gain unwavering eye contact. 'Yes, Catalin used to be around quite a lot. I feel something has befallen him and finding out what, exactly, is just one of your missions.'

'Catalin is a mission?' Glitch said; his face creased with confusion. 'I always thought he was an important Mage of the Light of some kind.'

'Glitch, do be quiet,' said Sheratz with exasperation. 'It is common knowledge that Catalin is the first of the original Chosen, of which there are six in total.'

'That's enough information on that subject, Sheratz,' Nexus said, exchanging a glance with the red dragon leader that Ionuin could not interpret. 'Let's not confuse them more than they are already.' He turned to Glitch. 'Yes Glitch, Catalin is very important, and if the Dark has consumed him, we have lost a hero. I digress, though; what was I saying initially?'

'You were telling us about the prophecies, father,' Spuddle said, 'and did you mention a mission?'

'Ah, yes, the prophecies,' said Nexus. 'Putting the original authors aside, they kind of appear through resonance, infiltrating the sentient thoughts of men and dragon alike. As for them being trusted, you don't dare doubt they are the truth, not now. To my knowledge they have never been wrong, although vague, admittedly, until the events occur, often in an unexpected manner, then prophecies reveal their true worth, but believe me, all of you, they can be trusted.'

'Nexus is right,' said Sheratz. 'I have knowledge of them myself and when interpreted correctly, I know them to be a valuable commodity for deciphering the future.'

'Thank you, Sheratz,' said Nexus, grinning up at the red dragon. 'So, you four can stay here on Merm, do nothing, allow the Darkness to have its way, which it will. Or you can fulfil the prophecies and go from this place and seek out the Others.'

'What about the mission you mentioned?' Glitch asked.

'Never mind the mission, who are the Others?' Ionuin questioned, now very uncertain as to where all this talk of Chosen, prophecies, missions and Others was actually leading.

'Others like yourselves,' Nexus said. 'There are more Children of the Light, most are hardly aware of their true nature, living ordinary lives, only half suspecting they may be a little different.'

'I always wondered about that third section of the book,' Taj said, nodding his head. 'So that's what it means when it speaks of *The Others*. I often thought the words were alluding to monsters of some kind,' he said, shuddering.

'So, Taj, you've read these prophecies too?' Ionuin asked.

'Many times,' Taj answered. 'They're scrawled in a book we secretly call Herald's Knell. Apparently, only three copies exist and-'

'Taj, enough,' snapped Nexus.

Taj looked uneasy. 'Ahem, yes, sorry, my Lord, got carried away there.'

'Perhaps I ought to know more of these prophecies,' Ionuin said, 'especially if they concern me.'

'All in good time,' Nexus said, re-examining his wound that was already healing over, a grimace of discomfort etched onto his face. 'Presently, we have other issues that need settling; urgently settling, for time is short.'

'Taj, you will tell me about the prophecies, won't you?' Ionuin whispered from the corner of her mouth.

Taj shrugged his shoulders. 'Another time,' he whispered back, nodding towards Lord Nexus and shaking his head. 'Truly, though, there is not much to tell, most of it is unfathomable, but at last, I do understand some of it.'

'You understand more than me then,' said Spuddle, grinning nervously, still fidgeting with his talons.

'Enough of the book and its meaning,' said Nexus. 'You must find these *Others*, they are important. You must journey through the portals and once together you will be strong. Support each other and you will be unassailable.' Nexus turned to the central part of the stone circle and released a heavy sigh. 'And the time to go, I'm sorry to say, is now at hand.'

'You mean when we are grown, don't you?' Spuddle said, looking as uncertain as Ionuin felt.

Nexus shook his head and touched Spuddle on his shoulder. 'No, my only son. I mean, right now. You must leave this place and venture to other worlds. First of all, you must find Fyrdraca. Ionuin's enchanted sword is also important and it will make you all even more powerful.'

Now Ionuin felt interest building. 'My sword is enchanted?'

Nexus took hold of Ionuin's hands, his talons clicking lightly against her gold bracelets, his eyes conveying warm gentleness. 'Allegedly,' he said. 'Although, I know little of such things apart from what I have read, but, the enchantment comes on good authority, you can trust me on that. Then, seek out Catalin, he will guide you to the Others.'

'So, where do you think my sword could possibly be?' Ionuin asked, her hand instinctively going to her hip where she wanted to touch the hilt, her fingers brushing against an empty scabbard.

Nexus shrugged. 'I have to conclude that the powers representing the Dark have got it hidden and undoubtedly, they will try to corrupt its magic. The sword has much power that could be useful: it must be found.'

'So, let me get this right,' said Ionuin. 'I knew Fyrdraca was special, my father said as much, but you are claiming it is enchanted and has magical powers?'

'Very much so,' said Nexus, nodding his head in confirmation.

'So, how will we find it?' Taj asked.

'Ionuin will do the finding,' Nexus answered. 'Ionuin, when you pass through the portal, think of the sword; it will guide you. Be not afraid of what awaits you. We have many friends ready to assist your cause, but you must go now.'

'Without even saying a proper goodbye?' Spuddle asked. 'Without, without even attending the victory feast? Without discussing-'

'Now!' Nexus repeated, rather sharply. 'The night is waning, the moon is up and the portal will close very soon. Once closed, it can still be used, but it could take you anywhere on a whim and it will be another quarterly turn of Merm for it to be fully opened to the guidance of the traveller once more.'

'I agree,' said Sheratz. 'Glitch, my son, and Royal Prince of our Red Brood, please make me proud.'

Seraph kissed her dragon child. 'You will, won't you, Glitch?'

'I, I don't want to go,' said Glitch. 'Really, I don't, there are still humans here to hunt, I mean, find and aid; and-'

'Shush,' said Sheratz, hugging his son. 'Stop this bleating. You must go, this is my command.'

'I don't want to go either,' Spuddle said, looking to his friend for support.

'We must,' Glitch said, sighing, placing a comforting wing around Spuddle. 'We can hardly disobey the words of our betters.'

'I can,' Glitch hissed.

Taj laughed. 'Yes, well ordinarily, but not when so much is at stake.'

'Yes, Glitch is correct, we must go,' Taj said. 'I actually feel it is right.'

'Hmm, I'm not so sure,' said Ionuin, folding her arms across her chest.

Taj unfolded Ionuin's arms and hugged her. 'Ionuin, trust me,' he whispered in her ear. 'I can feel this is right, this is what we must do. Do you not feel the same?'

Ionuin wriggled free of Taj's embrace, her eyes searching his and finding he was deadly serious. She looked at Glitch and Spuddle, then Sheratz and Nexus and finally back to Taj. 'I, I don't know,' she said, hugging herself. 'I suppose I do feel something.'

'Also, you do want your sword back, don't you?' Taj said, cajolingly.

Ionuin nodded her head. 'Yes, of course, I do sense an urging for me to look for my sword.' She sighed heavily. 'There is also an unsettling sense that I should not really be here, which I find quite disturbing.'

'That's what I'm talking about, sister!' Taj said. 'These are the feelings to which you should listen! They are your natural instinct, your intuition.'

'I too feel like I should be leaving,' said Glitch. 'How weird, I suddenly sense a pressing need to go, and soon!'

'I don't,' said Spuddle, shuffling his feet in the dust. 'Well, I do, I suppose, but I only just came home and,' he sighed. 'I don't want to leave, but inside, I know I must do what is expected.'

'Bravely spoken,' said Nexus, 'then it is settled.'

'Fine,' said Ionuin, throwing up her arms in exasperation. 'I admit, I too sense that to leave right now is expected,' she said. 'For the first time in my life, I know this feels right! Just yesterday I would not have believed in any of this, but today, fate is calling to us and yet, I don't understand, and this a worry for me! A very real worry,' she laughed, her voice betraying her nervousness.

'So, we are agreed,' Taj said. 'Spuddle, Glitch, are you both ready?'

With emotion welling in his eyes, Glitch obviously didn't trust himself to speak, so he simply nodded.

Spuddle rushed to Nexus and hugged him. 'Father; do you know how much I will miss you?'

'I know, son, I know,' Nexus said, returning Spuddle's hug. 'You have to prove you are dragon, now, playtime is over. No more games. This is for real; a lot hinges on what you do, or fail to do.'

Spuddle stepped back from his father's embrace. 'I am ready,' he said, holding his chin high as he stood beside Glitch. 'I am dragon and I will prove my worth.'

Taj climbed upon Glitch's back and Ionuin clambered aboard Spuddle. Nobody said anything; it just seemed the natural thing to do, so they did it. Once the decision had been taken, it all happened very quickly. The remaining dragons gathered around the stones as Glitch and Spuddle took to the air and flew in ever-decreasing circles, spiralling towards the central altar stone.

'Farewell, my son!' Nexus bellowed. 'Take care of him for me, Glitch. Taj and Ionuin: watch over them both and find your sword, Ionuin. Find Fyrdraca and may the Light speed you all to glory!'

'Cooee, bye, Taj!' Beulah shouted. 'Be careful when dreaming of girls!'

Taj laughed as they began flying faster and faster, and faster, until the scenery blurred into insignificance. Then they were in the void, but unlike before, it passed by barely noticed and the overhead night sky, scorched orange with the flames from burning corpses, became transformed into a startling brilliant blue.

'Wow!' said Taj and Ionuin in unison.

'Fantastic,' said Glitch, his eyes wide with awe.

'It's a bit bright,' Spuddle complained.

The dragons slowed and took in the surroundings. They were still flying around a stone-circle, a different stone-circle, surrounded by tall trees stretching away in all directions as far as the eye could see. It was such a contrast to their own world that they simply kept on flying slowly round and gazing in wonderment.

'This is very much like the world my father once described!' Ionuin said, her voice filled with amazement at the sight before her. 'It's even more beautiful than I ever could have imagined. Very green! And so many trees! But still, so beautiful.'

'I agree,' Taj said, 'I wonder if it's a friendly place?'

'Hmm, I doubt it,' replied Glitch. 'In all sincerity, I utterly doubt it very much indeed, but, one never knows, does one.'

'Come on, let's get going,' said Ionuin. 'The first thing I need to do is find my sword.'

'What about my empty stomach?' groaned Spuddle.

Ionuin lifted her eyes to the heavens and they all laughed, none of them noticing the old woman dressed all in black seated on the altar stone, grimacing with distaste as she observed the new arrivals to her world.

Epilogue

'Great fight,' said Sireena, removing her playing pipes from her belt.

Cai, her opposite in all things and fellow Numina, watched her from across the stones. 'You think so?' he said, absently examining his fingernails.

'I do,' she replied, coughing theatrically on smoke drifting lazily through the air from the ashes of the pyres. 'Such a shame so many of your dragons died. Still, I now know, just from the stench of roasting meat, that if I actually ate, you know, food, I would be a vegetarian for sure!'

Cai smiled. 'Yes, if you say so, then it must be true, but I do agree; a jolly good fight, and I'm pleased we won, even though you cheated.'

Sireena did not acknowledge Cai's accusation and began turning the pipes over, examining them closely. It had been a while since she had used them for long-session playing, but now, she knew in her heart, the ruthenium-coated gold instrument would be blitzing some dazzlingly difficult tunes in the future. 'You know,' she glanced up to see Cai had his back to her and was gazing at the sky, 'I wasn't cheating, just getting even, sort of.'

'Sort of even?' Cai said, nodding then spinning on his heel, unslinging the guitar from his shoulder, his fiery hands slipping across the spider silk strings, causing a thin undulating wail to pierce the night. 'So, why is that, then?' His fingers danced along the lapis lazuli frets, their speed a blazing blur; fire flew from his fingertips as he crouched and pointed the neck of the black onyx guitar at the emerging stars. 'Care to elaborate?'

'If you wish.'

'Oh yes! I wish!' Cai shouted as the last notes died away. 'Way to go baby!'

'*Way to go baby,*' Sireena repeated, in a hushed whisper, her tone somewhat mocking. 'What kind of talk is that, dear brother?'

Cai turned to Sireena, brushing long wavy hair from his face. 'On a different timeline, there are these guys, Hendrix, Page, Iommi, Blackmore, Rhodes, a few others. I heard their stuff drifting across the sub-ether network, and guess what?' His fingers flickered with white flame as he strummed through a short riff of tumbling notes. 'They play better than me, and I'm practically a god!'

Sireena laughed. 'You are no god, Cai, and you never will be. Like me, you are simply a force. A manifestation of natural purpose twisted into elemental energy. Do not ever forget it; such a lapse could be costly.'

Cai grimaced. 'I did say practically, and you don't need to tell me about cost, but you never answered my question. Why were you getting even?'

Sireena blew some haunting notes on her pipes. 'Hmm, bit out of practice.' Her dazzling blue eyes pierced Cai's gaze. 'I don't see why I should answer. Tell me, Cai, where is your bow?'

'My bow?'

Sireena sighed. 'Before you changed the shape of your instrument you used to slide a golden bow along the strings; did you not?'

'Oh, yes, the bow!' Cai laughed. 'Momentarily surplus to requirements!'

'So I see, but where is it? Or would you rather not say?'

'You know exactly where it is, you minx, and that is why you cheated!'

Sireena smiled. 'Yes, I know, you transformed it into a silly Horn for that daft old mage, Catalin, and that's why I stole the sword.'

'You admit that you stole it?'

'No, not really. I simply acquired it, finders-keepers, you might say.' Sireena laughed.

'Hmm, stolen then, I would like it returned, if you please.'

'I don't please. Besides, I sent it somewhere, just until I can locate the Golden Horn; you do know where the Horn is, don't you?'

'Of course,' Cai replied. 'Far from your scheming clutches.'

Sireena laughed again, but her voice lacked any merriment. 'So be it, then I keep the sword.'

Cai strummed his guitar and raised his eyebrows theatrically. 'I forgot that your hobbies are being stubborn, flouting the rules and acting childishly.'

'I will find the Horn, Cai.'

'Hah! You think you will,' Cai scorned.

'I will, and when I do, I will use your own power against you as I did when you stupidly split the world.'

'I split the world as you left me no choice.'

'To echo your own words, Cai, there is always a choice. Fyrdraca will be returned when the Horn is recovered.'

Cai slid his fingers up and down the strings, his finger-work on the frets unimaginably fast. 'Don't bother yourself, Sireena. I have every faith in my Children of the Light and I do not doubt that Ionuin will find the sword. It is enchanted you see, belongs to her by right. Is an essential part of her. Catalin made it so.'

'I know,' Sireena, sighed. 'A trick for which Catalin is paying dearly.'

Cai ceased playing and eyed his sister suspiciously. 'You know?'

Sireena grinned lasciviously, the bottom half of her face splitting open revealing an array of razor sharp teeth. 'Ionuin finding Fyrdraca is my plan.'

'Your plan? But-'

'Bye, brother!' Sireena lifted her pipes to her stretched lips with an angry smile.

Cai was shocked. 'Sireena, why have you messed with Catalin and what have you done with the sword?'

'All in good time, brother,' Sireena hissed, her image beginning to waver.

'Wait,' Cai shouted, trying not to sound desperate. 'I did not make and unmake the Horn because I wanted to cheat! Look, coming back to cost, I was well within my rights; do you not see that?'

'Yes,' Sireena hummed, her mood switching from anger to cheerfulness in the blink of an eye, 'I see, and by me giving the sword to others who will make good use, well, bad use of it, is well within my rights, thanks to you.'

Cai's eyes sprang open. 'Sireena! What have you done?' With a loud thrash of his guitar, Cai vanished in a wall of flame.

'I've done what I could, dear brother,' Sireena said to the empty stone circle, playing her pipes while drifting into the inviting cool of calm, soothing, nothingness.

Nexus banked and swooped low on his return from the grave of Tharl. He had sensed, rather than seen, activity at the stones, even heard some odd noises, rather like music, but on investigating, he could see that whomever, or whatever, had been there, had now departed. His biggest fear was that remnants of the Dark Dragon army had decided they would attack again, or come seeking the relics. If they knew he was just about the only active dragon left on Merm, they would surely have paid a visit, but as the portal was on the verge of closing; both he and the sacred implements of power were nearly safe. Should Dark enemies appear now, they would be trapped until the next equinox, so he reasoned that he really had little to fear. They would not dare stay in this dimension for any length of time, if it could be avoided, as it meant their ultimate doom.

One thing that had not occurred, which he had been certain would happen, was that Logihjorr, once the fifth of the Chosen, and now the ruler of Brule on Tarsier, had not made an appearance. This was worrying. Around two thousand years ago, give or take a century or two, he had fought side-by-side with Logihjorr during the serpent wars in the liberation of Tarsier. Once the battles were won, the Anadarang army driven to the extremities of the central land mass, the dragons had left Tarsier, and for reasons unknown, Logihjorr had turned to the Darkness as an ally.

Thinking of betrayal, he also suspected that it could have been Bollfur and his sons at the stones, but oddly, they had simply vanished, and even flying around in the open he could sense nothing of their presence whatsoever. He reasoned that they must have ventured through the portal at some point, perhaps to ply mischief on Earth or Deburon, or even distant Tarsier with its border-roaming oddities and miscreant monsters. That Bollfur had changed sides, like Logihjorr, he did not doubt. The reasons why and wherefore, he did not know, but Bollfur was not his problem now, he had no problems. Nexus knew his time was over, had known since Ionuin had come wandering inside his inner sanctum. He had lived a good life, seen and done many things and made a difference. He would die happy and contented knowing that he had done his best and not wasted his life. He left the stones and journeyed back to Fire Mountain, flew through the entrance with ease, negotiated the long tunnels, and with a flick of his mind, disarmed the sentinels before coasting to a halt in the Great Cavern.

Other dragons would now take over his leadership role; Sheratz, Seraph, Beulah and even some dragons that had not been present at the Battle for Merm, Nubian and Xanthippe, just to mention two. Nexus sighed, his heart heavy at the thought of his friends, some of whom he would have enjoyed seeing again before his passing, but nobody, not even Dragon Lords, ever got everything they wanted in life.

He walked around the Great Cavern for one last time, circling a disc of rune-marked stones piled with objects of various kinds in the centre of the floor. An odd collection, he mused, dropping Iron-wolf, the sword of Tharl, onto the heap. He knew Iron-wolf to be enchanted, like Fyrdraca, as it too had been made by the Ealfynkind. Forged from seven beaten rods of twisted steel, hardened steel, originally hacked from asteroids that had plunged to planet Earth. It bothered him that Fyrdraca had gone missing so mysteriously, and he wondered if this was a bad omen for those he had sent to aid Catalin.

Taking care, using his newly forming leg, he limped behind his serpentine throne. Admiring the flecks of olivine in the arms for the very last time, he slumped down to sleep. He was so tired, and could barely recall how many centuries he had been awake. At the moment, time passed faster on Merm than on the other linked-worlds, much faster in some cases. No doubt this was apt to change in the near future, as he sensed the Clysm drawing ever nearer, and once that fatal day dawned, time would be synchronised on all three worlds, but he knew he need not worry, he would have solidified by the time this occurred and be nothing but a distant memory.

Even in death, he still had a role to play, be it a simple passive guardian, the 'Last Sentinel' as the 'Herald Knell' termed him, and he wondered if he had done the right thing by swallowing the body of Tharl. It just seemed appropriate, in an odd way. Now, as he gazed on the pile of relics, the book, Tharl's sword, crystal goblets, amulets, pendants and even a wand, among other things, he waited for his thick scaly skin to transform into a stone shell.

He doubted anybody would dare attempt to steal these goods, but great changes had been forecast for Merm; being in the direct path of an ice-storm that whipped through this part of the galaxy at regular intervals, anything could happen, anything at all. He sighed as sleep slipped inside his mind, teasing around the edges of an image of his sister, Saturnine, and his mate, Nadine. Both large females, curled together, locked in an impenetrable slumber, far, far, below Fire Mountain, in a sealed cocoon beside a pool of bubbling lava, warded by magic.

Nexus yawned loudly and barely noticed when Tharl's body twitched in the sleep chamber of his great stomach, for the Dark had been defeated this time, but what the future held: only time would tell.

Wizard's Wrath

A preview of the second book.

Volume Two of the Cosmic Warrior Series

Paul M Chafer©

For my Grand Daughters
Darla and Katalyn

Dreadnoughts and Chosen

Prophecies of the Ancient's decree,
Dark Pariah shall face the dragon,
In the Universal arena, heart's quail,
Worlds tremble as giant forces clash.

Cloying Darkness is stirring, awakening,
Shadows shifting within Darker shadows,
Snake-like tendrils slithering, pulsing,
A menace daring to reveal true purpose.

Brandishers of Light must stand and fight,
Resisting all temptation of offered power,
Battling against foul corruption: death,
Halting the slide into dank, filthy, pits.

Monsters stalking the innocent; feeding,
Drenched in blood of pain and suffering,
Spawn of Dreadnoughts bring carnage,
Will any stand against the slaughter?

The fabled sword twisted in torment,
Calling, calling; seeking a champion,
Searching out those who would dare,
Questing for the brave of the Light.

Light heeds the need, offers strength,
Dragon heart's beat, Champions arise,
Drums of war, thunderous, deafening,
As the Reckoning screams to be birthed.

Lyondell: The Scribe, Poet and Teller

Four Cosmic Warriors arrive on Deburon, one of four known worlds, in search of Fyrdraca, the magical sword of Ionuin that was lost before the battle of Merm where the Dark Dragon was confronted and defeated. Our warriors soon discover that they have become embroiled in the struggle for power between forces of Light and Dark. Once again, powerful destructive forces are at work. Should they be allowed to rage unchecked, whole civilisations will crumble. Personifications of Dark and Light are attempting to force the outcome they desire, placing the warriors of Merm in great danger.

Before the sun has even set, the warriors become separated as the indigenous people of Deburon strive for control. At the heart of the conflict, causing untold chaos, is Fyrdraca, Ionuin's enchanted sword, now a weapon working for the Dark. The ongoing Clysm erupts, blood is shed, lives are lost, kingdoms are about to fall and the Reckoning draws ever closer. Only our four warriors can make a difference, but first, they must unravel the mystery surrounding the troubling events that are unfolding, distinguish friends from enemies, and ultimately, risk their own lives in order to save the lives of countless innocents.

Despite their formidable powers, Ionuin and Taj are stretched to breaking point in torturous circumstances. The fighting prowess of Glitch and Spuddle become tested to their limits. Choices between life and death must be faced, sacrifices have to be made, and all is not as it seems as new protagonists, fearsome and deadly, emerge and enter the conflict that will decide the fate of the known worlds. Earth, the blue pearl, now awaits the outcome that will forge its ultimate destiny.

Prologue

Haunting notes threaded the air of Aztalan beneath a starless sky resembling a sheet of black satin stretched over a dark lake as flat as a mirror.

'What a sad tune, dear Sireena,' Cai said, seating himself on the sand beside his sister, his own stringed instrument strapped across his back. 'Almost a dirge, not quite, but almost.' He tried gauging her mood, tried establishing eye-contact, but Sireena kept her cerulean eyes firmly focused on the horizon, avoiding his gaze while she continued playing. The slow rhythm seeming to spiral out in all directions, taking on a physical aspect, giving rise to the image of a Dark Dragon, it's head swaying in time to the sombre symphony that appeared to be coming from a thousand pipes rather than just one instrument.

Cai considered joining Sireena, using his own music to eclipse hers, but she gave one last sonorous note before slipping her pipes into the folds of her skimpy translucent dress where they appeared to vanish.

'It was a lament for those who have fallen, not a dirge, but from one Cosmic Minstrel to another, thank you for the compliment, brother,' she said, still staring straight ahead, a slight breeze gently trifling with strands of blue hair that had fallen across her face. 'I shall treasure your kind words, for I doubt there will be many more, considering what I have done.'

Cai laughed. 'Ah, Sireena, you judge yourself too harshly, but then, you always were a hard taskmistress. I imagine you thought Ionuin would crumble on learning that she had lived a lie for fifteen years.'

Now Sireena turned towards him and a part of him wished she had continued staring straight ahead, for her glowing blue eyes seemed to lance his inner being and hold it prisoner.

'Cai, your jumped-up champions are nothing to me,' she hissed. 'You have already lost Nexus during our recent clashes and Tharl is little more than the echo of a ghost guarding ancient treasure. I could crush all the remainder in the blink of an eye, as I did Shogun, so do not tempt me: do you understand?'

Cai swallowed then nodded his head. 'Yes, I do understand,' he reached for Sireena's hand but she pulled away, wrapping her arms around her knees, gently rocking back and forth. He decided to choose his words carefully, now was not the time to pursue a course of undignified taunting mockery. 'It would be a gargantuan mistake though, look what happened with the Shogun fiasco, very little was gained; we just made the future a more uncertain journey. If you simply choose to destroy all life as you see fit, it only allows me to engineer more potent warriors.'

'Oh, I would not destroy all life, brother,' Sireena replied, 'just those of whom you have, somewhat unwisely, I might add, grown exceptionally fond. They may have slain my Dark Dragon and forced his conjured army to retreat to the very edges of the universe, but my own Chosen champions are not done; not yet, and I have taken the liberty of generating enemies of equal, and even though I say it myself, superior prowess to your dragons and pathetic half-lings.'

'Pathetic?' Cai said. 'I see; I did not realise you considered Ionuin and Taj 'pathetic' and I aim to change your mind about that, but, as you think of them so, it would be demeaning of you to snuff out their lives on a whim, not that I would willingly acquiesce to such behaviour.'

Sireena laughed, the sound akin to a tinkling of iced bells. 'Could you stop me, Cai?'

'I would give it every effort, sister,' Cai informed her, injecting stern authority into his tone, 'but do as though wilt. I will soon have more Cosmic Warriors flocking to my banner, many more. Their power is infectious and perpetuated through connected emotions, reaching out to all who treasure life.'

Sireena pushed her feet into the black sand, her toes wiggling deeper and deeper beneath the warm grittiness. 'I am aware of this, brother, but by revealing your opposition of my wanton slaughter, you betray your own feelings.'

Cai shrugged. 'I cannot help but hold feelings for them, it comes with the territory of fighting for the Light, but you know this.'

Sireena smiled mischievously. 'Yes, I do know, but by betraying your feelings you also betray your weakness.'

'Such a thing cannot be helped,' Cai protested.

'You have to become more hardened, brother,' Sireena told him. 'When will you learn that love is as transient as their little-lives and of such shallow value, that it becomes meaningless. Can you not see? You fight from a position of abject poverty, dear brother, and as such, you must fail.'

'I wholeheartedly disagree, Sireena, for love is all consuming and as such, stronger than you can ever imagine.'

Sireena shook her head with obvious disbelief. 'Cai, you know nothing of what I imagine.'

Cai held up his hands in mock defeat. 'True, but my position and my champions only appear weak compared to the strength with which you endow their opponents, but you forget; we Numina are also bound by the laws of physics, there is always an opposite effect for all actions.'

'I forget nothing, brother, power and the yearning for more power is everything!'

'You only see what you want to see, Sireena,' Cai stated calmly. 'The will to triumph shall be the true decider in the coming battles, not power. Your potent wickedness and evil can never overcome the element of faith my Cosmic Warriors have in themselves and their allies. My Chosen shall triumph while your Dreadnoughts will wither and die.'

Sireena stood erect in one fluid movement of lithe grace. 'You seem confident, Cai, but I have seen into your soul, which quails pitifully with uncertainty as you know the essential element of chaos stitched into the very fabric of the universe cannot be bargained with: not ever. I feel it now, like the hum of a tuning fork in my very bones, vibrating at a regular frequency, but offering an irregular future as it cares nothing for well-laid plans and meticulous preparation, or the values of love, honour and respect by which you set so much store. Although, it will yield to overwhelming binding command, commands that will compel it to obey the laws of superior strength, then, your machinations will fall into despair and ruin and the Dark Dreadnoughts shall triumph.'

'Now it is you who seem over-confident,' Cai said, rising to stand by his sister, but lacking her sinuous agility, which he so envied. 'You grossly underestimate the joy of what I represent, but this is what I expect from one such as you.'

'One can always expect the unexpected, brother,' said Sireena, a slight smirk twisting her beautiful ruby lips. 'Despite your recent success, I will defeat you and transform the universe back to its original state of calm tranquillity, beautiful symmetry, where peace, in all its total nothingness, shall once again reign supreme.'

'Peace without life?' Cai snapped. 'How unstintingly tedious, I much prefer the chaos of living energy buzzing around the stars, their glory shining with such wondrous vitality for all to see in this astounding cosmos.'

'Tedious, you say?' Sireena laughed, already fading. 'There is nothing tedious in the elaborate plans I have set in motion, brother.'

'Wait!' Cai shouted, but Sireena had already departed. He glanced over the unending vastness of the flat lake of Aztalan and hoped with all his heart that his acolytes did not yield and drown in utter despair from the coming misery Sireena would heap upon them. For if they believed in themselves, truly believed, then anything within the realms of reality, and often beyond, was surely possible.

Chapter One

Tenja, Chosen and long-lived prophet of the southern Pertha desert, observed the two young people before her. Dhakoo, a native of Pertha and her great, great, great grandchild, was dark and moody, lean, angular, rather tall, but with fine muscle tone, while his partner, Jazzlynn, stood nearly as tall. She was a picture of elegance; lithe, strong, short-cropped light blond hair, typical of the land of Dansk, with scrolled tattoos of silver and blue marking her pale cheeks, enhancing her looks to striking beauty. They were young and inexperienced, however, they were definitely Children of the Light and true Cosmic Warriors and she knew they would have to do, for options were so few. Interesting times were about to explode into life on Deburon and ready or not, all capable hands must be utilised if victory were to be secured.

She had decided whose side she would aid; not that the generous offers from Sireena and the Dark would have worked, for the power saturating the magical field would always have persuaded her of the right choice. In her own mind, there was never any doubt where her allegiance would ultimately fall. Unlike the traitor, Logihjorr, she was, Chosen and the Light was in her heart and soul. Many in the warm southern lands, where she dwelled, would not approve of her choice. They were fearful of the Dark enemies, who they would rather placate than fight, but not only was Tenja a talented prophet, with the art of foresight, she was also a Mage of renown. Others father north beyond the equator were relying on her attributes and she was fully aware of what was to come, that is, if others also made the right choices. The future is not carved in stone, or happened already, as some believed, but is continually flapping around, rather like a flag in a summer breeze, susceptible to the unpredictable winds of change.

She stood and approached the pair. 'You both know what to do?' she asked, though she already knew the answer. They both nodded. 'It is summer in the northern hemisphere, but it will still be cold at night, wrap up warm, won't you, and once you find the one you seek, use your instincts as a guide.' Again, they both nodded. 'It is imperative that you exercise freedom of choice.' She leaned forward, stretched up and kissed them both on their cheeks. They were people of few words, these two young warriors, but deeds are what would mark them in the coming conflict, not words.

They bowed slightly, turned, strode out of the giant tented-desert-palace of Temple Bellwood and leapt onto their winged mounts. The horses snickered, reared, and galloped off into the night, becoming airborne in moments. Tenja went back into her tent. She had done what she could; now it was up to the other Chosen and the enlisted Cosmic Warriors already fighting through the portal from Merm. She just hoped they were capable fighters, wise decision makers, or all could be lost in the blink of an eye. She pulled up short as a blue darkness flashed before her, then was gone in an instant. 'Too late, bitch,' she hissed, 'much too late.'

'They have gone, Mistress?' asked a robed servant from the open tent flap.

'Yes,' Tenja replied, flapping her hand at him to be silent, her mind running on the wind, soaring, climbing, brushing the edge of the atmosphere, coasting down over the northern land of Trogg where the remaining Dreadnoughts sat in council.

I see you, Chosen, said a light voice, hissing through Tenja's thoughts.

It was Corn, the silent one, always friendly, but deadly, perhaps the most deadly of all the Dreadnoughts as few suspected her true talents. *Hello, Corn,* Tenja sent back, *I see you are having a party.*

Yes, but it is very dull, Corn complained. *Do not worry, I will not reveal you can broach our wards, what a flap that would cause and truly, I cannot be fussed with recalibrating the sentinels, just do not try to enter Trogg, especially the Ashermist Palace, I would have to kill you and that would be most upsetting, I like you too much.*

Likewise, Tenja replied, withdrawing before Lussker, their leader, discovered the tenuous link. Tenja had learned what she needed to know. The Dreadnoughts were preparing to fight and would offer strong opposition in the coming struggle. Well, the Light had more than a few surprises for them should they dare to venture too far from home, physically or mentally.

'Mistress, are we done here?' asked the servant.

Tenja nodded. 'Yes, yes we are done, I am tired, using my art to stand and walk even a little way is so taxing, take me down below to the Inner Temple, please.'

The servant bowed, a giant of a man standing two spans high, scooped Tenja up in his thick arms and carried her out of the tent. Tenja disliked being disabled, but it was surprising what the mind could accommodate when the body began to fail, very surprising indeed.

The dragons hovered in the air above the centre of the stone circle, hardly able to believe the greenery stretching away into the distance on all sides. Their riders too were stunned by the abundance of natural beauty, and the sky was so bright and brilliantly blue that it hurt their eyes to stare directly into the vaulted heavens.

'Look at the sun,' said Taj, shielding his eyes. 'Much bigger than our sun back home and fiercely hot too.'

'Well, don't look at it,' said Ionuin. 'It will burn out your eyes for sure; just feeling its warmth is enough.' She had never seen such a thing; the sky on their home world was usually a watery pink and the sun only half the size of this one. 'Can anyone see my sword?' she asked. Then her senses prickled; someone was watching. 'We're not alone,' she said, pushing out her thoughts, but finding nobody in her projected web of life. Then she heard someone yell from below.

'You lot took your time, didn't you?'

All four gazed at what appeared to be an old woman seated on the altar stone. She was dressed in black from head to toe, complete with a broad-brimmed pointy hat. The dragons slowed and with a few steady wing-beats, floated to the ground. Ionuin and Taj dismounted and stood before the old woman. She had a wrinkled face, a big nose, an almost toothless grin and more warts than could be counted at a single glance, but she seemed friendly enough.

Ionuin again pushed out her thoughts, but sensed nobody and wondered if her hunting senses were unable to function on this world, wherever this world may be. Feeling brave, she stepped forward. 'I am Ionuin, daughter of Tharl,' she said. 'This is my brother, Taj.'

'Hi,' said Taj, and smiled.

'What about the beasts?' asked the old woman, pointing to the dragons. 'Are they pets or just handy means of transport?'

Spuddle and Glitch exchanged hurt glances.

Ionuin's eyes visibly widened. 'The beasts, as you unkindly remarked, happen to be our friends.'

'Really!' said the old woman.

Ionuin nodded. 'Meet Glitch and Spuddle. They're dragons and-'

'-I know what dragons are,' interrupted the old woman, 'just never seen such weedy-looking tame ones before.' She sniffled and wiped her nose on the back of her hand.

'Tame! Weedy-looking!' Taj gasped, very affronted.

'Excuse me!' Ionuin snapped, her hand reaching for the hilt of her sword, more for comfort than anything, but only finding an empty scabbard. 'Like Taj and I, they're Children of the Light,' she continued, 'and the bravest creatures I know. Do you have any idea of the ordeal we have just been through, madam? No! You don't so-'

'-ooh, aren't we all Miss-Big-Britches then,' interrupted the old woman, cocking her head, re-examining the four of them.

'Pardon?' Ionuin said, not understanding the old woman's statement, but thinking she had the gist of it.

The old woman waved her hand dismissively. 'Nay mind. So, apart from the sword you just mentioned, do you know why you are you here?'

'We are Children of the Light,' said Taj proudly, actually puffing out his chest slightly.

'Children of the Light, eh!' replied the old woman. 'Catalin spoke of such beings, but you're the first I've ever seen. My name is Ethyl, by the way. Ethyl Wierwillechekme, but most round these parts call me, The Witch. S'not a personal thing, but it does mean that I'm left well alone and that's how I prefer it. Now, you're just in time for the task. Are you all prepared?'

'Wait, wait, you know of Catalin?' Taj said, stepping between Ionuin and Ethyl.

'Said as much, didn't I?' Ethyl said, folding her arms over her thin chest.

'Taj nodded, as if weighing up the situation. 'Hmm, you are obviously more than you seem, Ethyl, but I still don't understand. We are here for Ionuin's sword, what is this task you mentioned?'

'We know of no task,' Ionuin said, nodding in agreement with Taj. 'We're only here to find my sword; Nexus asked me to focus on Fyrdraca and told us that we would be led to its whereabouts.'

'Nexus, eh!' Ethyl said, her tongue flicking out, wetting her lips. 'Now there is a fellow I should like to meet, now that's a dragon is that.'

'Nexus is my dad,' said Spuddle. 'He was almost slain by the Dark Dragon back on Merm in the big battle we just won. Well, I say 'won' but, just fought, apparently. It appears there-'

'What is a witch?' Glitch asked, looking to Spuddle and shushing him before he could protest about such a rude interruption.

'Hah! The dragons talk!' Ethyl exclaimed, 'I did wonder if that would have changed over time.'

'Changed over time?' Spuddle said, looking around at everyone else in puzzlement.

'Course we talk,' said Glitch. 'We're of royal blood. I'm the Prince of the Red Dragon Brood, I am!'

'Ahem, I am the King in waiting of the Green Dragon Brood,' said Spuddle, shouldering Glitch aside. 'I am important, more important than Glitch, as one day I'll be a Golden Male. What do you mean by-'

'-yes, yes, I'm sure it's very nice for both of you,' said Ethyl, cutting Spuddle off, stifling a yawn. 'I have no time for dragon politics, such a bore.'

'Do you have dragons here?' Ionuin asked, leaping in with a question before Glitch or Spuddle could voice complaint at Ethyl's obvious rudeness.

'We have dragons, somewhere in the north, although they are rarely seen these days. Intelligent creatures, and much like me, keep pretty much to themselves.

'Do you know of the Dark Dragon?' Taj asked.

Ethyl shook her head. 'Nope. Something Dark is upsetting things here though, and I suspect the sword you mentioned on your arrival is deeply involved.' Ethyl then faded, almost disappearing altogether. 'Oh dear, I'm winking out.'

Ionuin took a precautionary step backwards, dragging Taj with her. 'What the . . . ?'

'She's not real!' Taj exclaimed, his voice awash with uncertainty.

'Course I'm real,' Ethyl scolded. 'I'm just not here. What you're seeing is a projected image.' She faded again then flickered back into view. 'Oh dear, look, you must stay here; don't go into the trees, there is much danger; do you hear? Stay right here until I can . . . .'

The image of Ethyl vanished along with her fading voice.

'She's gone!' Glitch said, walking around the altar stone where Ethyl had sat, as if she were a queen on a throne.

'She never answered any of our questions!' complained Spuddle, petulance evident in his voice, 'and she was so rude.' He looked about the stone circle. 'Anyone know where we are? I don't like this. What is this task she mentioned? What could be the danger from trees? Can they move, do you think?'

'Moving trees? Don't be daft,' said Taj. 'You'll be trying to eat your own foot next.'

Glitch grinned and nudged Ionuin. 'Taj is referring to Des, the daftest dragon in the history of Merm,' he hissed.

'Never mind 'foot munching Des,' I mean it,' said Spuddle. 'There are too many trees. Did you ever think there could be so many trees?'

'Imagine what we could do with all this wood!' Taj said.

Glitch sniffed the air. 'There are also strange smells.'

Ionuin twitched her nose. 'The smell is perfume,' she suggested. She sniffed deeply. 'Or rather, that from what perfume is made. I should know; I once saw a stall at a travelling bazaar back on Merm. It's the scent of flowers.'

'Why are we talking about flowers?' Taj asked. 'Spuddle is correct, you know; we are in a situation about which we know nothing! I expected to find your sword waiting for us, but, according to the old woman-'

'-Ethyl,' said Glitch, turning his head, his nose now swivelling around.

'Yeah, Ethyl,' Taj continued, 'Fyrdraca is responsible for some Dark happenings on this world and she thinks we're here for a task. What task? Whatever is going on?'

'Those flowers, that is what is going on,' said Ionuin. 'They are so overpowering. Can you not smell them, Taj? I've got to find them, I want them, need them, such a beautiful fragrance, hmm.'

'Flowers?' Spuddle said. 'Why the sudden interest in smelly flowers?'

'She's a girl,' Glitch said, 'can't help herself. Female dragons are the same: flowers, babies, sunsets; all that kind of stuff. It's a kind of female magic, a mysterious appeal beyond our masculine fathoming.'

Ionuin, with her nose in the air, wandered to the edge of the stone circle. 'Glitch, that statement is rhubarb. Boiled rhubarb, in fact and I think the smell is coming from beyond those trees.'

'Rhubarb or not, I think you are right concerning the whereabouts of the smell,' Glitch said, spinning around and following Ionuin.

'Whoa!' Taj said, grabbing Ionuin by the arm. 'Did you not hear what Ethyl said? There is danger outside the stone circle! We're not to go into the trees, any of us, understand!'

Glitch leapt up onto the lintels, his neck arching as he nosed the air. 'Oh yes, yes, I like that, a kind of fruity shallowness with an undertone of, of. . . .'

'Honey,' Ionuin suggested, trying to remove Taj's hold on her arm.

'Er, Glitch?' Spuddle said, leaping up beside his friend. 'I thought you said this was a female thing? Beyond our fathoming?'

Glitch looked at his friend. 'Did I? I'm sure I don't recall saying that at all.'

Spuddle furrowed his brow in puzzlement. 'But, you did say it, just now.'

'Taj, let me go,' Ionuin snapped, trying to smack away her brother's hand.

'No, I won't,' Taj replied, insistently, gripping her all the harder. 'Spuddle, Glitch, come back down here, now. Something is happening that I don't like. Get back inside the circle; your heads are over the edge. Ethyl said there's danger in the trees; did you not hear her?'

Glitch glanced back at Taj. 'Are you talking to us? You surely cannot be talking to us, two royal princes who are superior to you in both age and birth, for if you were talking to us, I would have to take issue with you, Taj.'

'Glitch! What are you on about?' Taj said, feeling exasperated and hardly able to believe what he was hearing. 'Also, why are you talking like that?'

'Talking like what?' Glitch asked, peering at Taj down his snout.

'As if you are a pompous arse!' Taj snapped. 'Have you lost it?'

'Yes, good point, Taj,' said Spuddle, looking from one to the other, finally focusing on Glitch. 'Have you lost it? This is Taj, son of Saturnine, your oldest friend. Whatever has gotten into you? What is all this rubbish about 'Royalty' for goodness sake, snap out of it, Glitch!'

'I will not 'snap out of it' I am Royal, and will be treated as so,' said Glitch, his voice sounding even more haughty than before.

'Let me go!' Ionuin wailed, kicking Taj, who held her firmly, one arm now encircling her waist. 'I want to follow the smell: let me go!'

Like the sudden breaking of a summer storm, it suddenly dawned on Taj what was going on. 'It's the flowers! The, the scent!' he cried. 'It's having an effect!'

'An effect?' Spuddle questioned.

'Yes, it's affecting these two. Don't you see? I can't smell it as I damaged my nose in Bollfur's chambers and, Spuddle, no disrespect, but your senses are still dull due to your renewed growth, but these two are intoxicated by the smell! Quickly, Spuddle, knock Glitch back into the circle.'

'I do beg your pardon,' said Glitch looking at Spuddle, 'but if you lay one talon on me, I shall-'

'You shall do nothing,' Spuddle said, who was smaller than Glitch by a good third in weight and height, but he spun on one foot, his tail smacking into Glitch's legs, upending him so he fell on his back. With a grunt of effort, he then thumped into the red dragon with his whole body so they both came tumbling back into the stone circle. Glitch fell head first, giving his skull a hefty crack on the inner stones, even rocking one lintel wildly, he then lay quite still.

Ionuin looked shocked at what had happened, her hand going to her mouth. She tugged away from Taj and knelt beside Glitch. 'Glitch? Glitch, are you all right?'

'He'll be fine,' said Spuddle getting to his feet apparently unharmed.

Taj hovered over his sister. 'Spuddle's right, don't worry, it's only a little knock. I once rolled a boulder onto Glitch's head that was almost as big as me and he was all right, once he came round.'

Ionuin looked up at her brother. 'You did what?'

'It was a laugh, a game we were playing on the slopes of Fire Mountain. He's a dragon, Ionuin, very hard to hurt, in other words.' Ionuin glared up at him, shock very evident on her face. Taj grinned at her apparent innocence and knew she was still affected by the flowers. 'Sister, please allow me to prove my words.' He reached down and nipped her nose between his thumb and forefinger.

'Yeah, rock solid,' confirmed Spuddle, his gaze lost in memories of better days.

Taj grinned. 'Yeah, rock solid. Have to be, originally, dragons were partly made from rock, had you forgotten that?'

Ionuin reached up to remove Taj's hold on her nose, then rocked back on her heels and rolled sideways. Taj kept a tight grip on her nose going to his knees so he could follow her down to the long grass growing amongst the stones.

Ionuin's eyes suddenly shot open wide, one hand going to her temples her other hand knocking away Taj's fingers. 'What, what just happened here?'

Taj crouched beside her. 'Not exactly sure, little sister,' he looked up at Spuddle who shrugged his shoulders, 'but I think the perfume was luring you and Glitch from the stones.' He rested his hand on her shoulder. 'How do you feel?'

Ionuin nodded. 'Just a little drowsy.' She sniffed the air. 'I can't smell it down here; whatever it was, it's, it's gone.'

'What do we do now?' Spuddle asked.

'We do what Ethyl told us,' said Taj. 'We wait.'

Chapter Two

Flickering torches adorned the grey stonewalls casting an irregular light around the cavernous chamber, breathing animated life into the cheerless, spectral, shadows. Shadows, drenched in untold wickedness, lingering beneath the much-feared rack, eagerly soaking up the stresses and strains of the stretched victims, some of whom had always yearned to be taller, but in retrospect, would have willingly settled for being short.

Other dark malevolent patches frequented the area around the Iron Lady, preferring to feast on the pools of dried blood, continually drinking in the slightly coppery flavour. Further absences of light languished in discreet alcoves, allowing their dark tendrils to pore over such heinous implements as the boot, assorted thumbscrews, and a varied selection of pokers. Pokers that had glowed red-hot before doing their dastardly work, punishing those responsible for gross acts of treason, or in one misguided case, found guilty of keeping library books beyond their due date of return.

In the uninviting atmosphere of these subterranean torture chambers, three wizards plotted, their thoughts flitting amongst the shadowy-chicanery, feeding from the centuries of misery. Two of them, Tintinere and Salongwee, planned to bring about the downfall of the remainder of the Gramrye region in the land of Pagonis, and eventually, the whole of Deburon. The third wizard, Ven, the youngest of the three wizards by far, observed their exulted leader, Tintinere, who was pacing the dimly lit chamber and seemed totally unaware of his own deranged chuckling. Ven wondered what depraved act of madness he was going to insist that they indulge in today? Truth be known, he had experienced all that his mind and body could take, more than he could take, and now, he just wanted out of this mess. He never joined up for this craziness, and began pondering how it had come to this, before finally wondering if he was truly evil? He knew for certain that both Tintinere and Salongwee, the so-called 'second in command,' were evil, more than evil, utterly wicked and heinous seemed a more apt description.

'You feeling all right, Ven?' Salongwee asked.

To Ven, he looked alien and very strange as he was a southern wizard from the warm land of Thailite. A people and place of which Ven had very little knowledge, but if they were all like Salongwee, he vowed he would never go there, not ever. Feeling uncertain, Ven simply shrugged.

'You thinking you happy,' said Salongwee, wagging a spindly finger in Ven's direction. 'I always second guess people's thoughts, it a gift of mine, tell me it is so, young Ven.'

'It, it is so,' Ven lied. 'I am quite happy, sir.'

Salongwee clasped his hands together and leapt into the air squealing with delight. 'Oh, my, I'm so, so good!'

Dud, would be more like it, thought Ven, but said nothing, for he was the furthest from happy he had ever been in the whole of his short life.

Tintinere suddenly stopped his pacing and peered at Ven from beneath quizzically arched brows. 'Hmm, you don't look happy,' he said.

'Ah, could be something I ate,' said Ven, rubbing his stomach theatrically.

'You should have had the queen's eyeballs,' suggested Salongwee, licking his lips. 'They were delicious.'

'Hmm, not really into eyeballs, as such,' said Ven.

'I've only seen you eating pies,' said Tintinere. 'Come to think of it, you never did join me and Salongwee when we feasted on the inhabitants of the palace, maybe you will join us tonight? There are still quite a few torsos remaining and plenty of arms.'

Ven coughed and could feel the blood draining from his face at the thought of eating a fellow human, and had to consciously fight very hard to control the gag reflex. 'Yes,' he said, his voice sounding meek. 'Perhaps, perhaps I will.'

'Oh, good!' Salongwee exclaimed. 'It be like real party, I shall make us paper hats, but mine must have yellow ribbons, I insist on yellow ribbons on things, do I not, Tintinere?'

'Yes, you do,' replied Tintinere, resuming his pacing.

Salongwee actually leapt into the air, unable to contain his excitement. 'So what now?' he asked, stroking his dark thin drooping moustache, his slitted, darting-eyes, flitting between his two companions. 'I mean, you have magic sword from Mistress, we've conquered Yorvic, their pathetic capital, and achieved ultimate power; so what else we can do?'

'Search me,' said Ven, who only wanted to escape.

Salongwee laughed. 'What strange expression, thing is, me do indeed wonder, what else is there to do in stagnant dump?'

'What indeed?' Ven said; he was feeling rather nervous at the thought of more bloodshed. He had only joined the newly founded 'Magic Society,' for a laugh, but somehow; things had gotten out of hand. 'Maybe we should have a nap?'

'A nap!' Tintinere snapped. 'A real wizard does not nap, Ven, you know that.'

'Yes, yes, silly me, I just forgot,' said Ven, wracking his brains for a more plausible suggestion. 'Well, I suppose we could proceed with more torturing; but I suspect everyone in the palace has already been tortured.' He looked to Tintinere, the High Grand Wizard - as he liked to be called - for confirmation, for it was Tintinere who had orchestrated the carnage. Salongwee had joined in, reluctantly, at first, while Ven had mostly observed what was supposed to be fun. In truth, Ven still wondered why he had aided them at all in their dastardly deeds? But he had, and he was ashamed.

Tintinere suddenly snarled and leapt atop of a heap of dead and bleeding bodies piled against the wall. 'All right,' he grumbled, withdrawing the sword from his belt, wielding it as if he were a master-swords-wizard. 'How was I to know that this sword would make mincemeat of the opposition?' He placed the strangely curved blade in a rack alongside several gruesome looking torture implements and withdrew a long poker with a barbed point. 'And is it my fault that torturing isn't all fun and games? Is it my fault that these pathetic cretins confessed to everything we suggested? No!'

'You were rather hard on them,' offered Ven, averting his warm brown eyes from Tintinere's penetrating, steely, grey gaze and wondering why he did not keep his stupid mouth firmly closed.

'Rather hard on them?' Tintinere repeated, jumping down from his cadaverous perch.

'Ah, well yes,' said Ven, seemingly unable to stop himself from talking. 'I mean, the Lord Chamberlain, poor fellow, confessed to being an elephant, even using his arm as a false trunk for goodness sake, and the City Marshall gladly wet himself at your command; then claimed that he enjoyed it! So embarrassing, 'loved the warm glow,' I think were his exact words. Then the chancellor barked like a dog, got down on all fours and crawled backwards, actually wagging his head!'

'Hmm, highly amusing,' said Tintinere without even the flicker of a smile. 'I did command he behave like a retarded dog, maybe the chancellor thought a retarded dog would walk backwards and wag its head: who knows?'

'I like females best,' said Salongwee, still stroking his moustache. 'By the way, what-'

'You ate all the females,' said Ven, rather more quickly than he had intended.

'Do not ask about females,' said Tintinere, eyeing Ven suspiciously. 'Wizards do not need female company, do they Ven?'

Ven, who knew he resembled a slightly overweight cherubic schoolboy prankster, rather than a wizard, just shrugged his shoulders. He knew he wore the right garb; pointy hat, blue gown embellished with mystical symbols, red slippers that curled up at the toes, and he could perform small feats of magic, if pressed, but he suspected Tintinere did not fully trust him.

Tintinere suddenly clapped his hands, actually startling Ven. 'Now listen, you two, we are now more than just wizards, we are . . . we are the new Gods!'

Ven shuffled his feet uneasily. He'd never wanted to be a God, never wanted to be anything, not really, he just liked magic. During the torture and maiming, he had felt sorry for most of the victims, apart from the Overlord. He was nothing but a bloated pig that deserved to die because he had offered his own daughters to placate Tintinere and save his own miserable hide, which turned out to be a major miscalculation.

Tintinere harboured no carnal desires whatsoever and would have killed the girls on the spot if Ven had not intervened to save them. Tintinere had given him a funny look at the time, until Ven explained how he was saving them for later. Luckily, because of the slaughtering taking its toll, the princesses had been forgotten, for the time being.

'Ah, we could kill Overlord,' suggested Salongwee.

Tintinere groaned. 'Salongwee! The Overlord is dead, got it? He died begging for mercy, pleading with us to take his children!'

'Take them where?' Salongwee asked.

Tintinere repeatedly slapped his own forehead as he circled the chamber. 'If you must know, it's associated with female company, and we wizards always avoid such things; don't we, Ven?'

227

'Certainly do!' Ven exclaimed, while thinking he would really like to kiss Charm, the eldest of the Overlord's two teenage children.

'I know,' said Salongwee. 'Let's resurrect Overlord, then kill him again!'

Tintinere growled angrily. 'Salongwee; don't you listen? I already told you once, when we secured the palace and killed most of the inhabitants; the magical field became severely depleted due to our extravagant over use. Now, we have to allow some recovery.'

'Will one resurrection hurt?' Salongwee protested.

'Salongwee,' said Tintinere, 'you truly are irksome beyond belief. Let me explain. When the appointed time arrives, we need the magic field to call upon the Mistress. If we drain its power by playing pointless games with reanimated corpses, we will be unable to forge the necessary link: understand?'

Salongwee, whose hobbies appeared to be indulging in melodramatics and sulking, pondered over Tintinere's words, made as if to speak, then shook his head and pondered further.

Tales concerning the Mistress sounded incredibly farfetched and Ven disbelieved Tintinere's claims. If the Mistress existed, surely she would be here, guiding and helping. Having foolishly agreed to become involved in the Gramrye conquest, he had never dreamed they would actually succeed.

To Ven, the whole charade was just an elaborately engineered lark designed to embarrass a few dignitaries. Then, from thin air, the sword had appeared in Tintinere's hand and the three of them suddenly became invincible. A whole army slaughtered in a single afternoon, the dignitaries of Yorvic murdered, and Ven knew he was partly responsible.

He had saved the two princesses, but he needed to concoct an effectual escape plan before Tintinere decided he would like to drink their blood, or perform some other equally nasty deed. Ven needed help, but where this help would come from, he had no idea. Although, his gut feeling told him, help was out there, he just had to find it, somehow.

The shrouding darkness of night eased west, hotly pursued by the dawn of yet another day that would reign supreme, until it too became vanquished by the very force it sought to eliminate. Sunlight tentatively peeked above the low hills flanking the eastern side of Asvancum, before bursting upon the land with astonishing swiftness. Shadows skulked in secluded corners, hiding beneath dense foliage, taking cover under anything and everything. These small patches of silent darkness waited patiently, creeping around, following the movement of the sun that created them, and at the same time, banished them. Forcing them to lurk quietly, until the time came to emerge from hiding and reassert their alleged authority, coalescing into an all-encompassing mass, eventually defeating the light, temporarily reclaiming the very position surrendered at daybreak.

The sun only just having risen, that time was still a long way off. In fact, being the middle of summer, in this, 'The year of the Robin,' it was going to be another long hot day. Making it incredibly similar to the long hot days that had gone before. The days to come though, according to those in the know, in Yorvic, were expected to be . . . different.

A new order had, literally, floated in on a passing summer breeze and taken control. An order so powerful and merciless that all those who stood against it were ruthlessly slain. Well, almost all. A small band of men, remnants of the Gramrye army, trudged silently through the swamps between Yorvic City and Asvancum Town. They were hungry, dejected and tired, but glad to be alive and under the trusting leadership of Captain Dedge.

'Shush,' said Flint, cocking his wily head to one side.

'What is it?' Treetrunk asked, bumping clumsily against his comrade almost knocking him into an uninviting pool of stinking sludge. 'Is it more wizards?' There had been lots of wizards assaulting the walls of Yorvic, mostly illusions that could not be killed, but even those had possessed real swords that could kill. 'I don't like wizards,' said Treetrunk, 'they don't fight fair.'

'Shut up,' snarled Flint, backing away from the gurgling mud at his feet. 'There's activity ahead.'

Birds noisily took flight as Captain Dedge reached the two men who had led the group since entering the swamp. 'Flint? Have we got trouble?' he asked, peering through the surrounding squat trees.

'He doesn't know,' whispered Treetrunk, shrugging his huge shoulders. 'Nearly fell in that there hole full of mucky water.'

Flint scowled at Treetrunk before edging around his massive bulk on the narrow slippery path. 'Ahead Captain,' he murmured, jabbing his thumb over his shoulder. 'There's something happening amongst the trees.'

'Something?' quizzed the Captain, bewildered.

'Something?' Treetrunk repeated, he considered himself an expert on repeating very short sentences, or the final few words of long complicated sentences.

Flint again scowled at Treetrunk. 'I couldn't quite hear, but they seemed to be engaged in some sort of game. I suspect there's about four of them . . .' Flint saw the Captain nod his head, a good sign that he meant action, '. . . or possibly twenty,' he added quickly. In Flint's book of guerrilla warfare, action is to be avoided at all costs. Action usually meant close quarter fighting with sharp pointy bits of metal, against terribly ferocious opponents who liked hurting people. Not that he'd ever seen much action; just hearing about it was enough. 'What shall we do, Captain? If there are twenty of them, we could be overpowered and killed, or, or simply drowned in the swamp.'

Treetrunk growled and clenched his fists. The Captain rubbed his chin, bristling with an overnight growth of short greyish hair. 'We should investigate. If it's the enemy and in sufficiently low numbers, we could probably take 'em. We've got the element of surprise,' he tapped his sword, 'and we're well-armed.'

'Well-armed,' offered Treetrunk, sliding his thumb across the edge of his sharpened blade.

'But Captain,' Flint protested, 'there could be twenty of them.'

229

'Or four,' said Treetrunk, grinning eagerly. Treetrunk liked a fight, as long as when you hit the opponent, they fell down and never got up again until much, much later, which was usually the case when Treetrunk fought anyone.

'What's happening?' asked a shallow timid voice behind the Captain.

It was Dweeb. High on intellect, short on muscle and not allowed to march in the rain, according to his mum. He had been fetching up the rear in order to detect pursuers.

The Captain ushered him along the narrow path and brought him into the group. 'Flint says there's a group ahead engaged in some sort of game. We're going to scout around and depending on numbers, either attack, or flee to Asvancum.'

'Great,' said Flint despondently.

'Hmm,' said Treetrunk, enthusiastically.

'Wonderful,' said Dweeb, uncertainly.

Following the sound of muted voices, Captain Dedge led the way along the narrow twisting path until they reached the edge of a clearing. In the centre of this clearing, on a raised platform supported by thick stakes, a gathering of swamp-sprites huddled around a table where carved wooden pieces stood upon a chequered board.

'What on Deburon are they doing?' Captain Dedge whispered.

Treetrunk grunted and shook his head.

'Playing chess, perhaps?' Dweeb suggested.

'I knew that,' said Flint.

The other three passed him doubtful glances.

'I did!' said Flint.

They watched as one of the sprites placed a hollow tube to his mouth and blew, firing a small projectile, striking one of his opponent's pieces, sending it flying off the board. The other swamp-sprites cheered, threw their caps into the air and smacked their own bottoms three times before catching their caps. The sprite that had lost a piece now took his turn, firing what looked like a hard pea, just wide of the mark. The other swamp-sprites hissed, threw his cap in the air and slapped him about the head.

'So, that's chess, is it?' Flint said. 'The famous game of brains?'

'Pea-shooter chess,' Dweeb corrected him. 'The famous game of swamp-sprites who never learned to play properly.'

'How many do you suppose there are?' asked the Captain.

'Two dozen,' said Flint quickly.

'Three,' offered Treetrunk, his voice brimming with hope.

'Sixteen, counting the two standing behind us,' said Dweeb.

They all looked around to see two swamp-sprites armed with long sticks sporting sharp points, and looking very vexed. They waved wildly with the sticks and made strange chittering noises with their odd little mouths. The men exchanged puzzled glances.

Brilliant, thought Flint, just bloody brilliant! He looked around for a safe direction in which to run while Captain Dedge cleared his throat.

'Afternoon!' said, the Captain. 'We were, observing your game and . . . .'

The swamp-sprites scowled. Anger flared in their beady eyes and Flint knew they had trouble. 'Time to scarper,' he hissed in the Captain's ear.

Dedge shook his head. 'I've scarpered enough today, I am fresh out of scarper; get 'em lads!'

Flint was nudged aside as Treetrunk moved first, clutching the shoulders of the sprite closest to him, who squealed in fright, dropping his stick then yelping as he became suddenly airborne. The second sprite actually launched a clumsy attack that the Captain easily sidestepped, before pushing his adversary into a pool of stagnant water. Uproar broke out around the chess game as the sprite Treetrunk had launched over his shoulders came crashing down on the table, scattering chessmen in all directions.

'Er, now we scarper!' bawled the Captain, pushing Treetrunk and Dweeb in the same direction that Flint had already taken.

The well-armed group of the toughest fighting men on Deburon, who were afraid of nobody, ran through the swamp with a pack of squealing swamp-sprites at their heels.

Charm glanced across at her sister, Trace, in the murky gloom of the dank cell, lit by a small flickering torch ensconced in the wall. Poor girl was only fourteen summers, two fewer than herself, and she had said very little since the friendliest of the three wizards had locked them up.

What a life, she thought, perhaps a short one too, and she had expected to have a beau by now. There had been plenty of Dukes, Earls, and Marquises calling and offering their hands, but none had appealed to her, and to her father's credit, for once, he had not pushed the matter. She suspected he was holding out for a more worthy candidate, or rather, a more influential one from beyond Gramrye and even the Pagonis States. Now, she wondered if there would ever be anyone in her life at all. Trace appeared to be mumbling under her breath. 'Are you distressed sister?' she inquired.

Trace looked up, she had expansive brown eyes and a perfect oval face framed by dark locks that hung in waves. 'Distress? Why no, not at all, dear Charm. I'm just composing a poem.'

Oh no, thought Charm, may the skies open and rain so hard that we are washed to the sea in a torrential flood. 'Really! How nice, what is it about?' she asked, instantly regretting her question as the poems of her dear sister usually involved puppies, kittens, or the sadness of a lame horse, or the bleating of lost lambs.

'It's about our situation,' Trace replied, her lips again seemingly moving over the words forming in her mind. 'Would you like to hear it?'

Charm wondered if it would be worse than visiting the torture chambers currently occupied by the wizards; they had heard the screams even here, in their dimly lit cell. It occurred to her that if the wizards actually heard any of her sister's poetry, they may offer her useful employment as a torturer. 'Why yes, of course,' she said, smiling beatifically. 'I would be honoured to listen to your

231

words.' She much preferred music, music had soul; it jangled the nerves, soothed the heart, made the mind swing, allowed one to dance and what greater pleasure could there be, than to dance?

Trace cleared her throat. 'It's not yet finished, but here is the first verse, well, two, no three, actually. Charm, before I share it, do you think we are going to die?'

Charm could see the telltale sign of tears forming in Trace's eyes. 'No, no, I don't,' she said, rather convincingly, and surprisingly, she found she believed her own words. 'Please, tell me your poem, or what you have created so far.' She prepared herself for a mournful sombre tale of coming death, that involved at least one sad puppy, that had perhaps lost its mummy and daddy.

Trace actually stood up from the straw filled cot that served as a bed. 'I've called it 'Just to be'.' She cleared her throat, rather theatrically.

'To hear the child,
Through outpourings of tears,
Is to hear a child in need.
To help the lost,
To search within themselves,
Is to help them to succeed.

To recognise sadness,
Concealed in brave composure,
Is to know how far we fall.
To sense one's love,
Through layers of deep emotion,
Is to know, love conquers all.

To believe in oneself,
Despite latent natural desires,
Is to accept the Karma inside.
To rise above mortality,
Slipping free of safe shores,
Is to sail on the spiritual tide.

Charm was too stunned to speak.

'Ah, I think I now have the last verse,' said Trace, clasping her hands with excitement. Shall I share it now?'

Charm nodded her head in approval.

To forgive the listener,
Who cannot hear the word,
Is to mourn one who'll never be free.
To touch one's heart,
So breathing life into life,

Is to reveal what it is, just to be.'

Charm still felt stunned, for a girl of fourteen summers to write like that was impressive. Not only that, this was her baby sister who was hardly ever noticed.

'Do you like it?' Trace asked, her tone one of uncertainty.

'I, er, well, yes, actually. It's not like your usual rub . . . compositions. Yes, composition is the word I'm looking for, even though you've not written it down, yet, and . . . .' She got to her feet walked across the cell and embraced her sister. 'Trace, it's very good, and yes, I can see how it does sort of, well, I see how you found inspiration in our present situation.' She kissed Trace on the top of her head. 'Don't worry, Sis, I'm sure help will come.' She held her sister tight as her body shook with sudden sobbing and felt the wetness of the tears through her thin nightdress. 'Help will come, I am sure.'

'I hope so,' said Trace, stepping back and wiping her eyes. 'I know I said it's finished, but I think I might have two more verses yet to write, or maybe they could go in a new poem!'

Then they both laughed, hugged each other, cried together, and laughed some more.

Chapter Three

The day passed slowly for Ionuin and her companions as they lay beneath the hot sun, and despite being ravenously hungry, it was not long before all four of them fell asleep. It was not surprising, as they had not had a moment's rest since the battle with the Dark Dragon. Ionuin was the first to awaken, she stretched along the ground, viewing the strange looking sun through squinting eyes and guessed it was mid afternoon, maybe later.

Ionuin heard movement outside the stone circle and sat upright. Spuddle was snoring softly, as was Taj, while Glitch was turning restlessly. Taj and Spuddle had been correct when they had said Glitch would be fine, once the red dragon had recovered his senses, he thought it had been a very funny incident and even thanked them for stopping him venturing into the trees in search of flowers. He also made them swear not to tell another living soul about what had occurred.

Thinking she could avoid the potency of the aromatic flowers, that had almost led her to go running into the trees earlier that day along with Glitch, Ionuin crawled along the ground to investigate what she thought may be animal noises, unsheathing her boot-knife as she went, after all, it may be small game and food was desperately needed.

She squeezed between the upright stones of the inner circle and listened as she scampered to the outer ring of stones. She heard scratching, like that of a goat or deer rubbing horn or antler on wood or stone. She reasoned that if she could find exactly where, one swift pounce, a well aimed thrust of her blade, and dinner would be served.

Walking with her head bent low, she scouted the inner edge of the stone ring, the scraping getting louder until she came to a giant stone, one of two that formed an entrance, of kinds. It sounded like the creature, whatever it was, could be only a quick step away. She cast out her mental net, but drew a blank, it seemed such things did not work here, or she needed to practice more and find a way to make it work, until then, hunting skill would have to suffice. She held her breath, moved forward, tensed herself into a crouch, ready to strike, and peered between the stones. It was indeed a deer, but not a breed she recognised. They saw each other at the same instant and Ionuin leapt, making a grab for its rear end. The dear turned and fled with Ionuin dragging behind, clutching its tail as she bounced along the ground.

She tried to stab the creature in its rump, but could not deliver a decent swing of her blade as it sped into the forest. She tried to gain her feet, but the pace at which the deer was travelling prevented her from keeping her balance and eventually, her arm tiring and feeling exhausted, she released the deer and gave up. Once free, the deer bolted, leaving Ionuin to roll to a halt in a swathe of tall plants, where she lay panting. It was then that she realised the folly of her actions, leaving the safety of the stone circle.

'I'll just follow the trail back,' she told herself as she sat up and looked around. The sky was out of sight because of the forest canopy and the air felt cool amongst the trees. She heard tiny animals scurrying around in the undergrowth and kept her knife at the ready, then wondered what might be edible on this strange world?

On Merm, game was relatively scarce, but at least you knew your quarry and hunting and trapping was just a matter of persistence and patience. The other big change was the landscape. Ionuin was used to cratered, rocky plains, interspersed with sparse grasslands, frequented by giant insects, lizards, snakes and rodents. Here, the world was more enclosed, the huge trees restricting the view and dense foliage providing extra cover for the game. There were things here that could be hunted and eaten, of this she was certain; it was simply a matter of adjustment.

'I'm hungry,' said Glitch.

Ionuin spun around, waving the knife before her in a warding off gesture, her other hand flattening against her pounding chest. 'You damned fool!' she cursed. 'You nearly gave me a heart attack!'

'Sorry,' whispered Glitch.

Ionuin sighed. 'No, I'm sorry, Glitch. I had no cause to snap at you.' She reached out and gave Glitch a hug, pressing her face against the warm roughened scales of his neck. 'You say you're hungry, Glitch, but I tell you now, I am absolutely starving! Not sure what there is to eat here, though.'

'I was following the scent of the flowers,' said Glitch, his nose rising into the air.

Ionuin glanced at her friend. Even though he was barely a teenager, in dragon years, he towered over her when his neck was stretched to its full height. 'Glitch, I don't think that's a good idea. Remember what Taj said? There could be danger.'

Glitch edged forward, sniffing the air. 'Taj? Phooey, what does Taj know about anything? He overreacted, don't you think?'

'I trust his judgement on this occasion,' Ionuin said, 'and so should you, Glitch.'

'Bah, my judgement is fine. Anyway, what possible harm can the scent of flowers do to one such as me, hmm?' He stared down at Ionuin. 'I am a dragon of royal blood, the most feared creature ever to live, and you ask me to be wary of some, some pretty flowers?'

'Pretty? Glitch, how could you know that?' Ionuin asked, getting to her feet and following Glitch's gaze. She too could now smell the flowers and, oddly enough, they made her mouth water, the thought of food again swam through her mind.

'I can see them,' Glitch replied, pushing through the tall plants, moving onto a narrow trail where he had to squeeze between giant trees, so large, that ten men linking arms would struggle to span their enormous girth. 'Up ahead, flowers of gold, and red, and purple that are so, so beautiful!'

'I see nothing,' said Ionuin, actually leaping into the air to gain a better view.

Glitch stopped. 'Here, climb on my back; let me show you, are they making you hungry too? I have never eaten flowers but I'm willing to try anything.'

235

Ionuin, scrambled up Glitch's hind leg, edged along his back until she was seated on his shoulders, her hands clasped around his neck. 'I still can't see them, but yes, I am hungry, and yes, I have eaten flowers, not very tasty though. Come on, let's go see, they do smell good, don't they? It's the fruitiness of the scent that makes you hungry, I think.'

'Oh, I'm not keen on fruit,' said Glitch, following the trail, keeping the tantalising colours in sight. 'Fruit does not usually agree with me, unless it's boiled to a pulp and coating hot meat, now that's the way to eat fruit, my girl, hmm, yes. Although, if there is fruit; hey, I think there is! I can see something dangling beside the flowers.'

Ionuin strained her neck to see what Glitch could see, actually standing on his shoulders so her head was nearly the same level as his. 'Oh yes, ooh look at the flowers, Glitch, they are pretty, like globes, and they shimmer too, and look,' she pointed ahead. 'Could be scrub-berries, giant ones, I am sure they are scrub-berries.'

'I don't know what a 'scrub-berry,' is,' Glitch replied, as they reached a large bush of tangled vines with fleshy green leaves, coloured rounded flowers, and black knobbly fruit, 'but I'll accept your assessment.'

Ionuin reached out and picked a piece of the knobbly fruit that even felt like the berries found at home. 'I wonder if this tastes good. What do you think, Glitch?' Glitch did not reply, he was too busy drinking in the heady smell, now wafting from the flowers in such profusion that you could actually see it in the air, like tiny floating water droplets. Trusting her instincts, Ionuin took a bite.

'Well?' Glitch asked, his eyes closed, a dreamy look on his face. 'Does it taste like scrub-berry?'

'Hmm, yes, only, more succulent, juicier and there's a, a slight under taste that's, that's rather pleasant.'

'Really!' Glitch shook his head as if trying to clear his thoughts, opened his heavy lidded-eyes, picked a piece for himself, and bit into it. 'Yes, yes, as I said, I'm not a lover of fruit, but this is really nice.' He grabbed two more and chomped on them, then another piece, and another. 'Would be better on hot meat though,' he said, black juice dribbling over his lips.

They consumed several more pieces each before gathering armfuls of the juicy fruit for Spuddle and Taj.

'I feel great,' said Glitch, fruit tumbling from his arms.

'Yes, yes, I feel great too,' Ionuin confirmed, as she ate yet another piece before burping loudly. 'Ooh,' she smiled, 'pardon me.'

'Pardon granted,' said Glitch, laughing a throaty dragonish laugh, before noticing his arms were now empty and pieces of fruit were around his feet. 'Oops, now look at that, however did that happen, clumsy me.' he bent down to retrieve the fruit. Ionuin slid from his shoulders in one gentle movement and was caught by the reaching sticky vines before she hit the floor. 'Do you feel sleepy?' Glitch asked, as he lay down beside her, the vines creeping around his great bulk. Ionuin half nodded her head in affirmation, then answered with a loud snore.

Prior to the conquest of Yorvic, the wizards had pretty much kept themselves to themselves. People left them alone, and they left the people alone. Now, half the city had become entranced, while the other half had fled, or were hiding in the cellars and attics of their homes. It had all gone so horribly wrong, thought Ven.

'Something on your mind, Ven?' Tintinere asked, tapping his foot with annoyance. 'Thinking of the depravity in which you shall indulge once Mistress arrives, 'eh?'

'Something like that,' Ven lied, trying to grin malevolently.

Tintinere laughed, his face splitting almost from ear to ear, displaying an incredible set of sharp, pointy teeth. His eyes, that usually resembled carved chunks of blank obsidian, glowed red, while the tiniest slivers of delicate green zigzagged across the pulsing orbs.

Salongwee unfastened the lifeless body of the dungeon's chief executioner and torturer from his own rack. 'So, when this Mistress arriving?' he asked, tossing the executioner's dismembered arms onto a pile with the rest of the human detritus.

'Soon, very soon,' Tintinere answered, his merriment subsiding. 'Should really be here now; actually, I cannot think what the delay could possibly be.'

I am in way over my silly fat head, thought Ven. The whole escapade has spiralled out of control, but what could he do? People had died, and more deaths were likely. I need help, he thought, big help, and soon. Tintinere had become sucked into a power vacuum and he and Salongwee were hanging onto his cloak without a clue as to what was transpiring.

'I know,' said Salongwee, his face glowing with eagerness. 'Let's, just for laugh, torture those princess creatures, or, how bout, we eat them!'

'They're already dead,' Ven snapped.

'No they're not,' said Tintinere, a queer look in his eye that Ven did not much care for.

Ven had to think fast. 'Ah, those princesses.'

'You distinctly informed us that you were saving them for later,' Tintinere reminded him.

Salongwee squealed with obvious delight. 'Ooh goody! I think we eat them . . . alive!'

'Er, I'm not eating live princess,' Ven protested, folding his arms across his chest.

'Why not?' Tintinere questioned.

'In all fairness, I prefer my food not to watch me while I'm eating,' Ven replied. 'And besides,' he continued, his brain racing ahead, attempting to outpace the rising waffle that was preparing to spring free should he fail to think straight, 'the princesses are too skinny and, and all that hair! Far too much hair.'

Tintinere did not appear convinced.

'The youngest girl had plenty meat covering her bones,' said Salongwee, drool already dripping from the corner of his mouth. 'I not eaten hair, it might be nice! Eldest has dark blonde locks, like old straw, might be nice in wine sauce.'

Ven could not believe what he was hearing. He considered Salongwee to have lost all his marbles, and what little sense he had previously possessed, was now gone completely. 'I don't care,' he said, vehemently. 'I'm not eating live princesses, and I'm certainly not eating hair in a wine sauce.'

'Well, let's just torture them,' suggested Salongwee.

Tintinere looked thoughtful. 'Agreed; but let's make them last. The others died far too quickly, and were no fun whatsoever.'

Salongwee grasped one of the iron pokers in his elongated fingers and leered lasciviously. 'These look like they not been used for while.' He cast a ball of fire onto a brazier, igniting the heaped coals in a flurry of crackling sparks and spouting flame.

'Excellent!' Tintinere exclaimed, rubbing his hands. 'I'm looking forward to a loud session of pitiful screaming.'

Ven kept his head. To panic now would incur further atrocities to be performed upon the flesh of the innocents. 'I'll erm, I'll fetch them then, shall I?' he said, trying to sound incredibly enthusiastic.

'Oh yes,' said Tintinere excitedly, his eyes flashing back to their usual obsidian colouring. 'Salongwee will accompany you, won't you, Salongwee?'

'Ooh, it be my pleasure,' said Salongwee, striding towards the chamber door, his voice giddy with excitement. 'Come Ven, we have much fun, yes?'

Ven sighed quietly and leapt to his feet. 'Yes, so much fun,' he said, hoping Tintinere did not notice his reluctance.

Having escaped the unwanted attention of the swamp-sprites, Captain Dedge and his men were taking a well-earned breather on the banks of the river Swatter. The retreating summer afternoon surrendered to the onset of early evening and sleep had come easily to the tired men, the lapping river slipped gently into Captain Dedge's dream. A dream awash with scantily clad mermaids who beckoned him forward to take whatever carnal liberties he desired. The Captain moaned in his sleep, his inner-eye roaming over the inviting flesh of the nubile bodies writhing temptingly before him. His heart melted as he drank in the shapely female beauty closest to him, and any thoughts he had of resisting the pleasures on offer, drifted away with the turning tide of the passing river.

Captain Dedge never wasted time with small talk. He sauntered over to the rocks on which the giggling creatures were sitting. 'I'll take you first,' he mumbled, through sleepy lips, forcing out his incredibly heavy arms, ready to embrace.

'If you insist,' replied the mermaid, whose voice did not sound as musical as the Captain had imagined it might, but he pressed on regardless.

'Kiss me long and hard,' he implored, 'and you'll be mine, forever.'

'Just this afternoon will do, thanks,' replied the mermaid, leaping upon the Captain, ravishing his lips with extreme gusto until he couldn't breathe.

Gasping for air, the Captain awoke and stared into the startlingly green, yet very bloodshot eyes, of an ugly old crone.

'A, a witch,' the Captain mouthed under his breath.

'Ethyl Wierwillechekme is the name, my fine fellow,' said the witch, nuzzling her big, soft, warty, nose against his proud soldier's nose, continuing the kiss, actually nipping his lower lip gently in her wayward teeth.

Dedge struggled to free himself, but her knees had him expertly pinned against the riverbank, while her tongue explored every available corner of his mouth. Fearing for his life, he managed to twist away his face, and in a voice barely above a whisper, croaked for help.

'Help?' Ethyl repeated. 'Why, whatever's wrong with you? Are you having a heart attack?' She pounded her hard-knuckled fist into his chest, transforming his face from blushing pink to deep crimson.

'Um, w-what's happening?' Dweeb asked, sitting up, rubbing his eyes.

'He's having a heart attack!' Ethyl screeched, driving home another thumping wallop into the Captain's chest. 'I only just secured his undying affection, and he's dying!' She thumped him again, even harder.

'A heart attack!' Dweeb exclaimed, jumping to his feet. 'Does this m-mean, mean, he's ill?'

'Yes, yes, I think maybe it does,' Ethyl replied, looking up at Dweeb uncertainly.

'Ahem, then erm, kick him in the head,' Dweeb suggested.

'Kick him in the head?' Ethyl asked, her face etched with confusion. 'Why, I never heard of such a thing, especially for illness! Are you sure?'

'When someone can't perform guard duty, because they're ill, the Captain always says, *they want their heads kicking in,*' Dweeb explained.

'Not ill,' gasped the Captain, his voice sounding hoarse and desperate.

'What was that?' Ethyl asked, cupping her ear.

'Say's he's not ill,' said Dweeb, peering into the Captain's rolling eyes. 'He looks ill, a kind of, puce-ill, if you know what I mean.'

'Puce-ill, ah, yes, well, perhaps he's delirious with love! Puce, especially deep puce, is a very lovely affectionate colour,' Ethyl suggested, firmly grasping the Captain's jaw. 'He was okay when I began kissing him; then he came over all funny, like.'

'You, y-you . . . kissed the Captain?' Dweeb said, his face hanging, slack-jawed.

Dedge gasped, trying to draw air into his lungs as Ethyl puckered up her pink lips, wet and drooling with eager passion, fearing she was going to kiss him again.

'He asked me to kiss him,' said Ethyl, giving the Captain an almost toothless smile and pinching his cheek. 'A real charmer is our Captain. He says he wants me to love him forever, and ever.'

'H-he did?' Dweeb asked, his tone edged with uncertainty.

'Of course he did!' Ethyl said, looking gob-smacked. 'I wouldn't make a thing up like that. Let's see, Captain Dedge, and Mistress Ethyl Wierwillechekme. Hmm has a nice ring to it, don't you think?'

'Get her off me,' Dedge croaked, asserting some authority into his barely audible voice.

239

'Did he say, he loves me?' Ethyl asked, cupping her ear again while managing to suppress a wry grin.

'Madam, erm, Ethyl,' said Dweeb, offering his hand, but smiling. 'I appreciate your humour, but I suspect that the Captain has had enough of your . . . your attentions.'

Dedge saw Ethyl wink as Dweeb offered her his hand.

Ethyl quickly batted away Dweeb's fingers. 'Think you're right, young man,' she said, springing from astride the Captain's chest with one easy bound. 'Don't want to become too familiar on a first date. He might receive the wrong impression. Can't have wrong impressions about witches, can we now, Captain?'

'I quite agree,' replied Dweeb, diplomatically.

Free of Ethyl's restraining thighs, Dedge sat upright and inhaled deeply. 'Dweeb, you idiot,' he rasped. 'You were going to kick my head in!'

'Ah, in my defence, I was still half asleep,' Dweeb protested. 'I-I panicked! I had been dreaming about a fight! Y-yes, that's it, a fight.'

'Fight! I'll give you a bloody fight!' said Dedge, wiping his hand across his lips that were still dripping with drool.

'It was an error of judgement,' said Dweeb, defensively, kneeling beside Dedge. 'You know how impulsive I am. Besides; I would have only had a little kick. Just to see if anything happened.'

Treetrunk, who had slept through the whole incident, shot bolt upright and screamed loudly, causing a gaggle of nearby geese to take flight.

'It, it's fine, Treetrunk,' Dweeb assured his comrade. 'You're only dreaming.'

Ethyl tapped her foot impatiently. 'What a shower. I'm not surprised the other fellow took to his heels.'

Dedge looked beyond Treetrunk and groaned. 'Great! Private Flint has scarpered, what a spiffing day we're having! Not only do I have a deserter in the ranks, but I awaken to find myself being assaulted by a hideous gargoyle, and my only trainee wants to kick my head in. What else can happen?'

'I'll tell you what else can happen,' said Ethyl, rounding on Dedge with menace in her eyes. 'You ever refer to me as a gargoyle again, and I'll boil your brains inside your skull! Men! They're so abominably fickle! One moment they're offering to love you forever, then it's nothing but insults! I don't know why we put up with 'em!' She glanced around 'Anyone know why we put up with 'em?' Dweeb and Treetrunk simply shrugged. 'No, me neither.'

'Hold on,' said the Captain, struggling to his feet. 'Just who on Deburon are you, anyway?'

Treetrunk began mumbling. 'Er' who am I?' he asked, looking at his hands, a grave look of confusion wrinkling his face.

'You're Treetrunk,' said Dweeb, scurrying around the Captain and helping his friend gain his feet and his sense of being. 'I'm Dweeb, and you're Treetrunk: understand?'

'Treetrunk?' Treetrunk said bewilderingly, scratching his big square unshaven jaw. 'Oh, yeah, Treetrunk.'

'What incredible powers of recall you possess, private Treetrunk, you never cease to amaze me, never,' said Dedge, rather sarcastically.

Treetrunk pointed at Captain Dedge. 'And, and you're, you're Captain Dedge!'

Captain Dedge nodded. 'Good, good.'

'And I am, Ethyl,' said Ethyl, curtseying to Treetrunk who offered her a slight bow.

Dedge cleared his throat. 'Well, Miss Ethyl Wierwillechekme, we-'

Ethyl giggled and lightly punched the Captain on his arm. 'You can call me, darling; because I like you. I like you quite a lot!'

The Captain tried to laugh. 'But, but, you're a, a kind of witch; aren't you?'

Ethyl inclined her head and stood with her hips swaying from side to side. 'Ahem, 'a kind of witch,' how very quaint! Yes, well, some people, and a few other creatures, often say so, but most just assume I am a witch, mostly because of my pointy hat and black clothes, but, appearances are so deceptive; don't you think?'

Captain Dedge removed his hat and scratched his head. 'Well yes, I mean, I sort of guessed that you, you were a . . . but, surely, witches are, well, stuff and nonsense. Mythical creatures from children's story books, aren't they?'

'Are they?' Ethyl said, folding her arms, a glint of humour in her eyes.

Dedge cleared his throat. 'Well, nobody'd ever believe witches are real; would they?'

'You mean, like wizards?' Ethyl replied smartly.

'Yes, just like . . . ah, quite, hmm. I see what you did there, but yes, you do seem to have a valid point.' Captain Dedge gave Ethyl the once over. 'One more thing, even though you probably could've, you wouldn't really boil my brains, would you, eh?'

Ethyl shook her head. 'Not really. I enjoy kissing you too much, and besides, how will you lead the dragons into battle if you can't think? Trust me, one needs brains to think.'

Dweeb said. 'Pardon me, witch Ethyl, or whatever you're called, but, did you say, dragons?'

'The name is Weir – wille – chek – me,' said Ethyl, mouthing the words in slow motion, and yes, I did say dragons. Two dragons, to be exact, and two others, that are like people, but also like dragons.'

'Dragomans!' Treetrunk said, smiling affectionately. 'Me like dragons, perhaps.'

'Yes,' said the witch, scrutinising Treetrunk for the first time. 'Dragomans, very good. They arrived earlier today at the Sacred Stones. Said they'd come for a sword, or something. Kept mentioning a battle with a Dark Dragon on the planet Merm, but it means nothing to me. Knew they were coming though; picked it up from the sub-ether.'

Captain Dedge could hardly understand a word Ethyl said, but he knew of the Sacred Stones and wondered if the mentioned sword was the same sword owned by the chief wizard. It had appeared like magic, slaughtered all opposition, and seemed able to manifest itself into the hands of replicas of the chief wizard.

'You say, you say they came for a sword?' Captain Dedge asked. 'Perhaps a magical sword?'

'A sword was mentioned,' Ethyl confirmed. 'Don't know about magic. I told them to wait for further instructions.'

'How interesting,' said Dedge, trying to piece it all together and failing miserably. 'We'll have to meet them, these, er, dragoman folk.'

'I'll arrange for them to rendezvous with you in Asvancum, and it will only cost you one more kiss,' said Ethyl.

'Ron day boo,' Treetrunk muttered, pulling off his helmet and scratting at his unruly mop of dark coarse hair.

Dedge flapped a hand at Treetrunk to be quiet, before turning back to Ethyl. 'Ah, about the kissing, I think-'

'Don't apologize,' interrupted Ethyl. 'Many men would like to take advantage of my favours, and I think you displayed exceptional bravery and extreme cunning, taking me unawares as you did. Very clever, very clever indeed.'

'So do I,' said Dweeb, grinning wildly.

'Me too,' added Treetrunk, even though it was obvious that he had no idea what was being discussed.

'Shut it, you two,' snapped the Captain.

'Oi, don't be so touchy!' Ethyl warned, prodding the Captain in his chest. 'We've serious business to attend, and we can't be having senior players taking umbrage, now can we?'

The Captain was dumfounded. 'Serious business? Senior players? I have a question, Miss Ethyl. What do you know about all this upheaval? In fact, how did you know the dragons were coming? What's more, what is the sub-ether? And, and, well, who are you really? And, and how do you know of me?'

Ethyl circled around him, walking slowly. 'That is five questions, my lover, but I am willing to answer them. So, apart from you being my new lover, I suspect you're a Captain in the Gramrye army, the army that recently got arse-whipped by the wizards. Who I am, is unimportant. What is important, is that you need my help, and also the help of forces greater than ourselves. The sub-ether is a communication network that spans the galaxy and for use only by those in the know, meaning myself, and others like me.'

'There are others like you?' Dedge asked, his mouth wide open in disbelief.

'Yes, hmm, similar to me, not quite like me. Now, are you going to rendezvous with the newcomers in Asvancum?'

The three soldiers exchanged troubled glances as Dedge slipped into deep thought. Having suffered defeat, chances were, they could suffer defeat again if they faced the wizards unprepared. He also knew that the wizards were forming a militia of bandits to do their dirty work. Even though Ethyl seemed to be talking in riddles, they did need help, and she was willing to provide assistance, of a kind. Angry sprites, from whom they had narrowly escaped, roamed the swamp in which he had intended to hide, so Asvancum looked like the best bet. Then

242

there were the dragons, or 'dragomans,' as Treetrunk had labelled them. He had heard of these creatures, but never actually seen one, so now looked as good a time as any to make their acquaintance and hope, just hope, that they were friendly. For if they were unfriendly, he had heard they could be quite challenging. 'All right,' he said at last. 'It seems we have no choice. Let's go to Asvancum.'

Ethyl Wierwillechekme smiled. 'Captain, there are always choices; agreed?'

Dedge sighed and nodded his head, she was right.

Ethyl grinned her gummy grin. 'I also agree, some choices are often poor, others reside in abject poverty, while some might seem risky; it is simply a matter of making the right choice.'

'I agree,' said Dweeb, wholeheartedly, smiling and falling in beside the witch. 'My mum always told me . . . .'

The words of Dweeb faded as Dedge led the way along the riverbank and tried to think straight. All this, bizarre as it was, seemed over-familiar to him, as if he had lived through it before, as if he had been expecting it all to happen. Had he dreamt of the witch before? Were the dragons that kept flitting through his thoughts more than just his over worked imagination? And what about the great big black dragon that often spoke to him? Was it one of the newcomers they were going to meet in Asvancum? It all felt very mysterious to him, but, at the same time, perfectly all right. He then wondered if the witch had cast some kind of soothing spell on him. Glancing at her over his shoulder, it did seem possible. Out of everything though, the most surprising thing of all, was that he had kissed her. He controlled a sudden lurching movement in his stomach and quickened his pace, knowing that the others would keep up. He was a leader, and whatever happened, he would certainly lead.